My First

by

Melanie Shawn

Cover Design by Hot Damn Designs
Copyedits by Mickey Reed Editing
Proofreading Services by Tiesha Brunson, Deanna McDonald
Book Design by BB eBooks

Published by Red Hot Reads Publishing
Rev. 3.1

Table of Contents

Chapter One

Welcome home, Katie thought, sardonically, as she sat, eyes closed, in her rental car on the side of Highway 90. She had a paper bag pressed tightly against her mouth with one hand, a picture in her other hand, and a mantra running through her brain on repeat.

You can breathe. Just breathe. Breathe in and out slowly. You can breathe.

Katie had been back in Illinois for less than an hour and here she was, smack dab in the middle of her first panic attack in years. Concentrating on the feeling of her thumb running across the smooth cool surface of the photo, she tried to soothe her racing heart, to anchor herself to reality. Her tongue was tingling as she forced the rapid movements of her chest to be slow and deliberate.

This seems to be working, albeit slowly, she assured herself.

When the overpriced therapist, who taught her the breathing exercise and mantra, had laid out his plan of connecting to an object or smell that calmed her, Katie had wanted to roll her eyes. She had wanted to tell him that he clearly had no flipping idea what a panic attack really felt like if he thought that repeating a little magic spell in her mind while spraying a calming scent, was going to have any effect at all. She had wanted to tell him that panic attacks didn't feel like nervousness or butterflies you could just calm with the power of your mind. They felt like you were having a heart attack, like you were dying. Seriously, had anyone ever heard of someone having a heart attack curing themselves by simply telling themselves to *breathe* while holding a knick-knack or sniffing some aroma therapy that miraculously calmed them?

Of course, Katie hadn't said any of those things. She had smiled politely and kept her judgment of his professional aptitude (i.e., that he was a total quack.) entirely to herself. Then, like the good student she was, she'd gone home and practiced with the bag and tried spraying a few scents, but found they never made her feel any sense of calm and happiness, like holding the picture she'd had since sixth grade did.

After that visit, the panic attacks had stopped and so she hadn't had the opportunity to test out the technique and prove his quackitude with rock-solid evidence. Now that she was in the middle of one, and, the exercises actually seemed to be working…

Well, I'll move his status down to 'Jury's Still Out on the Level of His Quackosity' but I'm not nominating him for the Nobel Prize just yet, Katie thought. Of course, this wasn't even close to a *bad* attack. This one was fairly mild.

But, that's exactly how they had started ten years ago. They had begun as hyperventilating episodes; and, over time, had developed into severe attacks resulting in her being rushed to the emergency room—*twice*—both times having truly believed she was having a heart attack. Which had not been the case.

The E.R. docs were the reason she had ended up lying on the overpriced therapist's couch (metaphorically speaking; in reality she had sat in a plush leather chair). Once the doctors at the hospital had ruled out the possibility that anything was physically wrong with her, they had strongly recommended that she delve into the possibility that it was her psyche, not her body, that needed medical attention.

Even now, as the panic attack was subsiding, Katie was still feeling some of the physical symptoms. Her head felt as if it were floating away, her fingers were tingling as if they were being stabbed by a thousand tiny needles, and she was being bombarded by an obnoxiously loud ringing sound. She forced herself to anchor to the sensation of the paper bag digging into her lips and the glossy feeling of the photographic paper beneath her fingers in order to ground herself back into reality. She looked down into the large brown eyes staring back at her from the picture and kept repeating the mantra (which, she had to admit, was kind of growing on her).

You can breathe. Just breathe. Breathe in and out slowly. You can breathe.

Slowly, bit by bit, she drifted back to the present and into her body. Closing her eyes, she let herself appreciate the little sensations she was now aware of—the leather of the seat pressed cold against her back, the icy breeze from the air conditioning blowing refreshingly on her face.

Leaning her head back against the headrest, she felt the weight of her chest rising and falling. Her arms felt heavy. Lowering them to her sides, Katie was vaguely aware that the paper bag had slipped from her hand and landed on the console beside her, but she'd maintained a firm grip on her picture.

After several minutes, her breathing returned to normal and the ringing sound in her head grew sporadic. Katie searched her memory in an attempt to identify if 'sporadic ringing in the head' was a normal post-panic attack side effect. She hated that these horrible attacks used to occur with such frequency that she actually had a personal database of experiences to check her symptoms against.

Nope, she concluded, *the sporadic ringing is new.*

Turning her head to take in her surroundings, she saw cars whizzing by on the interstate. She squinted against the glare of the sun, which was shining brightly down on the pavement and bouncing off the car windshields speeding by.

Setting her picture carefully on her lap, Katie retrieved the paper bag and folded it up, returning it to her purse. She didn't *love* the thought that she might need to keep it handy for future use, but better safe than sorry. Katie had always dealt in facts, and the fact was she'd been off the plane less than an hour and had barely started down the highway towards Harper's Crossing and she'd had a panic attack. Did she really think she would be getting through the rest of the weekend unscathed? Not likely.

As she placed the paper bag inside her gigantic "in case of emergency" carry-on bag, she discovered the source of the ringing.

She felt like an idiot. On the bright side, at least she didn't have to add tinnitus to the looooong list of symptoms that characterized her panic attacks. On the flip side? Apparently, she no longer recognized her own cell phone's ring tone.

Picking up her iPhone, she swiped the screen to answer, saying warmly, "Hey Sophiebell!"

"Katie, where are you? I just called the house and they said you weren't there. I'm running last minute errands with Bobby, but I thought you would be here by now. Was your flight delayed? I can't wait to see you," Sophie squealed, the words tumbling out of her mouth one over another.

Katie smiled to herself. She had always thought that Sophie Hunter could paraphrase that old Army motto to adopt as her own: "I say more before nine a.m. than most people say all day."

"The flight was fine. I am on my way, and I will be there in less than an hour. I can't wait to see you, too."

"Okay, hurry," Sophie pleaded but then followed it up with the firm command, "but drive safe."

"I will. See you soon, bride-to-be." Katie tried to cover the stress in her voice with ebullience as she said goodbye and hung up the phone.

After replacing the phone in her purse, she gently lifted the picture she'd chosen for her object of security. It was of her and Jason Sloan, both eleven years old, at science camp. A knot formed in her throat and she bit her lip.

Why? That was the one word question that always filled her mind when she looked at this picture or her thoughts drifted to the boy whose big brown eyes belonged to the scrawny kid with his arm thrown around her as they posed in front of Whisper Lake the summer before she'd met Sophie's brother Nick. Before she'd been Nick's girlfriend. Before Nick's accident. Before Nick's funeral. Before the night of Nick's funeral.

Why?

Why had *that night* happened? Why had she done what she had? Why hadn't she been able to face up to, and own, her actions? Why had she let one night define the last ten years of her life? And considering all of those things, why did *this* picture bring her the comfort that nothing else could?

Taking a deep breath Katie tried to mentally prepare herself for the fact that this weekend, whether she wanted to or not, she was going to have to face her past and the brown eyes that had haunted her for a decade.

Jason Sloan.

Jason had been her friend. Her best friend. At least, until that fateful night when she'd made the biggest mistake of her life. Jason had also been Nick's best friend. The entire town had lovingly nicknamed them 'The Three Musketeers.'

The same town that she hadn't been back to since the day they buried Nick.

It had been ten long years since Katie Marie Lawson had set foot in Harper's Crossing, the town of her childhood and her youth. She had never meant to stay away this long.

When she originally left for school in California a decade ago, her plan had been to come back at Christmastime. Sitting at L.A.X., waiting for her flight that first holiday away from home had been her first experience with a bout of hyperventilation. She never got on the plane. The next episode occurred as she booked her flight that same year for spring break. That time, she hadn't even made it to the airport. Then, they'd started to happen more frequently any time she was under stress. It took several years to get the episodes under control, during which she refrained from making travel plans.

Then, after she graduated from law school at Pepperdine University, she immediately started working at

Wilson, Martin, Gregory, and Associates, a very prestigious law firm in San Francisco.

The first three years at the firm flew by in a blur. Katie worked 80+ hours a week and even worked every holiday, including Christmas. She'd barely had time to breathe, let alone go out of town.

Last year, even though she was on the fast track to make junior partner, she had taken a vacation. The plan had been to take a few days for herself—to decompress—and then head back to her hometown. She had booked her flight and the experience had been incident free.

That was progress at least.

Katie had then spent the first four days of her vacation in her apartment, so it was really more of a 'staycation'—but still. She cleaned, cooked, slept, and had a Julia Roberts movie marathon.

At the end of the four days, the morning she was scheduled to fly back to Illinois, she had been called into work because a fellow associate had come down with the flu. And well, if she was being honest, she had been *more* than happy to go back to work on Wednesday instead of being on a direct flight from SFO to O'Hare.

Bottom line, she hadn't made it back home since 'the incident.'

Until today.

She was here. In Illinois. Headed back to Harper's Crossing. She had done it. Because this weekend wasn't about her—it was about Miss Sophie Hunter, who was getting married to Bobby Sloan, Jr., the youngest of the five Sloan boys. Sophie had called her, *ecstatic,* three months earlier to announce her engagement to Bobby and to ask Katie to be her maid of honor. Bobby was Jason Sloan's youngest brother and Jason was the best man in the wedding.

Nerves, unlike any she'd ever felt before, bubbled up inside of Katie. Looking down at the green LED lights on her dashboard she saw that it was 8:30 a.m. Today was Thursday and her return flight to California was not until 7:00 p.m. on Sunday. All she needed to do was get through the next four days—preferably without having a nervous breakdown—and then she could wing her way back to her lovely, safe, predictable life in San Francisco.

Let the countdown begin.

✦ ✦ ✦

Jason leaned his hands on the cool tile of the shower wall as steam rose up around him. He inhaled deeply through his nose as he let the pounding heat of the water hit his tense shoulders and back. Adrenaline raced through his veins like the white waters of raging rapids, nerves whirled through him like the Tasmanian Devil on speed. Rolling his neck from side to side he tried his best to just relax.

Never before in his life had he felt this amped up and anxious. Jason was an easy going, laid back guy.

Always had been. Until today.

This was it. The day that Jason had been waiting for, for over a decade, was finally here.

Katie Lawson was coming home.

Dipping his head once more under the heated shower stream, Jason reached down and turned the silver knob to the left, shutting off the water. He shook the excess water in his hair out as he pushed open the glass door and grabbed the towel he'd hung on the wall. As he quickly dried off, he heard his phone buzz for probably the tenth time in the last five minutes.

Grabbing his jeans, he pulled them on and swiped the screen on his iPhone. He had twelve missed calls. Three voicemail messages and two texts. Pressing his thumb on the icon to pull up the first text he saw it was from his oldest brother Seth. It read:

Is the kid really going to go through with this?

Jason sighed. None of his other brothers, *or* his dad, *or* any of the crew at work believed that Bobby was doing the right thing. Jason did. He saw the look in Bobby's eyes when he talked about, looked at, or was even thinking about Sophie Hunter. Jason recognized that look. He knew it well, from personal experience. It was the look of a guy that was in love with his soul mate.

Jason's thumbs flew across the screen as he typed back:

Yes. He is.

Bobby was twenty-four years old, a grown man. Yes, he may be the youngest of the Sloan boys, but he was still a man. Jason was sure, beyond a shadow of a doubt, his baby brother knew what he was doing.

A loud buzz once again sounded as Jason's phone vibrated in his hand. He looked down to see that it was another text from Seth.

You can't talk him out of it?

Jason inhaled slowly through his nose as he typed back:

No. And I wouldn't even if I could.

A part of Jason knew that Seth, and his other brothers Riley and Alex thought they had Bobby's best interest at heart. But Seth and Riley, had left for the Marines just days after their high school graduation and had been gone since Bobby was still in elementary school. Alex had only just returned home a few months ago after being in the Navy for the past six years. His brothers had been absent for years and didn't know Bobby, not the man he was today.

Jason was tired of having this conversation with people. Just this morning, a few guys on the construction crew had called to run the idea of kidnapping Bobby at his bachelor party tonight to "Stop him from making the biggest mistake of his life." Jason had quickly squashed those genius's abduction plan.

Scrolling through his missed calls he saw that a majority were from Laura, a girl that he'd been seeing off and on for the last year—until three months ago when Sophie and Bobby announced their engagement. Since then, Jason's social life had come to a screeching halt. No way was he going to return her call. He wasn't trying to be a dick, but she'd been calling a lot the past couple of weeks hinting (not so subtly) that she wanted to be his date for Bobby's wedding.

Yeah, that was *not* going to happen.

She hadn't been the only one who'd called, though. One voicemail was from his foreman on the Slater Street site and the other was from Sophie.

Lifting the phone to his ear Jason pressed play on the message from his soon to be sister-in-law while he reminded himself that as much of a milestone, a game changer, an event Katie Lawson's return was in his world, this weekend was not about him. It was about Bobby and Sophie. Bobby had chosen him to be his best man and Jason didn't take that responsibility and honor lightly.

Sophie's bubbly voice sounded through the speaker, "Hey Jas, just wanted to see if you can get to mom and dad's a little early. Bobby and I are still out running errands and Aunt Wendy is dealing with last minute wedding details. I just talked to Katie and she'll probably get there in about half an hour, before I can make it back. I wanted someone to be there when she gets home. You know like a welcome party, even if it's just a party of one. Can you believe it? Katie's actually coming home!" He barely registered Sophie's high pitch squeal of excitement followed by her quick, "Thanks, Jas. You're the bestest!"

Jason's mind replayed Sophie's words, "*Katie's actually coming home*!"

Yes, he was his brother's best man and he planned on being the best damn best man there ever was. But that didn't change the fact that Jason was finally going to get the opportunity to see Katie again. Apologize for that night. To tell her all the things he never had. To set the record straight. He wouldn't be on best man duty every minute of every hour over the next three days.

Jason looked at the time that Sophie had left the message. Thirty minutes ago. It must have been when he was out for his morning run.

He finished getting dressed, grabbed his keys, and was out the door in record time.

He had no idea what was going to happen when he and Katie saw each other again. What it would be like. What they would say to each other. But, there was one thing he knew for sure, he'd waited a decade to find out, and now, finally, the wait was over.

Chapter Two

As Katie drove past the sign marking Harper's Crossing city limits, her heart was racing as she tried her *best* not to think about the *best man* and instead focus on the reason she was here. Sophie's wedding.

Sophie (or 'Sophiebell,' which had been her nickname since Sophie was six and had decided that she was Tinker Bell) was the closest thing Katie had to a sister. And there was *nothing* Katie wouldn't do for her. And panic attack aside, she was *really* excited to see her. Other than a brief trip out to California after Sophie had graduated high school four years ago, Katie hadn't seen her since she left home. But they'd kept in touch, talking or e-mailing several times a week.

Katie was an only child. She and her mom, Pam, had gone to live with her Aunt Wendy in Harper's Crossing when Katie was four, immediately after her parents' divorce.

Craig, Katie's dad, had come to visit his daughter exactly one time since she'd moved to Harper's Crossing. One month after she and her mom had arrived,

Craig had taken Katie to Tasty Treats for a double scoop of mint chocolate chip ice cream.

He had talked about how much he loved her and assured her that the divorce and the move had nothing to do with her. He had also promised to see her once a month. Suffice it to say, he didn't keep that promise.

Katie had not seen her father since that cold October Saturday, twenty-four years ago.

Growing up, she'd always assumed that he had stayed away because he and Aunt Wendy "did not see eye to eye," as Katie's mom always said (although, now, as an adult, she was leaning towards the theory that it was because he was a shitheel).

Honestly, if Katie's memory served, she hadn't really seen a lot of her dad even when he and her mom were still together. It seemed to Katie that 'pre-divorce,' it was just Katie and her mom and then 'post-divorce,' it was Katie, her mom, and Aunt Wendy.

She never really missed her dad. Sometimes she would miss her *idea* of what having a dad in her life would be like. But never the man who had fathered her. She really never knew that man, and what she had known had been unpredictable. Promising to visit her once a month and then her never seeing hide nor hair of him again really just seemed par for the course where he was concerned. It was simply the last in a long line of broken promises that had characterized their father-daughter relationship, and—even at four years old—Katie didn't remember being terribly surprised when the months rolled around and he didn't.

She had always credited the fact that she didn't miss him terribly to how full her life had been, how utterly surrounded she was by people who loved her. Although, she would sometimes get lonely in Aunt Wendy's house. Aunt Wendy had a full-time job and Katie's mom usually held down two jobs just to make ends meet, so there was a lot of time that Katie had been alone with just her imagination and books to keep her occupied.

As she made her way down the highway, a smile crept across her face because, oh boy, how that changed the summer before Katie's seventh grade year.

That was the summer that Sophie Hunter (aka Sophiebell) had moved into the house next door to Aunt Wendy. And right away—literally, starting immediately on moving day—Sophie had become Katie's shadow. Not that she'd minded. Katie had loved finally having someone, anyone other than a doll, to dress up and play tea party with.

Sophie's dad, Mike, was a fireman and her mom, Grace, was a nurse. Katie had babysat Sophie when Mike and Grace's shifts overlapped. Katie's house felt a lot less lonely with a bouncing, laughing, full-of-life four-year-old in it. But Sophiebell wasn't the only distraction the Hunters had brought with them when they moved to Harper's Crossing. They also brought Nick, Sophie's older brother and Katie's first love.

Nicholas Hunter was three months older than Katie

and he had never let her forget it. He had sandy blond hair and the most beautiful green eyes Katie had ever seen.

The day before school started in seventh grade, two weeks after the Hunters had moved in, Nick came to Katie's door to get Sophie for dinner. She'd never forget that day. Before he left the porch, he looked over his shoulder, his green eyes sparkling in the sun. They were even extra green due to the fact that he was wearing his favorite Fighting Irish t-shirt. *Swoon.*

He asked, "Hey, do you think you would want to be my girlfriend? It's a lot easier to start a new school when you already have a girlfriend."

He then proceeded to shoot her a smile that—she would later come to know—had gotten him anything he'd wanted since he was an infant. And with good reason—it was one helluva doozy of a smile.

As much as Katie had wanted to act as if the smile didn't affect her, she knew the heat she felt in her cheeks meant they were bright red. No way could she hide the evidence.

Still, that didn't mean she had to acknowledge it. So, she'd done what any super-cool eleven-year-old girl would have done when faced with Nick Hunter's dreamy proposal.

She'd shrugged and said, "Yeah, whatever."

"Sweet," he smiled. "I'll be here at 7:45 so we can walk to school together tomorrow."

He then jumped off her porch before she could say

another word. She slowly closed her front door and, once it shut, started to scream and run around in circles until she fell on her couch in utter exhaustion. Katie always did lean towards the dramatic.

Katie had no way of knowing, then, that the relationship she had just entered would last for the next six years of her life and end in tragedy.

Katie's chest constricted tightly and tears stung her eyes at the thought of the senseless tragedy. The summer after Nick and Katie's senior year of high school, Nick had been out late one night joyriding and had tragically driven his truck off Spencer Point.

Hours later, when the police pulled the truck out of the steep embankment, they found a nearly lifeless body inside. Nick lay in a hospital bed in a deep coma for three weeks following the accident. Katie and his family were by his side every moment the hospital staff would allow them to be.

Finally, his parents, Mike and Grace, made the most horrific decision any parent could ever have to make. They took Nick off life support.

His funeral was held three days later, and Katie left that very same night to go stay with her grandmother in Chicago. She'd needed to escape. That was the last time she had set foot in Harper's Crossing.

Katie breathed out a long sigh as she turned onto Main Street. She needed to get her head on straight and pull it together. Facts—that was what she needed to focus on. Facts had always comforted Katie.

Fact: she wasn't a teenager anymore. Fact: she was an adult. Fact: she could handle this.

After Sophie called, Katie had decided to go and see another therapist to determine if she could pick up any tips for the panic attacks associated with returning to Harper's Crossing. She'd gone a grand total of eight times. Most of the things she'd told Katie had been fairly generic, but there were a few things that had stuck out. The therapist had explained that Katie had two very strong sides to her personality. One side was very fact, truth, rules oriented. It gave her security when making decisions and also made her a very good lawyer. The other side was a carefree, fun, sensitive side. Which made her care about and connect deeply with people and gave her a great capacity for giving and receiving love.

Those two sides of her had collided when Katie had left Harper's Crossing and she had never dealt with that inner conflict. The danger in returning to Harper's Crossing, for her, would be that all the memories and everything she had been hiding from and pushing down would now be flooding back because she would be in familiar surroundings with people that really knew her.

So, Katie's lawyer side, "the fixer," would say, *okay, we're finally going to face this, great! Time to face it = time to fix it—good let's get it done.* But she had to realize her emotional side would not be able to do that. She needed to be careful and take it slow, or she could be completely overwhelmed and just shut down, or possibly, even have a small breakdown.

A maid of honor having a mental breakdown was not the YouTube video moment that Katie wanted to occur this weekend.

Driving through the town as she took in her surroundings, Katie barely recognized it. The last time she had been in Harper's Crossing, it contained two traffic lights and one four-way stop. Today there seemed to be a traffic light or four-way stop at every intersection.

Katie's eyes scanned the area where Pickler's Field had been. She was shocked to see that the field she had learned to ride her bike in when she was five, played tag in when she was seven, attempted and failed to smoke a cigarette in when she was thirteen, and spent almost every Friday and Saturday night parking in with Nick after he turned sixteen and got his black Chevy truck, was now a strip mall.

Coming up to yet another stoplight, Katie did a double take. The quaint, one-story hospital she had been admitted to when she had suffered from chicken pox and had a temperature of 104 at age six, had her tonsils removed when she was eight, and spent three weeks keeping vigil beside Nick's motionless body as he lay in a coma, was now a four-story hospital that looked to be straight out of the pages of Architectural Digest. And if the exterior was any indication, it was now state-of-the-art.

As she continued on, she mentally counted four

McDonald's, three Burger Kings, and two Taco Bells since she had entered the city limits. This was quite a contrast to her days in Harper's Crossing, when there had only been one fast food restaurant in town—a Dairy Queen. It had been the local hang out for all the pre-teens and teens. Katie noted sadly that the Dairy Queen, which was another place that held so many of her teenage memories, had also been obliterated at some point in the past decade. It was replaced by an Office Depot.

But, as different as everything looked, it also looked the same. Harper's Crossing was still surrounded by lush rolling green hills on one side, quaint downtown buildings still gave it its character and a large river running through the center of town still gave the town a picturesque postcard feel.

As Katie made the left turn onto her childhood street, she audibly exhaled in relief.

From what she could see, nothing had changed on Harper Lane. Certainly not the houses, which were still all painted in one of three color combinations – blue and yellow, green and white, or blue and white.

And judging by the few neighbors she saw out on their lawns, the people hadn't changed either. Mrs. Belmont stood watering her yard in that same pink and green moo moo she had worn since Katie could remember. Mr. Peters still mowed his lawn in white shorts that were two sizes too small and black socks that he pulled all the way up to his knees, a cigarette precariously dangling out of his mouth.

As she pulled into the driveway of her aunt's two-story home (painted in the white with blue trim option, for that Mediterranean flair), she felt a confusing combination of relief, nostalgia, sadness, and anxiety.

This was it. Katie was home.

She opened the door to her rented blue Honda Accord, took in a deep breath, and let out a cleansing sigh. The air smelled of a familiar combination: sweet from Mrs. Greyson's beautiful flower bed and fresh from the trees that lined the street. Katie let her head fall back, soaking in the warming rays of sunlight. The sun in the sky may very well be the same one that shone in California, but somehow, standing in her Aunt's driveway, it felt different. It felt comforting.

With a renewed sense of calm, she moved to the back of the car, popped the trunk, and reached in for her suitcases. As she pulled them from the car, she was stopped cold in her tracks by a familiar voice.

"Need a hand, Kit Kat?" the deep voice sounded from behind her.

A shudder rippled through her body and the hairs on the back of her neck stood up. Her carry-on slipped from her shoulder and dropped with a thud on the cement driveway.

"Jason?" she said, her voice a whisper of disbelief.

Katie had known she would have to face Jason at some point on her trip home. He was, after all, the best man in Sophie's wedding—which made perfect sense, seeing as how Sophie was marrying Jason's little brother, Bobby. She didn't need to possess psychic powers to foresee that their paths would cross. She'd just thought she would have had a little more time to prepare herself before she came face to face with him.

She had also been banking on the theory that when the inevitable face-to-face occurred, she would have the benefit of a room full of people surrounding them to serve as a protective shield, a buffer. However, that did not seem to be the case.

Nope. Here they were. Alone.

She stood, frozen, with her back to him, staring down at her pink and black suitcase, wishing with all her might that she could just climb into the trunk and hide. Logically, she knew that plan was probably not the most mature response to this encounter—also, shall we say, not the most subtle. Still, it was tempting. Because as the realization sank in that the extra time and buffer-people she so desperately needed to get through this encounter with Jason *were not flipping forthcoming*, Katie felt as though the air was literally being sucked from her lungs.

Great. Panic attack number two. Here we go. And right in front of Jason. The hiding-in-the-trunk option was sounding better by the second.

Her mind raced as she tried to mentally prepare herself for seeing Jason again.

Jason Andrew Sloan had chestnut brown hair, whiskey-colored, soulful brown eyes, and a smile that could, as her Aunt Wendy always said, "melt butter in a freezer." He was also the first person Katie had met in her kindergarten class at Harper's Crossing Elementary.

23 Years Ago

It was the first day of Kindergarten and Katie was paired up with a boy as a table buddy.

A BOY! Could this day get any worse? The class's first official assignment as kindergartners was to write their names on the white paper sitting on the desk in front of them and then tape it to the back of their seats.

Katie wrote her name in all capital letters and rainbow colors and taped it on the back of her chair, just as she had been instructed to do. She was proud of finishing her assignment in time to go out for recess. She noticed her table buddy (The Boy!) had not.

After the first recess, when the kids came back into the classroom, she saw a few of them standing around her chair—laughing. As she walked up behind them to sit in her seat, she saw that the 'ie' at the end of 'Katie', on the nameplate she had been so proud of, had been crossed out, and the word 'Kit' had been written in front of the 'Kat' that remained of her original creation.

She was so embarrassed. Why would anybody ruin her name paper? She looked over to see her table buddy Jason (The Boy!) smiling a toothless grin from ear to ear as he patted her chair "I think this is your seat, Kit Kat," he said.

All the kids started laughing and Katie just slumped

down in her chair, furious at her table buddy aka The Boy aka Jason Sloan.

Jason never admitted to being the one who had defaced her beautiful rainbow-colored name paper but she knew, deep down in her heart, he was the culprit. And she would never forget it, just like no one ever forgot the nickname. From that day on, Katie Lawson was Kit Kat.

Well, to all the kids in Harper's Crossing Elementary anyway.

Present Day

His deep voice interrupted her thoughts now.

"Wow, all this time and you know it's me without even having to turn around. I guess that means I still got it," he said with his trademark cocky tone. A tone that had always amused Katie, not that she would ever let him know that. His ego was big enough.

Jason had had girls swooning over him for as long as she had known him. In fact, Katie maintained to this day, that even their sixth grade math teacher, Mrs. Carson, had had a crush on him. Whenever Jason would turn on the charm, usually to get out of detention for not completing his homework or being tardy, Mrs. Carson would just smile as her cheeks turned a light shade of red and say, "Oh, Jason, if you were just ten years older…"

Mrs. Carson never finished the sentence but Katie always knew what she meant, and Jason never got detention—at least in that class.

It's not like his charm only worked on older women either. Jason had always had girls eating out of his hand and he knew it. There wasn't a single girl in Harper's Crossing who wouldn't do just about anything to get Jason's attention.

Well, there was one girl. Katie.

"Oh yeah, you still got it, Jas," Katie said, forcing herself to speak, trying to buy herself even a few more seconds before she would have to face him. Katie's words sounded strained between her shallow breaths even to her own ears. "If by 'it' you mean the maturity of a five-year-old, then, yes, you definitely still have it."

She realized they were falling into their patented Jason-Katie banter, which was a good thing. Right? Out of all the ways that seeing Jason again could go, him being his usual arrogant self and her calling him on it was definitely not the *worst* scenario. Now, if she could just stop her body from short-circuiting at his mere presence, she'd be all good.

With each second that passed, it appeared that was going to be easier said than done. Not only was she having trouble keeping the oxygen from escaping her lungs, it also seemed as though all of the oxygen had somehow disappeared around her. Deliberately and methodically, she slowly breathed in through her nose and out through her mouth, trying desperately to remain as calm as possible.

She reminded herself, firmly, that she *had* to be calm in hopes of staving off panic attack #2. She absolutely couldn't think about how humiliating it would be to fall to pieces in front of Jason or fear would take over—her heart would start to race, her breathing would quicken, and it would all be downhill from there. Reaching up with heavy arms, Katie shut the trunk of the car so that she could lean on it for strength.

"Come on Kit Kat, you know you always loved that nickname," Katie heard Jason say playfully, but his voice sounded as if it were coming from a long distance, across a great expanse. She felt his hand grasp her arm, and then she felt her body being turned in his direction.

As Jason's fingers wrapped around her arm, they caused tingling sensations in places located much lower south, and not nearly as innocent as the place where he was touching her. Hmm, that wasn't a very good sign. It also wasn't doing a whole heck of a lot to help her in the campaign to keep her heart rate under control and slow her breathing. Nope. Not one little bit.

As she turned, her eyes alighted on a broad chest that—oh my, yes—filled out his white t-shirt quite well. Her mouth instantly filled with saliva like one of Pavlov's dogs. *Hmmm,* she thought, *so this is what they mean when they say something looks 'mouth-watering.'* She totally got it now. In an effort to avoid drooling, she swallowed, but to her own ears it sounded like a shockingly loud gulp.

Slowly, Katie moved her eyes up the length of the

solid, strong, statue-like figure standing mere inches away from her. She paused momentarily to admire—against her will—the smooth olive skin at the base of Jason's neck. She couldn't help herself. It just so nicely contrasted with the stark white color of the t-shirt's v-neck it was peeking out of.

Unconsciously, she licked her lips and saw the pulse on Jason's neck jump. Her eyes darted up to meet his golden brown ones, which caused the aforementioned tingling places to start pulsing.

Katie felt her heart beating so hard she thought it might beat right out of her chest. And the mantra began.

You can breathe. Just breathe. Breathe in and out slowly. You can breathe.

✦ ✦ ✦

As Jason stood in front of Katie, who was wearing a simple grey tank top and blue jeans, he was momentarily paralyzed with shock at the effect she had on him.

Suddenly he was back in Mrs. Garcia's kindergarten classroom.

23 Years Ago

It was the first day of kindergarten—finally. Best. Day. Ever.

Putting his backpack in his cubby, he felt a brush of something that tickled his arm. He swatted his arm and felt the softest, silkiest thing he had ever touched.

When he looked up to see what it was, he couldn't believe his eyes. There she stood, a real-life angel. Rays of sunlight from the window streamed through her long, blond hair, and she was looking down at him with the biggest blue eyes Jason had ever seen in his life.

The earth stopped spinning and everything stood still. Nothing existed except this amazing creature. She slowly reached her hand to her neck and flipped her long, blond hair behind her back as she placed her backpack in her cubby.

Jason could not speak. This was a new phenomenon for Jason, as the spoken word had always been one of his greatest gifts.

Since the time Jason was able to put two words together, he always knew just the right thing to say to either get out of trouble, get what he wanted, or just put a smile on the faces of the women in his life. Even before he was old enough to speak, he had exuded a natural-born mojo. The first word ever used to describe Jason in the nursery was charming. All of the nurses in the infant care ward would fight over who could hold him. Even as a newborn, he had a twinkle in his eye and a little smirk on his lips that the opposite sex just couldn't get enough of. But in this moment, five-year-old Jason could not even remember how to say, 'Hi.'

But luck was on his side, as it usually was. Yes! He was assigned to the same table as this heavenly being. Jason could barely sit still next to her. He fidgeted and couldn't keep his eyes off of her.

She, on the other hand, sat totally composed next to him, completely ignoring him, working on their first assignment, the name paper.

Jason had tried all morning to get her attention somehow, but to no avail. When she finished her paper, she looked so proud of it as she taped it to the back of her seat.

When she sat down again beside him, he had the sudden urge to pinch her just to see what she would do. Anything to get her attention. He was desperate to have her acknowledge him.

But reason prevailed, and he realized that pinching her wouldn't be the best course of action. He had to keep thinking. Before another plan could take shape, however, she was out the door to recess.

Finally, genius struck. As he sat in his chair while all the other kids were at recess, he decided he would 'redecorate' her name paper to give her a nickname. That would be a way he could start to talk to her—an ice breaker of sorts. He knew that would get her attention. And it would be special. If he gave her a special name paper decoration, she would know, for sure, how special he thought she was.

He looked at her name page, which so beautifully read 'Katie,' and the first thing that came to Jason's mind was Kit Kat—the best candy bar in the whole world. He quickly changed her paper to read just that.

He had not expected any of the other kids to notice it when they came in from recess—or to think it was funny. It was supposed to be a special, inside secret between him and his blond angel.

In fact, to be honest, he had completely forgotten that

any other kids were even in their class. No one existed in the room for him but Katie.

But after the look on Katie's face when the other kids were all gathered around her desk in giggles, Jason knew he had made a huge mistake.

Okay, he had to fix this and quick. The only thing he knew to do was try to relieve some of the tension by stating the obvious. It was part of his charm. Jason was always being accused of saying what everyone was thinking. Instinct kicked in and he simply said, "I think this is your seat, Kit Kat."

He was shocked to see a look of anger and embarrassment that suddenly appeared on Katie's face. He didn't know how things had gone so terribly wrong or why his charm and wit had not gotten the smile that always appeared on the opposite sex's face whenever he spoke. But the one thing he did know was that he had never met anyone else who made him feel the way this girl sitting next to him made him feel.

And he hadn't known it at the time, but he never would.

Present Day

The same feeling, that paralyzed him upon seeing her for the first time in their kindergarten class, washed over Jason now, as he stood in front of Katie. His world stopped spinning and she was the only thing that existed.

Katie had grown into the most beautiful woman he

had ever laid eyes on. Standing five foot three, with a petite figure that had curves in all the right places, she still had incredible long, blond hair and the most intoxicating blue eyes in existence.

And when he looked at her, he still saw his angel.

✦ ✦ ✦

Still unable to get her breathing under control, Katie stood stock-still, staring wide-eyed at Jason, who was totally silent. That was very un-Jason-like. He always had *something* to say, usually of the smart-ass variety.

The quiet between them felt electrically charged and Katie was desperate to say something to break the super-charged silence, but she just wasn't sure she could speak through her choppy breaths. Also, she wasn't sure she even remembered what they'd been talking about. Katie instinctively closed her eyes in hopes that she would have an easier time focusing without the overwhelming distraction of the much too-tempting man Jason had grown into. Also, maybe without the enticing visual stimulation, she could actually take in a steadying breath.

She took a deep breath in slowly through her nostrils. So far, so good.

So what were they talking about again?

Oh, yeah. The *nickname*.

Focus restored, her eyes flew open, sparking with fire, "No, Jason, *you* always loved that nickname, which I have to say surprises me, because—as witty and creative as you claim to be—I would have thought you could've come up with something just a little more original."

She strove to keep her voice light and even, but she could hear the tension in it as tight as a wire. She concentrated on keeping her breathing steady, on trying to remember to pull her voice back into a tone that sounded as casual and nonchalant as if she were merely taking note of the weather.

However after several seconds of melting into Jason's enticing stare, she concluded that she was failing miserably and that the casual demeanor she was striving for could be better maintained if she avoided direct eye contact with him. She looked away. Even without eye contact, a rush of heat washed over, causing tiny bumps to raise on her skin. Still feeling his potent effect, Katie reassessed thinking maybe it wasn't in his eyes after all. Her eyes darted back to his. The tiny glance solidified the fact that she was right the first time. Her cheeks flushed and her breathing threatened to gallop out of control again.

Yep. No eye contact. No eye contact was definitely the way to go.

Katie stared across the street. She just needed to look anywhere but into those big, sexy, soulful eyes. What's that saying? Oh right. "*The eyes are the window to the soul.*" Nope. Not a good idea. The last thing she needed was Jason looking directly into the gateway to her soul, thank you very much. She was going to go ahead and keep that tidal wave of feelings to herself.

Growing up, Katie had always thought Jason was cute. In a mischievous boy sort of way. But the specimen that stood before her, now, was no boy. No sirree. Nope. This was definitely a man. And the sexiest man Katie had ever been in the presence of, at that.

"Who said I came up with that nickname?" Jason asked with playful innocence coloring his voice. She knew that he knew *exactly* what he was doing. For some odd reason, frustrating Katie had *always* been Jason's favorite pastime. Katie never understood why.

"Come on, seriously? Are you *still* going to deny it?" Shaking her head, Katie's voice wavered between irritation, at once again visiting a topic that was well-covered ground, and amazement that Jason had not changed at all.

Instantly, Katie's breathing returned to normal and her lightheadedness vanished. Hmmm. *I guess being in the sweet spot between irritated and amazed calmed the beginnings of a possible panic attack,* she mused. *Good to know.*

Now that she had confidence flowing through her veins like liquid lightning, Katie turned and tilted her face up to Jason's, planning to continue her diatribe about his denial of the origin of the nickname, but she immediately froze in her tracks.

Big mistake. *Abort*! Her first instinct had been correct.

Note to self: avoid eye contact with Jason Sloan at all

costs this weekend.

Katie realized, in that moment, that no matter how strong and self-assured she felt going into it, eye contact with Jason would always be a supremely bad idea for a couple of reasons.

First, she didn't want him to have any inkling of the powerful effect he was having on her body—or, for that matter, on her mind and soul. It was going to be hard enough to put her past behavior in the water-under-the-bridge category without adding new indiscretions to the list.

Second, well, let's just say she still felt more than a little embarrassed about the way she had behaved the last time she saw Jason. But, mostly, she felt guilty down to the core of her being. A little embarrassment was nothing compared to the heartbreaking fact that, in one moment of weakness, she had betrayed not one, but *two,* of the most important people in her life. Even now, she could not come close to reconciling her behavior that night with who *she* was.

Loyal. Trustworthy. Caring. That was who she was. Except on *that* night.

Katie took a deep breath, steeling herself as flashes from the past started flooding her mind like a slide show from Hell.

It was the night of the funeral for Nick, her boyfriend and Jason's best friend.

Jason had come over that night to check on her and things had gotten a little out of control. A little…um…heated. Yes…heated.

They had been interrupted, but Katie had promised to meet him at the Dairy Queen at 8 a.m. the next morning. She hadn't. By the time 8 a.m. rolled around, she had been sitting in her Grandma May's sunny yellow kitchen over one hundred miles away.

She hadn't gone to the D.Q. to know whether or not Jason had, in fact, shown up. But in her heart, she knew he had. Jason faced things. It didn't matter if the situation was uncomfortable or awkward—he faced it head on. She had always appreciated and admired that about him.

If she could go back to that night, she would do so many things differently—starting with not running away.

A chill of awareness ran down her spine as more memories from that night populated her mind. Her body warming beneath his. His hands on her skin. His mouth on her neck. The feeling of overwhelming passion.

Then, new snippets hit her. What had come next. The footsteps on the stairs. The panic that had flooded them, causing them to spring out of bed and begin the frantic dance of pulling clothes on at top speed.

Jason's refusal to leave unless she promised to meet him. Her hurried acquiescence so they didn't get caught. His sinfully sexy smile as he disappeared out her window.

As soon as her mom and aunt had opened the

door—about one millisecond after Jason's head had disappeared from view through the window, thank God—Katie had turned around, shell-shocked, and announced that she wanted to go and stay with Grandma May for the rest of the summer.

She had thrown some clothes in a bag, hopped in her reliable, little used VW bug, and was sleeping in her Grandma's guest room by one in the morning.

Her mother brought the rest of her clothes the next weekend, and at the end of the summer, she went off to college. She never again set foot in Harper's Crossing—until now.

The flash flood of memory lane had her feeling more than a little lightheaded and slightly disconnected.

Katie moved her hands. Reaching behind her, she touched the steel solidness of the trunk, bringing her back to the present moment. *Facts,* she reminded herself. *Focus on the facts.*

Fact: she wasn't a teenager. Fact: she was an adult. Fact: she was standing toe-to-toe with one very grown-up Jason Sloan. Fact: she was trembling and trying to control her rapid heart rate.

Okay, maybe not *all* the facts.

Even in her heightened state, the irony was not lost on her that the very person who had sent her running off to Chicago all those years ago, scampering off out of Harper's Crossing like a scared bunny—the very person she had no idea how she could possibly face again—was the very first person she saw upon her return all these years later.

Okay, she told herself sternly. *Pep talk time. Shake it off, Katie. No more avoiding this. It's time to face your demons...pay the piper...walk the plank...cowboy up. It's go time.*

Take a deep breath, she reminded herself, *and...talk.*

Katie opened her mouth to speak, but nothing came out. She snapped it shut. She tried again. Same result. She imagined she looked like a trout on the bank of a river, flapping her mouth open and shut for no apparent reason.

The realization of how silly she must look gave her just the extra edge of courage she needed to jump off the cliff.

Looking down at the cement driveway, she quietly began, "Jason, I...I wanted to...I need to tell you that...I am so sorry... I can't begin to tell you how much I regret—" She shook her head in frustration. This was all coming out wrong. Why did she sound so formal? This was Jason. She wasn't deposing a witness.

As she took a deep breath, her palms moistened as nerves bubbled up inside of her. She tried again. "I am *so* sorry for just...you know...how I...and then when I..."

Katie stopped herself again. Stammering like an idiot was not the apology Jason deserved. She needed to abandon her self-imposed no-eye-contact rule and look Jason straight in the eye and apologize. Because this was

Jason. Yes, he might give her a hard time about it, but then they could move on past this awkwardness and get back to being *them.*

Gripping her fingers tighter against the trunk of the car, she braced herself for what she knew her physical reaction would be as she forced herself to look up into those gorgeous brown eyes, which reminded her of endless pools of warm and melty milk chocolate…

When she raised her eyes, the expression on Jason's face caused her to momentarily abandon her crucial apology. She narrowed her eyes.

"Why do you look like that?" she asked suspiciously.

"Like what?" he asked, his tone mirroring the arrogant expression he wore.

"So…" She paused searching for the right word. "Smug."

Rather than answering, the corner of his mouth tilted up as he bent down, putting his mouth right next to her ear. His hot breath assailed her neck, her lips started tingling, and she began to feel lightheaded again.

Wait…was this…*oh no.* Panic attack #2 might very well be on the horizon.

Not in front of Jason. Please *not in front of Jason,* Katie begged the Universe. It seemed like the Universe must have more important things on its mind because—oh, Lord. Now the shallow breathing was starting.

Jason's breath on her neck, however, was anything but shallow. It was deep. And heavy. And warm. It felt *so* good. And…oh, man, that lightheadedness was just getting worse and worse.

Jason moved a slight step forward. Reaching out, he rested his hands on either side of her body against the car, effectively pinning her inside his all-encompassing stance. Her mind was screaming at her to push him away and *run* as fast and as far as she could. She had done it before, and it had worked. Her body, however, was sending her some very different signals.

"I'm not smug, Kit Kat," Jason informed her, his deep voice rumbling in his chest.

"Wha…huh…?" Katie mumbled.

Jason laughed lightly. "I was just saying that I'm not smug. Just happy to know that I still get you all flustered."

Katie didn't respond. She didn't even really hear what he said. She'd stopped trying to pay attention to the words. Stupid words. They just got in the way of listening to his voice—that silky, low voice.

Reaching up, Jason brushed a stray hair that had flown across Katie's face. After he tucked it behind her ear, he traced his thumb down the back of Katie's neck slowly, sensuously, and then continued across her shoulder and down her arm. The work-roughened pads of his fingers grazed against her skin, causing an unwanted awareness of just how amazing his touch was.

When he reached her waist, he slipped his large

hand around her easily, spreading his fingers deliberately and firmly, grasping her back with a familiarity that felt as intensely dangerous as it did erotically comforting.

His thumb began to gently massage the small of her back, sending sharp zings of electricity ping-ponging off of her nerve endings. She wanted to stop those little zings of pleasure in their tracks. She wanted to ignore, suppress, deny—anything.

Her knees began to buckle beneath her as her head spun like a windmill on a blustery day.

She needed to push him away and get some distance so she could think straight. That is what she needed to do. *Any time now,* a little voice in the back of her head whispered. *Any time you want to get a jump on creating that distance would be perfect.*

That was, however, not what Katie did. No matter how hard her lizard brain screamed at her to push him away, step away, jump away, *dance* away even, all Katie found herself doing was looking up into his heavenly brown eyes as she melted into his embrace.

As her body brushed against his, Katie heard a low moan escape from Jason's throat, and she was suddenly hyper-aware of how close their lips were to each other. A shiver ran through her as she contemplated the nearness of those delicious, sexy lips.

Katie's breathing became more labored, but not in an out-of-control, panic-attacky kind of way. No, it was more of a body-coming-alive-for-the-first-time-in-years kind of way.

She vaguely wondered what was going to happen next but couldn't make herself focus too much on the future. Not when the present was this spine-tinglingly interesting.

Her brain might be telling her to get out of this situation, to think about the consequences, but her body was perfectly content to ride this little scene out and see where it went.

Why did it seem that she was utterly incapable of listening to her brain in any situation where Jason Sloan was involved?

Chapter Three

"Katie, you're here!"

A familiar loud female voice shook Katie (mostly) out of the spell Jason had somehow managed to cast on her, leaving her feeling woozy and a little discombobulated.

The next thing she knew she was being yanked away from Jason by the strong, sure arms of Aunt Wendy.

As soon as she managed to wrap her head around what was happening, she was filled with joy being in her aunt's warm, comforting embrace.

"Aunt Wendy, it's so good to see you." Katie's voice coming out slightly muffled as she was crushed against her aunt's broad, sturdy shoulders.

Since Wendy stood five-foot-nine barefoot, no one was ever going to miss her in a crowd. But Aunt Wendy was not the kind of person who hunched her shoulders and attempted to mask her height. Quite the opposite, as a matter of fact. Wendy wore her physical distinction as a badge of pride.

In addition to her height, there was also the fact

that Wendy had always loved bright colors, and that passion had bled into her clothing and hair choices.

And her personality? Katie smiled as she thought about it. Wendy's personality was as big as her frame, as loud as her voice, and as bright as her clothing.

As Katie was released from the crushing bear hug, she took in her aunt's appearance. Growing up, every day was a spin of the roulette wheel as to what Wendy's wardrobe might consist of. It was anybody's guess. Trying to predict her aunt's wardrobe was a game Katie had loved to play when she was little.

Today, Wendy's short bob cut was colored bright red, and she wore a sunshine yellow blazer paired with a white shirt. This topped black slacks and pair of bright red heels.

Katie felt warm from the inside out. Aunt Wendy was one of a kind and she had really missed her.

"What are you doing here?" Katie asked. "I thought you would be at work." A broad smile spread across her face as she said the words, but she was surprised to find that inside, happiness fought with disappointment at the arrival of this chaperone. Hadn't that been exactly what she had wanted—a buffer?

"Well, honey, I am at work!" Wendy exclaimed. "And I can't believe my peepers. Bless your heart, you've made it back to Harper's Crossing. You've finally come home, and all it took was a couple of kids gettin' hitched."

Wendy beamed at her niece, and Katie felt the glow

of her affection and pride warming her like rays of sun.

Then, Wendy abruptly turned her attention to Jason, saying, "Come here and get in on the action, Romeo."

And with that, Aunt Wendy pulled both Katie and Jason into an embrace, creating a three-way bear hug. Jason's arm came around Katie's waist as his fingers pressed into her jean-clad hip. The pressure of his possessive hold felt…good.

Oh boy, this hug was a *little* too close for Katie's comfort.

✦ ✦ ✦

As soon as Katie was ripped from his arms, Jason felt the emptiness like a physical blow. He immediately missed the weight of her against his body, the warmth of her against his skin.

What the hell had just happened here? He seriously needed to get a grip.

Damn. If Wendy hadn't interrupted them, Jason very well might have stripped Katie down, picked her up, wrapped her legs around him, and taken her—right there against her rental car—in front of God and everyone.

This was sure not how he had envisioned Katie Lawson's homecoming—and he'd had plenty of time to think about it since the last night he saw her over a decade ago.

Not only did he have a lot of things that he needed

to tell her, he also had questions he wanted answered. Not about the night she left or the years she had stayed away. Jason took full responsibility for that. He knew that was his fault. What still haunted him was her behavior leading up to that fateful night.

During the three weeks Jason's best friend—and Katie's boyfriend—Nick, lay in a hospital bed, lifeless and barely recognizable, Katie hadn't said two words to Jason. She hadn't even looked at him. He had always considered her one of his best friends—people called Nick, Katie and Jason 'The Three Musketeers.' Yet when they had needed each other most, she had completely shut him out. Whenever he had tried to speak to her, she would abruptly get up and leave the hospital room.

Every attempt he had made to stop her or confront her was always met with the same reaction, no matter who was in the room with him. People would always grab his arm and say things like, "Just let her go," or "She just needs space," or "Give her time," or "She'll talk when she's ready."

Why the hell had people been trying to protect her from him? Didn't they know that he had just wanted to make sure that she was okay? He had needed to know that she was all right more than he needed to draw his next breath.

What really pissed him off was all of the whys. Why had he listened to all of those people? Why had he let her go? Why had he given her time?

Why wasn't she speaking to him? Why couldn't she look at him? Nothing but questions. It had driven him absolutely insane.

From the first day he met her, Katie had never had a problem telling Jason exactly what was on her mind—and then some. So why hadn't she spoken to him—or even, seemingly, been able to bear looking at him—at the time when they had needed to lean on each other like never before?

Had Katie blamed him for Nick being in the car accident? Had she thought that Jason should have been with his friend on the late night joyride?

Or his deepest, worst fear—had she wished it were Jason lying in the bed instead of Nick?

10 Years Ago

It was after the funeral, and Jason simply had to talk to Katie. He didn't care what anyone said. He had to find out why Katie couldn't even look at him or speak to him—but most importantly, he had to find out if Katie was okay.

He was in the middle of trying to formulate a plan to get around all of her 'guardians' when fate struck and the Universe plopped an opportunity right down into his lap in the form of a phone call from Aunt Wendy saying that she was stuck catching up at work.

She obviously felt guilty for having to be at work—that was clear to Jason because she was talking a mile a minute. She was explaining that important issues had been neglected for far too long due to everything that had gone on in the last few weeks and that Katie's mom was working a swing shift, so could he please go over and stay with Katie because she didn't want to leave her alone for so long?

Jason supposed that all of the explanations must have registered somewhere in the back of his mind, but in the moment, all he heard her say was 'go stay with Katie.' Everything else after that was a buzzing blur.

Jason jumped at the opportunity. He rushed to Katie's house, heart pounding and palms sweating, having no idea what he was going to say when he got there but thrilled at the opportunity to say something, anything, to her.

When he arrived, he knocked on the door but no one answered. Jason let himself in, calling out Katie's name. There was no response. He felt his heart begin to beat a little faster as the very beginnings of fear began to flutter in his veins. He rushed upstairs to find her, struggling not to give in to the slow panic that was building with every stair he climbed.

As Jason opened the door to Katie's room, his eyes darted to every dark corner, straining to see. Still, he didn't see Katie, so he called her name again. He could hear the panic in his voice and he angrily told himself to get a grip.

Jason noticed a thin bar of light bleeding out below the bathroom door that opened from the far side of Katie's bedroom, and he took two large steps across the small space. It felt like it took him an hour to reach the door, even though, in his mind, he realized it must have been no more than an instant.

He knocked forcefully on the door to Katie's bathroom, noticing that it was slightly ajar. As his knuckles struck the wooden surface, the door slid open slowly.

Jason took a deep breath and stepped inside. He decided that he should cover his bases in case she merely happened to be wearing headphones or some other equally mundane explanation for her silence.

"I knocked and no one answered, so I let mys..." He stopped dead in his tracks.

He couldn't finish his sentence. He saw Katie sitting in her bathtub, her arms wrapped around knees that were drawn up to her chest, her head lying on her knees and lolling to one side.

She was, if he was not mistaken, naked.

He stopped breathing, he stopped moving, he stopped thinking. He just...stopped.

Until he began shivering. He felt the chill in the air and realized that the temperature in the house must be in the fifties, if not below. He felt air blasting out of all of the vents.

"Katie," Jason said firmly, trying to get her attention. "Katie." he tried again, his voice even louder and more insistent, but she didn't move. Didn't even open her eyes. He walked slowly to the tub and knelt down next to it. He touched the top of her head and realized that the wet strands of golden hair atop her head were ice cold.

He then reached out to trail his fingertips along the surface of the water, but the instant his skin made contact, he immediately pulled back his hand. The water was freezing.

"Katie, what are you doing? Are you okay?" he asked stupidly. Now the panic was not merely hovering around the edges of his voice—it had overtaken it.

She didn't answer. Damn it! She obviously was not okay.

Without a second thought, Jason plunged his arms into the bathtub and lifted her limp body up and out of the freezing water as the icy liquid splashed at his feet.

Katie was shaking, trembling like a leaf, and when he looked down at her face lying against his shoulder, he saw that her lips were slightly blue. Jason frantically glanced around the bathroom for a towel but none was in sight.

He tightened his grip on her and rushed back into her bedroom, making a beeline to her bed and gently laying her down on it.

As he sat next to her, he could not help but look down at her body. He was only human. God, she was incredible.

Jason, knock it off, he chastised himself. God. What was he doing. He had to make sure she was conscious.

"Katie, wake up! Katie! Wake up, baby!" he said loudly as he shook her shoulders.

Her head rolled to the side and her eyes fluttered briefly and then shut again. He took that as a good sign.

"I thought it was you. I thought it was you. I thought it was you, Jason," Katie repeated in a raspy whisper. She then, opened her beautiful blue eyes wide and made steady eye contact with him. When he saw that she was both conscious and present, he let out a breath that, up until that moment, he had not even realized he was holding in.

"It is *me, Kit Kat. It's okay, I'm here," he said in a*

deliberately soothing and comforting tone.

"I'm so cold. I was so hot. Now I'm so cold," Katie mumbled, and then her teeth started chattering.

Jason instinctively pulled off his shirt and lay over her, encompassing her icy skin with the warmth of his body.

He had learned in the Boy Scouts that the fastest way to raise a person's body temperature to normal levels was by using your own body heat. That was the only reason why he was doing this.

He mentally shook his head at himself. Sure, Sloan. Anything you need to tell yourself to not focus on the fact that you're laying on top of her and all you can feel is her breasts pushed up against your chest.

Oh yeah. He was a real Boy Scout.

Her tiny body was shivering beneath him and he did everything he could to just lie still and warm her. Of course, there was one (very insistent) part of his body that was not quite on board with the "lie still" plan. His jeans were growing tighter by the second.

Jason lay in that state of suspended animation, every tiny move she made torturing him, as the seconds passed inexorably. Finally, he felt her breath start to warm on the side of his neck. He sighed with relief of more than one variety.

Jason lifted himself off of the bed slightly so that he could look her square in the face as he asked, "Are you warm enough, Kit Kat? Are you okay?"

"I thought it was you. I thought it was you, Jason," she repeated, but this time her voice was no raspy whisper. It was as strong as it was anguished, and tears filled her eyes

and slipped down the side of her face as she spoke.

Oh, dear God in Heaven. Katie was naked and crying. How was he ever going to survive this?

"Katie," he said firmly but gently, hoping to comfort her, but also to lead her back to reality. "It is *me. I am here."*

As he said this, he lifted his hand and wiped away the tears that had fallen down her face. She sucked in a shallow breath as his hand touched her cheek and then she pressed her face against his palm. His breathing quickened. He felt like he was in a dream. The next thing he knew, her lips were pressed against his.

He wasn't sure if she kissed him first or the other way around, but that was something he could worry about later. Right now, all he cared about was that they were lip to lip.

Jason trembled. It was all his aching muscles could do to hold himself above her, to hold back the floodgates of lust and passion even a little bit. Her soft lips tasted so sweet as her tongue lightly brushed against his bottom lip.

He groaned. Before he could stop himself, he opened his mouth and slipped his tongue into hers, deepening the kiss to maddening levels. As his tongue moved hungrily inside her mouth, he felt her arms shaking as she ran her hands up his back.

Calling upon every ounce of will he possessed, he pulled away from her and asked, "Are you okay? You're shaking."

Present Day

And that was the beginning of… Jason shook his head. Never mind what that was the beginning of. He tried not to let himself think about what happened after that.

And he certainly couldn't afford to break his decade-long habit of attempting to avoid those memories while he and Katie were locked in Aunt Wendy's loving death grip.

Chapter Four

"Well, I swan. It's a little piece of heaven to see you two out here visitin' in the yard. Just like the old days. Have you two youngins had a chance to catch up?"

Aunt Wendy chattered happily as she released them both from her hold. Even though Aunt Wendy had grown up in Harper's Crossing and lived there most of her adult life, she spent six months living with a boyfriend in Alabama when she was in her early twenties and still liked to pepper her speech with Southernisms—especially when she was happy or excited.

"Actually I just got here, like, just a few minutes ago, so…not really, no." Katie could still feel the flush heating her face. Luckily, Aunt Wendy didn't really seem to notice.

"Well, Mr. Sloan, have you ever seen any girl as beautiful as my Buttercup?" Aunt Wendy asked as she looked at Katie, her eyes shining with pride and love.

Katie leaned her head against Aunt Wendy's shoulder, feeling safe and warm as she listened to her speak.

Unlike Kit Kat, a nickname that had always annoyed her, Buttercup was something Katie loved to be called. It made her feel special and cherished. Aunt Wendy had been calling her that for as long as she could remember.

As a little girl, Katie had been obsessed with the movie *The Princess Bride*. Aunt Wendy always thought that, with Katie's long and flowing blond hair, she looked a lot like Princess Buttercup herself.

As she rested against her aunt's comforting shoulder, she waited for Jason to answer her aunt's well-meaning question with a joke at her expense.

"No, I can honestly say I have not," Jason responded sincerely.

Wait, what? Did he just say something nice? About her?

Katie felt her cheeks start to flush again, and she shook her head to clear it. *Down girl,* she thought sternly. *You need to lock that kind of physical response down before it gets out of control.*

She looked up at Jason, trying to search for some clue as to why he was behaving so un-Jason-like. His rich brown eyes bore into hers with a complicated intensity. If she wasn't mistaken, there was desire in those eyes as well as something else she couldn't quite identify. Something…primal. Just as Katie was beginning to fear that she could not take one more second of the heat of Jason's intense gaze on her, she was saved by the bell. Well, a horn actually.

Katie turned her head to see Sophie and Bobby pulling up in the driveway of Sophie's house next door. Sophie burst out of the car before it even came to a full stop.

Sophie ran up to Katie at full speed and threw her arms around her.

A warmth spread through Katie as she returned the embrace. Even though Sophie was now a full grown woman who stood a good two inches taller than her, when Katie saw her flying across the yard with her wide open smile and her honey blond hair bouncing around her face, all Katie had seen was the four-year-old little girl who used to follow her around like a shadow and who she used to dress up like a doll.

"I am soooo happy that you are finally here." Sophie exclaimed as she pulled back from Katie, cheeks flushed. Katie smiled. This picture was only enhancing her view of Sophie as the adorable little moppet she used to be.

Sophie turned excitedly to the handsome, solemn young man who had been steadily following in her tornado-like path from the car. She exclaimed, "Bobby can you believe it? Everyone is here now. Let the wedding festivities begin. Woo hoo!"

Katie had to give herself a little shake as she took in the sight of, not only a grown-up Sophie before her, but a grown-up Bobby as well.

Bobby Sloan, Jr. was Jason's youngest brother. The youngest of the famous Sloan Boys. Of course, the

Sloan Boys weren't famous anywhere but in Harper's Crossing. But in Harper's Crossing? They were nothing short of legend.

There were five boys in the Sloan family: Seth, Riley, Jason, Alex, and Bobby.

Katie had always teased Jason about having "middle child" syndrome—always trying to do crazy things because he craved attention.

Seth and Riley had left for the military as soon as they graduated high school, so Katie didn't know them that well—although she knew all the stories about them well enough. One thing that had become even more obvious now that both men were adults was that Bobby was just about the spitting image of Seth. Physically, they were the only two of the boys with striking jet black hair and blue eyes. Coupled with smooth, olive skin, these features made them seem like movie stars from another, more elegant age.

But it was more than just their outward appearance that made Seth and Bobby seem so similar to Katie. They had always had the same manner about them. They were both quiet observers, always taking in their surroundings, always making unseen connections and observations. When you looked into the eyes of either Seth or Bobby, you were met with a mask of unidentified emotion. Katie had always thought of them as the "silent, brooding bookends" of the Sloan boys.

Come to think of it, Katie wasn't sure that she had heard Bobby speak more than ten words in her entire life. He'd always just been there—nice, reserved and quiet.

It was hard for Katie to think of the taciturn Bobby and the effervescent Sophie together. Talk about polar opposites. Though, when it came down to it, she guessed that the old saying was true—opposites attract.

Bobby raised a hand in greeting and smiled a smile that reached all the way to his expressive blue eyes. "It's good to see you, Katie," he said warmly, and when he spoke, Katie got a shock. His rich baritone voice was one of the deepest she had ever heard.

She felt her mouth fall open as her hand flew to her chest. She laughed involuntarily and exclaimed, "Holy smokes, Bobby. You are, like, really a…*man*!"

She reached up to give him a hug and heard Jason clear his throat in irritation as Bobby's arms encircled her.

"Okay, okay, enough with the hugging. Everybody knows everybody. Everybody looks good or older or fill in the blank. Don't we have some meeting or something to get to?"

Jason sounded more annoyed than Katie had *ever* heard him, and when she glanced over to where Aunt Wendy and Sophie were standing to see if they had taken note of his reaction, she saw them exchanging little conspiratorial grins.

Hmmmm…

Wonder what that's about?

But Katie didn't have an opportunity to contemplate it further, because as soon as Sophie took note of the puzzled look she was throwing them, she jumped in to fill the silence.

"Right, right," Sophie agreed crisply, suddenly sounding very mature and adult. "Okay, Aunt Wendy did you bring the notebook?"

Katie blinked at the stark difference between bubbly, bouncing Sophiebell and business-like, efficient Sophie.

"I sure did," Aunt Wendy confirmed proudly, "What kind of a doggone wedding planner would I be if I didn't have the wedding planning notebook?"

"You're a wedding planner?" Katie burst out. She tried to keep the shock out of her tone. But regardless of how successful she might be at not expressing the shock, there was nothing she could do to keep from feeling it.

It wasn't just that organization was *not*, shall we say, one of Aunt Wendy's strong suits. She had also never been married and would never be mistaken for a 'romantic.' In fact, she was such a pragmatist that she had often been known to refer to romanticism as "hogwash"—not what Katie would think of as the seeds from which a wedding planner would one day sprout.

"Well, yes, Buttercup. Don't you read my blog?" Aunt Wendy asked, sounding a little hurt.

Ouch. Busted.

She could try to explain that the life of an associate on the partner track didn't leave a whole lot of time for perusing web journals, but somehow she didn't think that would ease her aunt's hurt feelings. So instead, she shared a lesser almost-truth she thought would be more meaningful to Aunt Wendy—which was still no less valid just because it wasn't the main reason.

"Actually, Aunt Wendy, I don't," said Katie with all the sincerity she could muster. "When I read it, I just…I get really sad. It's just really hard because I miss you and Mom so much."

Sharing this small (mostly-true) vulnerability had the desired effect of distracting Wendy from her own hurt feelings entirely and focusing her energy elsewhere.

"Oh, my poor little Buttercup-girl, all alone in California. It must be so lonely for you, out there with no family around. Well, don't you worry your pretty little head, darlin'. I'm gonna get you all caught up on what's new with me and every other living soul in Harper's Crossing while you're here," Aunt Wendy said as she slammed her hand down on the trunk of Katie's rental car for emphasis. Katie had no doubt that her aunt would keep that promise.

Aunt Wendy continued her speech. "But as for right now, let's put a pin in that. Romeo is right. We need to get inside and nail down the nitty-gritty of this spectacular shindig."

Katie smiled at her aunt's vernacular. When Katie was little, she had asked her aunt why she talked like that even though she'd only lived in Alabama for a few months, and Aunt Wendy had just shrugged phlegmatically and said, "It stuck."

"I'll be right over. I haven't even brought my bags into the house yet," Katie pointed out, gesturing to the suitcases still sitting beside the car.

She wanted to buy a little time. All these people, all this emotion, all these changes. All this Jason. She suddenly felt very overwhelmed. She needed a moment to regroup.

Well, let's be honest, she needed more than a *moment*, but she wasn't greedy. She would take what she could get.

"Okay, Buttercup, you go put your things inside and we'll meet you next door after you get settled," Aunt Wendy said briskly, in full "wedding planner" mode.

"Great," Katie said gratefully.

"Romeo here will help you with your bags," Aunt Wendy continued, patting Jason's chest as she walked past him.

Alarms started going off in her head.

Alone + Jason = bad idea.

Fact: she did *not* trust herself.

"No. No, that's okay. I've got it. Really." Katie said, trying to keep the desperation out of her voice. But it was too late. Sophie, Bobby and Aunt Wendy were already halfway across the yard that separated Katie's house from the Hunters', and they were deep in wedding-related conversation.

"Looks like you're stuck with me," Jason said with

an oh-so-very-pleased-with-himself smile on his face.

Not knowing what else to do, Katie grabbed her suitcases and popped open her trunk. She threw her luggage inside unceremoniously and said faux-brightly, "I can get settled in later."

Slamming the trunk, Katie turned and looked up at Jason with the brightest smile she could plaster on her face. *Keep it light, Katie,* she told herself. *Don't leave any room for the intensity, hormones or emotion to creep back in.*

"Wow, the idea of being alone with me is that scary, huh?" Jason said casually, but if Katie's spidey senses were correct, there was the barest hint of hurt at the edges of his voice.

Katie paused for a moment, taken aback, but then realized her powers of deduction must be on the fritz because Jason did not get hurt feelings. Ever. So she maintained her faux-cheerful demeanor as she brightly chirped, "Yep, Jas, you're reeeeaaaal scary. I'm terrified to be alone with you. That's it!"

With that, she spun on her heel and began to practically jog across the lawn.

Alone. Ha! Right, like that was going to happen.

Katie's heart raced and her stomach was full of butterflies—*no,* she mentally corrected herself, *not butterflies.* Those lovely creatures flew around gracefully, sweeping their wings in wide, slow arcs. Whatever had invaded her belly was a lot more manic than innocent little butterflies. Maybe hummingbirds. *Yeah,* she thought, *hummingbirds*. Their wings going a mile a minute and shredding her stomach lining sounded about right.

But, she amended, *it's like they're not even just flying around in there. Maybe they are having some kind of Gladiator death battle, or an orgy, or...stop it, Katie.*

She *had* to stop thinking about sex! At the mere thought of even a few moments alone with Jason, her mind had sunk into the gutter and her body had exploded with uncontrollable tingles. Up and down her arms, zinging along her spine, but mostly...between her legs. She sighed. Yep. Especially between her legs.

Her own body was betraying her.

She had not had a reaction to anyone like this since, well, um...that night after Nick's funeral. The night when Jason had found her semiconscious in her bathtub, had laid her in her bed, and then stripped off his shirt to warm her up.

Oh, Lord. That night. At the mere thought of it, she wanted to bury her face in her hands. She couldn't begin to imagine what Jason must think of her after how she had behaved that night.

She could not believe she had put him in that no-win situation. Sure, he hadn't been complaining then, but that was in the heat of the moment. Once they were interrupted and he had the opportunity to view events in the harsh light of day, he must have had horrible regrets.

Not that she'd had any. She had tried so hard to

feel regrets for that night. But she simply couldn't.

She knew that he *must* think awful things about her, though. And deservedly so—he had every right to. Not only for her actions that night, but also for the way she had behaved in the weeks before Nick's funeral. Jason had constantly been trying to connect with her, trying to get her to talk to him, trying to get her in a place where they could lean on each other like they always had, and all she had been able to do was shut him out.

Shaking her head as if her brain were an Etch A Sketch and her painful memories were as easy to clear away as the thin grey lines on its screen, she ordered herself to put a stop to this line of thinking.

This was *not* the time to embark on a trip down memory lane. No need to dredge up the past this minute. Moving forward. Onward and upward. Here and now—that was all she had any control over.

Her main priority this weekend was to be there for her Sophiebell, focus on the wedding, and be the best maid of honor she could be. Secondarily, she would find the exact right words to let Jason know how deeply, truly sorry she was—just as soon as she figured out how to control her ridiculously out-of-proportion hormonal response to him.

As they were crossing the yard to the Hunters' house, Katie felt Jason's arm wrap around her waist. This caused a shiver (or rather, *another* shiver) to run from her head right down to her toes, one so powerful that it almost caused her to break her stride. Okay, come on. Who was she kidding? It almost knocked her flat on her ass.

Good night, nurse!

What was he? Electrically charged or something?

Her body grew tense at its response to his touch and Katie naïvely hoped that he would get the drift and release his arm. He didn't.

Instead, he leaned in and whispered in her ear, somewhat condescendingly in her humble opinion, "Not a big blog reader, huh? You get 'really sad,' do you? Good save, Kit Kat."

Immediately Katie's body relaxed. Irritation seemed to have that effect on her. As soon as annoyance began to flow through her and a retort began to form in her mind, her body reacted like an athlete about to run out onto the court. She was ready, armed with facts.

He hadn't seen her in ten years. He had no idea what was going through her mind. Maybe she really *had* meant what she had said to Aunt Wendy.

She opened her mouth to give Jason a piece of her mind when she realized that they were standing at the front door of the Hunters' home, and that realization derailed her defense.

She looked around at the porch, the door, the yard from this perspective. She felt like she was having an out-of-body experience.

It was surreal how familiar and yet how completely foreign this place felt to Katie.

The last time she had stood at this door was after the funeral. Nick's mom, Grace, had given Katie Nick's football jersey. She had handed it to Katie, wordlessly, the weight of grief etched on her face. Katie had taken it in her hands, reverently, tears streaming from her eyes. She had turned and walked down the porch steps without a word, the entire ceremony conducted in silence. The two women could feel how sacred it was.

She hadn't known it at the time as she walked down those steps, but by the next day, she would be gone. It was the last time she would stand on that porch.

Until today.

This realization hit her all at once like a ton of bricks. She tried to move her feet but she couldn't.

"It's okay. I'm here. We'll go in when you're ready," Katie heard Jason's voice say behind her, and she felt his arms wrap her tighter. Her knees were so wobbly that it felt like he might be the only thing holding her upright.

Katie took a deep breath. Her palms became clammy, and her feet felt like someone had dipped them in cement, but she knew she had to do this. She just needed to push forward. Yep. Forward momentum was the only thing she could count on to get her through this door. Through this *weekend*, for that matter.

"I'm as ready as I'll ever be," she said with a decisiveness she did not yet feel. Still, she pulled open the screen door and stepped inside.

"Katie, you're here."

"We've missed you so much."

"Honey, you look so pretty."

"Oh my gosh, it's really you!"

"Can you believe this one's getting married?"

"Katie, you're so beautiful."

"You're all grown up."

"I don't believe my eyes."

Katie's head swam as all the voices and people came flooding at her, all at once. The room was a sea of faces, but several stuck out from the crowd.

Katie saw Nick's parents, Grace and Mike. She also spotted Alex, one of the other Sloan boys, as well as their cousins, The Quad Squad: Jessie, Haley, Becca, and Krista. The Quad Squad had all been born within a five-year span. Katie had always thought Jason's Aunt Sandy was a saint.

Grace immediately pulled Katie into a warm embrace. Katie tried to return it, but so much was going on. She barely heard Grace's warm voice say, "It's so good to see you, sweetie. We've missed you so much."

Katie couldn't catch her breath. She felt the room starting to spin, and there was a growing sense of dread in her gut.

Wouldn't having a panic attack in front of all of these people she hadn't seen in ten years be just the *perfect* reintroduction?

It was starting to begin in earnest when she heard a gruff voice break through the melee. "Now, now. Let's give the girl some breathing room. She's had a long flight, and besides, you all know she is only here to see me anyway."

"Grandpa J," Katie whispered as she finally exhaled, and relief flooded her body like a soothing balm. The crowds parted, and she saw him sitting in the same brown recliner she remembered always seeing him in.

Emotion washed over her, and before she knew what she was doing, she ran up to him and threw her arms around him, tears falling down her face. Talk about forward momentum. She didn't care how silly she looked. This was Grandpa J.

Colonel James Hunter, or "Grandpa J," was really the only grandfather Katie had ever known. Her grandfather on her mother's side had been gone even before she was born, and her father's parents had passed when Katie was a toddler. She wasn't sure if she had ever met them or not, but if she had, she didn't remember it.

When Grandpa J came to live with the Hunters the first Christmas after they had moved to Harper's Crossing, Katie had naturally gravitated towards him. It wasn't just the idea of having a grandfather, any grandfather at all, that had drawn her to him—Grandpa J was special.

And for his part, Grandpa J had no problem adopting Katie as his own honorary grandchild. He always said that he was enough Grandpa to go around.

Katie loved listening to him talk for hours about his

time in the military—the fun he and his friends would have going out on the town, all dressed in uniform and looking as dapper as could be, and the shenanigans that would ensue.

He talked about hitchhiking from Florida to New York and all the interesting people he met along his two-week journey. But Katie's favorite story to listen to was the one about the very first time he saw his future wife, Marie Elise Gallo.

Katie never got to meet Grandma Marie, who passed away before Grandpa J came to live in Harper's Crossing, but from what she'd heard, Grandma Marie knew how to keep Grandpa J on his toes. Despite having never met her, Katie had always felt a special connection to Grandma Marie.

Katie's middle name was Marie, and growing up, she used to fantasize that she was named after Grandma Marie. She couldn't imagine a higher honor. As an adult she wanted to believe that it had actually been fate giving her a much more special nod—the assurance that her connection with this family had been preordained.

Katie could remember spending hours on end looking through Grandpa J and Grandma Marie's wedding album. She would imagine that it was her in the simple white satin and lace gown, smiling adoringly up at Nick in his dapper dress uniform. Well, she'd thought it was Nick. She realized now that the groom's face had always been a blur in those fantasies. But...of course it was Nick. Right?

As Grandpa J held her in his comforting embrace, Katie was overwhelmed with the realization of just how much she had missed him.

As if reading her mind, he spoke softly into her ear, saying "I missed you, Katie. I missed my girl."

"I missed you too, Grandpa J," Katie said, holding on to him as if for dear life.

Their reunion was broken up by the brisk and businesslike voice of Aunt Wendy as she began the meeting. Katie could tell that she was relishing the role of Woman in Charge.

"Okay, now that I have everyone here," Aunt Wendy said as she began handing out brochure-style schedules, "we can get right down to business. Here are your itinerary packets for the weekend. They are color coded, so make sure you take note of your assigned color on the front of the packet. The activities you are expected to be at are noted in the same color."

"Wow, you really outdid yourself, young lady," Grandpa J said. Katie smiled warmly. His tone was lightly teasing, but Katie could hear real admiration there as well.

The rest of the crowd got lost in reading the packets and softly conversing with each other about them, so Katie gratefully took the opportunity to melt into the background and study the itinerary unobserved.

She immediately noted, to her relief, that she really wouldn't have a minute to herself all weekend—thank

God. That was really for the best. She didn't want any free time to sit and marinate in her thoughts, emotions, and memories. No good could come of that.

Aunt Wendy continued. "So first up, we have the bride and bridesmaids' final fittings. Men, you have an hour before you are expected over at Richard's Formal Wear. Don't be late. Colonel, you are in charge of getting the young men there at 11:00 a.m. sharp."

"Yes, ma'am. They will be there. Don't worry your pretty little head," Grandpa J said with a wink.

Aunt Wendy actually blushed. Grandpa J had an amazing ability to compliment a lady and make her feel like the most special woman in the world, and he did it even with the simplest of words. It was an aura about him, an energy he would send across the room. Katie smiled to herself and thought, *He's got "game," as the kids would say.*

"Okay, bridal party, you have your schedules. Now, everyone behave, and let's make this the best wedding anyone has ever seen," Aunt Wendy said, her voice carrying equal parts enthusiasm and warning. She turned to the group of women standing behind her, of which Katie was a part, and said, "Ladies, let's get a move on."

As everyone in the room began to move towards the door, Katie felt an arm wrap around her waist and heard Jason's voice in her ear. She stiffened. She had begun to like the feeling of blending in with the anonymous crowd. It was relaxing. Now the sound of

Jason's voice reminded her that she was the target of his laser focus. Still, she couldn't help but be thrilled at the feel of his hot breath on the back of her neck and his strong hand on her back, firmly guiding her forward.

"You okay, Kit Kat? You look a little flushed."

"I'm fine," Katie said, her voice betraying her by allowing just a bit of tremulousness to dance around the edges. *Come on*! She just wanted to make it out the door without looking at him.

Just as she felt Jason pull her closer, Sophie came bounding up to her, much like the way she did when she was four, joy and excitement radiating from her smiling face as she let loose with a stream of chatter Katie also recognized from when she was a child.

"Katie, you're riding with us. My mom is just going to make a phone call and then we can go. In like, ten minutes, okay? Did you get your stuff all settled?"

"No, I didn't actually," Katie said, pulling away from Jason's oh-so-tempting hold. "I'll go run next door and be back in a few."

With that, she virtually flew out the front door. Alone.

She made it to her car and let out a sigh of relief as she popped her trunk and removed her suitcases once again. That relief, however, was short lived. As she closed her trunk, she heard *his* voice again and just about jumped out of her skin.

"I am not saying that this is the right time, but don't you think at some point this weekend we need to talk?" His tone surprised her. It held none of the cockiness or the teasing that was always present when he was speaking to her. In fact, he sounded earnest—almost plaintive.

No, no, no!

Katie was *far* from being ready to handle that.

"'Bout what?" Katie asked in her best faux-innocent tone. Fauxnicent. It was her specialty. She should copyright it. She had the legal knowledge to be able to do that, and it was, after all, her "go to" move.

She turned to look up at him and froze. Oh. Dear. God. He looked so amazing in the sun. She couldn't quite come to terms with how handsome and sexy he had become. Whenever she and Jason were exchanging their normal banter and she had her back to him, she could safely think of him as the 'cocky little kid she had grown up bickering with.' When she laid eyes on him, not so much.

Her brain couldn't seem to process the information her eyes were sending it.

He leaned in close to her ear and she could once again feel his breath on her neck.

Really. Did he really have to keep doing that?

And more importantly, did it really have to feel so good?

"Okay, Kit Kat. Have it your way," Jason said into her ear, his voice taking on a slow and languorous quality that was nothing short of mind-blowingly sensuous. "But just remember, I am more than ready to talk about this whenever you stop being a big chicken."

That snapped her out of her sexy-thoughts-brain-fog quickly enough.

"I am *not* being a chicken. I just asked what you wanted to talk about. And *stop* calling me Kit Kat."

Katie dropped her suitcases and stood there as tall as she could with her hands on her hips, her body radiating with irritation. Jason Sloan was the *only* person in this world who could cause Katie to go from being perfectly happy to extremely irritated in under zero point five seconds. It was truly a gift.

Jason took a step back and looked her up and down, his eyebrows raised in surprise. Katie was just beginning to wonder if she hadn't reacted just a *bit* harshly, and she started to feel just a tiny bit bad about maybe hurting his feelings—when he burst out laughing.

Seriously?!

"What's so funny, Jas?" Sophie giggled as she came bounding across the lawn.

"Yes, *Jas*, I was just about to ask the same thing," Katie said through a large smile and clenched teeth.

"What can I say? It's just that Kit Kat is still just as easily riled up as always, and even after all these years, it never ceases to amuse me."

Jason chuckled as he reached out and took her suitcases, as if his observation were the height of hilarity.

"Wow, I always wondered why God put me on this earth," Katie said sarcastically, "and now I have my answer. Clearly it was to amuse you, Jas."

As she looked up at him, trying to maintain a cool composure, he leaned down and stared intently into her eyes. Then, in a low and oh-so-sexy tone only she could hear, he said, "Well I've always known that God put you here for me. You might be a little slow on the uptake, but I'm just glad that you finally realize it, too."

Katie stood stock-still, having lost the ability to move or speak. The words that were coming out of his mouth did not make any sense. That could almost kinda-sorta be a compliment. But this was Jason. Jason didn't say nice things to her.

But he also didn't touch her all the time. And he was certainly doing a lot of that. Had she inadvertently come home to some weird-bizarro-alternate-reality version of Harper's Crossing where Jason Sloan complimented, flirted with, and constantly *touched* her? And where she suddenly had the raging hormones of a sailor coming home after being at sea?!

She barely heard all of the commotion and the voices surrounding her as Aunt Wendy corralled everyone, getting them into their assigned vehicles. It all just sounded like white noise.

All Katie could manage to do was stare into Jason's mesmerizing eyes and try to remember to breathe. Even though there were probably fifteen people buzzing around them, Katie felt as if she and Jason were the only two people on the planet.

"Katie...Katie..." She heard Sophie's voice as if it

were traveling to her from a million miles away. But when she slowly came out of her Jason-induced fog, she looked over and was surprised to discover that Sophie was still standing right next to her.

"Huh?" Katie heard herself ask. Sophie smirked a little, good-naturedly, and that was enough to bring Katie all the way back to herself. As she quickly became more aware of her surroundings, she said briskly, "Oh, right, okay. Are we ready to go? Let me just put my suitcases inside."

She reached to take her suitcases back from Jason, but he didn't let them go.

"That's okay, Kit Kat. You go ahead. I'll take them inside. I don't have to be at my fitting for an hour."

Katie tugged at the luggage.

"No, that's really okay. I can do it. I got it, Jas," Katie insisted as she pulled the handle harder.

"Now, Kit Kat," Jason said in a seemingly sincere yet somehow dangerously close to being condescending tone. "You don't want to make the bride late for her final fitting, do you?"

"Oh, just let Jason take them in, Katie," Sophie said, as she pulled Katie towards her aunt's white SUV. "Aunt Wendy's in the car and Mom already left. We gotta go."

"But…you can't get in," Katie said, her last ditch attempt at an argument, even though she had already been dragged almost all the way down the driveway and knew in her heart she was fighting a losing battle.

"I have a key," Jason said with a wink as he was turning and walking up the porch. "Now you go on and have fun. I'll put them inside and see you later."

"You have a key?" Katie yelled as Sophie was shoving her through the car door, but Jason didn't turn to answer.

Chapter Five

After having been forcibly placed in the SUV, Katie put on her seatbelt and felt the cool blast of air conditioning hit her face. She could either spend the entire ride to the bridal shop freaking out over her uncontrollable lust for Jason or she could get some answers.

She went with answers.

Katie turned towards Aunt Wendy and directed the same question to her that she just had to Mr. Must-Take-Suitcases-At-All-Costs.

"Why does Jas have a key to your house?"

"Well, what with all the work he's been doin' around the house and with his hours being so different than mine and your mama's, we just thought it would be easier if he had a key. That way, if he had time to work, he could let himself right on in," Aunt Wendy explained as she was pulling out of the driveway.

Katie took a deep breath. Now, she was in litigator mode. She only wished she had a yellow legal pad and a number two pencil in her hands to make her feel more at home.

"What kind of work needs to be done around the house? Why didn't you just tell me so I could hire someone to do it? Why didn't you just—"

Aunt Wendy apparently did not care to hear the rest of Katie's follow-up questions and interrupted her, "Well, sweetie, I don't want to put a fly in your pie, but you haven't really been around for the daily happenings in these here parts for quite some time. And there was no need for you or anybody else to hire somebody. Jason is more than willing and able to do the job even though he's a big shot now."

Aunt Wendy sounded proud as she said that last part, as if Jason, and *not* Katie, was related to her.

Katie immediately recognized her aunt's leading statement and figured she would play along, "A big shot, huh?"

Aunt Wendy continued animatedly. "Oh, yes. He is the Vice President of Sloan Construction."

"He's working for his dad?" Katie asked in surprise. When they had been growing up, all Jason had ever talked about was how he was *not* going to get sucked into the family business. He wanted to live, to experience the world. He *didn't* want to get stuck in Harper's Crossing.

"He's been there ever since his dad's heart attack," Sophie chimed in while texting on her phone from the front seat.

Katie sat in silence for a moment. That's right. Jason's dad had had a heart attack and she hadn't even sent a card.

Well, let's add that to the list of things she needed to address in her apology to Jason.

Wendy clapped her hands together as they pulled up to a stop sign, "Now, let's talk wedding details. Have you had a chance to memorize your schedule for the weekend?"

"Memorize?"

"Yes," Aunt Wendy clarified, "Commit to memory."

Katie laughed, thinking her aunt was joking, but Wendy didn't join in. Katie cut off her laughter quickly.

"Uh, no, not really," she stammered. "I mean, I just…I glanced at it earlier…but I will." Aunt Wendy was really taking this whole wedding planner thing seriously.

"Well no time like the present, Buttercup," Aunt Wendy said briskly. "I need you to be up to speed. As the M.O.H., you need to be on top of things."

"Okay, I'll take a look at it now," Katie agreed. She was grateful, actually, to escape the odd conversation. Why was Jason still working for his father? Why was he doing odd jobs for her mother and aunt? She needed a distraction to keep these questions, and more, from swirling through her brain and taking up all of the available real estate.

As Aunt Wendy and Sophie went over last-minute wedding details, Katie opened the folder and started to peruse it. She could not believe how well-organized it was. She was impressed. Maybe Aunt Wendy had found her calling after all.

Hunter/Sloan Wedding

THURSDAY:

Thursday: 10:00 a.m. Bride and Bridesmaids Fittings – Mona's Bridal Boutique

Thursday: 11:00 a.m. Groom and Groomsmen Fittings – Richard's Formal Wear

Thursday: 1:00 p.m. Bridal Luncheon – Salvatore's

Thursday: 8:00 p.m. Bachelorette Party – The Grill

Thursday: 8:00 p.m. Bachelor Party – McMillan's Pub

Katie mentally checked off each item against her one criteria—did her path cross with Jason?

Check, check, check, check, check. Nope.

So Thursday didn't seem like it would be so bad. She wouldn't have to spend any more time with Jason and she would be kept pretty busy. Hopefully those two factors combined would also keep any thoughts of Nick from rearing their ugly heads.

Okay. Next page.

FRIDAY:

Friday: 1:00 p.m. Check-in at Whisper Lake Hilton

Wait…Whisper Lake.

"Um, I have a quick question. Who is checking into the Whisper Lake Hilton?" Katie asked, trying to sound as blasé as possible.

"Oh!" squealed Sophie, "I can't believe I forgot to tell you. We are getting married up at Whisper Lake, just like Grandpa J and Grandma Marie did. Isn't that just the most romantic thing ever?" Sophie swooned, clasping her hands in front of her heart.

Romantic. Yep. Exactly the word she'd been thinking of.

"So romantic..." Katie agreed, smiling around the knot she felt forming in her throat.

She couldn't count how many nights she and Nick spent planning their wedding up at Whisper Lake. She had spent every summer there since she was in 4th grade. Sometimes with her mom and Aunt Wendy, a couple summers with the Hunters, and sometimes with the Sloan Boys and their cousins, the Quad Squad.

Of course, it made sense that Sophie and Bobby would be getting married up there. They spent summers together there, too. *This is not about you and Nick,* she reminded herself for the thousandth time that day. *This weekend is about Sophie and Bobby, not you and Nick...or Jason.*

Katie took a deep breath.

Okay. So, yeah. Whisper Lake. She could handle that. It was just one weekend.

All right, moving on.

FRIDAY:

Friday: 1:00 p.m. Check-in at Whisper Lake Hilton

Friday: 3:00 p.m. Facials and Massages (Entire

Wedding Party) – Hilton Spa

Friday: 5:00 p.m. Rehearsal

Friday: 6:00 p.m. Rehearsal Dinner – Malone Steak House (At the Hilton)

SATURDAY:

Saturday: 10:00 a.m. Bridal Brunch

Saturday: 2:00 p.m. Makeup and Hair (Bridal Party) – The Spa

Saturday: 5:00 p.m. Arrive at Church

Saturday: 6:00 p.m. Ceremony

Saturday: 7:00 p.m. Reception

SUNDAY:

Sunday: 12:00 p.m. Wedding Party checks out of hotel

Katie felt a sense of determination come over her as she read the schedule for the weekend. Of course, there was some Jason interaction on that list. It was to be expected. She was the maid of honor, and he was the best man. She just had to think about how to best minimize the impact of that time, which, if her first encounter with him was any indication, meant she may need to try to keep her distance.

She thought for a moment and then nodded to herself. Okay. All she needed to do was spend as much time with Sophiebell as possible–which was technically her job as M.O.H. anyway. And, she needed to steer clear of Jas, with the exception of a short face to face for her apology. Simple. Easy.

Good game plan. Go team Katie!

✦ ✦ ✦

As Jason opened the door to Katie's childhood home, a surge of nostalgia swept through him. He had been spending a lot of time here recently, trying to help Pam and Wendy save money by taking care of some repairs. But as weird as it might be to say it, the place felt completely different since Katie was back in town. It was like even her house was breathing a sigh of relief that she was back where she belonged.

As he walked up the stairs to put Katie's suitcases in her room, he actually felt a little nervous. He wondered why for a moment and then realized that he hadn't been in Katie's room since the night she left Harper's Crossing.

As he opened the door, he was surprised to see that, in ten years, nothing much had changed. Her dresser still held pictures of Katie when she was growing up, Katie with her friends and with Sophie, Katie with her mom, her Grandma, and Aunt Wendy—and, of course, Katie and Nick.

He did notice that one picture was missing. It was one of Katie and him. It had been taken at science camp, they were standing in front of Whisper Lake, and right after the picture had been snapped he'd thrown her in the lake. Jason knew she had kept it in a small frame at the edge of her dresser while she was growing up because he had clandestinely looked at it every chance he got when he and Katie and Nick had hung out in here together as teenagers. He didn't see it now, though.

Great. That probably meant it got tossed in the garbage on the fateful night Katie left Harper's Crossing. He didn't blame her.

A sick feeling began to form in the pit of his stomach as that night's memories started playing in his head, spreading inexorably through his torso and his extremities like a dreaded cold front that was hell-bent on taking over his body.

He knew that it had taken him a long time to forgive himself for what had happened that night, but right now–standing in the middle of the scene of the crime–he thought that maybe he still hadn't *entirely* forgiven himself after all.

He still wasn't sure if Katie had forgiven him, but he was going to find out this weekend. He was tired of wondering. As much as he knew, logically, that he should have handled things completely different that night, he could still never truly regret what had transpired. In fact, that was a big part of what made him feel so torn and guilty when he thought about it. How could one of his most precious memories also be one of his biggest regrets?

He took two slow steps across Katie's floor until he was standing directly in front of her bed. He set her suitcases down with a deliberate motion and just stood there, staring at her bed.

He closed his eyes against the memories that were flooding his consciousness. Memories of the last time he had been there, of Katie's naked body beneath him as he warmed her with his bare chest. How small and delicate she had felt in his arms. How alive, despite the iciness of her skin. How she melted against him. How her breath felt against his neck.

He had never experienced a night like that before or since. It had taken on a somewhat dreamlike quality in his recollection, as if it hadn't even really happened, like it was just a beautiful figment of his imagination. But even as he wondered, bittersweetly, if it might be all in his head, he remembered the taste of her lips as she sweetly touched her mouth to his. The way her body moved beneath him as she molded into him, becoming one with him. He knew it was real.

Standing there reminiscing had his jeans tightening by the second, and he decided that this wasn't the best time for a walk down memory lane. He needed to keep his hormones in check this weekend if he had any hope of fixing what he'd broken.

He shook his head. His mind and heart were both on board with that plan, but the region below his belt had other priorities for the weekend. He just needed to work on keeping his head in charge.

Jason had really thought he was prepared to see Katie again this weekend. As soon as he saw her standing at the trunk of her car with her back to him, that shining golden hair of hers streaming down her back, well, all of his careful preparation had gone right out the window.

He had always known that Katie had a powerful effect on him. He had just hoped that after ten years, some of her potency would have worn off. Unfortunately, that did not seem to be the case. If anything, the power of her effect on him had been amplified in her absence.

Now, as Jason left Katie's room to head over to Richard's for his fitting, he realized that there were two critical things he needed to accomplish this weekend.

First, be the best best man he could possibly be. That was a given. That was job one. Second, get some closure in the Katie Lawson department.

In the time that she had been AWOL, he had tried to go on with his life. He wasn't the kind of person to dwell in the past. He wasn't a "wallower" by any stretch of the imagination. But now that she was back, he could see clearly what he had known in the back of his mind all along—he had some serious unfinished business with Katie.

He'd always suspected that she was the reason he could never seem to maintain a serious relationship. Why he seemed to lose interest in women as soon as they showed signs of wanting to settle down. Jason knew deep down he wouldn't allow himself to take his relationships to the next level because the only person he'd ever wanted that with was Katie.

He shook his head again. One thing was for sure—

he needed to deal with this, and the upcoming weekend was probably going to be his only opportunity. He was sure that, come Sunday, Katie would be hightailing it back to San Francisco. That was her M.O., and who knew the next time he would see her?

Yep, he decided. Whether Katie wanted to or not, she would be dealing with him, and it was going to happen this weekend.

Chapter Six

Driving up to Mona's Bridal Boutique, Katie chatted with Sophie and decided to put everything but wedding business on the back burner of her brain. She consciously refocused her attention and vowed to herself to keep it where it belonged.

As they parked, Katie smiled as a flutter of excitement hit her. She was about to see her little Sophiebell in a wedding dress. What could be more special?

Getting out of the car, Katie smiled, finally feeling present and engaged, when she suddenly felt a chill crawl down her spine. She stopped short. The telltale tingle of goose bumps rising on the exposed flesh of her arms and the hair on the back of her neck stood up.

Someone was watching her. She was sure of it.

She spun slowly and looked around, but she did not see anyone looking her way. In fact, she didn't see anything out of the ordinary at all—just a cheery block of Harper's Crossing's downtown street, populated with the kinds of people you might expect to see there. A mom and her two little ones were crossing the street. Mr. Anderson, who owned the Sweet Tooth Candy

Shoppe, was sweeping up in front of his store. Some teenagers were hanging out in front of Dick's News Stand. Various other patrons of the quaint little shops lining 10th Street were shuffling up and down, each involved in their various errands.

The one thing they all seemed to have in common was that none of them were paying a lick of attention to Katie, much less watching her.

Trying to shake off the eerie feeling, Katie turned to Sophie. "So, pretty girl, tell me all about the dress I'm about to see. Is it strapless or halter or spaghetti straps?"

Sophie clasped her hands in front of her heart, which seemed to be a gesture she had embraced since falling in love. She dreamily expounded, "It has capped sleeves. I'm wearing Grandma Marie's dress but we had to make some adjustments."

Sophie beamed as she swept into the front door of Mona's. She enthusiastically greeted her soon-to-be cousins, the Sloan girls aka the Quad Squad. Haley, Jessie, Becca, and Krista returned her greetings just as enthusiastically, and they all cheerily chattered about the upcoming nuptials.

Katie was just steeling herself to go and join the group with her best plastered-on smile, but she felt Aunt Wendy's hand at her elbow, holding her back from the crowd for a moment.

Katie's false smile began to falter when she looked into Aunt Wendy's compassionate eyes as she said,

"Buttercup, Grandpa J told me that you've had your eye on that dress since he first showed you his wedding pictures. I'm so sorry, sweetie. You sure you're okay with all of this? Is it starting to be too much for you?"

As she spoke, Aunt Wendy ran her hand through Katie's hair, the same way she had thousands of times before, ever since Katie was little.

Katie put on her best brave face. Her voice only trembled a little as she said, "Of course I'm fine, Aunt Wendy. I wanted to wear Grandma Marie's dress when I thought Nick and I were going to have a happily-ever-after. I haven't even thought about that dress in years."

Aunt Wendy looked unconvinced, so Katie bolstered the cheer in her voice even further as she continued, "Honestly, I swear, I'm great. I'm just here to be the best M.O.H. I can be. This weekend is all about Miss Sophiebell."

Katie wasn't sure if she was trying to convince Aunt Wendy or herself.

"Okay. You just let me know if you need any little thing. I may be wearing my wedding planner hat a lot this weekend, but you know that I *never* take my Aunt Wendy hat off."

As she gave this sweet speech, Katie had to laugh as she watched Aunt Wendy mime putting on and taking off the imaginary hats. She almost expected her to end with a flourish and take a bow. In a spontaneous fit of affection, Katie threw her arms around her aunt's neck and squeezed tightly.

"I know, Aunt Wendy, and I love you for that. But I really am fine, I promise. Let's just head on in and get this wedding party started."

Aunt Wendy smiled and gave her one last squeeze before heading into the shop, but Katie hesitated. She paused and glanced around the street one more time, unable to shake the primal sensation that she was being observed.

She still didn't see anything out of the ordinary, so she shook her head and turned towards the door. *Oh well,* she figured, *it's probably just anxiety bubbling up from my subconscious, wanting to be dealt with. This being my first day back in town, and all of the ghosts I've had to face in just the last ninety minutes…it's no wonder.*

Maybe it was good, Katie reasoned, that she was being forced to face things now. Maybe she could finally close this chapter of her life, once and for all. This would let her start fresh. She could approach life without the past weighing her down, something she had never experienced as an adult. She sighed. A girl could hope.

As she walked into Mona's, she saw that the girls were already in dressing rooms trying on their dresses. She took a seat on the comfortable deep green sofa that backed up against the storefront window and settled in to wait for her turn.

Aunt Wendy bopped efficiently from dressing room to dressing room, making sure that each bridesmaid had everything they needed. Katie was impressed by her aunt's organizational abilities and enjoyed the chance to sit back and watch her in her element. Everything seemed to be running as smooth as silk, and as far as Katie could tell, they owed that all to Aunt Wendy.

As Becca and Haley made their way out of the dressing rooms and onto a small pedestal at the back of the shop that was surrounded by a three-way mirror, Katie laid eyes for the first time on the dress she would be wearing in Sophie's ceremony.

The knee-length and form-fitted strapless lavender silk creation was as trendy as it was beautiful. Katie smiled a bit as her eyes moistened. She should have known that Sophie would choose lavender as the color of her wedding. Sophiebell had always said that lavender was her "signature color." She had stolen that line from Katie's favorite movie, *Steel Magnolias.* Even though in the movie, the Julia Roberts character, Shelby favored pink instead of lavender, Sophie had made the necessary adjustment so that the phrase suited her own tastes.

Whenever Katie had babysat Sophie on a Friday night, no matter what other movie they watched, they always fit in *Steel Magnolias.* It was tradition.

Katie was beginning to think that there wasn't going to be *any* situation, this entire weekend, that was not chock full of memories.

"All right then, honey, it's your turn," came the no-nonsense voice of Mona, the stout woman who owned the bridal boutique. She strode purposefully towards

Katie with a dress in her hand that she had just grabbed from behind the counter.

Katie's eyes widened. She hadn't seen this woman since Nick's funeral. Mona had always had a soft spot for Nick, ever since their junior year when Nick had been trying on a tuxedo at Richard's Formal Wear, the shop next door that was owned by Mona's husband.

Katie had heard the story many times. When Nick came out of the dressing room, he found Richard lying on the ground, holding his left arm, and gasping for air. Nick—rather than freezing up or panicking as most kids his age would have done—immediately called 911 and then began administering CPR.

Nick had learned this valuable skill during his lifeguard training, but as far as Katie knew, he had never had to put it to the test while performing his duties the previous summers up at Whisper Lake.

When the paramedics arrived, they said that if Nick hadn't been there and started CPR, Richard most likely would not have made it—and would probably not have even survived the ambulance ride. Mona always called Nick her "guardian angel" after that.

Needless to say, he never paid for another tux.

"Oh my goodness, look at you," Mona said, her voice an almost reverent whisper as she recognized Katie. "You're so grown up. You look so beautiful."

"Well, what did you expect her to be?!" Aunt Wendy blurted out. Katie couldn't tell if this was her natural outspoken nature coming to the forefront or if she was trying to save Katie from yet another maudlin scene, but whichever it was, Katie was grateful. "Of course she's beautiful. She's as pretty as a picture. She comes from good genes. Now, Katie, you go on and try this dress on. You're the last one and I need to get you checked off my list."

"It's good to see you, Mona," Katie smiled as she was shuffled into the changing stall by Aunt Wendy. She continued to talk, knowing that she could be heard clearly on the other side of the curtain. "You look great, too. How is Richard doing?"

"Oh, Richard. He is just fine, thanks for asking. All thanks to Nick, of course, God rest his soul. Your brother is still my guardian angel, Sophie."

Mona yelled this last part to Sophie, who was in the dressing room with her mom and Haley.

"I know. He is to all of us, too. Right, Mom?" Sophie replied.

"Right," Grace agreed readily, her voice calm and steady. "He's always watching over us."

Katie felt a hitch in her breath and had to pause for a moment and steady herself with a hand against the wall. She concentrated on breathing deeply and slowly, centering her emotions. Whoa! That little exchange had taken her by surprise. It was so odd for Katie to hear people talking about Nick so casually, not crying or speaking in whispers. Just mentioning him as a part of everyday life.

But, she realized that must be what happens when

you stay and deal with something instead of running away like she did, moving to another state where no one even knows who Nick was, let alone ever mentions him.

It was also odd to think of Nick watching over them, and it was a concept Katie had never thought of before. Maybe that's what she had sensed outside of the shop. Maybe the feeling of being observed was Nick watching over her.

She shook her head. *No, no, no.* She was letting her imagination work overtime. That crazy feeling was probably just her subconscious trying to deal with all of the emotions she was feeling today. All of the stress she had been under didn't just disappear—it had to surface somewhere.

Suddenly, the curtain to Katie's dressing room was whisked aside briskly by Aunt Wendy.

"Hey!" Katie said in surprise. "I could have been naked in here."

Aunt Wendy waved this away like it was a small concern. "Oh, please, honey. Do you think I don't have the sense God gave a grasshopper? I knew you'd be taking a minute to collect yourself before you started undressing. But come on out now before you try on your dress. Sophie's ready for everyone to see her. You can finish after."

Katie nodded and stepped back out into the main part of the shop.

"Okay, is everyone ready to see the most beautiful

bride in the world?" Grace asked as she pulled the curtain covering the entrance to Sophie's dressing room to the side.

As Sophie stepped out of the dressing room, the entire shop was so silent you could have heard a pin drop. Everyone just stared, speechless.

The sight of Sophie took Katie's breath away. She was a vision, gorgeous.

Sophie had altered Grandma Marie's dress, modernizing the feel by transforming the three-quarter sleeve into a cap sleeve. But other than that one small adjustment, the gown looked exactly as Katie remembered. It was incredible, and Sophie looked as if she had stepped right out of a sepia-toned formal wedding portrait and into the real world.

"So..." Sophie asked nervously, clearly unnerved when she was greeted by nothing but silence. "What do you think?"

At this question, the room exploded with comments.

"You're beautiful."

"You looked like you just stepped out of a bridal magazine."

"You took my breath away."

"You are perfection."

"You have never looked so beautiful."

"Bobby is going to cry when he sees you."

"You look amazing."

"You are what a bride is supposed to look like."

Sophie didn't look as relieved at the barrage of positive comments as Katie thought she should have. As everyone was still speaking over each other, Sophie turned to Katie and said, voice trembling a little, "Well, what's the verdict?"

"Oh, Sophiebell," Katie cried, grasping the younger woman to her and holding her tight. "You're gorgeous. You took my breath away."

"Oh, good," Sophie joked, the relief she felt at Katie's approval evident in her huge smile, "because it's too late to change the dress now."

"You look beautiful, Soph. My brother is a lucky man," Katie heard a familiar deep voice intone from a few feet behind her.

Oh no. Jason was here.

Immediately, Katie slipped back into the dressing room and took her sweet time (as Aunt Wendy was wont to describe it) trying on the bridesmaid dress. She could hear the other groomsmen arriving, and Katie hoped that this was enough to distract Jason and lure him out of Mona's. She also heard Sophie being rushed back into her own dressing room so that Bobby wouldn't see her when he arrived at Richard's, since the two stores were connected by a wide-open breezeway. She heard all the voices start to die down and rushed herself into the lavender sheath. She was just about to walk out when Aunt Wendy threw the curtain back yet again.

"Buttercup, what is taking you so dad-blamed long?

All the girls are done and dressed and ready to head over for some yummy Italian eatin'."

"Again," Katie intoned dryly, "could've been naked in here."

Aunt Wendy swatted away this sentiment as if she were swatting at a pesky gnat. Her attention immediately focused on the voluminous dress hanging on Katie's thin frame.

"Oh, sweetie, you're swimmin' in that dress. You might as well be doing the backstroke." Aunt Wendy fretted and then yelled, "Mona!"

Katie looked down and realized that Aunt Wendy was right. The dress fit pretty well around the chest, but she definitely did not fill out the rest of it. It would need quite a few adjustments. Katie felt a wave of nausea as anxiety overtook her. It was Thursday—the wedding was on Saturday. Would there even be time for adjustments?

"I'm here. I'm here," Mona said as she shuffled around the corner. When she spied Katie, she cried, "Oh dear, honey. I am going to have to take that in."

"I know, but do you think that there is enough time?" Katie worried, twisting and turning in front of the mirror to try to get a better look at herself. "I mean...it's not *that* big. Is it?"

"Yes and *yes*," Mona said firmly as she began taking pins from her pin cushion and sticking them into Katie's dress.

Katie stood perfectly still as the dress she was wearing was tugged and pulled and pinned.

Aunt Wendy's phone began to chime the notes of "Sweet Home Alabama," and Wendy hustled outside to take the call, looking at the screen and muttering something about a flower emergency and getting better reception outside.

When Wendy passed the front door, Katie was, for all intents and purposes, alone. Mona was there, but she was laser focused on her tailoring work. Katie made the most of the opportunity to take one more cleansing breath and steel herself for this weekend. It looked like it was going to be one hell of a ride.

✦ ✦ ✦

Jason had walked into Mona's Bridal and immediately saw Sophie, his soon-to-be sister-in-law. He stopped just inside the door, she looked gorgeous. It was still hard for him to see her as an adult woman sometimes and not the little girl who was Katie's constant shadow he had always known—but not at that moment. She looked all grown up and beautiful.

As he pointed that out to her, he saw a flash of long blond hair rush into a dressing room out of the corner of his eye. He shook his head, thinking about the golden-haired blur. *Oh, Kit Kat,* he thought with an indulgent half smile growing across his face. *You can run, but you can't hide.*

As he waited for his brother at Richard's, he decided to set the whole idea of Katie aside. He would deal with that situation later. Right now, he needed to just focus on his brother and being there for him. He was the best man, and he took that role seriously.

The fitting went quickly and all of the guys were in and out in less than twenty minutes. Jason smiled. Those ladies had still been there an hour after their fitting had started. It was good to be a guy.

As he looked at the schedule while he walked through the parking lot, Jason was happy that he had some free time to kill until his next obligation. It was a good chance, he decided, to stop by the Slater Street building site and finish up some paperwork he needed buttoned down before he took off for the weekend.

Just as he shut the door of his truck with a satisfying slam, he saw Aunt Wendy waving him down from across the parking lot in front of Mona's. He pulled his truck out of the space it was parked in and swung over to her, pulling up beside her and rolling down the driver's side window.

"Hey, Wendy. What's up?" he asked affably.

"Well, Romeo, I have a huge favor to ask. Everyone else has already left to go get ready for the luncheon. I just got another panicked call from the florist and it seems like someone has changed all the numbers on the corsages and boutonnieres. I really need to get over there and straighten this out, but Katie has just started getting her dress altered. Can you give her a ride when she is finished?"

Jason began nodding before Wendy had even finished talking. "No problem, Wendy. Get over to the florist. I'll take care of Katie."

"Thanks, Romeo," Aunt Wendy swooned, giving him a little chuck on the chin. "You're a lifesaver."

"No worries. It's my pleasure." Jason couldn't help adding a silent 'literally' to himself, but he did manage to keep even the hint of a smile from showing on his lips.

Chapter Seven

Katie walked back to the waiting area of Mona's wearing her street clothes and looked around the empty space. Everyone was gone, it seemed. She stood alone in the room with Mona, who was busily working on her dress and didn't seem to notice her.

"Hey, Mona, did you see where Aunt Wendy went?" Katie asked, puzzled, as she continued to glance around the shop and then strain her neck to look into Richard's side of the space. Maybe, Katie figured, Aunt Wendy had stopped by to help the men out.

Nope, it was empty. Hmmm…

"I don't know where your aunt is, sweetie pie, but it looks like you *do* have a driver waiting on you," Mona said, and the playful tone in her voice set off red flags of warning in Katie's mind.

She turned slowly and saw Jason leaning against his black Chevy truck, looking like he was a living, breathing movie poster.

Katie was so stunned by the sight of him that it took her a moment to register anything about his truck. It wasn't the truck he had in high school.

Again, she felt a rush of emotion. That was becoming the theme of the day.

Of course it made sense that he wouldn't be driving the exact same vehicle ten years later. She certainly wasn't. But, somehow, it had never even entered her mind that Jason would drive anything but his black Chevy truck, the one that had formed a matching set with Nick's. The idea of Jason had become inextricably linked in her mind with the thought of that shining, beautiful black truck.

He and Nick had bought their matching set of trucks on the same day. They had nicknamed the identical pickups "the twins." They thought that double entendre was pretty clever. Katie had never thought too much of it, but looking back on it now, she could certainly see why two sixteen-year-old boys would find that particular nickname pretty amusing.

Katie steeled herself for another conversation with Jason and determined that she was going to keep it light, no matter how irritating (or sexy) he was. She breathed in deeply and put on a bright smile before stepping, confidently, out the door.

"Hey, Jas, have you seen Aunt Wendy?" Katie asked, cheerful tone firmly in place.

"I did, actually. She asked if I could give you a ride. She had a floral emergency that she needed to take care of," Jason said as he gallantly opened the passenger side door of his truck.

"Oh, okay," Katie said, resolutely refusing to abandon her cheerful tone even though she now felt virtually bathed in regret for not insisting that she drive her own car here. As she walked past Jason to get into the truck, she felt goose bumps rising all up and down her arms, and she realized that riding in this truck with Jason—even if it wasn't technically one of "the twins"—might be too much for her.

"On second thought, Jas…it's a beautiful day. I think I'll just walk," Katie chirped, scampering away from the truck and down the sidewalk as quickly as her feet would carry her.

"Really?" Jason's laconic tone made Katie stiffen as he called after her. He remained casually leaning against his truck. "You think that you have enough time to walk all the way back to Harper Lane, change your clothes, and then make it back downtown again by the time the luncheon starts at Salvatore's?"

She knew Jason was just pointing out the obvious, but the thought of being alone, in a confined area with Jason kept her legs moving in fast-paced strides.

"Fine, then," Jason said, his voice oozing with disappointment. "If you want to disappoint Sophie. I mean, it's not a big deal. You're just the maid of honor. I guess I'll just drive over to the restaurant and tell her you turned down a ride, so you'll be a little late. I mean, she probably won't care. And you probably won't be more than, what? Forty-five minutes? An hour late? You never minded being late, right Kit Kat?"

Katie stopped walking, her shoulders slumped. She

knew when she was beaten. She heard a door shut and the truck start up behind her. When it pulled up beside her, she looked over and saw Jason grinning behind the wheel. With his grin still plastered firmly to his face, he leaned over and popped the door handle. Katie sighed. It was going to be a long afternoon.

"Yeah, I guess you're right," Katie mumbled as she pulled the door the rest of the way open and slid into her seat. She leaned back and closed her eyes, resigning herself to the fact that she was going to be in a small, confined area with Jason for a fairly protracted period of time.

"You're welcome," Jason said cheerfully as he pulled away.

"Thanks, Jas," Katie said quietly as she lifted her head and looked out the window.

The truck moved along the familiar streets, carrying them closer and closer to Katie's childhood home, and she began to feel a little guilty for sitting in total silence when Jason was doing her a favor. After all, at one time she considered him one of her best friends, and she hadn't seen him in ten years. It wasn't Jason's fault that she didn't trust herself around him. It was hers. She needed to "drink a can of suck it up" as Grandpa J always said.

She only had to spend this one weekend with Jason, so she might as well try to get through it with dignity and class. No matter what Jason might think of her now, she was still holding out hope that all the years they had known each other prior to that fateful night would somehow trump that incident in his memory. Maybe then they could go on being friends.

In just the few short hours that she had been back in town, she had realized (if she were being completely honest with herself) just how much she had actually missed Jason.

And she didn't think this was just her hormones talking either. In fact, she wished they would just *shut up* already.

Nope, what she missed was his smile, his voice, his eyes—heck, she even missed their back and forth battling of wits. And then, of course, there was the fact that he *always* seemed to be around right when she needed something. She had forgotten that.

Although Katie could see him sneaking little glances over at her, Jason was also silent on the ride back to the house. Katie was not used to that. Jason *always* had something to say.

Was he upset that he had to play the role of chauffeur? No. That was not something that would bother him. Jason was, by far, the most 'go with the flow' person Katie knew.

As Katie stealthily watched him, silently driving down 10th Street, she was momentarily distracted by how ruggedly handsome he had become. As he looked into the rearview mirror with intense concentration, the sunlight beaming through the windshield hit his eyes, and Katie could see gold flecks surrounding his pupils.

She was mesmerized.

"Katie, I said, 'do you know him?'" Jason snapped.

"What? Who?" Katie asked, returning to her senses.

"The guy on the motorcycle about two car lengths back," Jason explained, tension tightening his voice in a way Katie had rarely heard.

Katie looked back and saw a young guy on a motorcycle a few yards behind them. He was probably in his early twenties, well built, with blond hair and sunglasses. There was an air of familiarity about him, Katie thought, but she couldn't quite nail down what that might be from or where she may have crossed paths with him before.

"He looks familiar, but I can't put my finger on it. Why? Who is he?" Katie asked, shrugging. She assumed it was someone they had known as teenagers, a friend's younger brother or cousin or something like that.

"I don't know, Katie. That's why I asked if you knew him," Jason said, his tone even more tense than it had been before. "He was across the street at Cup O' Joe nursing a coffee when I pulled up to Richard's. I noticed him staring at Mona's store so I walked in there to see what he might be looking at. The first thing I saw was Sophie in all of her bridal glory, so I just assumed he was looking at the soon-to-be bride.

"But while I was waiting for you, he just sat across the street, sipping away. Until, you came out of the shop and started walking down the street and away from my truck. Then, he got up and started walking the pavement. When you got in my truck, he doubled back, put his helmet on, got on his bike, and now he's behind us."

"That's weird," Katie said, remembering, a shiver running down her spine (and not the good kind), "because when I pulled up to Mona's, I had the strangest feeling that I was being watched. I convinced myself I was being paranoid because when I looked around, I didn't see anyone."

"You probably didn't see him because he was holding up a paper and pretending to read it. I saw him raise it a couple of times when he saw Mona's door open."

"Should have been my first clue," Katie tried to joke, "Who reads the print edition anymore?"

Jason did not participate in her frivolity, apparently not looking at this as a joking matter. He asked with an edge in his voice, "Any reason you would have some hot shot following you?"

"Come on, Jas. I'm not exactly the 'girl who gets followed' type. It's probably just a coincidence," Katie answered, trying to downplay.

Although…now that she thought about it, at the law office where she worked, they recently hired security to walk everyone to their cars and also held a mandatory self-defense class when a female associate was attacked in the parking garage after a rapist she had helped put away was paroled.

But that was in California. A whole world away.

Now she was back in Illinois, and she was sure any potential trouble that had started brewing in the Golden State would not have followed her here. At least, that's what she told herself.

She did start unconsciously thinking through all of the cases she had been on in the past two years. They were like a brimming file drawer in her head and she shuffled through them one by one.

She was so involved in her mental case review, in fact, that she did not hear the sound of either her phone ringing or of Jason's voice as he tried to get her attention.

"Your phone's buzzing," Jason said as he continued to drive, "and Mr. Motorcycle just turned onto Green Briar."

"Oh right, my phone," Katie said, startled out of her reverie. She rummaged through her purse until she found it. Sure enough, she had a text message. How had she not heard her phone? Man, she really had to get her head in the game. This whole 'checking in and out of reality' thing was unnerving.

She looked at her phone. The text message was from Sophie:

'Katie can u do me a huge favor please! I am really running late & I need u to stop by the drugstore and pick me up some tampons. Can u believe my luck, aunt flo coming to visit two days before the wedding!! Let me know if u can, MOH Thx XOXO'

Katie immediately texted back:

'Of course I will Sophiebell. See you in a little bit. <3'

Well, Katie thought to herself with a small smile, *I guess I know for certain it's not a shotgun wedding.*

"Um, Jas? Can you make a detour to CVS? I need to get something before the luncheon." Katie looked up at Jason when he didn't answer right away and saw that he was still looking in his rearview mirror every two seconds.

When Jason noticed her watching him, he replied, "Sure. Is everything okay?"

"Yeah, it was just Sophie. She needs me to pick something up for her. She doesn't have time to get it before the luncheon," Katie said, returning her phone to her purse and crossing her fingers that no more text-mergencies would be forthcoming.

"I can drop you home so you can start getting ready. Whatever she needs, I'll go get it for her and swing it by Salvatore's. That way you can change before lunch," Jason said.

Katie looked down at her plain grey tank top and jeans and knew that she was going to have to dress *slightly* more upscale for lunch at Salvatore's. At the same time, she didn't think that Jason would be game for this particular errand.

"I think it's better if I pick this up, but thanks anyway," she hedged.

"Come on, Kit Kat. What is it, something girly? Makeup, nylons, hair spray? I can handle it," Jason sounded much more like his normal, easygoing self since the mystery man was no longer following them.

Katie turned to look at him, a small smile playing at her lips, "Oh, really, Jas? Because it's tampons."

"Oh."

"Still think you can handle it?" she teased, waiting for one of his trademark witty comebacks.

To her surprise, he merely shrugged nonchalantly. "Sure. I mean, if you tell me exactly what brand and any special instructions or whatever, I can pick them up."

Katie, taken aback by his blasé attitude about something that would have unsettled most of the guys she knew, insisted, "No, Jas, its fine. I can get them."

Jason shrugged as he turned off 10th Street towards the nearest CVS. "Suit yourself. Well, hey. At least now we know it's not a shotgun wedding."

"Jas!" Katie said, shocked, as she slugged him in the arm.

"What? You know that was the first thing you thought." Jason raised his eyebrows and fixed her with a lightly accusatory stare, albeit one that was tempered with a smile.

"No comment," Katie replied, looking forward to hide the small smile on her face she simply couldn't contain. She had always appreciated the fact that Jason said what was on everyone's mind. It was part of his charm.

"I have to admit, though," she said thoughtfully, "I am really impressed that you would be willing to get them. You get props for that. Most guys would not be so cool about it."

"Well if you remember correctly, this is not my first experience with someone unexpectedly getting her period," Jason said as he pulled into the parking lot of the local CVS.

"Oh. My. God. That's right. I completely forgot about that," Katie said, covering her face with her hands as the memory of the first time she got her period came rushing back to her.

16 Years Earlier

It was the middle of sixth grade and Katie had just received a new pair of white Guess Jeans. She was sitting at the lunch table with her friends Chelle and Mallory, feeling like pretty hot stuff.

She was eating her lunch, giggling, gossiping, and talking about all the things eleven-year-old girls talk about. She was enjoying herself immensely when Jason, Pete, and Sam came over to their table.

At first, Katie had been annoyed because the boys were always so loud and obnoxious. She thought they would ruin lunch, her favorite part of the day.

Jason sat right beside her and started in with his usual shtick, making everyone laugh and—of course—getting all of the attention. She had just about all she could take of them, thankyouverymuch, and was about to stand up to throw away her tray when she felt Jason pull down hard on her arm, roughly returning her to a sitting position.

"Ouch, Jas! That hurt!" Katie protested angrily, pulling her arm away from his insistent grasp.

"Katie," Jason whispered intensely as he leaned in close to her ear, "look down at your lap."

Katie knew he really must be serious because Jason NEVER used her real name—he always called her Kit Kat.

As she looked down, she saw red staining the jeans between her legs. Katie started to panic. She was bleeding. Oh, God.

Jason, clearly seeing the horror spreading quickly across her face, leaned over to her and said calmly "Don't freak out. You just started your period."

Katie closed her eyes in relief and sighed, "Oh, thank God," under her breath. But then a new thought occurred to her, setting off a fresh wave of panic. How was she going to get out of the cafeteria without someone seeing her blood-stained attire? She didn't even have her backpack to try and hide behind.

If anything, she thought she might be more scared about this scenario than she was when she thought she was dying. After all, the only thing at stake there was death. Now we were talking about humiliation!

"Jas, what am I going to do?" Katie asked in a desperate whisper. "I can't get up without someone seeing me, and I need to go the nurse's office to go home."

Jason looked straight into Katie's eyes and said, in an authoritative tone she had never heard come from the joke-a-minute Jason, "I've got a plan. Just follow my lead, okay?"

"Okay," Katie agreed shakily as she tried to hold back tears of embarrassment.

The next thing she knew, Jason was on top of the lunchroom table pounding his chest, letting out a series of primal screams, and yelling "Me Tarzan, me Tarzan!"

Her eyes widened as she witnessed the scene. She felt nothing but shock, which quickly led to despair as she realized that Jas wasn't going to help her after all. He had gotten distracted by starting to pull one of his crazy pranks. But what was the point of this one? It wasn't even funny. It was insane.

Just when she thought he had completely lost his mind, he took off his shirt, throwing it to her and yelling, "Me Tarzan! You Jane!"

Relief flooded through her as she realized his plan.

He started jumping from table to table, making the rounds of the entire cafeteria via tabletop, as he yelled, "AHH AHHEAEA."

Taking advantage of the distraction, Katie slipped into his shirt, which fell almost to her knees. As every eye in the cafeteria focused on Jason's shenanigans, she escaped the cafeteria completely unnoticed. She made a beeline for the nurse's office and said that she had a horrible stomachache. Then she called her mom to come and pick her up.

Pam arrived within ten minutes and Katie gratefully piled into the car, desperately wanting to get as far away from the school as possible. When her mom looked at her with concerned eyes and put a hand to her forehead to check her temperature, Katie began to sob and spilled the entire sordid story of humiliated woe in one long, tear-

filled rant.

She didn't know what her mom's reaction would be. She might be sympathetic or she might be annoyed with Katie for lying about the stomachache. Katie just didn't know. She wasn't sure what it meant when Pam just smiled the tiniest of grins as she pulled away from the curb and commented casually, "That Jason sure is a great guy."

Katie didn't really think anything of it at the time because she was so busy wallowing in mortification at what had transpired. But after school, Katie had gone to return Jason's freshly laundered shirt to him. When she knocked on the door, Seth—the eldest Sloan brother—opened it and said that Jason was still at school because he had detention. When Katie asked what he had done, Seth said that he wasn't really sure, but that it had something to do with a stupid stunt he had pulled at lunch. He also added that their dad was going to "rip him a new one" when he got home.

Katie's head began to spin. She never, even for one second, had thought that Jason would get into any trouble for helping her. God, he was always doing crazy things and usually people just laughed. Sometimes adults would shake their heads, but they always looked amused. He had never suffered any repercussions because of it.

Now he was in detention and he was going to get in trouble at home. Katie didn't know what to do. She decided that the best course of action was to go to school and try to reason with Jason's teacher—even the principal if she had to. She would do whatever was necessary to get him pardoned.

She took a deep breath then, thinking about what she was going to have to deal with after she had dealt with the school. She was going to have to fess up to Jason's dad, Bob. Oh, man.

He was not going to be as easy to deal with as Principal Jenson.

She began to formulate a plan, a step-by-step blueprint of what she would do. She tried to come up with some story that would explain Jason's odd behavior. After discarding several lame versions of why Tarzan had made an appearance, however, she was forced to come to the conclusion that maybe the best thing to do would be to abide by the old adage 'the truth shall set you free.'

Yep, *she decided.* Honesty is the best policy.

She trembled in anticipation of having to relate her tale of humiliation to adults. To adult guys, no less. Oh, God.

The only way she could get through it was to really downplay the whole 'I just started my period in white jeans' part. Yeah, she would just rush through that part and make a point to emphasize how Jason had rescued her from complete and total humiliation.

Humiliation that would have endured for years to come.

Then, she would enlist Nurse Parks to come in and back up the fact that Katie had come into the office and gone home with a very bad "stomachache"—and (additional proof) that she was wearing Jason's shirt at the time.

However, as it turned out, none of that was how it went down at all.

As she turned the corner to Great Oaks Middle School, she saw Jason's dad's white Chevy Blazer parked in the teacher parking lot. Oh God Oh God Oh God! Maybe it wasn't his?

No. She knew it was, because it said Sloan Construction on the side.

Oh no, she was too late. Katie's breath began to quicken and her eyes began to well. She couldn't let this happen because of her. It was so unfair. She had to do something to try to diffuse the situation—and if that meant describing the entire embarrassing chain of events to a few adults gathered in a room, including Jason's dad (who was very intimidating.) then…okay, yeah. So be it.

Katie took a deep breath, pushed back her shoulders, held her head high, and pushed open the heavy double doors that led to the school's administration office.

She was immediately bombarded by the sound of laughter coming from Principal Jenson's office. Whoa! Not what she expected to hear.

She peeked unobtrusively around the corner and saw Principal Jenson and Bob Sloan hysterically laughing as Principal Jenson relayed the events of Jason's impromptu lunchtime performance. Katie breathed a sigh of relief when the Principal ended the recitation by saying that he would call the detention classroom and have Jason come up to the office so that he could leave with his father.

Katie smiled to herself. Hopefully this was a good sign. No need to humiliate herself after all if everyone was going to take Jason's prank in stride. She decided to let herself off the hook for that and just find Jason so she could thank him and return his freshly laundered shirt.

She knew that detention was being held in Mrs. Kimball's science lab this week so she started down the far left hall to see if she could intercept Jason on his way to the office.

That's when she saw it.

There, in a corner formed by a bank of lockers and an outcropping of the wall, halfway hidden in shadows, was Jason. Making out with Callie Martin. The single most stuck up, obnoxious, popular girl at Great Oaks Middle School.

Katie stood there, dumbfounded. Not only was she disgusted that Jason was kissing Callie, she also couldn't quite believe that Callie would be kissing Jason. Callie was an eighth grader. And she had all the eighth grade boys (and even some freshmen) drooling over her. Why would she be kissing Jason, a lowly sixth grader?

Obviously, Jason didn't need (or probably even want, the rat fink) Katie's help or apology. She spun on her heels and headed towards home.

Present Day

She had never returned Jason's shirt. In fact, most nights she still slept in it.

One time, during their junior year, Nick had been hanging out while she was doing laundry. He spied the shirt while she was folding her clothes and wrinkled his forehead in puzzlement. He asked why she had a guy's Def Leppard shirt, and she lied and said that it was an old shirt of her dad's that she kept because she didn't have that many memories of him.

He looked at her strangely, but didn't pursue it. She didn't care, though, because she knew for a fact that Nick would have never seen Jason in the shirt. Nick had moved to Harper's Crossing just before their seventh grade year began, and the shirt had been in her possession since the middle of sixth grade.

Now, sitting in Jason's truck parked outside of CVS, Katie realized that she had never thanked Jason for his jungle-tacular heroics that day.

She turned to him and slowly pulled her hands down from where they were providing protective cover for her red face. She said, "Oh my gosh, Jas…I don't know what I would have done if you hadn't been there and noticed my situation. Actually, now that I think of it, how did you see the problem? I was already sitting down when you came over to the table."

"I noticed when you put one leg over the bench to sit down. I could tell by the way you were talking and laughing that you had no idea, so I stayed at my table until I came up with a plan," Jason said in a matter-of-fact tone and then shrugged modestly, adding, "and then I went over to help."

"You already knew what you were going to do before came over to my table? Your Tarzan plan was premeditated?" Katie asked in disbelief, her jaw dropping slightly.

"Premeditated." he chuckled. "Whoa. Now, listen,

counselor. I knew that you would be too busy freaking out to figure out what to do about the situation once it was brought to your attention, so I figured I had to be the one to think rationally and devise a plan.

"I would think that instead of picking apart my M.O. you would have been kissing my feet for saving you an entire childhood of humiliation. You know, come to think of it, I never even got a thank you for being your knight in shining armor."

Jason said this in a lightly teasing tone, but when Katie looked at him, she definitely saw a challenge in his eyes.

Katie narrowed her eyes, she'd always hated it when he gave her that look. It was a look that said, "Checkmate. Your move." It was like he already knew he had won.

Well, not this time buddy.

She took a deep breath, squared her shoulders, and began her rebuttal.

"I wasn't saying that 'premeditated' was a bad thing. In fact, I am even more impressed that, *one*, you weren't too embarrassed to do anything, and *two*, you even noticed in the first place.

"*Three*, you did not decide to use the information to humiliate me, as you easily could have done. And, honestly, I really do want you to know how incredibly grateful for that I am," Katie finished sincerely.

Then she continued on with her speech, moving into the part where she was going to play a little hardball.

"Which is why I went to your house after school to tell you all of that on the day it happened. Seth said that you had gotten detention and that your dad was not too happy about it. Feeling bad about my role in your detention, I went down to the school to try to get you an early parole hearing by explaining how you had been my 'knight in shining armor.'" A small smile tugged at her lips. "My Tarzan in shining armor, if you will."

"By the time I got there, your dad was already in the office with Principal Jenson and they were laughing so hard that Principal Jenson could barely finish telling your dad the story. Then I heard Principal Jenson say that he would send for you to come up to the office, so I figured I would meet you in the hall."

She stopped and stared at him expectantly. He looked puzzled.

"What?" he asked, "Is that your whole story?"

Her eyebrows rose. "Well? What do you think I saw when I turned down the hall towards the science lab?"

Jason looked honestly perplexed. He shrugged and shook his head. "No idea," he said.

Katie gave him a punch on the side of the arm. "I saw you playing tonsil hockey with Callie Martin, you traitor. You didn't really look like you would want to be interrupted so I turned around and went home. And as far as never thanking you, I was eleven, and starting a conversation with someone by saying, 'Thanks for saving me from complete humiliation and social suicide the first time I started my period' isn't really the easiest thing to do.

"But you're absolutely right. You do deserve a proper thanks. So thank you, Jas, for saving me from years of humiliation. Happy? Or did you want me to kiss your feet?"

Jason still had that look in his eye, the one that made her insane. The one that meant he thought (knew) he was winning this round.

"Wow," he said in a lightly amused tone. "You said all of that in one breath. Now I'm the one who's impressed. Now, let me explain a few facts of my own to you."

Jason leaned in so close that he was barely an inch away from Katie's face. Her heart began beating double-time in her chest.

"*One*, of course I noticed. I notice everything about you. *Two*, I appreciate the fact that you came to rescue me from detention. That's sweet. *Three*, I would never do anything to humiliate you, Kit Kat. I wish you knew that about me.

"And as far as Callie Martin, well, she came on to me. I was just an innocent bystander in her plan to dominate the entire male population of Harper's Crossing. That's all that was."

Jason leaned back a little. The challenge was still in his eyes, but now a smile was deliberately spreading across his face, covering it as slowly, but surely, as melted butter coats a pan.

Finally, he said, "I have to admit, though. I'm pretty happy she did, all things considered. I like seeing the jealous side of you."

Katie's jaw dropped, and not just a little this time.

"I am not jealous!" she protested hotly. "I only even *mentioned* it because it was a pertinent part of my explanation. You know, as to why I didn't thank you."

Jason ignored Katie's outburst and brushed the side of her face with his fingertips.

"And *four*," he continued as if she hadn't even spoken, "I'd much rather you kiss my lips than my feet."

With that, he closed the gap between them and pressed his lips to hers firmly enough to show her that he meant business, but gently enough to make Katie want more…and more…and *more.*

Before she knew what she was doing, her hand was behind his neck and she was pulling him closer to her, deepening their kiss. She heard a low moan coming from deep within Jason's chest.

The sound made her bold, and she parted her lips and traced her tongue along his bottom lip. Her entire body was consumed with delicious tingles, her heart was racing, and her skin felt like it was burning up. She was engulfed in overwhelming sensations, and she never wanted to climb out of it. If this was drowning, she didn't want to be rescued.

Just as Jason's lips parted and their tongues made

their first electrified contact, Jason's cell phone rang. The sound shattered the bubble that had formed inside the cab of the truck and brought Katie back to her senses.

She quickly pulled away, turning in her seat to face forward. Jason just stared at her, his breathing labored, until Katie blurted out, "You'd better check that."

Shaking his head, he begrudgingly looked down at his phone.

"It's Bobby," he grumbled as he put his phone to his ear. "This better be good," he barked.

Chapter Eight

Katie sat there for a minute catching her breath, listening as the boys went back and forth with their usual brotherly bickering. Well, Jason's bickering might have been a little surlier than normal, but that was to be expected under the circumstances. When she felt like she had gotten herself under control, she slipped out of the truck and quickly walked into CVS.

Not only did she desperately need a break from Jason, but she also had to get what Sophie needed and get going so she wouldn't be late for the luncheon. She looked at her watch. Damn. It was 12:30. She couldn't remember if the luncheon was at 1:00 or 1:30. She prayed it was 1:30. Where the hell was her itinerary packet?

How could she not remember? Her colleagues had nicknamed her Polaroid, because they said she had a photographic memory. Which was an exaggeration, but she normally remembered and stored information better than most. It seemed her return to Harper's Crossing was apparently the kryptonite to not only her sanity, but her memory as well.

Whew. She felt like this day was spinning out of control. She couldn't remember basic details or find a program she had been given mere hours ago. She needed to get a grip. She was the M.O.H. She needed to be bright, cheery and on time. Disorganized, late and horny were not on the list of "Top Ten Most Desirable Qualities in an M.O.H." that she was sure Aunt Wendy had included somewhere in her packet.

Katie shook her head, hoping to clear it. What she could *really* use was a shower, both to cool down and to get her head on straight. She always sang in the shower, too. No matter what was going on in her life, a good shower concert was all she needed to get recharged.

She reached into her purse and dug around.

Bingo!

She pulled out the wedding festivities packet and took a quick look. Hmmmm. No schedule was in the packet. She had taken it out to study it in the car. Had she tucked it safely back inside when she was finished? She couldn't remember.

Either way, chances were that no shower concert was going to be on the agenda at any point during the day.

Hurrying to the appropriate aisle, Katie made her selection, got to the checkout stand, and paid for her purchase. She rushed back to the front of the store, scurrying quickly so as to get back on the tight timetable.

She was just about to step through the pneumatic

double glass doors that fronted the store when she stopped in her tracks. She caught sight of Jason leaning against his truck and talking on the phone, and it took her aback. He was laughing, completely unaware that he was being observed, without a hint of artifice.

Dimples. How in the world had she forgotten he had such deep dimples?

She had also forgotten the way that, when he was just being his relaxed and funny self, he radiated joy more purely than any person she had ever met. It was infectious. Just being around Jason when he was in that mood put a smile on your face—a real one. The kind that went all the way to your toes.

Man, she thought wistfully, *when was the last time I smiled like that? An all-the-way-to-my-toes smile?*

Probably not since the last time Jason made me smile like that.

In high school, she was always studying, always pushing, always trying to get the best GPA she could so she could get into a good school.

And then in college, although that should have been her time to cut loose and be carefree, she had continued to bury herself in academics. Now, looking back, she realized that it was a way to escape facing what had happened with Nick and the overwhelming guilt of feeling like she had betrayed him with Jason.

Lord Almighty. To this day, she still had a hard time believing what she and Jason had done. Jason and Nick had been best friends—inseparable—but Jason obviously did not have the same issues that were haunting Katie. He seemed genuinely happy and content with his life.

Granted she had only been back in Harper's Crossing for a few hours, but even with all of the wedding hustle and bustle, Jason seemed content. Not stressed at all. But that was Jason's way.

Seriously, Jason, she thought. *How on earth do you manage to do that?*

Katie had never understood how, no matter what was going on, Jason always stayed cool, calm and collected. Katie was usually uptight and worried about things like rules and schedules. That had always been their dynamic, even before Nick's accident.

After the accident, while Nick was lying in the hospital, in a coma, Jason tried to reach out and be there for Katie. But, for her own reasons, she couldn't let him in. She kept him at arm's length, pushing him further and further away.

And hadn't that proven to be the right thing to do, considering how things turned out? The night that she *did* give in to the sweet temptation of letting herself 'lean on him,' things ended up going *way* too far.

She had only herself to blame. That was why she had to keep her guard up. Jason had some kind of voodoo spell hold over her or something. She wasn't quite sure what. It was like he was a magnet and she was made entirely of metal, like the Tin Man from *The Wizard of Oz*. The big difference there, of course, was that the Tin Man had wanted to be granted a heart he didn't have. Katie had a heart, all right. It was her inability to control it that was the problem.

How could she have let him kiss her? Seriously, what if someone had seen? To this town, she would *always* be Nick's girlfriend. She didn't want anyone to view her act of kissing Jason, even after all these years, to be "cheating" on Nick, even if only in spirit.

Nick had basically been sainted in this town. This *small* town where people loved to gossip. This weekend was supposed to be about Sophie and Bobby—not a Katie/Jason/Nick love triangle.

✦ ✦ ✦

Jason hung up the phone and slowly took a deep, steadying breath in through his nose and out through his mouth. Damn. That kiss had shaken him up. He wished that he could control himself when he was around Katie, and he had promised himself that he could and that he *would*—but recent evidence proved quite the contrary. In fact, it showed that, not only could he not be trusted around her long-term, he could not even be trusted with her on a short car ride.

In his defense, of course, he had been pretty much head over heels in love with the girl since they were five.

They just needed to get some things sorted out before he let anything else happen between them physically.

He needed to set her straight on exactly how he felt about her—past, present, and future. She wasn't going to like it, but she was going to hear it. Not only that, he was going to make sure she listened with her heart, not just her ears. If that kiss was any indication of her feelings for him, she couldn't keep denying what they had between them. It was too raw. Too powerful. Too real.

Having a talk with her, where he laid his true feelings bare, was years overdue. It's not as if he hadn't always known the feelings were there. Growing up, Jason had always known he felt something special for Katie.

In elementary school, he had shown it the way most little boys did—by picking on her. They had been friends, but their friendship had mostly been based on him teasing her, followed by her snappy comebacks.

Then it had changed. Deepened. When Jason's mom passed away, the summer before middle school, it had sent him reeling. His behavior and his life spiraled into a tailspin. His mom hadn't even been in his life for years before she passed, but her death had still had a profound effect on him.

The year after her passing went by in a blur. He'd felt as though he were on the verge of drowning every single minute, and each day was just a long series of bumbling efforts, big and small, to keep his head above water.

The only time he felt okay, like he was hanging onto a lifeline, was when he was around Katie. But being eleven years old, and a boy to boot, he was unable to process those strong emotions and his reaction actually came out as anger and frustration at Katie rather than gratitude for her stabilizing presence.

Over the summer between sixth and seventh grade, Jason and Katie had seen a lot of each other. Down at the Riverwalk, at the Boys & Girls Club, and at friends' birthday parties.

They had even played Seven Minutes in Heaven at Rachelle Thomas's twelfth birthday party. They spent the first five of their allotted seven minutes just talking. Then, because Jason was always so 'smooth' when it came to Katie, he announced that he was bored so they might as well kiss.

She just stared at him in shock. Interpreting her silence as agreement to his plan, he went in for the kill without encouraging further discussion. Jason had kissed plenty of girls by the time he was with Katie in the closet. His first 'real' kiss was in fourth grade. But he had never felt the true power of a kiss until his lips met Katie's in that dusty closet.

During the last few weeks of summer vacation, he couldn't get the kiss out of his mind. Jason had even gone as far as purposely avoiding Katie in hopes that he could erase the event. It hadn't worked.

All day, every day. Every hour. Every minute. Jason did nothing during all that time but remember kissing Katie, dreaming about kissing Katie, and planning ways to create an opportunity to kiss Katie again.

Ultimately, he had made up his mind that the very next time he saw her, on the first day of school, he was going to ask her out. Which, in middle school, basically just meant that she would be his girlfriend. They wouldn't actually 'go' anywhere, per se.

Even now Jason could remember walking up to Great Oaks Middle School that brisk September morning and seeing something that hit him like a punch to the gut. Katie Lawson was holding hands with some blond-haired kid and giggling whenever he said anything.

Jason quickly learned that Nick was the 'new kid in school.' At first, he befriended Nick because he wanted to know exactly who this guy was that had swept in and stole 'his girl.' It was a 'keep your friends close and your enemies closer' tactic. But the thing was, Nick actually turned out to be a great guy. He and Jason quickly became best friends.

Jason had honestly *never* expected Nick and Katie's relationship to last as long as it had. Seriously, what kids that get together in middle school manage to last all the way through their senior year of high school? Jason had initially thought that he was just biding his time for the few weeks or months it would take for the novelty of the 'new kid' to wear off for Katie. Or maybe for Nick to meet some girl he hadn't come across yet when he had asked Katie to be his girlfriend before even setting foot in the school.

It had seemed like a solid plan at the time.

Unfortunately, neither of those things had happened.

As the years went on, Jason's feelings for Katie did not diminish one iota. In fact they only grew stronger. He knew that Katie and Nick's relationship was not going to survive through their college years. Nick loved Katie in his own way, but Nick loved Nick more. And he definitely had his flaws. Jason was of the firm opinion that, as great of a guy as Nick was, Katie still saw him through rose-colored glasses and that her vision would clear once she started getting to know the big, wide world outside of Harper's Crossing.

As it turned out, one of the many gut-wrenching consequences of Nick's death, for Jason, was that now he would forever be clothed in the protective, softening cloud of memory where Katie was concerned. How could Jason compete with a saint?

Before the accident, there were so many times that Jason had almost confessed his true feelings for Katie. One thing always stopped him, though. Katie seemed happy. Still, there were a lot of ways Jason did not feel that Nick treated Katie right, and he'd told Nick so. But Nick had something Katie needed, and it was something that Jason could not give her. Nick had a big, happy family that had adopted Katie as their own. He knew that was something she had always wanted.

Sure, Jason had his dad and brothers, not to mention that Uncle Pete and Aunt Sandy were around with his four cousins pretty often. But Nick had the perfect Norman Rockwell fantasy family to offer her: a mom and a dad, a little sister who adored Katie, and—the cherry on top—Grandpa J.

Jason couldn't compete with that, and he didn't want to take that 'family' experience away from Katie. She always went on and on about how fun their family dinners were. Jason knew it was true. Once or twice a week, he would stay at the Hunters' for dinner and witness, firsthand, just how much Katie enjoyed her time there.

He could see the happiness written all over her face, glowing from within her, causing her to shine the way only basking in love and acceptance can. He wasn't going to be the guy to rob her of that joy.

Now, as he watched Katie walk from the store to the truck, an odd sensation swept over him. He wasn't quite sure how to describe it or categorize it—even to himself. He just knew, now, more than ever before in his life, that the feelings he had for Katie were not puppy love and they weren't going away—so he had better decide exactly what he was planning to do about it.

He had always operated on the assumption that the straightforward approach was the best and most effective in any given situation. Say what you mean, mean what you say.

The only problem with that plan of action was that Katie seemed very skittish, even for Katie standards, at the moment. Going with straightforward might just send her running for the hills.

He needed to pace himself. He had the whole weekend to wear her down, and that was exactly what he planned to do.

Chapter Nine

Katie could feel her heart pounding out of her chest as she made her way back to the truck. She automatically started reciting her handy-dandy mantra inside her head.

You can breathe. Just breathe. Breathe in and out slowly. You can breathe.

Oh. Dear. God. In. Heaven.

Why, why, *why* did he have to look so gorgeous in the sun? It was like God himself was Jason's own personal lighting technician.

How in the world was she going to make it through this weekend without a repeat of what happened the night she left Harper's Crossing? She was just going to have to keep focused on the wedding and *not* focus on how amazing that kiss had made her feel.

"Did you get everything you needed?" Jason pushed off from where he had been leaning against his truck and opened the passenger side door for her.

"Yep, I'm all set." Katie's jaw tensed, but she made a valiant attempt to sound as unaffected by the ridiculous nickname as she possibly could. She knew that part of the reason (most of the reason) he insisted on calling her by it was that he loved getting a rise out of her.

Reaching under the seat and feeling around as she got in the truck, Katie realized the program had not fallen out in Jason's truck. She asked, a touch of despair tingeing her voice, "Jas, have you seen my itinerary? I need to know what time the luncheon is."

"The luncheon is at 1:00 and, no, I haven't seen your itinerary. Do you think you could have left it at Mona's? Maybe it fell out of your bag during your fitting," Jason sounded matter-of-fact and logical but also distracted as he pulled out of the CVS parking lot and made a right onto the parkway.

"Yeah, it probably did," Katie sighed, looking at her watch and already knowing the answer to her next question. "So…I guess I don't have time to get freshened up before heading over to the luncheon, do I?"

"Not unless you want to show up fashionably late. But if I recall correctly, and I believe I do, you were always somewhat anal when it came to punctuality," Jason replied with that challenge-hiding-behind-a-tease tone to his voice he knew was always good to get her riled up.

Well, she wasn't going to oblige him. She was going to keep it calm, cool, and collected.

"Just because I enjoy being on time for things does not automatically equal being anal," Katie responded, her tone measured and even, although it *did* kind of drive her crazy that he always had to make such broad statements about her. Yeah. Come to think of it, that was *really* aggravating.

"No, I guess it's not fair to call it anal," Jason teased. "I know *lots* of girls who show up to the prom by themselves because their date is fifteen minutes late to pick them up."

"Oh, come on. You cannot be serious. Just because I didn't want to be late to my senior prom does *not* mean that I am anal about being punctual. And can we *please* stop using that word? I've always hated it."

Katie saw a flash of amusement cross Jason's face, and that sent her irritation meter shooting from five to ten.

"I thought 'panties' and 'moist' were at the top of the 'perfectly valid words Katie hates' list."

"Those, too. But don't try to distract me when I'm on a roll."

"Is that what you're on?"

"Yep. And might I point out, while we're on the subject, that it was a certain Mr. Jason Sloan that was responsible for the aforementioned tardiness incident. I do believe that *someone* forgot to pick up a corsage for his date and forced the limo all of the guys—my date included—were riding in to go into town and stop by The Flower Pavilion so he could pick up the flowers. Sound familiar? Hmmm?"

Katie felt unreasonably pleased with herself that, for once, Jason was going to have to take responsibility for something. *Let's see you charm your way out of those facts,*

Jas.

To this day, Katie couldn't quite believe that on prom night, of all nights, Jason would forget something as important as picking up a corsage. Nick had made her promise not to harass Jason about it at the time because he didn't want their night to be ruined by her and Jason fighting. But what the hell? They weren't at prom now, were they? And truth be told, she was probably more excited than she should be at the opportunity to finally confront him about it.

"I mean, really, Jason? Really? There were four other couples taking that limo, and the fact that you would disrupt everyone else's night just to get yourself out of the doghouse is beyond me. Really and truly beyond me. And don't even *try* the 'I was too busy with sports' excuse because Nick played just as many sports as you and he managed to find the time to pick me out the most amazing wrist corsage made of the most incredible and beautiful calla lilies I'd ever seen.

"But, nooooo. Mister 'fly by the seat of my pants' couldn't be bothered to plan ahead, even for senior prom. Even when nine other people were counting on him. Didn't you even consider the fact that I might want to show up to my senior prom on time? Did that thought even cross your mind?"

"Are you finished?" Jason asked dryly as he pulled off the road and into a small parking lot Katie did not recognize.

"Yes. Yes, I think I am," Katie confirmed, not even

bothering to hide her self-satisfied grin.

"Well then, let me set a few things straight, counselor." Jason turned to face Katie after parking his truck in an empty space at the very corner of the lot.

They were hidden under a canopy of trees, and it felt...intimate. It felt like they had entered another realm—a fantasy forest filled with wizards and fairies, where she was the beautiful princess and Jason was the dashing knight.

Katie tried to push that vivid imagery from her mind. Fairy tale situations were the last thing she needed to be thinking about. Those fables ended in happily-ever-after, and there was no way that's where *this* was headed.

Turning towards Jason to focus on the here and now, on reality instead of magical realms, the cab of the truck suddenly seemed very small and very warm. Katie felt the hairs on the back of her neck stand up as Jason's eyes bore into hers. As much as she knew she ought to, she could not bring herself to look away.

Holy cow—how was it possible that this man had such a hold on her? He was just a person, for heaven's sake—he wasn't supernatural. No one else in the entire world affected her this way.

Katie prided herself on always being in control of her environment and *especially* of any conversation she was a part of. She wouldn't have made it very far in the legal profession if she couldn't get the upper hand in a conversation with an untrained civilian—it was, literally, how she made her bread and butter. Stay in control, never let the power balance shift, and don't get flustered—these were all techniques she had mastered.

Being a lawyer, she could say that she was, in a sense, a professional argument winner. Yet with Jason, she had never quite felt in control of anything, and from that look in his eye, she already knew she was going to lose this argument.

"I bought Krissy Anderson, *my* date, a pink pin-on rose corsage the Wednesday before prom," he began calmly but intensely, "and when Nick got to my house to get ready for prom, I asked him where his corsage for you was. He said—and I quote—'Katie doesn't even like flowers and the corsage I bought her for junior prom just got in the way all night. She couldn't stop fidgeting with it.'"

Jason lowered his hands from the air quotes he had been shaping and his right hand came to rest on Katie's thigh. Her breathing quickened. She wondered if the placement of his hand had been deliberate but then stopped wondering and simply started panicking, because, oh boy. The weight of Jason's hand felt waaay too good resting on her leg. She could feel the pressure of his long fingers as they wrapped around her thigh and it felt…amazing.

"There was no way I was going to let you go to your senior prom without a corsage just because numb nuts Nick didn't bother to get you one. So, I had the limo driver stop at The Flower House, Flower Emporium, and finally The Flower Pavilion. Want to know why we made more than one stop, Kit Kat?"

Katie simply nodded because she was unable to speak, distracted by the reaction her body was having to Jason's touch.

"We made more than one stop because I didn't want to get you a simple rose corsage. I remembered that in fifth grade, we were walking across Lincoln Park on the way home from school and I picked you a rose. You said that you thought roses were overrated and common. And I was not about to settle on anything that you considered 'overrated and common.' I did find a chrysanthemum corsage at The Flower House but it was a pin-on and I knew that you had a chiffon dress and that you wouldn't want to put holes in it. Plus, I remembered that you'd had a pin-on for junior prom and that was probably why you were fidgeting with it. So I made the driver take us to one more stop and that is where I found the calla lily wrist corsage.

"Oh and as far 'considering the fact that you would like to be on time to your senior prom,' I bribed the driver $50 extra to speed to your house, and I wouldn't let any of the other guys pick up their dates, or my *own* date for that matter, even though two of them were on the way to your house. Why? Because I knew you would be pacing the floor every minute that we were late. How did I know that? Because I know *you*, Kit Kat.

"We came screeching up to your house only to have

Aunt Wendy tell us that you had left with your mom five minutes before we got there because you didn't want to be late. So in answer to your question, yeah. I guess the thought of you getting to prom on time did cross my mind."

Katie heard the words that were coming out of Jason's mouth but she couldn't quite wrap her head around what he was saying. The story he was telling her didn't sound much like the Jason she'd known since the first day of kindergarten. It sounded more like something Nick would have done for her.

It was all very confusing and hard to believe.

Not to mention the fact that there was no way she could hold together a cohesive train of thought with Jason's hand sitting on her thigh and the stare of his whiskey brown eyes sending shockwaves of bliss erupting through her body. Still, even with that hormonal distraction, she knew there was one thing that wasn't adding up and needed clarification. Facts to back up this story. Not that she thought Jason was lying. He might be a lot of things, but a liar was not one of them. She just needed to make sense of it all.

"How did you know that my dress was chiffon? I didn't tell anyone what my dress looked like except my mom and Aunt Wendy. I wanted it to be a surprise."

He didn't even blink, much less hesitate. "I was at Richards's getting fitted for my tux and I heard your laugh coming from Mona's. I looked around the divider and I saw you standing on the pedestal in the middle of the room, swishing back and forth in your strapless, royal blue, floor-length prom dress. It was the single most beautiful sight I had ever seen in my life."

Katie was starting to feel lightheaded. He had an answer for everything, but things still just weren't adding up.

"Wait," Katie said, when we had the 'switch partners, ladies choice' dance and Krissy chose Nick, leaving me to dance with you, you were *clearly* pissed off to be stuck with me. You weren't even talking to me. I remember it perfectly because you seemed so *upset* about dancing with me that I tried to make you smile by telling you that you looked nice. Then I asked if you thought I looked okay, and you practically yawned as you said, 'You look as good as you can look.'

"Then when I hit you on the arm, you said 'Hey, don't ask a question if you don't want the answer.' That is a far cry from,"—Katie now adopted the air quotes technique Jason had used earlier—"the 'most beautiful sight you had ever seen,' like you claim."

Jason shook his head, looking slightly past her as if lost in the memory. She had rarely seen him look so pained. Her heart squeezed at the sad, almost tortured, look that she saw in his eyes.

"What was I supposed to do, Katie? Admit that I put Krissy up to asking Nick to dance just so I could have an excuse to have *one* dance with you? Tell you that you were by far the most gorgeous girl at that prom, or anywhere, for that matter? You were dating my best friend, and you had been for six years. My hands were kind of tied."

As Jason gave this impassioned speech, he gently squeezed his hand where it rested on her leg and then proceeded to start rubbing his hand up and down on her thigh as he continued.

His gravelly tone washed over her like an erotically charged breeze as he spoke, "Do you have any idea how it drove me crazy seeing you and not being able to touch you or kiss you or even just tell you how beautiful you were."

Katie felt her core begin to pulse with heated arousal as Jason's large hands ran up and down her thigh, each time getting a little closer to her center. She knew she should push him away, make him stop, but why did this have to feel so good? And how could she bring herself to pull away from him after the things he had just told her?

Her head was spinning. She was confused yet also thoroughly enjoying the thrilling pleasure racing through her body. She couldn't seem to catch her breath.

Oh good Lord, if she was going to have a panic attack, she just wanted to get it over with already. Screw the mantra.

"Jason," Katie said. She had been aiming for a warning tone, but it came out more like a moan.

"What?" he replied, sounding as innocent as a newborn lamb.

But when she looked over at him, she saw the look of intensity in his eye. He was nowhere near innocent and certainly not going to stop because of a warning tone, particularly one as weakly delivered as what she had managed.

This had to stop. She couldn't let this go further until she had a chance to figure out what in the world was going on with her raging hormonal response to Jason's every touch, every look, every smile. She felt like she had stepped into an X-rated version of *The Twilight Zone*.

She moved in her seat, fully intending to shove his hand away, pick up her purse, and get out of the truck. That's what she *planned* to do anyway. But as she reached down to push his hand off of her thigh, he used her shift in position to slip his hand further up her thigh, not stopping until it was snuggly resting between her legs. The side of his index finger was pressed against her center, and he began gently rubbing his thumb lightly back and forth over the area above her core.

Katie froze, uncertain about what to do next, as Jason began pressing his fingers against her, massaging her intimately. She felt the most overwhelming sensations starting to wash over her. She closed her eyes and laid her head back. She couldn't think, couldn't rationalize what was happening. She could only feel.

As Jason's sensual touch moved directly over the apex between Katie's legs, an intense pressure began to build within her belly, waves of extreme pleasure radiating out like shockwaves from the epicenter of an earthquake.

She had a vague realization about how inappropriate this behavior was, but she felt nearly powerless to act on it. She forced her eyes open to turn away from Jason and made one last valiant effort to move his hand away from her body, but to no avail. Her muscles were weak with arousal, and her half-hearted efforts at pushing his hand away amounted to little more than a light brush against his forearm. When she exerted every ounce of her remaining will to wrench her head to the side, hoping to free herself from his magnetic power, she ended up looking directly into those oh-so-amazing eyes. Lifting his free hand he cupped her jaw, pulling her face towards him and capturing her mouth with his in a blisteringly hot kiss.

Katie gasped at the assault on her senses. Her head was spinning, and her heart was racing. She couldn't make sense of any of this, and she was almost beyond even wanting to. The longer the encounter went on and the more her body was overtaken by sensation, the stronger her desire came to just surrender to the power of Jason's hands, Jason's lips—to just surrender to Jason altogether.

As soon as his tongue slipped inside her mouth, an explosion of passion, unlike any she had ever felt, was released through her entire body. His tongue was searching her mouth, probing, sweeping back and forth insistently. She found herself matching his intensity jab for jab and parry for parry.

He wasn't just kissing her. He was devouring her. He was owning her.

His hand had found exactly the right spot between her legs and he was expertly manipulating her flesh. The fact that she was still fully dressed and he was touching her through denim didn't slow Jason down in the least. In fact, if she wasn't mistaken, he was somehow using it to his advantage.

His fingers started moving faster, applying ever-increasing pressure, and she felt the waves of pleasure rolling inside of her increase to Category 5 Storm levels.

That little voice in the back of her head, the one that always wanted to follow the rules and made her a pretty successful lawyer, kept telling her that she should stop. But...she couldn't bring herself to pull away. She wanted nothing more than for him to keep touching her, keep kissing her, keep making her feel more alive than she had felt in so, so long.

Katie heard sounds coming from the back of her throat she didn't even recognize. Her heart felt like it was beating to the rhythm of his fingers. Her entire body felt infused with spine-tingling bliss.

Just when she was thinking that this couldn't possibly get any better, that she was at the outer edge of pleasurable oblivion, Jason pulled his mouth from hers and began kissing his way down her neck. He licked, trailing his tongue down her burning skin, and stopped several times to suckle the sensitive little niches on her throat. This sent jolts of electricity directly down to the exact place his fingers were working their magic, and to her shock and amazement, she found that she had not yet reached the outer edges of this pleasure landscape. No, Jason was taking her even further into unexplored territories of bliss. He kissed a trail back up her neck, alternating sucking and licking the whole way, stopping at her jawline.

"Jason," Katie thought she heard herself say with a hint of pleading in her voice. She felt as if she were floating without an anchor, as if she were going to be set adrift in this sea of pleasure. She reached up and grabbed his shoulders so that she would have something to hold on to.

"Say that again," he growled against her ear.

The sound of his voice vibrating in her ear almost pushed her over the peak.

"Jason," she said again, and this time she was definitely pleading, more than just a hint of desperation coloring her voice.

"Damn, Katie. I love how you say my name. Now, come for me, baby," Jason commanded seductively as he lightly bit down on the sensitive area right below her ear.

That was all it took. Katie went up and over the edge, a cry tearing from her throat. She dug her nails into Jason's shoulders and gasped as every part of her body was flooded with mind-numbing pleasure. She held on to him tightly as her body shook, burying her face in his neck as she climaxed. He held her tightly against him as she rode out her orgasm—the single most intense orgasm she had ever experienced.

As the dense, sexual fog that had taken up residence in her brain began to slowly dissipate, the painful awareness of what she had just done began to seep into the edges of her consciousness, piece by tiny piece.

Katie found herself clinging to Jason for dear life. Her face buried in the crook of his neck, resting her head on his shoulder. His fresh, manly scent filled her senses as she luxuriated in the soft sensation of his skin against her cheek. His arms surrounded her in a cocoon of safety. She could feel his chest moving in and out against her body, his labored breathing the only sound in the cab of the truck.

After several moments, the bubble of intimacy she'd been floating in was popped when Jason shifted, moving his hand from between her legs so it was now resting again on her upper thigh.

In a split second of awareness, embarrassment and shame flooded Katie. She abruptly pulled away from Jason and covered her hands with her face. She couldn't face him. She was mortified.

From the relative safety of hiding behind her fingers, she managed to blurt out, "Oh my God, what did I just do? How could I? What was I thinking? How could this…this is not really happening. I don't do things like this."

Katie, trying with all her might to make sense of all

of what was going on, let her thoughts flow out loud with hardly any filter as she hid her face and shook her head back and forth.

She heard Jason's voice, sounding irritatingly amused, as he said, "FYI, I can still see you. Covering your face does not make you invisible, Kit Kat."

She kept her hands in place but managed to retort, "I realize that you can see me, Jason. I am not delusional. A slut maybe, but not delusional."

She forced a bark of laughter after the last statement, trying to make herself believe that she'd only meant it as a lighthearted joke.

Then, just to make herself feel better, she added for good measure, "And don't call me Kit Kat."

"Take your hands off your face," Jason commanded in a surprisingly authoritative tone.

Katie shook her head, she barely recognized herself in this moment. These were not the actions of a lawyer, or even an adult. Nope, she'd just acted like a horny teenager and because of that, she was sitting here, covering her face like a child who was pouting with embarrassment.

Even *knowing* that she was being ridiculous, she couldn't seem to snap out of it. She just wanted to get out of this truck. Now. "No. Just hand me my purse and I'll go. Please, Jason."

Then, taking just one hand off her face, still keeping her eyes tightly shut, she stuck out her hand to retrieve her purse.

Rather than placing her pocketbook in her outstretched hand, Jason took her hand in his and repeated his directive. "Katie, open your eyes and look at me."

"Would you *please* just hand me my purse and let me go?" she begged as she tried to feel for the door handle, still refusing to open her eyes.

Had anyone actually died from mortification? No? Well, there was a first time for everything.

"Kit Kat, it's just me. Come on. Just turn around and open your eyes." Jason's voice was calm and in control, almost as if he were trying to sooth an unruly child.

Which made sense since she was acting like a bratty kid. But hey, bratty kid was still better than brazen slut.

Feeling none of the confidence she had in a courtroom or mediation, she kept her eyes shut. She couldn't look at him. She just couldn't.

Katie sat there, unmoving, facing the window with her back towards him and her hand reaching back so she could retrieve her purse. When she was met with only silence, she waved her hand back and forth insistently to illustrate how serious she was.

"Fine, Kit Kat. Go ahead, run away," Jason muttered as Katie felt her purse being pushed into her hand. He then added, pointedly, under his breath, "I guess some things never change."

Katie spun around without thinking, eyes narrow and blazing, and spat out indignantly, "Are you kidding me? This is not the same thing. I have to go to the bridal luncheon. I don't have time to deal with this right now. If you honestly can't see the difference between those two situations—"

"See? I knew you could be a big girl." Jason cut off her rant, and Katie noticed for the first time that he had a very satisfied grin on his face.

Frustration filled her as she realized she'd been had.

"Fine. You win, Jason. Does that make you happy? Mister Calm and Collected, teasing me with 'See? I knew you could be a big girl' and then sitting back to enjoy the show." Katie mimicked him, making her voice as deep as she could. "You enjoy this, me all flushed and flustered and you completely unaffected." Katie got more and more annoyed the longer her speech went on and the more and more she attempted (unsuccessfully) to pry open the passenger's side door handle.

She felt her hand being grabbed, and before she could pull it back, her palm landed on something hard and thick. Instinctively, she wrapped her fingers around it at the same time her eyes darted down to see the evidence that, *oh yes*, Jason was, in fact, *very* much affected by what had just occurred. His jeans were so tight that it looked as though he was going to burst out of them.

She pulled her hand away as fast as if she had touched a hot stove. She looked up into Jason's eyes, shocked, as he calmly stated, "Well I think that takes care of the notion that I'm 'unaffected.'"

"Oh well, um…okay," Katie stammered, trying to come up with an exit strategy that would still leave her with (even a tiny bit of) dignity. It wasn't easy, especially since her palm still tingled from her intimate touch of his arousal. Katie held her head high as she said, "Alright, well affected or not, let me just say that I am sorry for my behavior. I am not quite sure what came over me. I don't seem to be acting much like myself today."

She sat for a moment in silence. She expected Jason to respond, but he didn't. He just kept watching her.

Maybe he realized she had more to say. In a small voice, trying to make it sound like an aside, even though she realized as she said it that it was the true heart of the matter, she added, "I can't even, and don't want to, imagine what you must think of me."

She heard Jason take a deep breath in through his nose and out through his mouth. If Katie wasn't mistaken, Jason was…irritated. *That is weird,* she thought. The Jason she had known never let anything get under his skin. Maybe he wasn't acting like himself today either.

As she slowly turned in her seat to face him, her suspicions were confirmed. Yep. That was definitely the face of one *perturbed* Jason Sloan. He clearly had something on his mind that he was dying to say, so Katie decided to just be silent and let him get it out.

He took a deep breath and launched in. "You're really something, you know that? So let me 'just say' that you never—*never*—have to apologize for that kind of 'behavior' with me, past or present."

He looked out the front windshield of his truck and slammed his palm against the steering wheel. He then visibly re-centered himself, took another deep breath, and continued. "Look. I'm sure you feel a little off balance and out of your comfort zone. That must be scary. But you've got to know something—*that's* the Katie I've always loved. Not the 'cool, calm, and collected' follow all the rules, black and white version most of the world sees. That's for them. With me, you can be yourself.

"I know you, Katie, better than most. I know you inside and out. I've seen you at your best, at your worst, and everywhere in between, and I love it all. Every bit. So don't apologize to me for letting go and losing yourself. That's what's special between us—the fact that you can lose it, and you are just you. You are acting like there is something wrong with that and *that* pisses me off. It's not a bad thing. It's special, and I wish you could see that.

"We have a past that has included good times and bad. But I have been, I am, and I always will be, here for you. That's a given. That's a *fact*. To speak your language, you can consider it a legally binding agreement. No matter what you think—even though you know I love to give you a hard time—you never have to be embarrassed around me. Ever."

Katie was speechless. She tried to respond, but

when she opened her mouth to speak, words would not come out. Hell, *sounds* wouldn't even come out.

Jason continued his speech as he started up the truck. "Now, Kit Kat, as much as I would love to continue this conversation—and believe me, I have a lot more to say—the girls are waiting at Salvatore's for you and I don't want you to be late. So you need to get to the luncheon and have fun, and we'll talk more soon."

"Jas." Katie cleared her throat and made every attempt to choose her words carefully. "I just want to make it clear that this"—she waved her hands back and forth between them as she swallowed hard—"can never hap—"

"No." Jason interrupted, raising his voice to Katie for the first time she could remember. "You are not going to do that. You are not going to make ridiculous statements like that. We *are* going to deal with this, whatever this"—he waved his hand back and forth between them, mirroring her gesture—"is. You and I are going to deal with it this weekend like the mature adults both of us are and at least one of us is acting like, and that is happening whether you want it to or not. And just so we're clear, that's not a request—it's a statement."

Jason reached across her lap and opened the passenger door. "You're close enough to walk. Now go have a nice lunch, and I'll talk to you later."

Katie was overwhelmed. She had never expected

things to play out like this. And Katie Lawson *always* thought of *every* possible outcome before entering into any given situation.

She had prepared herself for several outcomes in facing Jason this weekend:

Scenario 1 – Jason would ignore her and she would suffer through several awkward situations they would naturally be in as part of the wedding party.

Scenario 2 – Jason would still be upset about *that night* and have a few choice words to impart. She would apologize, he would accept (because that's the kind of guy he is), and they would get through the weekend and part on newly-reconciled terms.

Scenario 3 – Jason would appear to have forgotten all about what happened ten years ago. He would say that it was great to see her, and she would say the same. The customary small talk would ensue, and Jason (being Jason) would slip in some sly comment that made an oblique reference to the night oh-so-long ago. By doing so, he would let Katie know that, while he *did* remember, she was, for all intents and purposes, off the hook. She would return to San Francisco unscathed and with a huge weight lifted off her shoulders.

She could have lived with any of those three scenarios. Some would have been more pleasant than others, but they all had one thing in common—they fit within the narrow box she had relegated Jason to in her mind.

This…did not.

Never in Katie's wildest dreams did she prepare herself for:

> Scenario 4 – Katie and Jason see each other again and there are more sparks than the Fourth of July. He almost immediately brings up the fact that they need to talk, and he confesses within hours of her arrival that he did not one, but *two* incredibly "knight in shining armor-esque" feats during their childhood. He then proceeds to not only kiss her silly, but also to give her one of the most incredible orgasms of her life. Fully dressed. In broad daylight. In a parking lot.

Yeah, not the sort of thing that fits in a carefully crafted box. This was definitely some outside-of-the-box material.

Dear Lord, what could possibly happen next?

No. She stopped herself. She definitely could not let her mind go there. She needed to get away from Jason and process all of the events that had occurred in the past four hours. Then she needed to prepare herself, mentally and emotionally, for any future out-of-the-box onslaughts that may come flying at her over the course of the rest of the weekend.

As she turned to say goodbye to Jason and exit his truck as gracefully as possible, she was stopped dead in her tracks by the look of pure and utter amusement in his eyes. That was the *exact* smug look that got her goat. For some reason, that little I-know-something-you-don't-know-and-it's-really-damn-funny expression had always irritated her down to her bones. It could definitely take her from zero to furious in about 2.5 milliseconds.

"What?" she snapped before she immediately wished she could just once have a normal civilized response to him.

"I could practically hear the wheels turning in your head as you sat there trying to compartmentalize everything that's happened between us this morning," Jason said, his tone light and amused.

"Oh, please. What are you, a mind reader now? You don't know me *that* well, Jas. I was actually just thinking about how underdressed I am going to be at the luncheon. There was not a single thought in my mind that had anything to do with us," Katie lied, her tone steady and controlled even though her brain was screaming, *You know he's right.*

"Sure there wasn't. Just keep telling yourself that and maybe one of us will believe you."

Katie opened her mouth to respond, but Jason immediately went on.

"But speaking of being underdressed, I got so, well, let's say distracted, that I almost forgot to tell you.

While you were in CVS, I made a call to my friend. Her name is Amber, and she's the owner of Bella. She is holding a dress for you. I told her you were a size four. You can go in through that back door." Jason pointed to a door painted a deep red.

Katie's eyebrows rose in amazement. It seemed like every time she got frustrated or irritated with him, he went and revealed some over-the-top, knight-in-shining-armor gesture he had put together and took all the wind out of her annoyance sails.

"After you change, just head out through the front entrance, and Salvatore's is right across the parking lot." He grinned before adding, "Now get going. We both know how anal you are about being on time."

"Okay," Katie said as she stepped out of the truck feeling dazed and more than a little off balance. After a few steps, she realized she needed to at least *try* to handle this with a scrap of grace. She took a deep breath before turning to say, "And...thanks for the ride and thinking of the dress and...everything."

"By 'everything' I am assuming you mean the mind-blowing orgasm," she heard Jason say just as he pulled the door shut and roared off, giving her no chance to have the last word.

"Oh. My. God." Disbelief in her current circumstances ran through her as she stood in the empty parking lot.

She closed her eyes as she wondered how she would ever survive until Sunday.

✦ ✦ ✦

Pulling out of the back parking lot behind Bella, Jason was again shocked at what had just transpired. Never in his wildest dreams had he imagined *that* would happen. Well, all right, maybe in his *wildest* dreams. But certainly not in any dream he'd ever thought would come (no pun intended) to fruition. He never expected what had happened to actually come (that pun somewhat intended) to pass.

It had taken every ounce of self-control Jason had within him not to pull Katie down beneath him in the cab of the truck, push her jeans down, and finish what he'd started.

He'd never meant for things to go that far. But it was becoming blatantly obvious that when he was around Katie, he could *not* control himself. Normally, he lived by the creed that if you couldn't control a situation, then you shouldn't to try to. 'God grant me the serenity' and all that. If a situation was beyond your control, you should just go along for the ride.

He wasn't sure if that was the best course of action when it came Katie, but he *was* sure that if he didn't start showing some small amount of self-control around her he might just push her away again. This time, it might be for good.

He tried to get his body under control as he headed towards the construction site. This was the largest job that Sloan Construction had undertaken and he needed to stay on top of it this weekend, wedding or no wedding. Bob, Jason's dad, was semi-retired, and Jason felt more than certain that, if everything went well with this build, his dad would finally hand over the reins of Sloan Construction to him.

The fall after high school graduation, Jason had headed to college. With Nick's death and Katie's disappearing act, Jason was more than ready to hightail it out of Illinois and get to NYU to study journalism. He had loved NYU. He had loved the fast pace of the city. He'd loved feeling like he was in the middle of something *bigger* every minute of the day. He'd felt like he was really learning a lot about life, and about himself.

Jason came home to Harper's Crossing that Christmas break, secretly hoping that Katie would have returned to visit her mom. But sadly, that was not the case. After speaking to Pam, Katie's mom, and finding out that Katie had changed her plans and opted to stay in California for the holiday, Jason had made a spur-of-the-moment decision to book a flight out to the Sunshine State to face Katie and discuss what had gone on between them the previous August. He needed to see her, to make sure she was okay.

Pam had told him that she and Wendy had gone out and visited Katie during Thanksgiving break and that Katie seemed to be dealing with her grief the same way that Katie dealt with everything—by burying herself in her studies. She did soften that somewhat, however, by saying that Katie genuinely seemed to love her school and that she had decided to apply to law school after she graduated.

All of this information should have eased the knot Jason had not realized, until then, had been in his stomach since that fateful night in August. But it didn't. So many things were happening in Katie's life that Jason didn't have firsthand knowledge of. He didn't like that feeling. He was used to getting all of his information straight from the source—from Katie. He didn't like having to hear about her life from a third party, even if the third party was her mom. His mind was made up. He had to speak to Katie in person and look her in the eyes to make sure she was okay.

He booked a flight from O'Hare to LAX that left Christmas Eve. He felt comforted just knowing he held the ticket. It would be only two more days and he would see his Kit Kat. He would beg for her forgiveness and—knowing Katie—she would lecture him and explain why their behavior was wrong, but she would forgive him.

He hoped.

Unfortunately, the day before Jason was to fly to California, his father had a heart attack. Jason had to step in and handle the business. His two older brothers, Seth and Riley, were overseas in the military. His two younger brothers, Alex and Bobby, were only sixteen and fourteen. Kids.

There was no one else but Jason. He had no choice.

It seemed like that had been his life's mantra from that point forward. *There's no one else but me. I've got no choice.* Yep. He might as well have had it tattooed across his forehead.

His dad's heart attack, as it turned out, was major, and Jason had to step even further into the business that spring, taking over all daily operations. What had originally been a plan to take a few weeks off turned into a semester, and that turned into a year. One year turned into two, and so it went.

At age twenty-four, after six years of working full time for his dad, Bob named Jason the new vice president and had basically spent the next four years grooming his son to take over when he retired.

Jason had made peace with it—he really had. He even looked forward to being the one in charge. He had so many plans for Sloan Construction, starting with a logo and a website. Bob was really old fashioned and believed that there was no need for a construction company to have any sort of "new" website or "fancy" logo.

Jason did not agree. He wanted an interactive website with 3D blueprints that were accessible to clients so that changes could be made and approved no matter where the client was. He wanted virtual tours of some of the past jobs. He wanted testimonials, for crying out loud. At the very least.

He thought that they should have Facebook and Twitter accounts. It was time for Sloan Construction to join the social media revolution. And they most certainly needed a logo. Something that could be put on signs and then hung on fences of the job sites they were working on. A little brand recognition could go a long way.

Jason also knew that his dad needed to retire. He looked as though he had aged thirty years in the last ten since his heart attack. He had worked so hard all of his life. God knows, owning his own business and raising five boys, alone, could not have been easy on the old man.

Not that Bob had ever complained. That would have been completely contrary to his nature. He just worked hard and made sure that there was food on the table, clothes on their backs, and punishments handed out if any of the boys started acting up or stepped out of line.

Jason knew that having your wife walk out on you when you had five boys ranging in ages from two to ten had to shake you up a bit, but Bob never let it show. Not that Jason could remember anyway.

Jason didn't have many memories left of his mother, Cheryl, now. Most of his memories consisted of a constant low-lying sense of dread. The knowledge that he had to be quiet all the time in the house because she was always resting. He remembered seeing her crying many times when he would go into her room to ask if he could have a snack or go out and play. She would never answer him. She would just wave a hand to dismiss him.

When he thought of her, in fact, that was the image that most often came to mind—her huddled under her covers and staring blankly at the wall, sniffling, tears flowing unchecked from her eyes for no apparent reason.

But then there was this whole other side to her that came out sometimes. She would come into his room in the middle of the night, wake him up, and they would go out and catch fireflies together. Or he would come home from school and find that she had baked a cake, and they would sit there and eat the whole entire thing together, just the two of them.

One time, she had been taking him to school when she suddenly turned to him, eyes lit up with a fiery glow, and said, "Let's blow this Popsicle stand. You wanna?"

Of course, being a very young child, he had just nodded. With no set plan in mind, she just started driving out of town. They didn't come home for three days. His father was worried sick when they walked in the door and had shaken five-year-old Jason by the shoulders, shouting, "Don't you ever do that again! Do you hear me? Do not *ever* leave and not tell me where you're going!"

Jason had noticed even at that young age that, although his dad was definitely furious with his mom, he didn't even bother telling her never to do it again.

It had obviously never even occurred to Jason, on

their impromptu vacation, that no one had known where they were or that he should have called his father. It was the first inkling he had that, despite his young age, *he* needed to be the responsible one in charge.

He didn't have any memories, at all, of his mother doing normal 'Mom' things like cooking dinner, tucking them into bed, helping with homework, or taking them to the park. Those were too mundane and stifling for her during her manic phases and far too much for her to handle during the depressed times. Which unfortunately seemed to be triggered by special events like birthdays or holidays. There was not one single picture of Cheryl with her husband and sons during those occasions. Not at Halloween. Not at Thanksgiving. Not at Christmas, even during the years she still lived with them.

Now that Jason was an adult, he knew and understood that his mom suffered from bipolar disorder. All of those crazy, spontaneous things she had done with him hadn't been driven by a sudden, passionate need to get in some mother-son bonding time with her middle child after all. They had been the product of her illness. Intellectually, he got that. Emotionally…he couldn't help it. He still treasured them. In her manic, fevered way, they *had* bonded. She could have gone off on her adventures alone. She hadn't. She'd brought him along, creating a weird and wonderful world that only Jason and Mom understood. Even in the throes of her illness, she had reached out to him, at times. That had to mean something. Right?

After his mom had left their family she moved in with her parents. About a year after that, she was placed in a psychiatric treatment facility as a result of attempting to take her own life. At the time, Jason was just told that his mom was in the hospital because she was "sick." Jason hadn't understood entirely. He just hoped that she would get better. Maybe if she wasn't sick anymore, she'd want to come home.

Well, rather than improving, she got "sick" four more times over the next three years. It got to the point where the whole thing seemed so abstract to Jason's young mind that he couldn't even bring himself to feel all that upset anymore when he was told about her hospitalizations.

Finally, the fifth time she got "sick" she did not recover. Jason was ten by then, and by that point he knew what getting "sick" was a euphemism for. They were talking about the crying jags, the outbursts, even the 'crazy fun' times—all the things that made her not like other moms.

Jason didn't cry at her funeral. His older brothers, Seth and Riley, did. Bobby and Alex did not. They were too young. They'd never really known Cheryl. The boys never spoke about it with each other and their dad never talked to them about it. In fact, the only person Jason had ever spoken to about his mother was Katie.

18 Years Ago

There were a lot of people at his house after his mom's funeral. All the adults were speaking in hushed voices, saying how young Cheryl was, how beautiful, what a shame this had to happen.

Jason sat on his living room couch listening to all the voices surrounding him, and with every passing moment, it felt more and more like the walls were closing in on him. The whole room was spinning. Everything kept going all blurry.

Then, all at once, he was saved. He felt a soft hand tugging on his elbow, pulling him up and off the couch. His body felt heavy as he was dragged through the house to the front door. The cold air hit him, like a slap in the face, as he stepped out onto the wooden porch.

He tried to breathe in the fresh air. He took a deep breath and then another deep breath and then another. But soon his breaths started coming too fast and hard. He fell to his knees and tried even harder to slowly breathe in and out.

The wind was completely knocked out of him. He couldn't get control of his breathing. He was starting to feel lightheaded, and a sensation swept over him like he was falling.

He began to panic and squeezed his eyes shut, willing the rest of the world to just disappear. Or maybe he was willing himself to disappear.

He was shaking his head back and forth, trying to make everything go away, when he felt his face being cradled by two of the softest hands he could ever remember feeling.

His whole body stilled immediately at the sensation of her hands on his face. He opened his eyes to see Katie kneeling on the grass in front of him, looking into his eyes. She was talking, but he couldn't hear her. All he could hear was a loud buzzing. He tried to concentrate. He tried to focus.

Slowly the buzzing faded out, leaving room for her voice to come through.

"That's good, Jas. Just look at me. Don't think about anything. Just focus on me. That's good now. Just relax."

He didn't even try to process what she was saying. He just held on to the soothing pattern of her voice.

He felt as if he were coming out of a deep sleep. The world around him started to gain clarity, bit by tiny bit.

Just when he was starting to get his bearings and feel like himself again, Katie removed her hands from his face and plopped down on the wooden porch beside him.

Jason wasn't sure what had just happened. He didn't know if he needed a doctor or…? He felt confused and embarrassed and he didn't want to turn his head and look at his great savior. He had no idea what she must be thinking about him. He was still battling with this quandary when he felt her slip her slim, soft hand into his and lay her head softly on his shoulder.

Jason felt the silkiness of her hair as it brushed down the side of his arm. He smelled the strawberry scent of her shampoo as she nestled against him. They sat like that for what felt like hours, neither of them saying anything.

He forgot about the funeral, the people's whispered voices in his home, about his dad seeming sadder than he had ever seen a man look, his older brothers acting angry with him, and his little brothers looking confused and lost. Basically, he forgot about the rest of the world.

It was just him and Katie in the little bubble of the front porch, and an incredible sense of calm came over him. He wasn't sad or scared or confused or upset. He just WAS.

When people started emerging from the house and making their way down the porch steps, the exclusionary bubble that had formed around the two of them burst. As his Aunt Lois came to say goodbye to him, he stood and felt the small hand that had been his anchor, fall from his grasp. He said goodbye to several other relatives, friends of the family, and even some people he didn't recognize. All the while, Katie stood beside him, quietly offering support.

After a few minutes, she grabbed his hand, once again, and dragged him over to the side of his garage. Picking up his bike, which was leaning against the wooden door, she shoved it towards him and then gracefully swung one leg over her own bike and began riding down the driveway.

He did what any ten-year-old boy would do and just followed her.

She rode through town, and he was right behind her the whole way. She rode over Craw Bridge, through old man Pickler's field, and up and over Gibler Hill until she reached the river.

He was breathing heavily as he skidded to a halt next to her. When he looked over at her, he saw that her face was flushed and pink. She dismounted from her bike, setting it to the side and walking out to the edge of the river. She slipped her sandals off and sat on a flat rock while her feet dangled in the water.

Jason hopped off his own bike, took off his shoes, and sat down on the rock beside Katie. Rolling up his dress slacks, he put his feet in the water beside hers. He didn't know what to say, so he didn't say anything. They sat in that silence for a few moments until Katie broke it, her voice matter of fact.

"My mom used to hyperventilate a lot," she said and shrugged. "It started right after we moved here actually. It would happen one or two times a week. Usually Aunt Wendy was there and she would talk her through it, but I had to do it a couple of times when Aunt Wendy wasn't around. If it gets really bad then you have to breathe into a paper bag and that usually does the trick."

Jason was amazed. He had just experienced one of the strangest, most embarrassing episodes in his short life—and the girl who had not only been witness to it, but also saved him from it, seemed to think it was as common as a headache.

Okay, well…he guessed that if she wasn't going to make a big deal about it, he shouldn't either. Maybe she even knew why it had happened to him. It couldn't hurt to ask. Attempting to sound as nonchalant as possible, he said, "So why'd your mom have 'em?"

"They were stress-induced," she said, obviously repeating a term she had heard adults use many times to describe her mother's episodes and feeling very adult herself now

that she was the one doing the explaining. She patted his hand comfortingly. "Losing your mom is a big deal, Jas. Even if she hasn't been around for a while. Maybe even more because of that. I know I would be upset if my dad died, and I haven't seen him in years."

"Yeah, I guess you're right," Jason sighed. "I mean, yeah. It's not like she was around or anything, but it's just weird to think that she is really gone forever. Like…I will never see her again. Like…all the things I might ever want to say to her…I can't now. Even though I couldn't before, because she wasn't here, it was still like…maybe one day she would be. You know?" Katie nodded sagely.

They sat in silence for a few more moments, and then Katie took his hand again and leaned her head against his shoulder. They sat there together, holding hands while they watched the river rush by and felt its power sweep past their feet, and Jason thought to himself, I'm probably the worst person in the history of the world for thinking this, but…this might be the best day of my whole entire life.

He thought that his mom might have understood his feeling that way. He hoped so.

Present Day

Katie's actions and words, on that day, still gave him comfort now. He couldn't believe he had let so much time pass and had not gone to see her. So many years he had wasted, not seeing her, not talking to her, not touching her.

Well, damn it, there's no use crying over spilled milk. Today was a new day and he was not going to let her slip through his fingers again.

Chapter Ten

Knowing she didn't have time for the nervous breakdown she deserved, Katie shook off what had just happened in the truck, hurried across the empty parking lot, and opened the back door Jason had instructed her to, stepping into what appeared to be a very upscale boutique. Looking around, she saw that she appeared to be in the employee break room, but it was much nicer than any employee lounge she had ever seen. There was a plush, red Italian leather couch and a flat screen TV. A massage table sat in the left corner of the room, and there was a state-of-the-art stainless steel refrigerator to her right.

Katie stood for a moment, taking in her surroundings and wondering what to do next, when she heard the sound of beads brushing against each other. Looking up, Katie felt her eyes widen as the most beautiful, exotic woman Katie had ever seen in her life walked through the black bead-curtained doorway, creating the illusion that she was magically taking form from the onyx baubles right before Katie's eyes.

The woman stood about five feet six inches tall, and

had long, thick, shiny black hair and gorgeous hazel cat-shaped eyes. Her flawless olive skin gave her the air of Middle Eastern royalty. Katie thought that she looked like nothing so much as an Arabian princess brought to life.

The woman was wearing a pair of fitted white linen slacks and a tailored black halter top with intricate beading along the neckline. The ensemble was finished with elegant black slingback flats. She looked like she'd just walked off the pages of Vogue.

Katie tried to be subtle as she glanced down at her own (distinctly underwhelming) ensemble and attempted not to feel like a peasant in the presence of nobility.

"Katie," the woman said warmly, and her smile revealed a row of the straightest, whitest teeth Katie had ever seen outside of a movie screen.

"Hi, um, yes, I'm Katie," she mumbled uncomfortably, slouching her shoulders unconsciously because she suddenly felt so frumpy and dowdy. "You must be Amber."

"Yes, I am. Wow," Amber enthused, looking Katie up and down. "It is so nice to finally meet you."

Oh, God, please don't look me up and down, Katie pleaded inside her head, feeling supremely uncomfortable under the stunning woman's gaze. Katie couldn't be sure if Amber was *really* happy to meet her or if this was like in middle school when the popular girls would tell you that you had the 'cutest skirt' and then as soon as you walked away, they would laugh behind your back and joke that you must have bought it at UglyMart.

Either way, she felt on display and it wasn't a pleasant feeling. Her breathing started coming in short pants. Wait, no—please no panic attack.

Katie pulled it together enough to manage to say (and not mumble), "Um, it's nice to meet you, too."

There was a semi-long, semi-awkward pause. Katie waited. Hey, she had said the last thing, right? It was Amber's turn. That's how conversations worked.

When it became apparent that wasn't going to happen, Katie cautiously continued. "Jason said you were holding a dress for me?"

"Oh, yes. Of course." Amber shook her head back and forth, her dark locks swaying as though she were in a shampoo commercial. "Sorry, I don't know where my manners are. I think I might be in a little bit of shock. It's just, I have been hearing about you for years now. Even seen a few pictures, but here you are in the flesh. It's surreal."

This didn't make Katie feel less like a bug under the microscope. Nope. Not at all.

Amber stared wonderingly for a few more seconds, but then she stepped back through the doorway, pushing the beads to the side and gesturing for Katie to follow her. She said, "I certainly am holding a dress for you, and I know you are in a time crunch, so let's get you in it."

Still in shock that this complete stranger seemed to

know who she was when Katie didn't know her from Adam, she mindlessly followed Amber down a short hall painted a muted shade of red. As they reached the dark wood door to the dressing room, Amber abruptly turned to her. As she opened the fitting room door, she said, "You should find everything you need in there, but if you need a different size or you'd like to try different accessories, just let me know. I'll be in the front closing up."

With that, Amber practically pushed her into the room and closed the door. Katie leaned against the door and took a deep breath. She really needed a moment to collect her thoughts and compose herself. Hmm, that seemed to be her theme of the day.

In this instance, ironically, the cause of her needing a few minutes was the same reason she did not *have* that luxury at the moment—Jason.

Always the pragmatist, she shook off those thoughts and set about the task at hand. She put her purse down and picked up the hanger from the ornately crafted hook on the back of the door. There was a lovely and feminine blue silk sundress with a sweetheart neckline and crisscrossing straps down the back, a white cashmere button-up sweater, and adorable white wedges with crisscrossing straps that echoed the pattern in the dress.

Quickly pushing down her jeans and removing her tank top, she slipped the dress over her head, luxuriating in the way the soft silk whispered over her skin. She got a sudden mental image of Jason's hands lightly trailing over her skin in all the same places the fabric was touching her and had to put a hand against the wall to keep from tipping over as her knees buckled.

No time for that now, Lawson.

She stood up straight, shook off the short moment of erotic dizziness, and turned to look at herself in the three-way mirror. She was pleasantly surprised by what she saw.

The dress fit her perfectly. It hung well, and the draping hit her curves in all the right places. She found herself starting to wish that Jason could see her in it and had to nip that in the bud. Best to move on quickly to the accessories.

She slipped her feet into the sandals and grabbed the sweater that was hanging on the back of the door. Katie quickly folded her clothes into a neat pile and placed her Converse tennis shoes on top. She grabbed her purse and headed out of the dressing room to the front of the store where she saw Amber behind an onyx counter top.

"Thank you so much," Katie said sincerely. "This is such a pretty dress and the shoes fit perfectly. Did you just guess my shoe size?"

Amber looked up. "Whoa, that was record time. You're like Wonder Woman. Well, damn, the dress looks amazing on you. And no, I didn't guess. Jason told me you wore a size five-and-a-half shoe."

"That's so weird," Katie mused. "How would Jason

know what size shoe I wear?" Katie suddenly noticed that Amber was locking up the register and gathering up her purse, and she put a hand out to stop her. "Oh, wait. Before you lock up, how much do I owe you? I didn't see any tags."

As Katie spoke, she was fumbling through her purse to try to retrieve her wallet at the same time as she was attempting to balance her folded jeans, tank, and sneakers. Oh, and not get her dress wrinkled, of course. She felt like a klutz. She was sure if Amber were trying this whole act, she would just wave her hand and her wallet would magically appear in her palm. But grace and elegance had never been Katie's strong suit.

"Oh, I took them off. And don't worry. The payment has already been taken care of." Amber smiled as she came around the counter. She was carrying her purse as well as a beautiful silver and white tote bag. She reached over, deftly grasped the jeans, tank, and shoes from Katie's hand, and placed them in the bag before handing the bag back to Katie.

Katie was confused and wanted to seek clarification, but at the same time her brain took a split second to stop and let the little voice in the back of her head point out to her, 'See? Told you she'd look graceful if she tried to handle those...'

She shook her head to clear it of that thought and then asked, "Taken care of? Wait, what do you mean? Did Jas...? No. I can't let him do that. How much do I owe you?"

Katie put on her 'insistent lawyer' voice and held out her wallet. She did not often deal with Jason or his Harper's Crossing minions, though, so she was out of practice when it came to talking to people to whom her 'insistent lawyer' voice meant exactly nothing.

"It's out of my hands at this point," Amber said in a cheerful tone, putting up her hands in surrender. "You'll have to take that up with Jason."

"Great. I need that about as much as I need a huge, sweltering cold sore," Katie mumbled, the good mood that had begun when she looked at herself in the dressing room mirror beginning to crumble. Then she stopped herself, realizing that Jason wasn't trying to one-up her or win—he was being…nice. She just wasn't used to it. It was a lot to process.

Making a concerted effort to brighten and look at the good side of a situation in which she felt increasingly out of control, Katie said, "Oh well, I guess this is as close as I will get to my own real life *Pretty Woman* moment."

She paused a moment, and then the meaning implicit in the reference hit her. Without thinking, she blurted out, "Not that I'm a prostitute."

Amber burst out laughing so hard that it caused her to bend over at the waist. Katie realized what she'd said might be considered to some a little amusing, but this reaction seemed a tad out of proportion.

Katie shrunk inside. Umm…clearly she had made some hilarious faux pas. Yeah. That grace and elegance thing had not gotten any better in the last five minutes, it seemed.

Amber looked up at Katie, wiping her eyes, and—clearly taking in her stricken look—said through her laughter, "Sorry. Oh, sorry, hon. I'm not laughing at you. It's just...that's exactly what Jas said that you would say. He told me—and I quote—'She will be upset at first but then it will probably remind her of *Pretty Woman*, minus the whole hooker thing.' It's like he's in your head."

"No, it's not." Katie automatically retorted and then realized that the extreme quickness with which she shot that answer back may have actually disproved the point she was trying to make. Backpedaling, she explained, "I mean...it's just, we grew up together, but you know...we haven't seen each other in years."

Katie was confused. She couldn't help the twinge of—if she didn't know any better—jealousy that swept over her when she heard Amber refer to Jason as Jas. Which was ridiculous. Everyone called him Jas or J. It didn't mean anything. But the familiarity in her tone just rubbed Katie the wrong way.

And even if it did 'mean something,' why should she care? Seriously. She had *no business* feeling anything about any relationship Jason had had in his life.

Realizing how her outburst must have sounded, she tried her best to recover. "I just mean, people change a lot in ten years. I knew Jason a lifetime ago."

"Okay, you just keep telling yourself that," Amber

said and flashed her a very knowing smile as they walked together towards the arched double doors at the front of the store. Why was that the second time she had heard that today? First Jason had said it, and now Amber. *Damn,* she thought. *What is with these people?*

As Amber held open the door for her to walk through, Katie said, "Well, thank you, again, for all of your help. I love the dress. You're a lifesaver, honestly. It was really nice meeting you."

"Thanks, and it was nice meeting you, too," Amber said as she turned to lock the door, "but if you wait just one second while I lock up, I'll head over with you."

Katie stopped and waited. "Oh, are you going to the luncheon?"

"Yeah, of course. Oh, I mean…I thought you knew. I am one of Sophie's bridesmaids."

Katie laughed. "You can add that to the long list of things I've spent my morning trying to play catch-up on. No, I didn't know. But please don't take it personally. I just got into town this morning and haven't really been brought up to speed yet. Were you at the fitting? I don't remember seeing you there. But then again, I was in the back most of the time getting my dress pinned."

"No, I couldn't make it. My assistant store manager called in sick this morning. It sounded like it might be more than a twenty-four-hour bug, and with me up at Whisper Lake for the wedding the next few days, I figured there was a good possibility the shop would be shut down for the rest of the weekend after this morning. I decided I'd better keep it open today, at least for part of the day. And it's a good thing I did. Otherwise you might have been going to this luncheon in jeans and a tank top." Amber smiled as they started off across the parking lot together.

"Yeah, that would *not* have been good," Katie laughed. She liked Amber and—other than the momentary insane twinge of jealousy—she was really enjoying her company.

It dawned on Katie that, in California, she really didn't have any friends. She talked to Sophie on the phone regularly but Sophie lived here in Harper's Crossing. In San Francisco, Katie had colleagues, but they were all so competitive that it didn't really count. Plus, they really didn't talk about anything that was not related to the firm, the law, and sometimes, briefly, certain reality shows they were interested in at the moment. *Hey, everyone needs some sort of mindless escape. If you could find it in forty minutes of Survivor, then God bless.* That was Katie's philosophy. But they never talked about anything personal.

Katie realized, with a jolt, that there were a couple of her associates—people that before this moment she would have described as being close—she did not even know the most basic of details about, such as where they had grown up or their marital status.

Damn.

She realized she had really missed having friends.

Not just 'friends,' but actual friends. "So how do you know Sophie?" Katie asked. She figured that, in a break from the pattern she had established with the people at work, she would start this relationship by finding out the details of Amber's life.

"Well, let's see…" Amber took a deep breath before she began, the first indication Katie had that this might be an actual Story-with-a-capital-S. "I moved to town about eight years ago. Right when Sophie started high school, actually, and we had, um, a…mutual friend, I guess you could say."

Amber looked down at the ground, avoiding eye contact with Katie, and Katie felt the return of the twinge, even though she had nothing to base it on but pure instinct. Amber shook her head a little and continued. "She was going through a pretty rough time. She needed a good listener and that just happens to be one of my specialties. Before I opened Bella, I was going to school to be a psychologist. Even then, though, fashion was always my passion. When I see people walk out of my store feeling like a million bucks in my designs, it feels like my own personal form of therapy.

"I hired Sophie part-time when I first opened the boutique. We always got along really well, but we got even closer when I lost my brother a few years ago." Amber finished the story, sadness coloring her voice when she reached the last part.

"Oh, I am so sorry." Katie touched her arm sympathetically. She had forgotten how easily people shared their life stories in small towns. She guessed she had been living in the 'big city' so long that she was really out of touch with small-town life.

"Thanks," Amber said with a melancholy smile. "He was a really great guy. He was in Afghanistan, and there was a car bombing. My mom still has a really rough time dealing with it, but I try to get through it by choosing to focus on the good stuff. He was only eleven months younger than me, you know. Sometimes we seemed more like twins than just siblings."

Amber was quiet for a couple of steps, and Katie sensed that it was best to just let her process her thoughts in that moment without saying anything. After a few beats, Amber continued. "Sophie really helped me get through that time. She taught me some really great coping methods she had learned in grief counseling. I love her so much. She's such a sweet girl. I'm so happy she and Bobby finally got together, aren't you?"

Amber turned to Katie as she asked the last question just as they walked into Salvatore's.

"Yep." Katie replied, maybe a little too enthusiastically she realized as she heard herself. It had just occurred to her as she processed Amber's question that she didn't even know what the 'finally' entailed. In fact, she had absolutely no idea what Sophie and Bobby's path to romance had been.

She knew that they had known each other since

grade school and that Bobby was a couple years older than Sophie. Sophie had told her when they had gotten together about six months ago and then gotten engaged three months ago. But a lot of times their conversations were short due to Katie's busy schedule.

Oh, she also knew now that this wasn't—as had immediately jumped to her mind in the CVS parking lot and Jason had been so quick to point out—a shotgun wedding.

She knew all of that. What she didn't know was their love story.

Dang.

She felt a little out of place and really sad that she had missed being around for such big chunks of Sophie's life. She truly considered her to be like a sister.

Reminding herself that she hadn't planned to stay away this long, didn't really make her feel any better.

Katie took a deep breath as they walked into Salvatore's. She let the wave of sadness she was feeling go ahead and wash over her unchecked because she knew it would be worse if she tried to push it down. Better to just feel it, acknowledge it, and move on.

She and Amber strode through the fancy restaurant and entered the banquet room in the back of Salvatore's. She put on a smile and resolved to let that smile reach down inside her and influence her heart, spreading its joy so that it became a reflection of her true feelings and not just the instrument she used to hide them.

She had missed out on so much of so many peoples' lives—people who she loved so much—because the past was just too overwhelming. But that was over. She was living in the moment now. For every single minute of the coming weekend she was going to enjoy being right here, right now. She was going to soak it in. She was going to bask. She wasn't going to think about the past or the future. She was all about the present.

Sure, she thought to herself. That would probably last until the next time Jason walked in the room. Then who knew where her mind, emotions, or hormones would stray. But who cares? She was making an effort now.

She looked around her. She was in a room filled with so many people she had known since she was a child. They loved her. She loved them.

But much like the people she worked with, she had been faced, today, with the very stark realization that she barely knew them now. She felt very much an outsider, and she was suddenly consumed with wishing she would have taken a different path. Starting with the night of Nick's funeral.

Then she remembered Jason—and his truck—and that old 'fight or flight' feeling came rushing back.

Holy confusion, Batman.

This weekend was turning out to be more of an emotional roller coaster than Katie ever could have prepared for.

She greeted the various ladies at the luncheon as she

made her way down the long table to find a seat, and a strange wave of rightness came over her. She began feeling less like someone on the outside looking in and more like an integral part. She belonged here. She may not have been here for awhile, but this was where she belonged.

She knew about half of the ladies in attendance. She was having fun greeting each new (old) face in turn. Even though the years had added maturity to their countenances (and in some cases, a few wrinkles or a couple of pounds), their essences remained the same. These were Katie's friends.

And she had thought that she didn't have any.

She took the first available seat she could find and was turning to greet the person seated to her left when she felt a hand on her shoulder.

She lifted her head and saw her mom standing there, beaming down at her. Her mom had always had a way of smiling that made Katie feel that, no matter what the world brought her way, she would be okay.

"Hey, sweetie pie," Pam said warmly, her voice infused with equal parts affection and excitement as Katie stood and hugged her tightly.

Katie had seen her mom about twice a year since she'd been gone. She and Aunt Wendy would come out to California to visit her. They had even stayed for an entire week when Katie graduated from college.

She knew that she missed her mom and always enjoyed the visits she was able to make. But in California, she was always so busy and there were just so many distractions. Even at the end of the visits she admittedly would feel sad when her mom and Aunt Wendy boarded the plane back to Illinois, but she never really felt *empty*. There was always work that she was eager to get back to, always another deadline fast approaching.

Or maybe she was so closed down emotionally that she had been numb for the last ten years and not really felt *anything*.

No matter what the reason, she definitely felt something now as she stood hugging her mom. She held her desperately, not wanting to let go, and she felt tears running down her cheeks.

"Is something wrong? Are you okay, sweetie?" Her mom's whispered voice was laced heavily with concern.

Katie slowly pulled away from her mother's embrace and took a deep breath. She was reluctant to leave the hug. She felt like she could have stayed there all day, but she knew that she needed to alleviate the concern she had heard in her mother's voice. She plastered her smile back on and said in as light a tone as she could manage, "I'm fine, Mom. I just really missed you."

Pam's eyebrows scrunched together suspiciously. When she spoke, her tone revealed that, although she was willing to let it go for the moment, she was by no means convinced. Stroking Katie's hair, she said, "All right, sweetie. If you're sure."

"I am, I promise," Katie said sincerely, looking into

her mother's eyes and grasping her hand as she spoke to emphasize her words. "It's just been a long day. And I've only been here a couple of hours."

A strained laugh escaped from Katie as she tried to end on a joke, which, she realized as the words were leaving her mouth, wasn't really a joke at all.

"I'm so sorry I couldn't pick you up at the airport or at least be there when you got home. I tried to see if Gertie could cover for me today, but she's already working my weekend shifts so I can head up to the wedding. As I'm sure you remember, she's not the most accommodating coworker," Pam said as she slid into the empty seat next to Katie, her voice lightening as she started to chat (gossip) about work.

Pam was one of four 911 emergency operators who handled all of Linden County, which included the cities of Harper's Crossing, Preston, and Mallardville. Gertie was the most senior operator at the station, and needless to say, she had not been particularly pleased when Pam had been promoted ahead of her.

But seriously, Katie thought, getting into the spirit of the gossip. She was, like, seventy-five. Did she really think she would be put in a position of authority when she should have been retired for at least fifteen years? Not to mention, she was so crotchety with callers that Katie was sure a recording of one of her calls was bound to go viral at any time. Nevertheless, since there were only four operators, the other three did still have to depend on her. Whether they liked it or not.

"Well, I am so happy that you got the weekend off, Mom," Katie said, relief flooding her voice.

Katie wasn't looking forward to the barrage of emotions that she would certainly feel this weekend, especially up at Whisper Lake, but knowing that her solid and supportive mom would be by her side did somehow make it more bearable.

As she sat next to her mother, the two of them surrounded by familiar faces and voices, everyone chatting and laughing and discussing the upcoming nuptials, Katie decided that it was not going to be another ten years before she returned to Harper's Crossing. That is to say…before she came home.

Chapter Eleven

Jason's boots sounded loud even to his own ears as he stomped up the three metal steps to his onsite office trailer, filled with renewed determination. As he was opening the door, ready to lose himself in a few hours of work before heading over to the bachelor party at McMillan's Pub, he heard the gravel kicking up in the small lot. As he looked up, he saw his brother, Alex, parking his white SUV beside Jason's truck.

Alex stepped out. "What's up bro? Why are you here? You slackin' on best man duties or what?"

"Aww, are your panties still in a bunch because Bobby asked me to be his best man instead of you?"

"Nah. I know the real reason that Bobby asked you and not me," Alex said confidently. Alex took the three steps of the metal stairway in one long stride, pushing past Jason, and said, "He couldn't risk having this perfection"—he waved his hand in front of his face—"standing beside him, stealing all of his attention. He had to go with his ugliest brother so he would look better."

Jason laughed and slapped his brother on the back

as he entered the office. Jason crossed to his desk taking his seat behind it.

Despite Alex's bravado, Jason knew that he hadn't taken Bobby's decision to overlook him for best man duties in favor of Jason all that well. Bobby and Alex were the youngest of the brothers and had been inseparable growing up.

But after graduation, Alex had left for the Navy. He had moved up the ranks quickly and was selected for the prestigious Navy Seal program. He served proudly for six years and had only recently returned home to Harper's Crossing, where he was now a firefighter and paramedic.

Jason was the one who had stuck around. He had been there for Bobby, helping to raise him. Giving him advice. Picking him up in the middle of the night from random parties so he wouldn't drive drunk or ride with anyone else who was. Making sure that he studied, stayed out of fights, graduated. And as soon as Bobby graduated he'd come to work with Jason at Sloan Construction.

Jason was also the one who'd recognized that Bobby had been in love with Sophie since they were kids. He knew the signs from firsthand experience. And he was the one who had encouraged Bobby to go for it, not wanting his little brother to make the same mistake with Sophie that he, himself, had made with Katie.

Once Bobby had finally gotten his chance with Sophie, he had quickly decided that he wanted to marry her. Their dad hadn't agreed with it—he said that it was too fast. But Jason had gone to bat for Bobby, defending him, saying that Bobby had known Sophie practically his whole life. He had argued that this was the real thing. Sure, they may have only technically been dating for a few months before they got engaged. But Sophie Hunter had been the sole keeper of his brother's heart for years.

So, yeah. Maybe Alex wasn't happy about the fact that Bobby had chosen Jason, but Jason sure as hell wasn't going to tiptoe around Alex's feelings just because he was butthurt about it.

"Actually, I stopped by to see how you were holding up," Alex said, plunking himself down in one of Jason's visitors' chairs, reclining back in it as far as it would go, and placing his feet casually up on Jason's desk.

"I'm good. Bobby's all set, and I'm just trying to tie up some loose ends on the Slater Street job before we head out of town tomorrow." Jason delivered this information as he reached across his desk and knocked Alex's feet off of it.

Alex smiled a knowing smile and raised his eyebrows. "I wasn't talking about your work schedule, although thanks for that boring little rundown. I was referring to the return of one blond-haired, blue-eyed hottie. I saw you driving away from Richard's with Katie after our fitting. How are you doing with *that* situation?"

Jason did not like where this conversation was headed. He didn't mind being a sounding board for his brothers and would always be there for them if they needed to talk, needed advice, or needed *anything*. But that was a one-way street. He wasn't going to sit in a construction office trailer and talk about his *feelings*. He didn't need to have an Oprah moment with his brother.

"There is no situation," Jason stated calmly, intending to end the conversation before it even got started.

"No situation, huh?" Alex said, amused. Jason could see his little brother was clearly *not* going to drop this.

Always one to cut to the chase, Jason looked his brother straight in the eye. "You got something to say, then say it."

"Hey," Alex said with a *who, me?* expression on his face and put up his hands in mock surrender. "I just wanted to let you know I'm here if you want to talk, and also I really wanted to make sure it wasn't messing with you too much, seeing her again."

"Katie and I have been friends practically our entire lives. It's good to see her again. End of story."

"Friends, huh? Is that what you kids are calling it these days?" Alex smiled again, that same superior and knowing smile.

Jason knew his brother was getting at something. He just wished like hell he would come out and say it already rather than sitting there like an asshole and hinting around at it with that damn smug smirk on his face.

Wait a minute.

That little speech sounded familiar—from the other side. Yeah. He suddenly recognized it. He'd been the recipient of that same complaint multiple times.

Well, shit. So was this what Katie felt like when he gave her that little grin he liked to give her, just so he could see her get riled up? Damn. He had thought it was charming. If what he was feeling right now was any indication, though, he was probably going to have to revisit that conclusion, because 'charmed' was the furthest thing in the world from what he was feeling right now.

"I'm gonna say this one more time. If you have something to say, say it. If not, shut the hell up," he snapped, his tone sounding harsh even to his own ears.

"Look, Jas, seriously. I didn't stop by to give you a hard time. It's just that the night of Nick's funeral, you know, I was staying at Chris' house. He lived right down the street from Katie. We were out in the front playing basketball when we saw you climb out of Katie's window and shimmy down that tree, *and* you didn't have a shirt on. If memory serves, Katie was gone by the next day."

"Gotta love small towns," Jason said tightly, never having felt more nostalgic for NYU than he did at that moment.

"And she's never been back to town since. Not even

once."

"Alex, if you have a point to this little trip down memory lane, you need to make it," Jason said, hoping he was succeeding at his goal—to keep his expression blank, not giving anything away.

"All right, fine. You don't want to talk about it, so I'll back off. I just stopped by because I wanted you to know that, even with Bobby busy with wedding stuff and Riley and Seth deployed, you do still have a brother to talk to if you want to."

Alex stood and turned to leave but looked back as he was opening the door. "Hey, you picking up Bobby tonight? You know the kid can't hold his alcohol for shit."

"Yeah, I am heading over there after I finish up here," Jason said, and then, feeling a little bad for shutting out his brother when he'd just been trying to help, he added, "Hey, you bringing a date to the wedding?"

Alex smiled and deep dimples appeared on his face. "Nah, bro. That would be like taking sand to the beach."

Chapter Twelve

Standing in the bathroom, Katie put the finishing touches on her makeup. When she had gotten home from the luncheon, she had been able to take a long, hot shower and she had sung her heart out. Shower concert *for the win*! She felt like a whole new person.

Yes, this day had not gone how she had planned, but she wasn't going to get bogged down with that now.

The luncheon had been a lot of fun. She had been able to catch up with everyone and really enjoyed being back with a group of people that really knew her. There was a shorthand in their communication that she hadn't even realized she'd missed until today. There was no way to develop that sort of unspoken understanding with new people, no matter how much you liked them. The only way to enjoy that kind of telepathy was by being with people who had known you forever and shared countless experiences with you.

The one teeny tiny piece of the puzzle that had tainted her complete and total enjoyment of the afternoon was her insane reaction to—and behavior with—Jason. It wasn't just what she had done—although it was definitely not something she wanted to dwell on. No, it was also how much she had missed him.

God, she *really* had missed him.

Well, nothing to be done about that now. Nope. Tonight, Katie was going to go out with Sophie, Amber, the Quad Squad, and Sophie's friends. She was just going to relax and enjoy herself.

Taking in a shaky breath just from the thought of Jason, Katie remembered to put her trusty paper bag in the purse she was taking tonight. Hey, no reason to tempt fate.

Just as that thought hit her, there was a knock at her bedroom door. *That's odd,* she thought. *Mom and Aunt Wendy are both out running errands. Maybe they forgot something.*

"Come in," Katie sing-songed from her bathroom.

She heard footsteps and felt more than saw Jason standing in her room. She opened the bathroom door a little wider and tilted her head to peek out.

"Hey, Jas..." She stopped in her tracks before she was even able to ask what he was doing there because holy moly mother of... He looked smokin' *hot.*

Jason stood in her room wearing charcoal gray slacks and a black button-up shirt. He had not shaved so he had a sexy stubble that was more pronounced than even this afternoon when she had seen him. He cleaned up well. He smiled and she melted, her insides dissolving into a puddle of mush. Lovely, tingly, euphoric mush.

"Hey, Kit Kat." His voice was deep and gravelly and she felt it run through her all the way to the tips of her toes.

"What are you doing here?" Katie asked, remaining in the safety of the bathroom. She honestly did not trust herself to step into her bedroom with him. Not after how she had behaved a few hours before in his truck and *certainly* not with him looking the way he looked right now.

"Bobby's next door with Sophie. He wanted to stop by because she thought there might be strippers at the bachelor party and she was upset."

Katie raised an eyebrow. "And does she have any reason to be upset?"

He stepped closer to the bathroom door and raised his hands above his head, resting them on the door frame.

Damn, he smelled good, too. And the way his shirt pulled taut against his biceps. *Oh my.*

"No," Jason replied, looking completely calm, relaxed, and oh-so-sexily confident.

Hmmm. Katie tried not to get distracted. She considered the way she had phrased the question and his answer, her friends had nicknamed her Sherlock growing up because she was always looking for clues in things other people took at face value and usually uncovered the truth. Best to be a bit more specific with her inquiry.

"So then, there is *not* going to be a stripper there?" Katie asked determinedly, trying to pin him down. Katie needed to get to the bottom of this because a big part of her duties as M.O.H. tonight was going to be calming Sophie down if she got upset. Katie knew that if Jason told her there wasn't going to be a stripper then there wasn't going to be a stripper. Jason didn't lie.

But the other reason she was asking was that, well, for some strange reason, the thought of a half-naked or (God forbid!) completely naked girl shakin' what her mama gave her all over Jason made her feel…not good. Not jealous, she assured herself. But not good.

But mainly she was asking for Sophie's sake.

Yeah, and if she believed that then maybe she could sell herself some ocean-front property in Arizona.

"I didn't say that," he (non-)answered.

"So there *is* going to be a stripper there?" Her tone sounded much more strident than she had meant it to.

He shrugged noncommittally. "I didn't say that either."

"Seriously, Jason. Is there going to be a stripper there or not?" He could be so frustrating sometimes.

"Why do you care?" He leaned closer, making direct panty-melting eye contact and smiling that sexy, enigmatic smile. His masculine scent was filling the bathroom. Suddenly, the space felt very small, almost claustrophobic. Katie's breath quickened and she wondered if just the sight of Jason Sloan in slacks and a button-up up was enough to bring on a panic attack.

Stealthily she ducked under Jason's arm, brushing lightly against his body as she passed him on her way out of the bathroom. It was just the briefest and tiniest of contacts, but it was just enough that her body was now humming with an electric current that felt dangerously close to arousal.

Jason turned towards her as she passed him, leaned back casually against the door frame, and crossed his arms, causing his sleeves to hug his well-defined biceps. She touched her mouth to make sure that she wasn't drooling. She should not be this turned on by him basically just *standing* in front of her.

"Well?" he asked, a little smile playing on the corners of his mouth.

"Well, what?" she heard herself snap back at him. She really didn't understand why his smug smile drove her crazy but…it did.

"Why do you care whether or not there is going to be a stripper at the bachelor party?"

"I don't care. I'm just asking for Sophie. I am the maid of honor, remember? It's my job to make sure that Sophie has a good time tonight, and if she is worrying about her soon-to-be husband being gyrated on then she will not be enjoying her bachelorette party."

"Well, I am the best man, remember? And maybe a stripper would be add significantly to Bobby's enjoyment of his bachelor party."

"Jason, quit playing games and just tell me yes or no, is there going to be a stripper there?"

"Yes or no, is there going to be a stripper there," Jason repeated. When she glared at him, his face looked as innocent as a choir boy as he stated mock sincerely, "What? You told me to tell you 'yes or no is there going to be a stripper there.' I'm just trying to be helpful and follow orders."

Katie shook her head in frustration and bent over to get her heels out of her suitcase. She unzipped the case and flipped open the lid, and as she did that, she saw that Jason's shirt, the one she'd had since his Tarzan impression in sixth grade, was sitting on the top. *Damn.* She hadn't even thought twice about packing it. She never imagined for a second that he would have an opportunity to see it.

She should have known better.

✦ ✦ ✦

Jason knew he should simply answer Katie and put her mind at ease. He remembered what it had felt like when Alex was putting him through the paces. But he just couldn't help himself—he loved seeing Katie Lawson annoyed. It was one of the cutest things in the world. The way she narrowed her eyes and tilted her head, the way her skin would get a little flushed and she would shake her head, trying to clear it of frustration.

Man, he had *really* missed her.

As she bent over to get something from her suitcase, he took the opportunity to enjoy the view. And what a view it was. *Damn.* Her sweet ass was molded perfectly by the skin-tight jeans she was wearing. He felt himself growing harder by the second and his brain began to fog over with lust, with need. He had a vague notion that he should try to clear his head, but that thought was getting further away by the second.

Katie suddenly slammed her suitcase down and turned and looked…guilty. Hmmm. That was interesting. Jason felt his lips curl up in a smile as he took a slow step forward.

"What's in the suitcase, Kit Kat?"

"Nothing." Katie's response came just a little too quickly. He saw her cheeks turn red and he knew she was hiding something.

"Tell me." He challenged playfully.

"Just clothes, Jas. Seriously." She looked him straight in the eyes, her face completely relaxed, her voice as smooth as silk.

He knew that, at least in her youth, Katie always pinched her lips together right before she told a lie, like her body was rejecting it. But she was older now, and top that off with the fact she was a lawyer. Yep, she could probably lie with the big boys now.

Either way, there was definitely something in that suitcase that she absolutely did not want Jason to see. Which, in Jason's mind, meant only one thing—he needed to see what was in that suitcase.

"Open the suitcase, Kit Kat," he said in an authoritative tone.

"What? No," she retorted, crossing her arms and looking annoyed. She jutted out her hip and said sassily, "You're not the boss of me, Jas."

"Now who's acting like a five-year-old?" he sassed back. "You win many arguments in court that way? I can just hear it now. 'But, your honor, that's not fair. Tell opposing counsel he's not the boss of me!' Very professional."

A flush crept up Katie's porcelain cheeks. Tinting her smooth, pale skin pink from either rising ire at his words or embarrassment over what was in the suitcase. Jason smiled wider. *Time to find out.*

He juked around her and was just in the middle of pulling the top open when Katie jumped in front of him and sat down firmly on top of the suitcase lid. She was grinning broadly, and Jason could see in her smile that she was proud of herself because she thought she had outsmarted him. He burst out laughing, which took a bit of the shine off of her smile.

"You think plopping your skinny little ass on top of there is going to deter me?" Jason laughed and then made a tsk-tsking sound and shook his head slowly back and forth. "Kit Kat, I'm hurt. Honestly. It's almost as if you don't know me at all."

Her eyes grew wide as he lunged forward to pick her up and toss her on the bed. She must have recognized the maneuver from when they were kids because a burst of competitive laughter immediately sprang forth from her mouth and her eyes came alive with a warrior's fire.

As soon as he lifted her, she interlocked her arms in his, the same way she used to when they would swim at The Plunge during the summer and he would try to toss her up in the air. Because of the way their arms were intertwined, he wasn't able to release his hold on her, and momentum sent him tumbling onto the bed with her.

When they came to rest, Katie was on her back, her golden mane of hair spread out across the pillows behind her head like a shining, silky cloud. Her eyes were wide, her skin was flushed, and she looked as beautiful as he had ever seen her look. More beautiful than any woman he had ever seen in his life.

Her clear blue eyes opened wide in astonishment, but whether that was in response to something she saw in his face or something that was going on inside her own mind and heart, he had no idea. Maybe it was combination of both.

He was immediately lost in those giant blue azure pools, as he always was any time he looked into them. His awareness of everything else in the world faded away—of the suitcase, of the fact that Bobby was next door, of the fact that they were in her childhood bedroom, of the fact that he was growing harder by the instant. He was not aware of anything but Katie's big blue eyes.

Hesitantly, Katie reached up and trailed her fingertips lightly over his face. Jason swallowed a moan. Damn, the sensation was almost too much to bear.

Her exquisite eyes filled with tears that shone like diamonds as she whispered, "Jason…" There was so much emotion infused in that one tiny, desperate whisper that he had to close his eyes against the sudden rush of his own intense feelings. Eyes closed, he pressed his forehead to hers, breathing hard.

"God, I've missed you so much," he whispered back to her, his intensity matching that of her own voice just a moment before.

He opened his eyes and looked into hers again. He saw in them that she wanted him as badly as he wanted her. Their lips were mere millimeters from touching. He slowly moved his head towards hers…

At that exact moment, the loud strains of, Sir Mix-A-Lot's "I Like Big Butts" filled the room, startling them both.

Katie jumped involuntarily, which caused her forehead to bang into his with a loud knocking sound. Jason reared back, moving his head away from the pain, and his hand flew up to where he had been hit.

This movement caused him to lose his precarious balance on the edge of the bed, and in one quick motion, he fell to her wooden floor, landing flat on his butt with a hard thud.

Sir Mix-A-Lot's party anthem continued to fill the room. *Damn Alex and his constant prank ringtone changing*. Loud pumping music filled the air but Jason could pick out one sound over the canned rap song.

He looked up and saw Kit Kat's beautiful face looking down at him. His mouth went dry. With her golden hair backlit by her bedside lamp, she really did seem to have an angelic glow about her. It looked like a soft, bright halo surrounded her glowing face.

Then he realized what the sound was that he could hear over the blaring ringtone.

She was laughing her ass off.

She looked so beautiful. Happy. Relaxed. Free.

In that moment, something happened that he never would have thought was possible. He fell even more in love with Katie Lawson.

Chapter Thirteen

Hearing the doorbell ring mere minutes after Jason had left, Katie ran down the stairs of her childhood home and opened the door to see Sophie standing on her porch like she had been a thousand times before. Katie was struck, once again, with the differences in beautiful Sophie's appearance.

She was no longer a bouncing four-year-old, a tomboy eight-year-old, or a pre-teen with a mouth full of braces. Sophie stood before her in stiletto heels, skinny jeans, and a sparkling black top, and she was a beautiful young woman.

"Ready to party?" Sophie asked mischievously, and Katie grabbed her and hugged her. "Are you okay?" Sophie asked next, concern lacing her voice as she rubbed her hands up and down over Katie's back.

Katie, for her part, was too choked up to speak for a moment. In all the drama that had been consuming her thoughts, she really hadn't let it soak in that her Miss Sophiebell was getting married.

"I'm fine," Katie assured her with conviction as soon as her voice returned to her. She gave Sophie one more hard squeeze before grabbing her purse and heading out the door. "I just really missed you, chickadee. I'm so happy to be a part of your big day."

As Katie climbed in the party bus filled with rowdy women eager to begin their night out at The Grill on the Riverwalk, Katie noticed something disconcerting. The guy on the motorcycle, the one Jason had pointed out earlier in the day, was sitting on his bike two car lengths behind the bus.

Hmm, that's odd, Katie thought to herself. She felt a little tingle at the back of her spine but put both the thought of Motorcycle Man and the twinge of fear firmly and deliberately out of her mind. This was Harper's Crossing. It was a small town, not like San Francisco, where seeing the same person twice in one day could almost never be random.

As the bus pulled away from the curb and headed towards downtown, she made a decision to keep thoughts of this weird little coincidence out of her mind for the rest of the evening and just concentrate on having a good time.

This resolution became ten times harder when the motorcycle pulled away from the curb immediately after the bus did and began to follow them.

✦ ✦ ✦

It felt so strange to Katie to actually be walking up the wooden steps to the bar portion of The Grill. She had never been upstairs before, although it had always held a place of reverence and mystery in her mind. But the last time Katie was in Harper's Crossing, she wasn't legal yet. Nick and Jason had snuck up there several times when they were all teenagers, but Katie had sat her butt in her seat at their table downstairs in the restaurant portion of the establishment and staunchly refused to go with them. It was against the rules and Katie *never* broke the rules.

She had always been curious about it, though, and was excited to finally get the chance to see it with her own eyes. As she handed her driver's license and ten-dollar bill to the guy working the door, she realized that, although she was twenty-eight years old and a practicing lawyer, she had never actually felt quite as "grown up" as she did at that moment.

When she stepped inside, her skin tingling with anticipation at what wonders the space might contain, she couldn't help but feel a little bit disappointed with what she saw. It wasn't the "den of iniquity" she had always imagined it might be, and it also wasn't the cosmopolitan oasis she had also, at times, dreamed it was. In fact, it didn't match up to any of the visions Katie had imagined.

In reality, it looked pretty much the same as the restaurant downstairs. It had the same wall coverings, the same tables, the same chairs, the same art on the wall. The only difference was a large dance floor in the center of the room and a glossy wooden bar that ran across the entire left hand wall.

Katie smiled to herself as she surveyed the space. It was exactly as it should be. She wouldn't have it any other way.

Seeing Sophie get carded was also a strange experience. Sure, logically she knew that Sophie had turned twenty-one the previous summer, but to actually *see* her in a bar was strange.

Who was she kidding? To actually see her drive a car was strange, let alone gain admittance into a bar.

There were about fifteen girls present that were all part of Sophie's party. Katie knew about half of them already and was looking forward to getting to know the rest during their night of debauchery. Amber was in attendance as well as the Sloan girls Haley, Krista, Jessie, and Becca. The rest of the attendees were girls that Katie remembered being Sophie's childhood friends.

As she stepped through the "VIP" area (which, in reality, consisted of a red rope sectioning off three tables. But, hey, this was Harper's Crossing) she spotted a girl sitting at the far table and did a double take.

"Chelle?!" Katie exclaimed and realized that, because of her surprise and excitement, it had come out a little louder than she had meant it to. But then again, with the music pounding from the speakers, even her enthusiastic exclamation was barely audible.

As the woman turned, Katie saw that it was, indeed, her Chelle. She screamed and ran over to her, pulling her into a tight embrace.

Rachelle Thomas (AKA Chelle) had been Katie's best friend since second grade. Rachelle had started at Harper's Crossing Elementary mid-year and so, of course, she was branded the "new kid," with all of the social stigma that entailed among vicious seven-year olds. Chelle had been really quiet for the first few months that she attended Harper's Crossing Elementary. Katie had thought about approaching her, but the girl had seemed so contentedly self-contained that Katie wasn't even sure what she would talk about with her.

Then it had happened. Chelle had gotten the dreaded chicken pox and had to miss several weeks of school. When she came back, she had worn not one but *two* badges of shame—now she was not only the "new kid," she was also the "chicken pox kid." The other members of their second grade class had descended on her at every playground opportunity, taunts at the ready, like a pack of blue-jeaned, pigtailed wolves circling an injured deer.

That pissed Katie off. Even at seven years old, she had a strict moral code. She didn't believe in being mean to people. Not only that, the teacher had said that they needed to welcome Rachelle back and show her some support. The teacher had *said* it! That made it a rule!

Katie mulled over what to do about the situation. She knew that explaining to the other kids that what they were doing was wrong was a losing proposition.

She also instinctively recognized that sticking up for Rachelle while the mob frenzy of mocking was in full effect would not have the desired outcome but would rather just make her a target as well.

Then she came up with the perfect idea. She wouldn't try to confront the bullies directly. She would just act in opposition to them. She would be as nice to Rachelle as they were being mean, and hopefully they would see the difference and be ashamed of themselves. Well, that was probably too much to hope for, Katie had decided, but at least Rachelle would have somebody being nice to her.

The very same night that she had that idea, she spent all evening making an elaborate card for Rachelle. On one side of the inside flap, it read "YOU ARE" in big, bold letters. On the other side of the interior, Katie listed all of the good qualities she had noticed about Rachelle in the time she had been going to school there.

The next day, as all of the class was filing in and taking off their coats, putting their backpacks away, and making their way to their seats, Katie walked up to Rachelle and wordlessly handed her the card. She wasn't trying to be mysterious. She was just nervous about what Rachelle's reaction would be. She sat down in her seat and stared steadfastly forward, waiting for the teacher to begin, and then lost herself in her work until morning recess.

As the class was filing out, Rachelle hung back to wait for Katie. She looked just as nervous as Katie felt, which made Katie relax a little bit.

"Did you mean that stuff?" Rachelle asked shyly.

Katie nodded with conviction.

"Do you wanna play on the monkey bars?" Rachelle asked as a follow-up.

Katie nodded again, and they scampered out to the playground together, where they spent that recess and every recess thereafter. They became fast friends from that moment on.

The mean kids stopped making fun of Chelle, preferring targets who were isolated and defenseless.

In middle school, they bought necklaces that had the words "Best Friends" written across a heart that was split into two pieces.

When Aunt Wendy saw the necklaces, she said that a lot of people have 'best friends' but very few had 'diamond friends.' She explained that 'diamond friends' were better than plain old 'best friends' because diamonds were not only rare, they were forever.

So, needless to say, from that day on, Chelle and Katie were 'diamond friends.'

Then, Chelle had to move the summer before their senior year because her dad got transferred. They kept in touch through letters for the first few months, but by the end of senior year, Katie got so busy that she hadn't written—and then she left for California.

She almost couldn't believe what she was seeing, that Chelle was really here. In Harper's Crossing. They hugged long and hard, and as they pulled away, Katie felt tears forming in her eyes. Oh good. More tears. At least she was consistent. Oh well, at least these were happy tears. She'd had enough angst.

"Hi, diamond friend," Chelle said with a big smile on her face and tears brimming in her own eyes. "How ya been?"

"I can't believe you're really here." Katie said aloud.

Chelle smiled and said in her signature dry tone, "Really? Because since I moved back here a year ago, the word on the street is that it's a lot more rare to see you around these parts than me."

Katie laughed. "Guilty as charged. Wow. So you moved back here? How did that happen?"

"Well, that's a funny story. You know David Price? Remember, from high school? He's running for City Planner now. Well anyway, we reconnected on Facebook a few years ago and started talking. It just turned into something…more, and now we're engaged." Chelle said happily, showing Katie her ring.

Katie struggled to keep the expression on her face positive—or if she couldn't manage that, at least neutral. Katie had always thought that David Price was a supreme douchebag. But hey, maybe he had changed. Right? As long as he made Chelle happy.

As Katie and Chelle caught up, it felt to Katie like no time had passed at all since they'd seen each other. They fell into an easy conversational rhythm, one that was uniquely theirs.

Katie learned that Chelle's older brother, Eddie,

was in the wedding, a last minute replacement. He and Riley Sloan were best friends, and when it became clear that Riley was not going to be able to make it back, Eddie had offered to fill in so that the ratio of bridesmaids to groomsmen would not be skewed. And since he also worked with Bobby and Jason as a project foreman at Sloan Construction, it had seemed even more natural.

Katie, in turn, told Chelle all about becoming a lawyer and being on the fast track to junior partner.

"That sounds exciting." Chelle enthused.

Katie nodded in agreement, but her manner was thoughtful. She replied, "Well, I don't know if exciting is really the word I would use. I mean, it's a lot of work, a lot of pressure. But it's very fulfilling."

"Oh, that's amazing." Chelle said with a wide smile. "It must be so cool to help all the people that come into your office, all of your clients. I know you always talked about wanting to help people who were in trouble. Just like you did with me. And now you're a lawyer. Now you can."

Katie nodded, although it was even more half-hearted than before, and said, "Well, yeah, I mean…our clients are corporate executives. I mainly work in corporate acquisitions. You know, preparing briefs, hammering out buyout deals, things like that."

Chelle nodded. There was a moment of awkward silence before they both burst out laughing. They laughed until tears ran down their faces.

"Okay, so I'm just gonna shut up then," Chelle mocked herself when their fit of giggles was over. "I'm putting my foot back into my Jimmy Choos before I can stick it in my mouth again."

"No, no," Katie said. "Really, it's fine. I mean, yes, I know that my life doesn't look like I had always dreamed it would. But it's nice, you know? I live in a beautiful city, I have a job I enjoy and am really good at, an apartment I love... That's a pretty damn good life, right?"

Chelle nodded enthusiastically. "It is. And are you happy?"

Katie affirmed that, yes, she was indeed happy.

Chelle paused a beat before saying quietly, "Well, why do you look so miserable, then?"

Katie opened her mouth to respond, but before anything could come out, Amber appeared in front of them and informed them that the party games were getting started. Katie was glad. She didn't have the first clue what she would have said to answer Chelle.

As Katie and Chelle settled back in their seats, the other girls all piled into the "VIP" area and sat down, forming a large circle.

Once everyone was seated, Amber announced, "The first game we will be playing is 'Same-Same-Shoot It-Shoot It,' the object of which is to find out a little bit more about each other. Well, the object of which is to get drunk. Who are we kidding?"

A raucous cheer went up from the girls at Sophie's

party, and she continued. "The way it works is you pass around a hat filled with general relationship questions. One person at a time draws and then answers the question. Everyone who has the same answer has to drink.

"For example, if the question is 'At what age did you have your first crush?' and the person says six, and six is the same answer for you, then you have to yell 'Same-Same!' and then everyone else will yell 'Shoot It-Shoot It!' Then the person who drew the question and everyone who had the same answer have to take a shot. Got it?"

The group nodded their understanding and the game began. Amber went first to demonstrate. She pulled a card out and read, "Have you ever had a one night stand?"

Katie noticed that a flush appeared on her olive toned skin as Amber nodded while announcing, "Yes. Yes, I have."

Several other girls yelled "Same-Same!" Then the rest of the group yelled, "Shoot It-Shoot It!"

Half-way through the first round, it became glaringly obvious that these girls had had quite a bit more experience than she had. It wasn't as if the statements on the cards were even all that racy. Over a half dozen girls had gone and Katie had only participated in a grand total of one 'shoot-it shoot-it.' She'd gotten several strange looks from a few girls when she hadn't yelled out 'same-same' on a few of the questions. It was odd, but it felt like these girls expected her to be much more worldly than she actually was.

Katie chalked their reactions up to the fact that she lived in California. People did generally have preconceived ideas about that place.

When the question-filled hat was passed to Katie, she actually got a little nervous as she pulled out a card, hoping for something innocuous. Thankfully, she was more than a little relieved at what she saw. Her question was easy-breezy-beautiful-Cover-Girl.

Happily, Katie read it out loud with confidence, "How old were you when you met your first love?"

She looked up at the girls, all waiting for her answer shot glasses in hand, and began to respond but, surprising even herself, Katie stopped herself before the reply that had automatically popped into her head had come flying out of her mouth. Her confidence dropped like it was shooting down a Slip-N-Slide on a steep hill.

What was wrong with her? She had met Nick the summer before seventh grade. So why was 'five years old' the first answer that had popped into her head? And why did that realization feel like a punch to the gut?

"I was eleven," Katie answered quietly, and several girls yelled, "'Same-Same!'" with everyone chorusing, "'Shoot It-Shoot It!'" immediately after.

Bringing the glass to her lips, Katie's head fell back and she downed the shot, ready to have her turn over as fast as possible. The liquid stung a little as it hit the back of her throat. A warmth spread through her as she gulped down the alcohol. Setting the glass down she could already feel her muscles loosening as she became more relaxed. Dang. Two shots and she already had a little buzz. Clearly a party girl she was not.

Chelle's turn was next, and her question was "Have you ever had an unrequited love?" Chelle immediately responded emphatically. "Yes."

Several people yelled, "Same-Same!" and the group called out a spirited, "Shoot It-Shoot It!"

Katie leaned in close to Chelle feeling a little loose from her participatory shots. "Unrequited love, huh?"

Chelle smiled enigmatically. "Hey, at least I told the truth."

Oops. Busted. Had she been that transparent? Katie tried to look as innocent as humanly possible as she turned to face her diamond friend, but with the buzz she was already feeling, it was a little hard.

"What? I told the truth." Katie protested, her lips pursing as she lied through her teeth.

"Nope, you sure didn't," Chelle insisted.

Katie tilted her head, still hoping to play it off. "Really? Okay then, diamond friend, what's the real answer?"

Chelle shrugged, and the alcohol was clearly starting to get to her as well. She replied with a small slur, "Haven't the foggiest. Ha ha. Get it? 'Cause you live in San Francisco now." Chelle chuckled and then waved her hand dismissively, "Anyway, I don't know what the real answer is. I only know that it wasn't what you said because you, Katie Marie Lawson, still have the same lying 'tell' you've always had."

"I do not," Katie argued.

"Then how did I know you were lying? That proves it right there," Chelle said proudly.

Katie shook her head, which was starting to feel a little fuzzy. "Your so-called 'proof' is based on a faulty premise. I *wasn't* lying, so your logic is flawed."

"Whatever," Chelle said cheerfully. "That would work in a court of law. But we're not in a court of law. We're in the court of tequila. And in the court of tequila, you and I both know you were lying."

Katie opened her mouth to continue arguing but just sighed resignedly. She shrugged. "Fine, what's my tell?"

"You purse your lips together right before you lie. It's like your body is rejecting the lie," Chelle chuckled.

"Whatever." Katie rolled her eyes.

"So what is the *real* answer?" Chelle persisted.

"Eleven," Katie insisted, not willing to give up the story. "I was eleven when I met Nick. What else could it possibly be?"

"Oh, I don't know," Chelle said airily. "How old were you when you met Jason?"

Katie's eyes widened, but she was saved again from having to provide an answer by being called back to the game.

"Katie! Chelle! Pay attention!" She heard Sophie's

tipsy voice ring out above the music. "You're missing all the questions."

"Sorry," they answered in unison, turning their attention towards the game.

Sophie drew next. "Have you ever had sex in public?" She immediately responded, "Yes." About half the crowd yelled, "'Same-Same!'" and so they 'Shot it-Shot it.'

The game continued, and Katie realized as the questions became more sexual in nature, that she had seriously been neglecting her love life. Or more accurately, her sex life.

She tried to tell herself that the reason she wasn't 'same-saming' and 'shoot-shooting it' was because a lot of the questions seemed to be not only sexual, but geographically specific in nature. Like your first time being under the night sky up at Whisper Lake. There were quite a few questions that involved Pickler's Field and the back of a black pickup truck.

Every time another question that involved that field and a truck came up, Katie was shocked at just how much Jason had done with these girls. He'd certainly lived up to his nickname. Romeo had nothing on him. His truck had seen more action than G.I. Joe.

Katie began to start feeling a tad self-conscious as she continued receiving strange looks whenever one of those questions came up. Then her Sherlock-senses kicked in, and she realized, of course, all these girls would of expected that she and Nick had done every dirty deed imaginable in that field in his truck. They hadn't. With each question her shock-slash-totally-irrational-irritation at Jason grew, she figured, *screw it.* Rather than stick out like a sore thumb, she would just, well, 'shoot it-shoot it.'

Chapter Fourteen

Jason leaned against the doorway while he nursed his beer and looked around the private back room at McMillan's Pub, which he had rented out for the bachelor party. All of his and Bobby's friends were there in the dark, wood-paneled room. They were drinking, throwing darts, shooting pool, and smoking cigars. Everyone seemed to be having a good time.

Jason should have been enjoying himself a hell of a lot more than he was. He couldn't get his mind off of Katie.

Damn.

Why did she have to be every bit as beautiful as the day she left? Every bit as smart. Every bit as fiery and funny…

And, she was leaving. Again. It had been bad enough the first time, when he'd lost the girl he'd loved practically his whole life. Now, after seeing the woman she'd become, he'd fallen even more in love with her. What in the hell was he going to do when she left this time?

Jason shook his head. This shit was making him

crazy. He felt on edge. Irritable.

"Strippers!" a loud, obnoxious cheer sounded in Jason's ear.

There were also a couple aspects of the party, itself, that was getting on Jason's nerves. Like David Price. That douchebag. He was running for City Planner and he hadn't aged one day (in terms of maturity) since junior high school. He was sloppy drunk and wouldn't shut-up about how Jason should have "ordered" a stripper. He referred to it the same way you'd order a pizza.

"I don't know what to tell ya, Davey boy," Jason repeated for what felt like the hundredth time. "It's Bobby's night, and he didn't want one. This is all about giving Bobby what he wants."

David threw his arm around Jason's shoulder, which upset the balance of both Jason's and David's mugs of beer. Of course, both drinks splashed down Jason's pants, leaving David's completely unscathed. Jason sighed as he pushed down the urge to punch this asshole in the face at Bobby's party.

How this jackass had ever managed to land a class act like Chelle Thomas, Jason would never understand.

Jason still remembered when Chelle had moved to Harper's Crossing and transferred into his and Katie's second grade class. Almost the entire class had been completely awful to her—including this douchebag she was now engaged to. Jason hadn't felt good about it, and he had certainly never joined in, but he never made a move to stop it either.

He still remembered the morning he saw Katie slip Chelle a piece of paper that looked like a card. She didn't make a big production of it. She just handed it to her while they were all filing into their seats. Jason only noticed because, well, he noticed everything Katie did.

He watched Chelle read the card. He saw her open it up, her expression blank. She probably thought it was going to be a mean trick, something to make fun of her. But as she read over the words once, twice, three times, her expression changed. He saw her smile for the first time.

When the teacher started class, Chelle quickly tucked the card inside her desk. However, as the class worked, he saw her take it out from time to time and, clandestinely, read it again. Every time, the same little smile would creep across her face.

When the class went out for recess, he saw Katie and Chelle run to the playground together.

Jason had to stay behind, as usual, because he hadn't gotten his work done in time.

When Ms. Lindsley told him that she was going to run up to the office and that she would be right back, he saw his chance. He *had* to know what that card said.

He rushed over to Chelle's desk, looking over his shoulder the whole time, and quickly pulled out the card. He opened it. The first part said "YOU ARE" in bold crayon letters. The second part was a list, one that used little stars, hearts, and flowers for bullet points. (Girls! Whatever.)

The list included items like "Really Smart," "Really Brave," "Really Funny," "Really Pretty," "The Best Speller In Class," and "Really, Really Nice!!!!"

That was Katie. His Katie.

As if reading his thoughts, David turned the subject to Katie. "So, have you seen that Katie Lawson's back in town? God, she has a great ass."

Jason felt every muscle in his body tighten at David's comment. He had to remind himself, *yet again*, that this was Bobby's party and he couldn't punch David Price out in the middle of it. Not to mention, if he won the City Planner election… Yeah, it wouldn't be great if the future president of Sloan Construction had a history of violence with the City Planner.

Jason nodded, ignoring the *ass* comment. "Yep. She's the maid of honor. I'm the best man. It would be kind of hard to miss her."

"Hehe…you said hard," David chortled, imitating the *Beavis and Butthead* cartoon show they had watched in junior high. "Hard. Katie's ass makes me hard. Katie. Katie. Katie."

Jason felt himself moving dangerously close to not giving a shit whether or not they were at his baby brother's bachelor party when Eddie, Chelle's brother, saved him by coming up and joining the conversation. Or so he thought.

"You guys talking about Katie Lawson?" he asked.

"Damn. I saw her at CVS, and she looks *good.* I know she was my little sister's best friend, but I always thought she was pretty hot."

This was going from bad to worse.

Out of the corner of his eye, Jason saw Bobby answer a call on his cell phone. His brother's animated movements and expression did not look like the conversation was going well.

"Catch you guys later," he said to Eddie and David as he gestured towards Bobby. "Duty calls."

With that, he made his way over to Bobby in several long strides.

"No, baby," Bobby was insisting into the phone. "There's no stripper here, I promise."

Even over the crowded room Jason could hear Sophie's inebriated, loud voice on the other end of the phone. She sounded like she was more than just a little tipsy. Thank God they'd listened to him when he'd suggested having the bachelor and bachelorette parties on Thursday instead of Friday so everyone would have a day to recover.

Bobby's face wrinkled in puzzlement and he said, "What do you mean Katie locked herself in the bathroom?"

Jason said, "What's wrong with Katie?"

Bobby turned away from Jason, waving his hand to signal Jason to be quiet.

Bobby spoke again into the mouthpiece of his cell phone, asking if Sophie was okay. Jason tried to wait out the drunk ass lovebirds assurances that she was okay and that there were no strippers at the bachelor party. But when Bobby and Sophie started a lengthy and drawn out session of I-love-you-more-no-I-love-you-more-no-I-love-you-more, Jason lost his patience.

Jason tried to interject again. "Is Katie okay?"

Bobby gestured for him to go away but the motion caused him to stumble over his feet and almost drop the phone.

Luckily, Jason had ninja-quick reflexes. He grabbed the phone before it hit the ground.

"Sophie? This is Jason," he said.

"Jaaaasssoooonnnn!!!!" Sophie exclaimed, her slurred exclamation long and drawn out. "You're the best best man. Haha. That sounds funny. The bestbestman…"

Jason sighed and rubbed his forehead with his fingertips. He'd been nursing one beer all night. Every time he found himself sober in a room full of drunk people, he remembered why he normally tried to avoid being sober in a room full of drunk people.

"Sophie," he said patiently. "Why is Katie in the bathroom?"

"Because she won't come out," Sophie promptly replied.

Jason shook his head. He couldn't fault her for factual accuracy.

"Why won't she come out?" he clarified.

"Ooooohhhhhh!!!!" Sophie said. "She's sick."

"She's sick?" Jason's chest tightened.

"She said she was feeling not so good and she went in the bathroom; and, Chelle has been trying to get her out and she won't." Sophie burped loudly then clarified, "Won't come out, I mean."

"Yeah, I got that part," Jason said, shaking his head. "Look, Soph, keep an eye on her if she does come out. I'm coming over."

"N-noooo!!" Sophie exclaimed in liquor-fueled despair. "You're the best man. You can't see us before the wedding. Wait...I don't know if...can you see us...or is that..."

"Just stay there," Jason said firmly.

Jason handed the phone back to Bobby, and as he was walking away, heard his brother say into the phone, "No, I love *you* more." God help him.

Jason walked back over to where Alex was now standing with Douchebag David Price and said, "Hey, Alex. I have to go check on something. You're officially filling in on best man duties till I get back."

Alex smiled broadly. "Well, that's a lucky break for everybody at this sorry excuse for a party. Let the fun begin!"

A whoop went up from all of the guys who were standing close enough to hear, and Alex's grin widened.

"Is the emergency that you have to go nail Katie Lawson while she's drunk enough to let you?" David snickered as he started to stagger over to pour himself another drink.

All right, Jason thought, *that's enough.* He wasn't going to punch him. It was still Bobby's party, after all. But he did extend his foot slightly as David was passing him and took great satisfaction in hearing his high-pitched little-girl scream as he went sprawling to the ground.

Jason had to admit he felt a small bit of satisfaction as he headed out.

✦ ✦ ✦

He took the stairs up to the bar area of The Grill two at a time. He couldn't get the knot out of the pit of his stomach and knew that he wouldn't be able to until he laid eyes on Katie and saw for himself that she was okay.

He nodded to Reece, the bouncer, and headed straight to the bathroom.

As he weaved his way through the maze of tables in the bar, Sophie ran up to him and blocked his way. She planted her feet firmly and put a hand on each shoulder. The look on her face was stern.

"Jason, I hafta ask you a serious question," she said, her voice revealing that she was way past tipsy.

Jason tried to be patient although his heart was racing. He said gently, "In a minute, Soph. I've gotta check on Katie."

Sophie stamped her foot, a move he hadn't seen her do since elementary school.

"Isss my party," she insisted drunkenly. "I getttta

aksss the questions."

Jason closed his eyes, shoving down his growing sense of panic, and said, "Okay. What's up, Soph?"

"You hafta be honest," she said, the alcohol in her system making her overly earnest.

"I will be," Jason assured her.

"Okay," Sophie agreed. "Then you hafta tell the truth."

Jason nodded.

"Was there really a stripper there? Jason? Honest? You hafta tella truth," she slurred.

"There was no stripper, Soph. I promise," he said as he stepped around his soon-to-be sister-in-law.

"Where are you going?" she asked as she grabbed his forearm.

"To check on Katie," Jason explained calmly.

"Oh good!" Sophie's face lit up with excited relief. She let go of her grip on his arm and scrunched her face as she hissed through her teeth. "Did you know she's sick and won't come out of the bathroom?"

Jason just shook his head and continued to the back where the restrooms were. When he reached the end of the hall, he found Chelle pounding on the women's door, asking Katie to open the door. All he heard coming from the other side of the door were groans.

When Chelle saw him walking up, her face immediately relaxed into a warm smile of relief. She said, "Hey, Jas, I'm so glad you're here. She's been in there for almost an hour. I think she might have gotten sick, and she isn't making much sense. I'm not sure if I should take her to the hospital or not. She's had quite a few shots."

"How much did she drink?" Jason asked, his stomach constricting with panic at the mention of the word 'hospital.'

Chelle's face looked a little sheepish as she said, "Oh, umm. Well, after I started counting, she did at least seven more shots. I'm not sure how many before that."

"Goddamn it!" he growled.

"No, it's not her fault, Jas," Chelle insisted, immediately jumping to Katie's defense. "We were playing this game and I think she felt like she had to…I don't know, like people expected her to…"

"Never mind. It doesn't matter," Jason said, shaking his head.

Stepping past Chelle, Jason pounded on the door. He demanded firmly, "Katie, open up!"

"No," she replied. She had answered immediately, which was encouraging. But her voice had sounded weak, which was not.

He tried the handle. No go. He pounded on the door in frustration. "Katie, open the door. If you don't, you know I'll just go get the key from Jack and open it myself."

There was silence for a few seconds, and Jason was just about to walk away to go and retrieve the key when he heard the lock click.

He pushed open the door and found a half-naked Katie slumped on the floor. She was holding her shirt up to cover her chest, her head slumped over. It was obvious that she was drunk as a skunk, but he was here. With her. He'd take care of her.

"So, Kit Kat, don't get me wrong, I'm enjoying the view, but just out of curiosity, any reason you're topless?" Jason asked, knowing that what he said would irritate her. His hope was to get a little rise out of her.

"This isss't funny, Jason." Katie wouldn't look up at him, and her slurred words escaped through clenched teeth.

He knew he shouldn't be enjoying any part of this, but his relief was powerful, like a drug coursing through his veins. He had been so worried that he would find her crying or vomiting—that finding her topless and frustrated made him almost giddy as a schoolgirl.

Lowering down, he bent his knees so that he was crouching down in front of her, resting his elbows on his thighs. He touched her chin to lift her face up, and that's when he saw that she had, indeed, been crying.

He felt a stab of pain rip through his chest. God. He couldn't stand seeing women upset in general (probably leftover shit from his childhood), and that was just random women. This was his Katie.

"What happened?" he asked gently as he ran his thumb along the wet streak running down her soft cheek.

She sniffled and pulled her chin out of his grasp, but continued to keep her head up so that she was facing him eye to eye.

"We were playing this game of shotsss, annn I took more than I could handle," she hiccupped. "As soon as I started feelin' sick ann on my way to the bathroom some idiot tried to hit on me. I felt wobbly and when he wouldn't let go of my arm I pulled away too hard and ended up knocking into a cocktail waitress who was carrying a tray of drinks that ended up all over my shirt..."

The lengthy narrative apparently wore her out. She dropped her head against the back wall with a loud sigh. "...which turns out to be see-through when wet."

Jason tried to keep his temper under control as he asked her, "What did the guy look like?"

"What?" She shook her head, clearly confused.

He spoke slowly and deliberately. "What. Did. The guy. Who put his hands on you. Look like, Katie?"

"Ohmigosh, Jason, isss fine, isss not a big deal. Ima big girl. I handled it myself."

Jason stood.

"Where are you going?" Katie asked, still slurring her words.

"If you won't tell me what he looks like, I'll find out myself."

"Jason, don't leave," she pleaded, grabbing his hand and holding on. "I dunno know whats to do. I can't put my shirt on."

Tears started filling her eyes. Dang it. Jason's Achilles' heel.

"Chelle's outside, she can help you," Jason offered. Achilles' heel or no Achilles' heel, his blood was boiling. He needed to get his hands on the asshole who thought it was okay to touch Katie.

"I don't want Chelle to help. I want you."

Jason knew, logically, that Katie was drunk off her ass and not choosing her words as carefully as she normally would. She wasn't thinking through all of the possible implications of what she was saying. She probably just felt that he could handle the situation better than her friend because he had always taken care of her, always fixed things for her in the past.

Sure. He realized all of that. But he couldn't help it. Hearing the words "*I want you*" come out of her mouth was a straight shot to his heart.

There was no chance he would leave her now, even in the capable hands of her childhood BFF, so he resigned himself to the fact that he just needed to get her home.

Pulling his shirt from his pants, he started to unbutton it.

Katie's eyes widened. "I didn't mean like that."

Jason rolled his eyes and grinned. "You should be so lucky," he teased as he quickly pulled his shirt off of his shoulders and wrapped it around her.

"Oh," she said quietly.

"Do you think you can walk?" Jason asked as he

helped her up.

"Of course," she answered, looking at him like he was a world-class idiot for even broaching the question.

But as she stood, her legs wobbled, and she would have fallen right down on her cute little ass if he hadn't been there to steady her.

Scooping her up into his arms, Jason stilled for a moment. Damn, if she didn't feel so good there. It was hard for him to believe that she'd had been back less than twenty-four hours. How in the hell had he made it through the last ten years without her?

She let out a small breath and her body relaxed as she melted against him. She just buried her face against his chest and wrapped her arms around his neck.

Double checking that she was all covered up, Jason opened the door and saw Chelle still standing there.

"I'm taking her home," Jason informed her. Then he asked with genuine concern, "Are you good or do you need me to call Eddie?"

"I'm good. Sophie offered to take everyone home in the Party Bus."

"Tell her I'mm sooo sorrrry, but I have to go home now," Katie said to Chelle.

"I will sweetie," Chelle answered comfortingly. Then, when Katie laid her head back against Jason's shoulder, Chelle mouthed a grateful, "Thank you," to Jason and handed him Katie's purse.

Jason headed out the back exit and down the stairs that led to the parking lot. No way was he going to go back through the crowded bar. He didn't want to deal with the comments from drunk assholes who would feel compelled to comment on either – 1) Katie's drunken state, 2) His shirtlessness, or 3) The fact that he was carrying a purse.

As he carried Katie's limp form down the stairs, her head lolled against him. As she took a deep breath and readjusted, snuggling her head deeper against his neck, she sighed, "My hero…"

Jason felt his chest puff out involuntarily, and the most intoxicating mixture of pride, affection and flat-out lust coursed through his veins at the sound of those words.

He reminded himself that she was drunk, that what she was saying right now didn't mean much.

Still.

Hearing her say that she needed him and that he was her hero…well, it felt pretty damn good.

Chapter Fifteen

Katie's head was spinning as Jason set her in his truck. She tried to clear it as she took in her surroundings. Hmmm, his truck. Just thinking about their afternoon made her hot all over.

Wait, she was mad at Jason. But why was she mad at him?

She knew she was really mad, but she wasn't sure why.

Katie looked down and watched as Jason pulled the seatbelt across her body and his knuckles brushed against her nipples. She sucked in a gasp.

Her heart started beating rapidly at his touch. Jason stilled for a moment but then clicked the device into place.

Katie took the opportunity of him stretched across her to breathe him in.

Mmmmm…

He smelled like aftershave mixed with…with…well, musky heat. He smelled like sex.

"You smell good," she heard herself say in a dreamy tone and went in for another smell.

She never got another sniff because Jason pulled away from her and shut the door without saying a word.

Well bully on you, Katie thought as she lifted the collar of his button up shirt that she was wearing to her nose. *I'll just smell your shirt then.*

Jason opened the driver's side door, got in, and asked as he started his truck, "So do you always drink like this or is this a special occasion?"

Bingo! She remembered why she was mad at him.

"*You*!" Katie pointed at him.

"Me?" He gave her a strange sideways glance as he pulled out of The Grill parking lot.

"Yes. This is all *your* fault," she stated as she crossed her arms in a huff.

"My fault?" Jason repeated in a calm tone.

"Yes! If youuu"—she poked his arm—"hadn't done it with Kylie, Elena, Tiffany, Lisa..." She was using her fingers to count them.

He cut her off. "Done what with them?"

"It!" she exclaimed. "We were playing 'Same-Same, Shoot It-Shoot It' and everyone answers questions about their 'experiences' and if you have the same ones as the girl who answers you have to take a shot," she finished as if that explained everything.

"Okay," Jason said slowly. "I'm still not following."

"Well, you did so much in your *'black Chevy truck'* at Pickler's Field and everyone just *assumed* that I would have done all of that stuff with Nick in his truck so they were all staring at me weird, expecting me to do shots when they answered. They don't know Nick wasn't a big pervert like you."

"Katie," Jason's deep voice sent goosebumps popping out all over skin.

"What?" Katie asked trying to ignore her body's response and hold onto her indignation.

"I never did anything with Lisa, Kylie, Elena or Tiffany. In my truck or out of it."

"Oh, come on. Yes, you did. Only you and Nick had black Chevy trucks." She shook her head in irritation, and tears started leaking from her eyes.

She stared at him. He didn't say anything. He was quiet, like he was waiting for *her* to say something. Crap. She really wished she were clear-headed for this conversation.

He took a turn and her stomach rolled.

"I think I'm gonna be sick."

Jason reached to the console and turned on the air conditioning. Then Katie felt his fingers brush the back of her neck as he pulled her hair off her neck, gently guiding her so the cold air was blowing directly on her face.

After a few seconds (or maybe it was minutes. She really couldn't tell) he asked, "Better? Or do I need to pull over?"

Katie's stomach no longer felt like it was in revolt and she answered, "Better."

He released her hair and a chill ran down the length

of her spine as the work-roughened pads of his fingertips grazed her sensitive skin. She felt confused and…horny. Mostly confused.

When she tried to make sense of what Jason had told her or why she wanted him to kiss her more than she wanted her next breath, her head pounded and everything started spinning.

Closing her eyes she rested her head against the passenger side window, enjoying the feel of the cold glass against her flushed skin. *Ohhh, that feels so good,* she thought as she took in a deep breath.

Who knew a window could feel so good?

✦ ✦ ✦

Katie had passed out cold on the short drive home. As Jason pulled up to her Aunt Wendy's house, he was seriously pissed at himself. He knew he should have just kept his mouth shut and let her believe that it was, in fact, him who had gotten his freak on with all those girls in his truck.

The truth would hurt her and the last thing he wanted was for Katie to be hurt. But at the same time, he was just about done with everyone thinking that Nick was the 'Golden Boy Saint' and he was the 'Romeo Womanizing Player.' If anyone deserved that title it was his brother, Alex. Not Jason.

Hopefully, Katie wouldn't even remember this conversation come morning, since she was three sheets to the wind. Maybe even four or five.

When he opened the passenger side door, she fell into his arms since she had been leaning against the window. She felt so right in his arms. Like she was made to be there.

As he approached the front door, it opened and a sleepy looking Pam stepped out.

"Is she okay?" she asked, her voice filled with concern.

"Yeah, she's fine. She just overdid it on the shots. Sorry if I woke you."

As Katie's mom moved aside to let him step into the house, she waved her hand. "Oh no, you didn't wake me. I was just resting on the couch so I could see my girl when she got home. I miss her so much, I thought, even if we just got a few minutes to visit…"

Jason smiled. "Well, unfortunately, I don't think that will be happening tonight."

Pam smiled back and nodded her head in agreement. "Yep, looks like catch-up time will have to wait. Do you want me to take her?"

Jason shook his head. "No, but if you could make her some toast and grab a few aspirin and a big glass of water and meet us upstairs, that would be great."

"Sure thing, sweetie." She patted Jason's arm as she headed off to the kitchen.

Jason had always loved Pam. She was subdued compared to Aunt Wendy, and she wasn't as overly nurturing and affectionate as Nick and Sophie's mom, Grace. But she had such a quiet strength about her, a solidness. She didn't get upset easily, and when she did, it was never in an overreacting sort of way. She was just steady and calm. It had always comforted Jason.

When he reached Katie's bedroom, he laid her down on her bed and smoothed her hair. She murmured something unintelligible and pressed her head into his hand. He pulled her desk chair over to sit next to the bed and keep watch.

He looked up when he heard Pam entering the room and then immediately vacated the chair, motioning for her to sit.

Pam smiled. "Thanks, Jason."

Pam sat down in the chair and set the water, dry toast, and aspirin on Katie's nightstand. She gently shook Katie awake and helped her take the aspirin and eat the toast, chuckling at all the nonsensical things Katie was mumbling.

"I admit, I used to tie one on every once in a while back in my day," Pam said ruefully, but Jason thought there was a touch of nostalgia in her voice. "There's nothing wrong with it if it doesn't become a habit."

After Katie had finished her piece of toast, Pam stood and excused herself, yawning all the while. Jason covered Katie with her blankets and was just about to flip off the lights when he heard her say, "I need your shirt."

He walked back over to her bedside.

"Katie, sweetie, you're wearing my shirt," he said gently.

She looked down at herself and pulled at his button-down.

"No," she said disgustedly. "Not your shirt. I need *your shirt.*"

Jason shook his head at that logic. He was trying to figure out what to say next when she made the very surprising move of pulling his button-down shirt right over her head.

"Whoa!" he exclaimed, turning his back out of sheer instinct. Ogling her in her impaired condition seemed like a shady thing to do.

"I need your shirt," she continued insistently.

Okay, so, maybe it was best to just follow along with her line of logic.

"Okay, Katie. Where is the shirt you want me to get for you?"

"Duh. In my suitcase," she replied like it was the most obvious thing in the world.

He walked over to her suitcase, being very careful to keep his eyes straight ahead not on her bare breasts, as much as he would have loved to indulge in just that under any other circumstance.

As he bent down to unzip her case, he said, "Okay can you give me a clue so I know which shirt it is you want to sleep in?"

"It's. *Your.* Shirt," she continued to insist. "The shirt I sleep in every night..."

He shook his head. She still wasn't making any sense.

He unzipped her case and flipped it open, getting ready to dig through her clothing so he could just find a comfortable shirt for her to sleep in. Even if it was her shirt and not 'his,' hopefully she'd be satisfied enough with it to settle down and go to sleep.

He was reaching his hand towards her bundle of clothing, when he froze, hand still in the air. His eyes saw what was lying in front of him but his brain was having trouble processing the information it was sending.

Was that…?

It couldn't be…?

It was his Def Leppard shirt. The one from sixth grade. The one he had felt so cool in because, while all the sheep he went to school with were wearing boy band t-shirts, he was sporting a vintage rock tee. The one he had taken off and given to Katie that day in the cafeteria.

Holy shit.

Could this be the shirt she wanted? *His* shirt?

The one she'd said she slept in *every* night?

He stood up and handed it to her, his eyes never straying below her beautiful face.

"Is this the shirt you want?" he asked quietly, his voice hoarse.

"Yes!" she exclaimed, "*your* shirt."

She swiftly slipped the shirt over her head and fidgeted as she pulled it down, then plopped down on her back and brushed stray hairs that had fallen in her face.

A few seconds later, he heard light snoring fill the room.

He waited for a moment and watched her sleep, all cuddled up in his shirt, sleeping like a baby.

A smile pulled at his lips.

Like a very drunk and soon-to-be very hung-over baby.

But that was fine. She was comfortable for the time being. And what had allowed her to calm down and drift off to sleepy time? It was his shirt. That was the only thing that had eased her restlessness.

He smiled wider.

She slept in it every night.

Yep. Any lingering doubts he might have had about whether or not Katie had more than friendly feelings for him were erased in one fell swoop.

She may not know it yet. She may be in denial. But Jason was sure, now more than ever, that this thing between them was real.

Oh yeah. It was on.

Chapter Sixteen

Katie felt something on her arms. Shaking her arms. Gently, but still, it was annoying.

She swatted at it. "Stop…" she moaned.

She became a little bit more aware and heard her mother's voice.

"There we are. Good morning, Sunshine. Time to get up."

Katie cracked her eyes open. Even with the shades fully drawn, the room was far too bright.

"What time is it?" Katie groaned.

"It's almost eleven. I've got to get to work, and you've gotta get on the road pretty soon," Pam replied.

Katie's eyes flew open. Eleven? Whoa! Sleeping in to her, was not getting up until 7:00 a.m. She couldn't remember the last time she had still been asleep when the double digits rolled around.

She heard her mom laugh and say, "Okay, I see that little tidbit's got you wide awake. I'm heading out to work, sweetheart. I'll be driving up to the lake after my shift. I probably won't get up there in time for the rehearsal dinner, but I will see you up there tonight."

Katie nodded, although it was painful, and Pam bent down and kissed her forehead. She heard her mom call out as she was heading for the stairs, "I'll call you on my break, baby—just to make sure you're up and around."

"Thanks, Mama," Katie called back weakly.

Katie gently rested back against her pillows and tried to remember what happened the night before even though the mental effort felt like it was driving shards of glass into her brain.

Closing her eyes, the previous evening's event started coming back to her in snippets.

She saw flashes of herself taking shots, beginning to feel sick, making her way across the bar, getting drinks spilled on her, and Jason coming in the bathroom.

Then…nothing.

She couldn't remember anything past that.

Ah. Katie hated the feeling of not being in control. There was a reason she had gravitated towards the legal profession. It was a world that was all about laws, which were the ultimate arbiters of control and rules.

Not being able to remember her own actions was the ultimate loss of control.

Gingerly, she pushed up onto her elbows. Squinting at the pain in her head, she forced herself to complete the task and come to an upright position. She tried to swallow, but found the task much more difficult than it should be because it felt like her throat had been coated down with cotton balls.

Taking in a deep breath, she lifted her arms above her head to stretch. As she did, she looked down and noticed that she was wearing her regular nightshirt. The Def Leppard shirt. She couldn't remember how she'd gotten home, let alone how she'd gotten into the shirt.

Damn, everything was so foggy. If it wouldn't be so painful, she'd shake her head to clear it.

Just then, she glanced at the clock and realized that it was about time to get this show on the road.

She climbed into the shower and let the hot water stream over her sore and aching muscles. She tried to sing a few times to clear her thoughts, but the rise in pressure it caused inside her head was just too great. It seemed her concert was going to have to be canceled.

After her shower, Katie made her way slowly back into her bedroom and repacked her suitcase. She felt like she was moving at a snail's pace, but she couldn't help it. She was just so sore, nauseous, and foggy-headed.

Her eyes, once again, turned to her nightstand to check the time and see how she was doing according to the schedule and was shocked by the realization that this was just a few hours past the time she had pulled into town yesterday.

God. So much had happened in twenty-four hours. Being home. Seeing everyone. Seeing Jason.

Coffee. Katie needed a cup of coffee.

As she made her way downstairs, the Sherlock in her was still trying to piece together the events of the night before; and, at the same time, she was silently praying that Mom or Aunt Wendy had made coffee already. If it was already made, she would have just enough time for a cup (or maybe two) before she got out onto the road.

Her head still felt fuzzy, but about halfway down the stairs, she did recognize the intoxicating aroma of freshly brewed java drifting into her nostrils.

Ahhhhh, yes, she thought. *Thank you, God.*

As she stepped into the kitchen, her energy spiked as she made a beeline for the coffee machine, just as she heard a deep voice behind her say, "Good morning, Sunshine."

Katie screamed and jumped two feet in the air, twisting as she did so, and landed so precariously that, before she knew it, she had fallen flat on her rear.

Her heart was racing like it was running from the cops as she looked up through the blonde strands of hair that covered her face like Cousin It. There, sprawled on the kitchen floor, beneath the curtain of hair, she saw that Jason was already beside her reaching down to help her up, laughing so hard, she was surprised he hadn't doubled over and fallen beside her.

Seriously? It wasn't that *funny,* Katie thought as Jason's strong hands wrapped around her and she was back on her feet.

Tingles spread through her at his touch and she tried to shake it off while she admitted to herself that yeah, it probably was *that* funny.

✦ ✦ ✦

As Jason helped Katie off the floor, he tried not to notice how good she looked in her red v-neck t-shirt and blue jeans, but *damn*, she did look good. The hint of cleavage that was peeking out of her shirt made his mouth water. Literally.

"Still unsteady on your feet, huh, Kit Kat?" Jason teased, trying to direct the conversation away from anything remotely sexual.

"I'm not unsteady on my feet," she declared defensively once she was standing upright again and had the leverage to push away from him. "*You* scared me. That's why I fell."

"Yet another thing that's my fault," Jason pointed out as he went to take his seat, once again, at the kitchen table.

Jason saw something flicker across Katie's face, but he couldn't decipher what it might have been. As fast as it had appeared, it was gone again. She groaned. "I need coffee."

He watched as she poured herself a cup and waited while she took a few sips. He had always known that talking to Katie before she was ready to listen was a mistake, so he waited patiently. Sure enough, after a few minutes, she asked, "What are you doing here? I thought you would already be headed up to the lake with Bobby."

"Well, Sophie wasn't feeling very well this morning,

so Bobby wanted to drive her up so he could take care of her and make sure that she had everything she needed."

"She's sick? Oh, no! Is it bad? Oh my gosh! I should be with her. I'm her maid of honor!" Katie quickly set her cup down and headed towards the front door. "I can't believe I got drunk last night. What was I thinking?!"

"Slow down, Kit Kat." Jason held her arm gently as she rushed past him. "Sophie's fine. It's just a bad hangover. And believe me, she would rather have my brother taking care of her anyway. They left a couple of hours ago, so they should just about be at the lake by now."

Jason felt all of the tension leave Katie's muscles. Her arms relaxed, her shoulders dropped down, and she let out a huge sigh.

She stepped back into the kitchen. "Well, if that's the case, then I need one more cup before I hit the road."

Jason stood, walked over to the fridge, and pulled out eggs, butter, cheese, veggies, and orange juice.

"Sit down. Drink your coffee," he said amiably. "I'll fix you an omelet before we hit the road."

"Are you headed up there right now, too? I mean, like I said, I thought that you would've left earlier."

Katie scooted by him to take a seat at the breakfast bar as she said this, and he felt her body brush against his back as she passed. The contact sent electricity surging through his body.

He tried to ignore it.

"I had a meeting with a surveyor that ran a little late. I was just headed out of town when I got a call from Grandpa J saying he thought you might need a ride," he said neutrally. He knew he would need to ease into this discussion carefully with Katie. She was *not* going to like this little turn of events.

"Oh, that's sweet of him, but really, I'm totally fine to drive," Katie assured him as she lifted her hand, waving it in a gesture of dismissal.

"That very well may be the case, but he wasn't calling into question your ability to drive. It was more a question of having the transportation necessary to do so."

Katie tilted her head and scrunched her nose the way she always did when something didn't quite make sense to her. Jason had forgotten how much he loved that face, it had always reminded him of a bunny. She was so adorable it actually made his chest hurt.

After she downed the last of her second cup of coffee, she sat up straighter looking more alert by the minute. Her innocent movement, however, was making his jeans grow tighter and tighter by the second. Katie was seriously filling out that red shirt and it was killing Jason not to be able to strip her out of it. He was beginning to sweat and it had nothing to do with the stove he was standing in front of.

"I have my rental car," she said, her eyebrows knitted together, totally oblivious to the internal battle her lovely lady lumps were causing him.

"Well, yeah, that's the thing," Jason explained as he plated her omelet and set it in front of her at the breakfast bar. He, then, went to retrieve the Tabasco sauce—Katie *always* had Tabasco sauce on her eggs. As he set the small, red bottle in front of her, he said, "There's no air in the back tires of your car."

"What?" Katie looked alarmed.

"Eat," he commanded as he pushed both the hot sauce and the plate closer to her and leaned his elbows on the counter. He waited until she took her first bite and then continued.

"Both of the back tires are flat. I called the rental company and they're sending out a tow truck, but they didn't know how long it would take. I told them that you had arranged other transportation, so they are only charging you for one day."

"Other transportation," her eyes narrowed, "...meaning you?"

"Yes, indeed," Jason confirmed cheerfully as he turned to wash out the pan he had used to cook the eggs. "So eat up, and we'll hit the road."

"That's so weird," she mused as she worked her way through the plate of eggs and sipped the orange juice. "I wonder what could have happened. Why would both back tires just go flat like that?"

Slipping off the barstool after finishing every last bite, she bumped Jason's hip with hers in a friendly gesture of camaraderie as she set her plate in the sink. "Thanks for the breakfast. I'm starting to feel human again. And also for taking care of the rental and the ride to the lake. Just…thanks, Jas, for everything."

He smiled and nodded at her. What he *actually* wanted to do was pick her up, set her on the counter, and kiss her so hard she wouldn't be able to think straight. But he knew she wasn't ready for that. Yet.

Things had gotten way too physical yesterday, and he needed to establish their connection on a non-physical level if he had any chance at not scaring her off again.

Her full lips tilted up as she smiled warmly at him as they finished up the dishes. After they finished wiping their hands on the dish towels that hung beside the sink, he turned to head out of the kitchen, but before he took a step, Katie threw her arms around his neck, lifting up on her toes, and pulled him into a tight embrace.

After the moment of shock wore off, Jason wrapped his arms around her and held her firmly against him. He inhaled deeply, breathing in the scent of her hair and just *feeling* the intensity of the moment.

As much as he was enjoying her being in his arms he knew that there was something going on with her, she was holding onto him like her life depended on it. Rubbing her back, he gently asked, "Hey, are you okay?"

He felt her chest rise as her breath caught and she

gave him one more squeeze before leaning back with a small, almost sad, smile on her lips. Tears brimmed her gorgeous baby blues as she whispered, "It's just really good to see you again, Jas."

Then, the next second, the moment was over. She patted him on the chest as she spun away. "I gotta go pee before we hit the road, Jack."

Damn.

He *really* didn't know what he was gonna do if—no, scratch that, when—she left again. Jason didn't want to think about that or even face it. So he decided to put the thought as far out of his mind as possible for the rest of the weekend.

Chapter Seventeen

Katie's muscles felt like they had melted on the drive up to Whisper Lake. Like she was floating on a cloud. In fact, she couldn't remember the last time she had been *this* relaxed. She and Jason were riding in companionable silence, his music was playing low in the background, and she was watching the beautiful and increasingly tree-lined scenery that was so familiar to her.

Katie used the time to reflect on how things were going this weekend, particularly with Jason. She had felt so overwhelmed when she hugged him. On the one hand, it had felt really good to be in his arms—safe and right. On the other hand, she had absolutely no idea what had possessed her to hug him in the first place, and that made her feel dangerously out of control.

She had just suddenly had this overwhelming desire to hold him—and she went with it. Which was not like her at all.

Jason had always been her friend. Nothing more. Well, until the night that all changed. Still, Katie couldn't understand—why was she was *feeling* so much for him now?

The feelings she'd been having since she'd heard his voice from behind her on the driveway yesterday were not of the friend variety. That much she could admit to.

Then, because she certainly didn't feel ready to dwell on why she felt that way, she decided to try to move on and piece together the night before.

Like any good mystery, she started with what the parts of the puzzle she knew as fact and figured she would expand from there.

The shots. Feeling sick. Getting drinks spilled on her. Locking herself in the bathroom. Jason coming in. Jason taking off his shirt—whoa, okay, that was a new one.

Katie vaguely remembered the sensation of being carried by him. Then leaning her head against his window. Then she started to remember being mad at Jason.

Wait.

Why was she mad at him again?

Why did the girls' faces from last night's debauchery pop into her head when she thought about Jason?

Oh. Yeah, that's right. The girls had done shots because they had all done various naughty things in Jason's truck. In fact, as the night had gone on, the girls who Jason had fooled around with made it a running joke to add 'in a black Chevy truck' each time they took out a question that had a sexual nature to it. It had been *really* irritating.

But then...why didn't she feel mad again right now when she remembered the truck adventures? Wait—she seemed to remember Jason saying he hadn't done anything with any of those girls.

Why would he deny it? Everyone knew how he was. His nickname was Romeo.

Better get to the bottom of this.

"Jas, do you remember last night when I told you why I had taken all those shots?" She saw his hands grip the steering wheel and his posture stiffen.

"Yep, Kit Kat. I wasn't the one who was smashed," he said tightly.

"Whatever. Anyways, did you tell me that you didn't do anything with Lisa, Elena, Kylie, or Tiffany?"

Katie watched as Jason nodded his head in the affirmative but remained silent.

Okay...

Talking out loud, Katie reasoned, "That's so weird. Why would those girls lie about that? It's not like they were trying to impress someone. We're not in high school anymore. I mean, we're pushing thirty."

She waited for Jason to reply, but there was no response from the peanut gallery.

"I mean, they *had* to be lying though, right? Because if they're not lying, that means that you're lying. And you don't lie."

Nothing. Crickets.

Shaking her head, she tried to clear the fog that was

in her brain. She felt like this was some kind of Sudoku puzzle of drunkenness. It would all come together if she could just find the one missing piece.

If she wasn't mistaken, her silent travel companion held that piece.

"Fine." She tried another angle. "So let's say they weren't lying. Maybe you let someone use your truck."

Silence. He did, however, shoot her a look that told her in no uncertain terms that theory was crazy.

"Right," Katie agreed with his unspoken criticism. "Neither you *or* Nick would *ever* let anyone else drive your trucks."

She stared at Jason's profile, hoping he would fill in the blanks for her, but it seemed that he was going to remain tight-lipped on this topic.

Although Jason certainly wasn't verbally offering any new insights, he wasn't exactly not communicating with her. His body language was screaming for her to drop it. But, she just couldn't bring herself to let it go. Something just wasn't adding up.

Man, she wished she hadn't drunk so much last night. It would be *so* much easier to figure all of this out if she didn't still have 'mush brain' from last night's overindulgence. Facts. She just needed to stick to the facts.

"Okay, so let's begin with what we know. The girls said they had several 'experiences' in the cab or bed of a black Chevy truck parked at Pickler's Field. They have no reason to lie. So let's proceed on the assumption that they are, in fact, telling the truth."

She waited to see if Jason would at least give her a nod of agreement, since apparently the cat had his tongue. But no. Not even the smallest gesture of encouragement.

Fine, then. She didn't need him. She could do this all by her lonesome.

"You told me that you never did anything with those girls, either in or out of your truck, and I know you don't lie."

An uneasy sensation came over her as she watched Jason adjust his grip on the steering wheel. She had a feeling that if she pursued this, she would be passing a point she couldn't come back from. She would be opening up a strange new can of worms that could never be closed. Could she face whatever was at the end of her yellow brick road of hoochies?

Grandpa J's voice sounded in her head. "*Better an ugly truth than a beautiful lie.*"

She couldn't count the number of times she'd heard him say that over the years. Maybe she should just face this. Whatever *this* was.

Honestly, Katie knew that none of this would be bothering her so much if the girls hadn't been giving her the strangest looks when they offered up their answers. It was such a weird vibe they were sending, and she just couldn't shake it.

She continued building her logic, taking strength from Grandpa J's words of wisdom.

"And you and Nick were the only two with black trucks."

Oh no. It couldn't be... Nick would never. A sick feeling welled up in her stomach.

Katie spoke slowly, trying not to jump to any conclusions, even though her brain was currently hopping like a bunny on the conclusion trampoline. "So if you didn't do anything, then...wait. Are you saying that *Nick* did all of those things with those girls?! That it was *his* truck? Are you saying Nick cheated on me?"

"I'm not saying anything. I haven't said a word during this entire investigation, Sherlock. That's all you." Jason said through a forced laugh.

Katie spun around at the tone in Jason's voice. He sounded more than a little mad.

Why would *he* be mad?

"Jason, I'm serious. Tell me. Is that what happened? Did Nick cheat on me?" She couldn't believe those words had actually just come out of her mouth.

She waited, but Jason didn't reply. He just stared straight ahead.

"Jason. Answer me. Did. Nick. Cheat. On. Me?" Although she was striving to stay calm, she heard the strain coming through in her voice.

"Katie, it was a long time ago," Jason said, his jaw tense. "Just leave it alone."

"Seriously. You *know* that's not going to happen." She could not believe that he wasn't answering her. Why wouldn't he just put her out of her misery? Was this some kind of a sick joke to him? "This isn't a joke. It's not funny. Come on, Jason, tell me! Did he?"

"It's not my place to say." Jason set his jaw in that stubborn way he had, and Katie could tell that he had no plans to tell her anything. Frustration bubbled up inside of her like lava ready to erupt from a volcano.

"What are you talking about? Of course it is. You were Nick's best friend and my...my..." her voice trailed off as she lost some of the steam powering her locomotive of indignation.

Jason took his soulful brown eyes off the road, briefly, to meet her gaze.

"I was your *what*?" he asked pointedly. His voice was low, harsh—almost dangerous in its intensity.

Hello!

At the tone of Jason's words, she felt a jolt...below the belt.

Wow, she must be losing her mind. Only a crazy person would get turned on in the middle of *this* conversation.

Katie's breathing was starting to get very labored, and her head was spinning. Perfect, just perfect. She was about to have a panic attack.

No. There was no way she was going to let that happen. Not before she got some answers, at least. She opened her mouth to speak but Jason beat her to it.

"I was your what, Katie?" he asked again, this time without the same edge to his voice, but with a lot more melancholy.

"You were my…you are my…" Katie hesitated, doing a Google search of her mind for the right words. She didn't know how to explain, how to make it clear, everything that Jason was to her.

Growing up she'd always just thought of Jason as her best friend. He'd teased her mercilessly and never showed any interest in her. She'd honestly never thought that she had deeper feelings for him. Yes, there had been the brief kiss, her first kiss, at Chelle's birthday party when they were eleven, but he'd treated her like she'd had the plague after that. He'd avoided her the rest of the summer.

Then, Nick had moved next door and Katie had put any confusion she'd had over her lip lock with Jas out of her mind. Katie had always compartmentalized things. Nick was her boyfriend. Jason was her friend.

The roles that Nick and Jason had played in her life had never confused her until the night of the accident. Since that night, things had not been so black and white for Katie.

At a loss of what else to say Katie opened her mouth and said, "You're my…Jason."

✦ ✦ ✦

Hearing Katie describe him as '*her* Jason,' caused emotion to well up in Jason like he'd never felt before. It was painful and constricting. Her words had reached inside his chest and squeezed it like a lemon.

She wanted to know the truth about Nick. It broke

Jason's heart to think that he was going to be the one to tell her this, but, at this point, he figured it was like ripping off a Band-Aid—quick and fast was the best way.

"Yes, Nick cheated on you," he stated matter-of-factly. He waited for her to cry, to yell, to do…something.

But she just stared at him. He could feel her crystal blue stare locked on him like a heat seeking missile. Jason waited, knowing that this was Katie and she would need time to process.

"And you knew. The whole time," her tone was even. It was more of a statement of fact than a question.

"Yes."

"Why didn't you tell me?" Katie asked in barely a whisper.

Jason raked his hand through his hair and took a deep breath. He really did not want to be having this conversation with her. After returning his hand to the wheel, his fingers opened and closed over the hard plastic.

"Because, Katie, it was complicated." Jason knew that no way was she going to let him off with that explanation, but he really had no idea what else to say.

"How 'complicated' is it to say, 'Hey, Katie, you know Nick has slept with half the female population of Harper's Crossing?' Doesn't seem that complicated to me."

Glancing over, Jason saw that those big blue eyes he

loved so much had fury beneath their surface and it was all directed at him. Shit, talk about shooting the messenger. If looks could kill, Jason would have been a man down.

Screw it. He figured he might as well start at the beginning. It would be the only way she might even *sort of* understand.

"Remember the summer between freshman and sophomore year that you spent at your Grandma's in Chicago?"

"Yes. Nick and I talked every day," Katie said. Out of the corner of his eye, he saw her blond head nodding, but her tone sounded borderline defensive.

"Well, one night about a week before you came home, we went to a party at David Price's house and we drank—a lot. I left with Krissy that night, and I didn't see who Nick left with, but the next day he came over and told me that he and Tiffany had hooked up."

Jason paused, he figured she might need a moment to let the information sink in. She didn't choose to take it.

"And?" Katie demanded stridently.

He knew that she wasn't going to like what he had to say but he also knew she would want the truth, the whole truth and nothing but the truth.

"And I told him he needed to break up with you. He said that he couldn't, that he loved you. I said that if he wasn't going to break up with you, then he, at least, needed to tell you what had happened. He wasn't happy about it but, finally, he agreed.

"You came home that Friday, and I really did think that he was planning on telling you. But, remember his mom made that big dinner? And you were so happy to be home and happy to see his family? He couldn't do it. He promised he would tell you the next day, but the next day turned into the next week, the next week turned into the next month. And he never told you.

"As far as I know, he didn't cheat again until the next summer when we were all up at the lake. Remember that lifeguard, Britney? Well, he hooked up with her. He said that it wouldn't happen again because we were leaving. I believed him. Again.

"Once our junior year was in full swing, I heard rumors about his extracurricular activities and confronted him. He admitted that he had been seeing some girls, and I told him that if he didn't tell you, I would. He promised he would. He never did.

"I don't know, Katie. Time kept passing and he never said anything. And I just didn't want to burst the bubble of happiness you were living in."

Katie was quiet. Jason wasn't sure if she was thinking and would rather be left alone, but he didn't want her to shut him out again.

"Katie, talk to me."

"What do you want me to say? That I was an idiot? That I was a fool? Seriously, Jason, did everyone at school know? Was it some big joke?" she asked.

"I don't think that many people knew. The girls

didn't want it getting around, and honestly, it was only a handful of them. And you were not an idiot. You had a boyfriend you trusted. That doesn't make you an idiot. If anyone was an idiot, it was Nick." Jason paused a beat and then added quietly, "To be honest, I never knew how he could even look at anyone else when he had you."

Chapter Eighteen

Even in her heightened emotional state, Katie couldn't help but be soothed by the gorgeous greenery that surrounded Whisper Lake as well as the quaint downtown area they had to drive through in order to get to the hotel.

This place had always been where she had come to heal her soul, and maybe it could do its work again, this time. She hoped so.

As they stepped out of the truck, she breathed in the clean mountain air and let it revitalize her. She felt it refreshing her body as it refreshed her spirit, and she gave in completely to its ability to do so.

Katie thought about what she had learned on the drive. Well...continued to think would be more accurate. After the big 'reveal,' she had told Jason she had a headache and wanted to take a nap. She had sat with her eyes closed for the last hour of the drive, faking sleep.

She realized during that meditative interlude that, surprisingly, she wasn't mad at Nick. At all. Maybe it was because so much time had passed—and since he was gone, it wasn't like she could confront him about it anyway—but really, she wasn't devastated or even *upset* that he had been with other girls.

But, she was mad. It was just that her anger was all directed in the very last place it should be. Pointed right at Jason. Which made no sense. Except for the fact that she had always trusted him, and it felt like he had betrayed that trust. She knew, logically, that he was not the one to blame, but apparently her logic had decided to stay in California because she certainly hadn't been behaving or thinking very logically since she'd landed in Illinois.

As she and Jason walked up to the hotel lobby, Katie stopped to text Sophie to let her know that she had arrived and to ask her how she was feeling. Before Katie had even put away her phone, Sophie texted back that she was feeling much better and that she would see her soon for massages and facials.

When Katie looked up from the text exchange, she saw Jason walking towards her with two key cards in his hands. "Got us all checked in," he smiled cheerfully. "Come on. You're on the third floor. I'll carry your bags."

A weak smile lifted on Katie's lips. She couldn't help it. It didn't matter that she was hurt or mad at Jason, she had no choice but to smile when he kept thinking of her, her needs, taking care of her. Growing up, he had never been so infuriatingly gallant.

Well, apparently he had… she just hadn't known

about it at the time.

They both remained silent on the trip up the elevator. When they arrived at room 318, Jason inserted the key and held the door open for her. After Katie had walked inside, he smiled and placed her bags just inside the door.

She saw something brewing in the chocolate depths of his eyes, but she couldn't quite place what it was. Before she figured it out, Jason pulled her into a quick hug and said, "Okay, Kit Kat, I'm gonna go and get settled in my room. Text or call if you need anything."

Katie nodded against the solidness of Jason's firm chest, feeling torn. As hurt as she felt right now, she had to admit that she didn't want to see him go. She wanted him to stay here with her. Hold her in his arms. When Jason's arms were around her, the world didn't feel so confusing. It felt right.

Still, she let him walk away without saying anything.

When the door shut, she stared at it for several minutes. Then, when Jason didn't magically walk back in, she shook out her arms and tried to focus. Unpack. That's what she should do. After that deed was done, she checked out the bathroom, opened up the tiny bottles of shampoo and conditioner and smelled them. She pulled aside the drapes and spent a few minutes enjoying the view of people hustling and bustling through the courtyard below.

Katie leaned her head against the glass as a sigh escaped her mouth. Anxiety was rushing through her veins and she was beginning to feel claustrophobic. So, she made an executive decision to head downstairs to check out the hotel grounds. After pocketing her key, she grabbed her purse and headed out the door.

She hadn't even made it halfway across the lobby before she saw a familiar face at the check-in desk. Chelle. Her diamond friend.

Joy filled her when she walked up and gave her friend a huge bear hug. Last night was still somewhat of a blur, but she did have clear memories of catching up with her long lost friend.

"Where's David?" Katie asked, careful not to let the cheerful tone in her voice waver as she pulled back from her hug.

"Oh, he couldn't make it. He had to work at the last minute. But that's okay, because I was able to bum a ride with Eddie so I didn't have to drive by myself."

"Yay! I'm so glad you're here!" Katie clapped her hands together and smiled from ear to ear, suddenly feeling like she was back in elementary school. That had been happening a lot over the past couple of days. Katie, honestly, hadn't realized just how much she'd changed since she'd moved away to college until she'd come back this weekend.

If someone would have asked Katie a year ago, a month ago, or even a week ago, if she was happy, she would have instantly replied, "*yes.*" But, she was starting to think that she wasn't, in fact, happy. The life that she'd made for herself was beginning to feel emptier and emptier.

After Chelle finished checking in, she turned to Katie and her big brown eyes looked filled with emotion as she said hesitantly, "There's something that I need to talk to you about."

"Okay," Katie agreed readily.

"Umm...maybe we should go sit down," Chelle motioned to the cozy couches that were positioned in front of a large fireplace with a roaring fire in the lobby.

Katie nodded in agreement and the two girls made their way over to them. On the short trip, something dawned on Katie. Apparently, even smack dab in her very own existential crisis, her Sherlock meter was at high alert. As they sat down, Katie asked excitedly, "Oh my gosh, Chelle! Are you pregnant?"

Chelle laughed nervously and said, "No, I wish that were all it was."

Katie's brows tightened in concern at Chelle's reluctance to tell her. She hated seeing her diamond friend looking so uneasy. "It's okay, whatever it is, just tell me. I'm a big girl. I'm sure I can handle it."

Chelle nodded and took a deep breath before diving in, saying, "Look...you know me, I am *not* about gossip and drama, but I really think you need to know something before you see everyone at the wedding tomorrow."

Katie nodded as she felt the all-too-familiar knot beginning to form in her stomach.

Chelle plowed forward. "Here's the thing. After you left The Grill last night, I overheard Tiffany and Kylie talking about how awkward it was for them to be taking shots in front of you…when it was about stuff they had done with Nick." Chelle looked worried and then said quickly, "I'm so sorry you had to find out like this."

Katie waved her hand dismissively, "Don't be, I didn't. I already figured that out and then confirmed it. Apparently Nick cheated quite a lot during our relationship, a fact of which I was blissfully and stupidly unaware."

"Not stupidly," Chelle corrected.

Katie appreciated her friend's support, but it didn't really change the facts. "Thanks for saying that. I can't help but feel like an idiot. I mean, I'm Sherlock, right? How did I miss that?"

"Because, you trust people you love. And I know that you loved Nick. You guys were together forever. You would have no reason to think that anything was up with him." Chelle paused for a minute, "No pun intended."

Katie looked at her friend, who sat with a totally straight face. Katie felt laughter bubble up inside of her as her head fell back and she began laughing harder than she had in a long time. Not only had Katie always thought Chelle was hilarious, she had always had a talent for knowing just what to say to lighten the mood.

As her laughing fit died down, Katie wiped under her eyes that had watered during her hyena impression.

Chelle smiled warmly at her as she asked, "But, seriously are you okay with all of this breaking decade-old news?"

Katie nodded, "Yeah, you know…it was a long time ago. Truthfully, I'm not even that upset at Nick. It's weird because mostly…I just feel betrayed by Jason. Which is totally ridiculous. Logically, I know he didn't do anything. But, I don't know. It's just…he was my friend, too! He was my friend for a lot longer than he was Nick's, as a matter of fact, and I just can't believe he didn't tell me."

"Hmmm," Chelle murmured noncommittally.

"What?" Katie asked.

Chelle shrugged. "It's just interesting. Even though Nick was the one who cheated on you, the only real emotion you feel about it is directed at Jason."

"Well, I'm probably just upset with Jason because…well, I mean, Nick is gone. So how can I be mad at him?" Katie tried to reason out her emotional wheel of misfortune that had randomly landed on Jason when she'd stepped up and taken her turn at life.

Chelle looked unconvinced. "I don't know. Last night when you locked yourself in the bathroom, you seemed *pretty* upset that Jason had been with all those girls. So here's the real question you need to answer: would it bother you more if it *had* turned out to be Jason that had messed around with all those girls? Or are you relieved that it was Nick?"

Those words hit Katie like an arrow in her chest. Chelle's question had unwittingly gotten straight to the heart of the matter. The reason she hadn't spoken to Jason while Nick had lied in that hospital bed. The question whose answer she still hadn't come to terms with, or had forgiven herself for, since the night her life had turned upside down.

Was she relieved it was Nick?

Katie felt raw. Exposed. She opened her mouth to answer and then closed it when nothing came out. She thought for a minute and then opened her mouth again to speak. Still nothing came out, and she closed it, having said nothing.

Concern filled Chelle's big brown eyes, "Katie...."

Before she was able to finish her thought, Katie's phone buzzed loudly. More than a little relieved for the distraction from a topic that, it was clear now, needed to be addressed, Katie pulled out her phone and saw that it was Sophie texting to say that all the girls were at the salon and asked where she was.

"Looks like it's massage time," Katie explained to Chelle as she texted back that she'd be right there. "We need to get over there."

Chelle nodded and grabbed her small overnight bag and they headed off across the hotel complex to find the day spa. Katie hoped that maybe a nice, luxurious massage would be just the thing to help her mentally refocus.

As the two girls walked into the upscale day spa, the first people they saw were the Sloan girls. They were sitting on a long bench talking with a very radiant looking Sophie. When Sophie looked up and saw Katie and Chelle, she squealed.

"Hey, Chelle. Katie. It's gonna be just a few more minutes. Katie, why don't you have a seat so we can grill you on your fabulous life in San Francisco? We haven't really had a chance to yet."

Haley Sloan interjected cheerfully, "Ooooo, yes. It was so loud at the bar last night we really didn't get to talk. So, Katie, what's it like being a big-time lawyer?" Katie laughed and sat down, as did Chelle.

Katie said, "Um, well, I've already bored Chelle with this, so sorry, diamond friend. You have to sit through it again. I'll be brief, no pun intended."

Chelle laughed and Katie smiled as she continued.

"Really, it's not as exciting as it sounds. I'm on the fast track, that's true. But honestly, when I think about making partner lately, it seems less like a dream job and more like, I don't know...prison. It seems like committing to twenty years of having no life. Which is bizarre, because I thought that's what I've always wanted."

The Quad Squad and Sophie exchanged knowing looks, and Katie said, "What? What was that look?"

Sophie smiled mischievously and said, "Well, maybe you're figuring out that there's something *else* you've always wanted."

Katie's eyes widened. She didn't know what to say.

They couldn't possibly be talking about Jason? Right?

She decided to try and play it cool and shrugged, "Maybe. In just the short time I've been home, I've realized how much I've missed everyone all these years. I think I've been really lonely, you know?"

"Oh, we know," Sophie and The Quad Squad all said in unison, and they all laughed. But Katie couldn't help but feel just a little unsettled that they were alluding to something she was *not* comfortable talking about. Or even, you know, *acknowledging*.

Just then, Aunt Wendy and Sophie's mom, Grace, popped their heads into the waiting room.

"Hey there, chickadees," Aunt Wendy sing-songed. "I just wanted to make sure all my little chickees made it into the coop on time. Are y'all good?"

"We're good," they all chorused.

"Are you staying for massages?" Sophie asked hopefully.

"Oh, gosh no, honey," Aunt Wendy waved off that idea. "We've got too much to do. We're busier'n a one-armed paper hanger. We just wanted to check in on you girls."

With that, the "Aunt Wendy Tornado" blew out again as quickly as it had blown in, Grace along with it.

Just as the two women were headed out, the guys came in.

Katie asked with surprise. "Are you guys getting massages, too?"

Jason laughed. "Kit Kat, did you read your itinerary? Did you even skim it?"

Katie swatted his arm playfully, and she definitely noticed Sophie and the Sloan girls exchanging knowing glances during this little exchange.

Before she was able to suss out exactly what all the covert glances meant, the day spa attendant came out and told the assembled crowd, "Okay, we're going to be calling you back in small groups. So first we have the couples' massages. That's..."—she consulted her clipboard—"Sophie and Bobby and...let's see...Jason and Katie."

Katie whipped her head around to look at Jason. "Couples massage?"

Jason put his hands up in a 'not me' gesture and chuckled, "Hey, maybe it's a 'best man/maid of honor' thing."

Sophie placed her hands on Katie's shoulders from behind and pushed her towards the open door to the back. She trilled, "Clerical mix-up, booking snafu, fate... Why overthink it? Just enjoy."

With that, she sent Katie off after Jason with one final shove.

As Katie walked towards the back, suspicious of the whole thing, she could hear the Quad Squad giggling behind her.

What was going on?

✦ ✦ ✦

Jason didn't know how he was going to make it

through this massage. Every time he turned his head, he got another little glimpse of Katie's uncovered flesh. A shoulder here, a thigh there. It was enough to drive a man crazy. His brain was so fogged with lust that he could barely string two coherent thoughts together. Luckily, he didn't have to, because Katie hadn't stopped talking since they laid down, she was like the nervous chatter Energizer bunny, she kept going and going and going. He had barely had to grunt agreeably every thirty seconds.

Katie's nonstop talkathon came to an abrupt halt, however, when the massage therapist had intervened, very politely suggesting that their massages might be a more relaxing experience if they were enjoyed in silence.

That was fine with Jason. He was worried that he was going to be held responsible for remembering some tidbit she came out with during that long, nervous monologue because damn, he would never remember one word that was said when he and Katie Lawson were naked, two feet away from each other.

Just the knowledge that nothing separated their bodies but two feet of air and two flimsy sheets… Aw, hell, who was he kidding? He was lying here wondering how he was going to make it through this massage when what he should be wondering is how he was going to make it through this weekend.

Chapter Nineteen

Katie headed back to her room to get ready for the rehearsal and just prayed that she wouldn't run into anyone she knew on the way. She was far too shaky and addle-brained from spending an hour next to Jason Sloan in the buff. Her mind and imagination had been over-sexed.

She shook her head to clear it.

Wow. She found that to be singularly ineffective.

The entire massage, all she had been able to do was think about the fact that Jason was within arm's reach with nothing but a thin sheet covering his naughty bits. It was just too much. She was overheated.

Thankfully, she made it to her room without being stopped and leaned against the inside of the door once she had closed it. *Just breathe.* She just needed to stop long enough to take a deep breath. Oh, man. She didn't feel like she had *really* been able to do that since she had arrived.

There was no time for it now either. She had to get ready for the rehearsal and rehearsal dinner afterward.

Lifting her hands, she rubbed them over her face

then pushed off the door and moved to the closet. Katie slipped on a sleek red dress and strappy heels before she freshened her makeup, straightened her hair, and added a delicate gold chain and bracelet to complete the ensemble.

As she looked at her reflection, she realized that she had chosen to wear two things that were red today. Hmmm…could that be a coincidence? Or was she subconsciously deciding to "dress to impress" a certain someone who really liked how she looked in red?

A small smile played on her lips as she remembered an incident that had occurred sophomore year of high school. She had come to school in a new red sweater with a little pep in her step. Katie had always loved the "high" that came with wearing new clothes or shoes.

That high didn't come close to competing with what she'd felt when she'd walked into English class. Katie would never forget how Jason had stared at her in a way she had never seen him stare at *anyone*. At first she'd felt uncomfortable and she hadn't liked it. But then, she sorta did.

When she'd sat down in her seat, Jason had leaned forward and said, "Kit Kat, red is your color."

Even now, she blushed thinking about how many nights she had played back that exchange in her head during high school. There was something so primal and intimate about the way he had said those six innocent words to her.

It wasn't even that it was some epic compliment or

anything. It wasn't so much about *what* he had said. No, it was more about the *way* he had stared and *how* he had said it.

Okay, she needed to backburner that mental topic. There was absolutely nothing good that could come from getting herself hot and bothered right now.

Moving on to less arousing, more stressful topics. Yep. That should do the trick. She knew she was going to need to talk to Jason about *everything* before she left this weekend. She didn't think her mental health could stand another ten solid years of not having some sort of closure.

Mentally, she made a list of everything that was in the clearing-the-air category. First up, she needed to address what went on the night of Nick's funeral and during the weeks she had ignored him leading up to the funeral. Also, she couldn't forget the most recent incident in the cab of his truck in the back parking lot of Bella.

She decided that, maybe after the rehearsal dinner, she would ask him to go for a walk or something. That way they could get all of it settled before the wedding so there wouldn't be any weird tension between them.

Proud of herself for making the decision to put her big girl panties on and face Jason, she headed down to the rehearsal with renewed confidence.

Katie arrived at the rehearsal, filled with determination. She could take control of her life. It was possible. Her whole body thrummed with purpose and the vibrant electric current it brought.

She was going to get the Jason situation under control tonight, come hell or high water.

She walked into the lobby of the small chapel where the wedding was being held to find a fun atmosphere of barely controlled chaos. The girls were standing together in little groups, chatting and laughing. The guys were joking around, Grandpa J keeping them from taking it too far. The older folks were sitting in the back pews, talking in low tones. Aunt Wendy was moving from one group to another, asking questions, imparting information, and making notes on her ever-present clipboard.

Katie felt a delicious tingle at the small of her back and the hairs on her arms and the back of her neck stood up.

She whirled around to see who was staring at her—and there was Jason. Smiling devilishly, like the sexy Romeo he was known to be.

His eyes were hungrily taking her in, and she felt her entire body coming to life. Any illusions she had worked up within herself about the prospect of 'taking control' over the effect Jason had over her all disappeared, like a David Blaine trick, with one look from those soulful brown eyes.

They stood there like that, looking at one another, heat burning inside Katie like sun shining through a magnifying glass, until Aunt Wendy clapped her hands loudly and said, "This is it, ladies and gents. Let's get this show on the road. We're starting from the beginning, when the fellas are up at the altar and the ladies are about to walk in. So go ahead and take your places—hens in the back, roosters in the front."

The crowd began to move around them, but Jason and Katie stood still. Katie felt entranced, mesmerized.

Finally, Jason strode slowly past her, catching her arm as he went. He leaned his mouth close to her ear as he went past and whispered huskily, "Red is *definitely* your color."

Oh boy.

✦ ✦ ✦

Jason stood at the front of the church, watching as the girls made their way down the aisle. He smiled at each of his cousins, in turn, and then at Amber.

Then…his heart slammed in his chest as Katie glided down the aisle, moving effortlessly, looking like she was walking on a cloud.

What was it about Katie Lawson that caused the whole world to disappear every time she was in the room?

What was it that made him care about *nothing* but seeing her smile every time he saw that gorgeous face?

Damn.

Jason made a decision right then and there. He had known that he and Katie were going to have to talk and put their cards on the table, but he'd been trying to be patient. Wait for the right time. Well, time was up. He was talking to Katie. Tonight.

About the weeks that Nick was in the hospital. About the night of Nick's funeral. About the ten years in between.

Because…damn. Just damn. There was no way Jason could survive another ten years without Katie in his life and it was time she knew that.

Chapter Twenty

Katie leaned back in her chair at the rehearsal dinner. She was surrounded by Chelle and the Sloan girls, and for the past hour had only suffered from passing thoughts of angsty talks with Jason. She was having more fun than she could remember having since...well, since the *last* time she'd hung out with Chelle and the Sloan girls.

But just as Katie thought she was enjoying a moment of Jason-free bliss, Chelle leaned over and said, "So I notice that a certain sexy Sloan brother has not been able to take his eyes off of you all night. Spoiler Alert: I don't mean Alex or Bobby."

"I don't know what you're talking about," Katie said with a shrug.

"I'm talking about Jason," Chelle clarified dryly.

Katie couldn't help but smile. "Yeah, I got that."

Chelle's eyes danced with amusement. "Jason can't stop looking at you."

Katie shook her head, and tried not to blush. "It's not like that."

Chelle eyes widened. "Oh, really?"

"Yes. Really." Katie confirmed quietly, hoping her friend would drop it before any of the other girls at the table picked up on their conversation.

She should have known better.

Instead of picking up on Katie's not-so-subtle cues, Chelle smiled as she suggested, "Well, then let's do what all the great scientific minds do when they want to test a hypothesis."

"Bust out a beaker and fire up the hot plate?" Katie asked.

"I think you're confusing freshman chem with great scientific minds, but, yes—the same principal. I propose an experiment."

Katie knew that trying to derail the Chelle-train once it had left the station was a losing battle and decided the path of least resistance would probably be the way to go. "What do you have in mind?"

"Well, he's looking over here every few seconds. Let's just pick a random point in time and then start counting. I propose that we will not get past five before he has to feed his Katie-glancing addiction."

"Oh my gosh. This is ridiculous." Katie felt her cheeks heat as her lips pulled up in a smile.

"No. It's not. Those peepers of his are hooked on some Katie Lawson. They're jonesin', man."

Katie shook her head again, feeling uncomfortable with all the attention, and secretly praying that Chelle was right.

Chelle's eyes narrowed as she said, "Okay, starting...*now*! 1...2...3..."

On 3, as if he had been programmed to, Jason gave a little glance their way. When he saw that they were looking at him, he raised his glass and his mouth turned up in his signature panty-melting sexy smile. Tingles spread through Katie's entire body at his gaze.

Hoping that she was hiding her reaction she raised her glass, at the same time Chelle did, back to him. Under her breath Chelle said, "Told you." Miraculously the girls managed to display enough good manners to keep themselves from doubling over with laughter until they had turned back around.

Katie *definitely* had not had this much fun in a very long time.

Sophie walked up to them, face flushed and glowing. She said, "Hello, lovelies. Wow, looks like you're having a good time."

Chelle and Katie both stood to hug Sophie and assured her that they were, indeed, having a great time.

"Oh, good," Sophie replied as Chelle and Katie both sat back down. "Well, you girls keep having fun. I'm heading to bed so I can be nice and rested for the big day tomorrow."

Katie sprung up out of her seat again. "Oh, I'll go with you, sweetie."

"No, no," Sophie replied a little too quickly. "I mean, that would be silly. I'm just going to sleep. I do that without help all the time, you know?"

There was a very suspicious blush creeping up Sophie's cheeks, so Katie decided to just drop it. "Okay, Sophiebell, but you know you can call me if you need anything. I've got my cell on."

"Oh, I know. I won't need anything. See you at brunch." Sophie said then turned and made an exit that would have left the Road Runner in the dust.

Before the door to the dining room had even shut from Sophie leaving, Chelle nudged Katie and motioned over to Bobby who was saying quick goodbyes and then heading out, too.

Chelle said, "Look at those two, sneaking off together. She's going to sleep, my ass. She might be going to bed, but I don't think she'll be sleeping."

Katie smiled. "Awe, I think it's romantic."

"You think what's romantic?" Jason's deep voice sounded behind her and every fiber of her being came alive with awareness. What was going on with her? She'd never been this sexually charged.

Chelle, thankfully, must have seen that Katie was not going to be keeping up her end of the conversation and explained smoothly, "Your brother and soon-to-be sister-in-law sneaking off together the night before their wedding."

"Yeah, they weren't too stealth about that little maneuver," Jason laughed as he brushed his hand over Katie's shoulder.

"Nope," Katie was, gratefully, able to get out, even with the chills running down her arms from the roughened pad of Jason's thumb grazing the base of her neck.

Jason gave her shoulder a squeeze as he asked, "Hey, Kit Kat, you want to go take a walk?"

His voice was deep and gravelly and Katie felt its effect shoot right between her legs. She tried to focus on the words he'd said, which was easier said than done, with the powerful arousal that was short-circuiting her senses.

Jason had asked to take a walk. Katie's stomach began to do somersaults. She felt her palms moisten. Her breathing began to get ragged. She quickly felt inside her clutch to check that she had, in fact, brought her trusty in-case-of-emergency paper bag and was relieved to find that she had.

"Yep, sounds good," she managed to reply over the large lump that had formed in her throat.

She felt herself being pulled into Chelle's arms as she whispered in her ear, "You're good. It's just Jason. Just talk to him."

Katie nodded against Chelle's shoulder and gave her one last squeeze before standing and heading out.

As they were walking out of the dining room, she asked Jason, "Do you think we need to tell anyone we're leaving?"

It was a stalling tactic, she freely admitted to herself.

"I think they'll figure it out. I have my cell, if they need anything," Jason said with a wink.

Jason reached out and intertwined his fingers in

Katie's as they stepped into the outdoor courtyard, which was lit up by twinkle lights. Katie shivered as they walked outside, partly from the drop in temperature, but mostly from the intense crackling of electricity she felt between herself and Jason.

Of course, Jason picked up on the slight tremor, since it seemed he noticed everything about Katie. He let go of her hand just long enough to take off his sports coat and wrap it around her shoulders.

She pulled it in front of her and he rested his hand on the small of her back as they made their way through the expansive garden area.

His thumb was rubbing small circles, and even through the jacket and her dress, his touch felt intimate.

Katie had no idea why she was so nervous. She had planned on asking Jason to talk anyway, so she should be prepared for this…but she wasn't.

They walked in silence until they came to a small bench in front of a waterfall feature. As they sat, Katie turned to face Jason. She was just about to speak but he beat her to it.

"Katie…"

Uh-oh, she thought. *No nickname. This must be serious.*

"I just want you to know how sorry I am—" he began.

"It's fine, Jas," she interrupted.

"No, it's not. In fact, I can't believe I did what I

did. I would completely understand if you couldn't forgive me." He looked so sincere, and it tugged at Katie's heartstrings.

"Jas, really, it's fine," she assured him. "I was upset at first, but I've been thinking, and I talked it through with Chelle, and I'm over it. Honestly. I mean, it's not like you were the one who cheated on me. You just didn't tell me."

Jason's brow furrowed. "What?"

"It's really not your fault," she continued, patting his hand. "I was just upset and you were there. I really just needed to process it. But you don't have to apologize."

He caught her hand mid-pat and held it firmly. "I'm not apologizing for not telling you about Nick cheating on you, Katie. I'm apologizing for what happened the night of Nick's funeral."

Katie felt her head start spinning. She tried to push past it and do what she should have done ten years ago. Words flew out of her mouth like they were being shot from a cannon, "You don't… Why are you… I should be… I'm the one who's sorry…"

She stopped and took a deep breath, closing her eyes against all of the crashing emotions that were pounding against her heart and her head. When she felt that she had herself under control, she opened them again and tried to collect her thoughts.

She decided to give her speech another try. "I'm the one who should be apologizing to *you* for that night.

And I am…I mean, I wanted to…"

She paused. Another deep breath and another crack at it. "Jas, I'm so sorry for what happened that night. I'm sorry for you finding me in the tub and…and after when, you know…we…you know. And then I just left."

She felt tears starting to form in her eyes. She took another deep breath. She could do this.

"Katie, don't. It's my fault. You didn't do any—"

She interrupted again "Please, Jas, just let me finish. I just need to get out what I have wanted and needed to say to you all these years."

Jason's gorgeous brown eyes were brimming with emotion but he nodded his head, gesturing for her to continue.

Katie lifted her hand and wiped her eyes before proceeding. "I'm not the kind of girl who hooks up with guys randomly. I don't do that. I don't know what happened. I just…I felt like I needed…I mean, you felt so…warm and…"

Her cheeks now felt like they were on fire. She dropped her head in her hands. This was not coming out the way she wanted it to. Why did she feel like she was back in high school? Where was the confidence she always had when she stepped into a mediation or courtroom?

"Can I say something?" Jason's soothing voice asked as he rubbed the small of her back.

Katie nodded, not taking her face from her hands.

When he did not continue, however, she cautiously looked up at him. His milk chocolate brown eyes were pooled with warmth, and Katie felt like she could drown in them.

"I know you're not 'that kind of girl.' I know that night was your first time."

"How do you know that?" Katie felt a panic begin to rise inside of her. She had believed that was a carefully guarded secret. Everyone had always assumed that she and Nick were sexually active and she'd never told *anyone* otherwise. Her mom had even had her go on the pill when she was sixteen.

"Because since Nick was doing, well, whatever he was doing, I made him promise me one thing—that he wouldn't be sleeping with you at the same time," Jason explained, his tone even and calm. "I just wanted to protect you."

Jason paused for a moment before he added with frustration in his voice, "Then I turn out to be the asshole who takes advantage of you. I don't know if you can ever forgive me. I know that's why you left and haven't been back."

He raked his hands through his hair, and his voice sounded nothing short of tortured. He looked so full of guilt and shame, and Katie knew he that didn't deserve to feel any of those things.

Time to step up and clear the air once and for all.

She sat a little straighter, trying to build up her confidence even though she felt none forthcoming. It didn't matter though. She needed to face this. She had to let Jason off the hook he had apparently placed himself on.

Taking a deep breath she figured, *Here goes nothing.*

"Jason, look. I am so sorry that you have been carrying around some misplaced guilt about that night. I am also very sorry that I didn't stay and meet you at the Dairy Queen. I'm sorry that I stopped talking to you when Nick was in his coma. I'm sorry that I didn't fly home the second I heard about your dad's heart attack. I'm sorry that I disappeared from everyone's lives for ten years."

Tears started falling down her cheeks as she continued on a roll, "God. I'm so sorry for a lot of things, Jas. But there is one thing that I am absolutely *not* sorry for. I am not sorry that you were my first. I will *never* be sorry for that."

Katie knew that it was time to fess up to something that until this moment she'd never truly come to terms with. "When my mom woke me up on the night of the accident"—Katie swallowed hard—"she said that she had taken a 911 call about a black Chevy truck that had driven off Spencer Point."

She took another deep breath and shook her head at the awful memory. "I thought it was you, Jason. I thought you were in the truck. And then when my mom told me it was Nick..." Katie felt tears pouring down her face. She quickly wiped them but forged ahead as she did so. "I felt... Oh, God, I mean, I was…relieved that it was Nick and not you in the truck.

"That's why I stopped talking to you, why I couldn't even look at you when we were at the hospital. I felt so guilty about that. And when you found me in the bathtub, I tried to tell you, to explain that I had thought it had been you. I hadn't slept in days, though, and I know I wasn't making much sense. But when I said that night that I needed you, that I wanted you…I knew exactly what I was asking, and it was exactly what I wanted. And who I wanted."

Jason brushed away more of the tears that were still flowing freely down Katie's face.

"But then we got interrupted, and I just… I couldn't face you. I had no idea what you must have thought of me. I had to get away. I couldn't even face myself for the feelings I had. I was confused and scared and devastated over losing Nick. It was just too much."

"Katie." At the primal growl in Jason's voice, tingles spread through Katie's body.

She looked into his eyes, and where there had been warmth just a few minutes ago, there was now hunger, desire.

He leaned close so that his forehead was resting on hers, and his breathing was ragged and warm against her damp cheek. Cupping her face in his large hands he spoke low, "I know that we have a lot more to talk about, but right now all I can think about is how much I need you. We've both been carrying around all kinds of misplaced guilt, confusion, and pain about that night. Please let me take you upstairs so I can make it right, make us right. Please, Katie… I need you."

He slid his fingers through her hair at the nape of her neck and tilted her head slightly. As he did, his lips covered hers. Heat rapidly spread through her.

She slid her hands up his muscular arms and heard a soft, anxious sigh escape her mouth. She felt overwhelmed by the sheer voracity of his sex appeal. And not just his body (although that was beyond swoon-worthy), but his soul, too. The way he took care of her. The way he knew her better than she knew herself. The way he was just Jason…all of that was sexy as hell.

Slipping her arms around his neck and gliding her fingers through his soft brown hair—that hair she had always loved—at the same time he was wrapping his strong arms around her, pulling her closer, crushing her body against his chest. She felt tiny in his arms, like a china doll when compared to his overpowering strength.

When Katie was in his arms, she felt that there was no danger in the world, no power, no destructive force that was strong enough to hurt her. Not when Jas was there, encircling her in his protective hold. It was the sexiest feeling in the world, she realized, to feel that loved and cherished and protected. In a flash of clarity, Katie knew that there was nothing Jas would not do for her, and that triggered a primal reaction in her—to do absolutely anything for him.

His soft but firm lips moved against hers, his hunger matching what she felt inside, his passion rising up to meet hers. The intensifying waves of heat exploding from her core came faster as the pace of his movements increased, their mutual need stoking the flames of their feelings for each other, their desires.

Her body felt like it was made of nerve endings. Every tiny move he made against her—every brush of his skin against her skin—lit her up like a wildfire burning across a dry and thirsty plain. Every sensation felt like it would overtake her, every one felt more intense and pleasurable than the last, and then (although it seemed impossible) the next one would be even more pleasurable still.

He slipped his tongue into her mouth, probing, exploring, and she met it with her own. She pulled him closer with her hands tangled in his hair, thrusting her tongue into his mouth, grinding her lips against his as she ground her hips into his thigh where their bodies met.

Just when she thought that the fire of her lust-filled passion could not be stoked any higher, he rose slightly, causing his chest to move against her, grazing her nipples all the way.

All of a sudden, Katie reached her breaking point. It was all too much for her. She felt the biggest wave yet, crash over her, and she knew she needed him. Badly.

His lips, his tongue, his hands, his skin, his chest—

she needed him, and not like this. Not on a bench, in public, where all they could do was kiss. She needed to have him, to be with him, to be naked with him, to press her body against him, to give him pleasure and take her own until they both cried with release.

She tore her lips away and looked into his eyes, intensity flooding every cell of her body as she gasped, "Yes, Jas. Take me upstairs…please, yes. I need you."

His only answer was a Jason Sloan Romeo smile. The next thing she knew she was up off the bench and being quickly guided across the hotel lobby with the same urgency she felt burning inside her.

Chapter Twenty-One

As Jason led Katie across the hotel lobby, he could barely believe that this was really happening.

Was this really happening?

He glanced back at Katie, giving her a small smile. She returned the smile, looking every bit as unsure and shell-shocked as he did.

But yes—she was there, she was real, and this was happening.

He just prayed that they didn't run into anyone on the way to the room that would soften Katie's resolve.

Please-no-please-no-please-no-please-no, he chanted in his head to the rhythm of their footsteps.

They stood in front of the elevators and Jason firmly pressed the 'up' button. He would have sworn that his hand was shaking—that he was, in fact, trembling all over—but no. He saw that his hand was steady as he reached out to push the button.

Damn. If he was completely still, then it must be the rest of the world around him that was quaking.

The elevator doors opened and Jason prayed—again—that there would be no one they knew inside.

He'd been waiting for this moment for what felt like forever. To have it derailed at the last minute because they ran into one of his cousins in the elevator would be just *too* cruel. And in a hotel that was practically overflowing with their friends and relatives… It felt like it would take a miracle to get to Katie's room without being seen.

Luck was on his side, however, because they arrived at Katie's door without exchanging so much as a smile or a nod with anyone known to them. Katie pulled her keycard out of her purse and fumbled with it, her fingers shaking, making the task difficult.

Jason stepped behind her, pressing his body right up against hers, placing his hands firmly on her upper arms. She froze in his embrace.

He began to move his hands down her arms, slowly, inexorably, and he heard her let out a little gasp. He felt her tremble beneath his caress. When his hands finally reached hers, he wrapped them around hers, his big, large hands covering her small, dainty ones entirely.

She stood still, frozen against him, although he could feel and hear her breathing quickening. When he felt that she was ready, he decisively moved their hands together to firmly slide the card in and out of the lock.

The light above the mechanism turned green, and Katie and Jason were inside the room in less than a heartbeat.

Jason backed Katie against the wall and pressed his

lips to hers. He kissed her passionately, desperately, almost aggressively. All of the pent-up desire of the torturous years he'd wanted Katie but couldn't touch her, couldn't kiss her, was pouring out of him.

He felt Katie's petite hands roaming his body. One minute they were tangled in his hair. The next they were clinging to his shoulders and back. Then they were grasping at his neck or caressing his face.

His hands answered her exploration move for move. He ran them through her silky, golden hair and trailed them up and down her arms, and he grasped the sides of her delicate neck as he began to trail kisses down it.

As his head began to move down her neck, she wrapped her arms around his neck, and in one small little jump, she hopped up into his arms with her legs wrapped around his waist.

God. Her body against his made him lightheaded.

He cupped his hands under her adorable and sexy ass and began to kiss her again, supporting her as he moved the two of them towards the hotel bed. When they got to the bed, he reached down and tore the covers from it, never breaking their kiss.

He lay her down gently on the bed and stood above her, gazing down as if she were a priceless and fragile treasure.

"Damn, Katie," he breathed, looking into her eyes. "I'm going to make you feel so good."

She smiled, tears shimmering in her gorgeous blue

eyes. She whispered, "You already are, Jason."

Moving over her, Jason began to gently kiss her again on her forehead, her eyelids, her cheeks, her chin, and down her beautiful slim neck. He was surprised at how he felt right now. A moment ago, he had been consumed by animal-like passion. He would have sworn that this encounter was going to be a tangled mass of grabbing at clothes, grasping each other desperately, and mindless ecstasy.

Now, just a few moments later, he felt content to take things slowly, treasuring every small touch, every sight, every taste of her on his lips.

He had waited to explore her body and take his time making love to her for so long, and he wasn't going to rush his opportunity now.

As he trailed kisses slowly down her neck and felt the vibration of her moans through his lips as his kissing became ever more insistent, he traced his fingertips over her body—up and down her arms, up and down her legs, and up and down her thighs.

She began to squirm harder, to writhe a bit even, and then finally she caught one of his hands in both of hers and pulled, causing him to look up at her.

She was panting, and the hair around her forehead was damp with the same sweat that was making her skin glisten. He felt himself grow even harder—if that was possible.

"Jason," she whimpered. "I need you. I need you so much. Please, just…right now. I need to feel you…"

God, he felt the erotic charge of her fevered exclamations to the very core of his body and soul. His erection pulsed heavily behind his zipper. His body screamed for him to strip her down and sink inside of her.

As he rose up above her, he saw her smile. He realized that she must think that he was giving in to her demands, speeding up and just taking her now like she wanted.

He grinned to himself.

Katie Marie Lawson should know him well enough to know that he didn't do things a certain way just because her bossy little butt said that he should.

Leaning down, he pressed his mouth against her ear.

"Katie..." he said.

"Yes?" she gasped.

"Do you trust me?" he whispered.

"Yes," her small frame shivered in response.

"Then you need to trust me now," he whispered hoarsely, his lips brushing against her ear. "Trust me that I'm going to make love to you tonight, and it's going to be amazing. Soul-shattering. I'm going to make your body feel things you didn't even know it was capable of. I'm going to bring you pleasure you've never even dreamed was possible—even in your wildest fantasies. But in order to do that, I need you to trust me. Do you think you can do that?"

He felt her nodding frantically, and he drew back

and resumed his mouth's slow journey down her body. He kissed and licked down her neck and across her chest. When he got to the neckline of her dress, he moved his hands up her outer thighs, drawing the hem of her dress up with them, and inched it up until it came free and he pulled it over her head.

He tossed it aside, his eyes moving up her body stopping at her heaving breasts, mesmerized by how delicate and beautiful they were. The creamy mounds were topped by stiff, pink points, their shuddering motion, as Katie's breath hitched, filling him with nearly uncontrollable desire.

Under the weight of his hungry, lustful gaze, he saw her china skin begin to color to a rosy pink all over her chest and belly. Her breathing became even more rapid, and her nipples hardened even further.

Her body's reaction to the way his eyes took her in, turned him on, driving him to heights of lust he had never before experienced. Her skin, her breath, her nipples—she was reacting as if he were touching her, kissing her, licking her. That was how turned on she was getting just from the way he *looked* at her.

It was too much. He couldn't hold out any longer. He had to touch her, to taste her.

He knelt beside the bed, leaning over and taking one of those tantalizing pink tips in his mouth, suckling at it, working it with his tongue. With his hand, he caressed her belly and her side and played with her other stiff, sensitive nipple.

He knew he was driving her crazy. She was wiggling back and forth on the bed, and her hands were grasping at the back of his head and on his strong forearm. She was murmuring unintelligibly, encouraging him—begging him. But he was proud of her. She was staying true to her word: she was trusting him.

As he continued to suck and lick at both of the sensitive peaks of her breasts, he moved his hand farther down, urging her thighs apart. She spread her legs open for him, willingly, eagerly even.

He trailed his fingertips in little circles and curlicues up the inside of her thighs until he came to the very center of her core. He could feel the heat radiating from her even through the flimsy material of her black lace panties.

As he lightly brushed his fingers up the fabric, he noticed that it was soaking wet.

Katie groaned and arched her back as she felt his light touch on the sensitive skin of her lips even through the fabric that covered them.

"Yes, Jas, yes..." she murmured. He heard the note of desperation in her voice. He smiled. He loved seeing Katie like this.

Hooking his fingers in the lace material at her thigh Jason slowly slid her panties down over her legs and threw them aside. Then, moving his hands up her inner thighs, he spread her legs and took a moment to fully appreciate her beautiful body. His eyes roamed across her perfectly full breasts, down the curve of her thin waist, sliding even lower past her hips, and finally landing on her center. Jason's fingers instinctively gripped her inner thighs as he gently nudged her legs even farther apart and watched her grow even wetter right before his eyes.

Arousal and need exploded through Jason as he stared at Katie's wet center. But, he ignored his own body's demands. For now.

Pulling Katie's hips to the edge of the bed where he knelt between her knees, Jason placed the palm of his large, strong hand flat on her lower belly and began to trail his thumb lightly along her outer lips, never penetrating the folds underneath. He felt her shudder under his featherlight caress.

"Katie," he said huskily.

"Yes…" she gasped, her head thrown back, her eyes closed.

"I have a question for you."

"Okay," she moaned.

"Do you remember the other day in the truck?" She nodded. Jason felt a grin pull at his lips.

"Say it," he commanded. There was a smile in his voice, but it was clear he was serious.

"I remember," she moaned.

He heard his voice grow thick with desire as he said, "Tell me what happened in the truck."

Katie sucked in a quick breath as her head fell back, but she didn't answer.

He waited. His rock hard shaft jumped in his pants

as he watched her bite her bottom lip, her breasts rising and falling, rapidly, from her labored breaths.

"Tell me what happened in the truck," Jason repeated as he continued circling her sensitized nub.

She moaned, "Jason…"

He slowed the movement of his thumb to a virtual crawl and she grasped his forearm desperately.

"Tell me," his low voice commanded.

"You…you made me…" she stammered before blurting out, "You made me come."

Satisfaction filled him as he began to move his thumb again. "That's right, I did. I made you come. Did you like it?"

Katie nodded furiously, throwing her head back again, eyes still closed. Her hands by her sides pulling the sheets in her clenched fists.

"It felt good?" he asked.

Another nod, and her back arched, stretching her breasts towards the sky.

"Tell me," he demanded.

She moaned as her head fell to the side, "Jason, why are you doing this?"

"Just tell me," he insisted.

Hoarsely, Katie finally admitted, "I loved it. It felt amazing."

"Good. I'm glad. I wanted to make you feel good. Amazing is even better. Now, Katie, here's the real question. Do you want me to make you come again?"

"Yes!" the cry tearing from her throat almost involuntarily, it seemed.

Jason smiled, perhaps the wickedest—and sexiest—smile he had ever smiled.

"Katie, if you want something, you have to ask for it," he teased. "How am I supposed to know what you want if you don't tell me?"

He loved making her squirm, both literally and metaphorically. He knew that, for Katie—the good girl, the color-inside-the-lines girl, the rule-following girl—talking like this was definitely stretching her outside of her comfort zone. That was what he liked about it.

He liked knowing that she wanted him so desperately, she was willing to follow him outside that comfort zone and that she trusted him enough to see what lay there.

"I want…" She squirmed, tossing her head back and forth. "I want…"

Then she surprised the hell out of him. It was like a determination came over her, a calmness. Her squirming and wriggling ceased, and she lay perfectly still as he touched her. She opened her eyes wide, looking straight into his. When she spoke, her voice was raw with desire, but there was no tremor in it.

"I want," she said, "for you to touch me right where your thumb is. I want you to keep touching me until you make me come again, Jason. I've never wanted anything more in my life."

Jason closed his eyes against the powerful wave of desire that crashed over him at these words. It was all he could do to keep from passing out.

He opened his eyes again and looked straight back into hers. He shook his head mock-regretfully.

"Well, you're in for a bit of a disappointment then, I'm afraid," he said. Without giving her a chance to wonder what he meant, he clarified, "I don't plan on using my fingers at all this time. Only my tongue."

Without waiting for her reaction, he dipped his head and covered her completely with his mouth. She tasted so sweet that he felt like he could spend the rest of his life devouring her. He ran his tongue up and down, again and again, alternating thrusting his tongue inside of her and working her sweet button of pleasure.

Finally, when he felt her motions become even more frenzied and heard a new note of urgency enter her cries, he knew it was time to release her from this exquisite torture he was causing to riot through her.

He broke his earlier promise and slipped two fingers inside of her snug heat, working her with them as he concentrated his mouth on her center of pleasure. He felt her inner muscles squeezing harder, clamping down on his fingers, and at the same time, she grasped the back of his head with both hands and thrust her hips up into his mouth, screaming, "Oh, Jason, yes! Yes! Jason...Jason...Yes, Jason...Jason!"

He stayed with her as her body milked his fingers while she rode out her release. He only slowed his movements as she slowed hers, bringing her down softly from the powerful orgasm.

When she was almost completely calm, she spoke his name quietly, "Jason? I need…"

He looked up to meet her eyes and saw that she was looking at him—clearly and directly.

"What, angel?" he hoarsely whispered. "What do you need?"

"To feel you inside of me," she stated matter-of-factly.

This time it was Jason's turn to groan uncontrollably.

He stood on shaky legs and began to undress, unbuttoning his shirt first. Katie watched him for a few seconds and then shook her head.

"Nope. Too slow," she concluded with a sly grin and sat up on the edge of the bed, her fingers working at his clothing. Looking down at her, watching her sit on the edge of the bed completely naked as she worked to undress him, was an almost unbearably erotic image.

When they had completely freed him of all of his garments, he slipped on the condom he had pulled from his pants pocket.

She smiled a little as he rolled it on. "Pretty sure of yourself, huh, Jas?" she asked.

He grinned back at her. "Yep. I knew if it weren't you, it'd be somebody," he teased.

She laughed and smacked his chest. "Shut up!"

Growing serious, he said, "But seriously, Katie. I feel like this is fate. You and me, this weekend—all of it. I feel like it's meant to be. I didn't know for sure in my head that it would happen. But I think in my heart, I always did. You're it for me. It's always just been you."

Katie's big blue eyes filled with tears again, and she didn't even reply. She merely scooted back gracefully on the bed, taking his hand and pulling him with her as she laid back against the pillows.

Jason moved over her as she began to kiss him again and run her hands all over his body. His shaft throbbed painfully at her exploration. God, he didn't know that it was possible to get this hard.

Before long, he felt her thin, delicate fingers grasp his length and guide him inside of her. Damn, it felt so perfect. She was warm and tight, and it felt as if he were being completely enveloped in her as he began to pump rhythmically in and out.

Soon, even that conscious thought was banished from his mind as his whole world narrowed just to the sensation that Katie's body was making him feel. He was vaguely aware of her hot breath on his neck, of her soft skin against his body, of her hands trailing over his back, and of her legs wrapped around his waist. But all of those sensations were secondary to the one overwhelming, overriding sensation in his consciousness—how it felt to be inside of her.

Her inner walls contracted tightly around him. She locked her ankles around his back, pushing him even deeper inside of her. He felt her heat pulsing around his steel-hard erection as he thrust in and out of her.

Her hips moved against his as their pace quickened. Her nails dug into his back.

"Jason. Oh God, Jason," His name came out as a plea on her lips.

He felt her core begin to spasm around him and his passion rose to a peak, and then he felt it break. He had never experienced an orgasm like this one before. This felt like the complete release of his mind, his body, his soul. This felt like the whole world was coming to an end, but at the same time, it felt like the whole world was just beginning.

Not even recognizing his own voice he heard himself groaning, "I love you. Oh, Katie, I love you. I love you so much..." as he rode out the wave of ecstasy crashing over him.

His world stopped spinning as he heard her gasping in his ear, "Oh, Jason, I love you, too. So much. I love you so much."

And in that moment, it was enough. It was all he needed to know.

Chapter Twenty-Two

Jason drifted awake the next morning on a cloud of good feeling, and he reveled in the sensation for a moment before even trying to figure out where it came from.

Why was he so happy again?

He sleepily turned his head and saw Katie's tousled hair on the pillow next to him. It all came rushing back, and he smiled a sleepy, silly grin—the grin of a man who'd spent the entire night making love to his soul mate.

Unfortunately, his dreamy good mood was shattered by the insistent chime of his text message alert. Pushing out of bed, he quickly searched through his pockets and tried to silence the phone before it woke Katie.

He finally found it and hit the button for the text message, but it was too late. Katie was sitting up in bed, looking like a Greek goddess with the white bed sheet wrapped around her, rubbing her eyes sleepily.

The moment their eyes met, her face turned up into a smile that was so beautiful it felt like his heart was breaking.

"Everything okay?" She asked between yawns.

Jason nodded. "Yeah. Or it will be. It seems boy wonder can't seem to locate the wedding bands. I think I'm going to have to be on best man duty this morning," he said regretfully.

"You were certainly on best man duty last night," Katie said, a sultry note in her voice.

He sighed. Damn. As he quickly pulled on his clothes, he wished he had time to follow up on that undertone and make a little somethin' happen, but he didn't.

He leaned down and kissed the top of her head. Who was he kidding? Best man or not, if he kissed her on the mouth—even a kiss goodbye—he wouldn't be leaving this room anytime soon.

"I'll see you later today," he said as he walked towards the door. "I love you."

"I love you, too!" she called after him, and he could not have asked for sweeter words to send him off.

✦ ✦ ✦

Katie headed down to the bridal brunch feeling happy, but confused. She was also sore in places she wasn't even aware she could be sore in. She smiled to herself. Her shower concert this morning had been extremely upbeat, favoring numbers like, "Walking on Sunshine," and "I Just Called To Say I Love You."

Just as she was about to round the final corner, she

realized that she had better put the kibosh on her glowing demeanor and mile-wide smile if she didn't want to have to answer a lot of very awkward questions.

She buttoned down her facial expression and walked into the brunch room.

The Sloan girls were already sitting at the table, and Katie saw Sophie walking in from the other entrance at the same time. Katie moved over to her and hugged her, saying, "Hello, beautiful bride. You look as fresh as a daisy this morning. I guess that 'solid night's sleep' did you some good."

Katie finished with a wink, and Sophie laughed, her cheeks turning pink. Then she smiled a wicked smile and leaned in closer to Katie. "From what I hear, I'm not the only one who got a 'solid night's sleep' last night."

Katie's eyes widened and she stammered, "What…who told you?"

Sophie grinned wider and returned her wink. "You just did."

Katie threw her head back and laughed. She said, "You're a lot sneakier than you used to be, missy."

Sophie smiled proudly. "I've been working on it."

"Seriously though, let's keep this between us. I don't want to steal your thunder. This is your day."

"Hmmm, thunder. Not a bad comparison," Sophie teased. "Sure. I'll keep your and Jason's little weather experiment to myself. But don't think for one minute that I believe you want it kept private all because of little ol' me."

And with that, Sophie spun and headed off towards the table, leaving Katie with no other option than to trail after her, eyes wide and mouth a little agape.

They settled into their seats and chatted for a while as the rest of the ladies arrived. Chelle came in, followed by Grace and Pam, and Katie jumped up to go give her mom a big hug, as well as Sophie's mom.

As she returned to her seat, she noticed that some other ladies had filed into her seat and the ones surrounding it, probably not realizing that she had already been sitting there. That was fine. In fact, she was kind of glad. This would give her a chance to visit with her mom and Grace. Trying to be as subtle as possible, she bent down and grabbed her purse from under the chair and returned to where Grace and Pam were seated at the end of the grouping of tables.

Pam looked up, happy. "Well, isn't this a pleasant surprise. I didn't expect to get the chance to visit more with my girl."

Grace looked equally pleased. "Katie, honey, I sure hope you're not gonna let it be ten whole years until we see you again. We sure do miss you."

Katie smiled, basking in the warm glow of being surrounded by loved ones.

Just as they were finishing up the last drops of satisfying coffee and conversation, Aunt Wendy swooped into the room like a tornado.

"Ladies, ladies!" she exclaimed. "It's time to go get

gorgeous."

A round of applause went up from all of the women at the table, including Katie. How had she forgotten how much she loved hanging out with this group of girls?

They all stood and filed their way down to the spa and salon area, and Katie felt tingly with the anticipation of the wedding drawing near. As they settled into their chairs and the stylists began to work on their hair and makeup, Katie continued to marvel at how gorgeous Sophie looked. She was the quintessential beautiful bride.

As much as she wanted to revel in the female togetherness, though, and enjoy the cozy nesting feeling that was building among the group of women as they all readied themselves for the ceremony, she couldn't seem to tear her mind entirely away from last night.

She didn't know what it meant. If anything.

Wait. That was a horrible thought. It had to mean *something*. Right?

Now she knew that she loved Jason. Not just as a friend. She must have always known it deep down, but last night had made that fact crystal clear.

So okay. She loved him. He loved her. Those were the *facts*.

But they had separate lives. She lived in California; he lived in Illinois.

She couldn't imagine just going back to San Francisco like it was nothing, resigning herself to not seeing him. That was utterly inconceivable. But on the other hand, how could it possibly work? She had a serious job. She was on track to become junior partner—and then partner—at a prestigious law firm in one of the United States' premier legal communities. It wasn't the sort of job you just walked away from. Jobs like hers were not a dime a dozen.

And Jason. Talk about being stuck geographically. He had his entire *family* depending on him to take over the family business. Plus, there was his dad's health to consider. There was no way he could just up and move.

She looked around her, watching all of these women who were dear to her as they got their hair and makeup done, had their nails painted, and talked and laughed with each other the entire time.

Her mother, looked so happy and content with her baby girl by her side. She'd never looked that way when she visited Katie in San Francisco. Katie realized that she hadn't actually seen her mother look totally relaxed in ten whole years. Not until Katie had come home.

Then there was Aunt Wendy. Crazy-haired, southern-speaking, bright-clothes-wearing Aunt Wendy who had apparently found her calling as a wedding planner. Katie could not be prouder.

There was Grace, Katie's second mother, who had welcomed her home like a long-lost prodigal daughter who had returned to the flock.

Then there was Chelle. Her rare diamond friend, a woman she had thought was lost to her forever but was now back in her life.

And, of course, there was Sophie. Sweet, beautiful Sophie, who Katie would never be able to see without also seeing the faint shadow of her four-year-old self hovering just behind like a double exposure image.

She shook her head, trying to control her sudden fierce emotion. Jason may be the person she had just realized she was in love with, but he was far from the only one she was going to have a heart-wrenchingly hard time saying goodbye to tomorrow.

Oh, God.

The thought froze her.

Tomorrow.

Chapter Twenty-Three

Katie walked with the rest of the bridal party down to the small lakeside chapel where Bobby and Sophie were going to be saying their vows at the exact same altar that Grandpa J and Grandma Marie had said theirs so many years ago.

The chapel was charmingly rustic, but its most wonderful feature by far was the large bank of picture windows that formed the entire wall behind the altar, giving the congregation a gorgeous view of the lake in the background as the ceremony was conducted.

As the group of bridesmaids headed down from the hotel to the chapel, meticulously making their way through the gravel and dirt in their high heels, Katie saw that Amber was making a special point to catch up with her. She slowed to wait for her.

"Hey." Amber smiled as she drew even with Katie. "How's it going?"

"Great," Katie replied politely with a smile.

"How are things with Jason?" she asked conspiratorially, her dark eyes twinkling.

Katie was sure Amber was a very lovely person and

all, but she simply didn't know her well enough yet to trust her. She said noncommittally, "Oh, you know, we're catching up with one another."

Amber giggled. "Making up for lost time is more like it."

Katie smiled but didn't respond.

Amber pushed on. "Can I just say that I've certainly never seen Jason look at *anyone* the way he's been looking at you this weekend? You're a very lucky girl, you know."

Katie nodded, not sure how to respond to this. She didn't know what Amber was getting at.

"Look, all I'm saying is...sometimes when things are right in front of us, we don't appreciate them. But if I ever had a man look at me the way Jason looks at you, well, I would think twice about letting him go is all."

Katie nodded again and was trying to formulate some kind of reply, but just at that moment, the group arrived at the front door of the chapel and Aunt Wendy began to line them up with her usual—and, thank God, distracting—flair.

When the bridesmaids were all in line, Aunt Wendy brought Sophie out from the side door of the chapel and she took her place at the end of the line.

Katie said, "You're the most beautiful bride that has ever lived, Sophiebell," with tears shining in her eyes.

Sophie threw her arms around Katie and whispered, "I love you, Katie. Thanks for coming home for me. I know it wasn't easy. I don't care what blood says. You'll always be my sister."

Oh boy. How was she going to leave tomorrow?

The strains of music began from inside the chapel, and Mike came out to take his place beside Sophie, ready to give away his beautiful daughter—if any father ever can be ready for something like that.

The bridesmaids that stood in line ahead of Katie began to make their way down the aisle, and Katie knew that her turn was drawing nearer.

The roller coaster range of emotions that were assaulting her as she stepped closer to the entrance of the chapel made it difficult for her to even think. Her head was swimming. She made a concerted effort to put off even trying to categorize them or process them in any way. There would be plenty of time to analyze later. Right now, she just needed to take a deep breath, square her shoulders, and walk down the aisle as Sophie's maid of honor.

As she took her slow and formal steps down the center aisle of the chapel, she saw Jason in his tux, standing next to Bobby, looking more devastatingly handsome than she had ever seen him.

He was staring at her as if she were the most beautiful creature he had ever seen. He smiled and winked at her, and just like that, all of her roller coaster emotions calmed. She kept her eyes on him as she walked towards the front of the chapel where he was standing, and it all felt like the most natural, inevitable thing in the world.

As Katie reached the front of the room, took her place, and turned around to face the congregants, the universally-familiar opening lines of "Here Comes The Bride" began to ring out from the organ, which stood on the far side of the platform and altar.

The wedding guests turned to face the back of the church, as one, many of the ladies preemptively holding handkerchiefs up to their faces in preparation of the sentimental tears that they knew they would be crying as soon as they saw Sophie start to make her way, on her father's arm, down the center aisle.

When Sophie and Mike reached the front of the chapel and stood before the pastor, Bobby stepped down and stood on the other side of Sophie, taking her hand. At the same time, Grace and Grandpa J stood up from their seats to walk over to stand next to Mike, and Bob Sloan stood and walked over to stand next to Bobby.

The pastor, in his deep and booming voice, said, "The marriage of Bobby and Sophie unites two families and creates a new one. Who presents this woman and this man to be married to each other?"

All of the standing family members answered in unison. "We do."

The pastor continued. "And will you receive Bobby and Sophie into your family and uphold them with your love as they establish themselves as a family within your own?"

The family members chorused, "We will."

Oh, Lord. The tears were already starting. There was nothing Katie could do to stop it. But as she looked around, she saw that she was far from the only one falling victim to the waterworks. All over the chapel, people were dabbing at their eyes—and not just the ladies.

As Grace and Mike walked back to their seats, a look passed between them that was all their own. It encompassed the entire range of emotions they must be feeling at that moment—bittersweet melancholy that their baby was all grown up, happiness that she had found such joy, and sadness that their son could not be there to see it.

At the thought of Nick, Katie glanced over to the small memorial to him that was set up at the far end of the platform. It was bright, happy, and beautiful—just as Nick had been. It was a simple photo of Nick and Sophie standing out in the yard in jean shorts and t-shirts, mouths red from the Popsicles they were holding, arms slung around each other. Katie remembered the t-shirt he was wearing. She'd been with him when he bought it. She realized the picture must have been taken in the last few months of his life.

Nick and Sophie were beaming out of the photograph, their happiness at being together palpable even in two dimension. A simple row of tealight candles burned below the photo.

Katie felt Nick's spirit in that moment. She felt that he was giving his blessing to the union of his beloved little sister and his best friend's little brother. As crazy as it sounded, she also felt that he was giving *her* his blessing, too—to move on, to be happy without him.

Nick had been a happy guy, above all else. He had lived for the moment and valued nothing above enjoyment, fun, and having a good time. He wanted that for himself, and he wanted that for the people around him as well.

Katie took in a shaky breath. Yeah. That was true. That must be why the whole cheating thing didn't surprise her very much or even make her all that mad at him. Because Nick was, in the best way possible, like a golden retriever puppy. He was adorable and silly, and he lived for the moment.

God. The thought that she would still be torn up about losing him, unable to move on with her life ten whole years later—Nick would have hated that. He would have laughed and said, "Katie. Seriously, move on. Let it go. Life is for living."

And then he probably would have jumped on his mountain bike or gone base jumping or any one of the other dangerous and thrilling things he loved to do. Which had, you know, eventually ended his life. But, while he'd been alive? He'd really lived. And he would have wanted that for her as well. And if she was honest with herself, *living* was about the furthest thing from what she'd been doing this past decade.

She shook her head. She wasn't entirely ready to let it go, she knew. But she was closer.

Sophie and Bobby moved to the altar, and Sophie handed her bouquet to Katie. Katie reached over and smoothed and adjusted Sophie's gown so that it lay perfectly.

She felt eyes on her, and as she straightened, she saw that Jason was smiling at her as he watched her with Sophie. She smiled back, and recognition of the significance of the moment and of their significance to one another passed between them. Katie's heart melted as she likened it to the unspoken communication Grace and Mike had shared.

Katie knew that what she had with Jason was rare and beyond special—there was no denying that. Now all she had to do was figure out what to do about it.

✦ ✦ ✦

Jason had tried to prepare himself for seeing Katie walk down the aisle, but *nothing* could have prepared him for the feeling that came over him as he watched her walk towards him. The light lavender shade of her gown was close enough to white that a momentary fantasy overtook him—that he was the groom and that he was lucky enough to be standing at this altar, waiting for Katie Marie Lawson to walk down the aisle and become his wife.

He took a deep breath and closed his eyes against those thoughts. *Don't get ahead of yourself, Sloan,* he admonished. *You don't want to scare her off again.*

He knew he should be paying attention to the ceremony, but he was mesmerized by watching her every movement.

He was so taken by her, in fact, that he didn't even realize the pastor had asked for the rings until Alex elbowed him. Hard.

He scrambled to get the ring out of his pocket quickly and handed it to Bobby.

Alex leaned forward and whispered in Jason's ear, "Just one more piece of evidence that Bobby was hitting the bottle when he asked you to be his best man. It all makes sense now. Stings a little less every day."

Jason shook his head. He could hear the mocking tone even through the whisper and knew his brother wasn't going to let him live this down for a very long time.

Still, Alex had a point. He was here to do a job, and that job wasn't to ogle Katie Lawson (although if he could figure out how to turn that into a job, it would be a pretty damn sweet one).

He tried his best to focus on what the pastor was saying. Every time he felt his eyes straying to Katie's beautiful face—or other parts—he pulled his attention back. But, *damn*, it was hard. She was breathtaking. It seemed that whenever she was in the room, the rest of the world faded away for him—even if the "rest of the world" consisted of his baby brother's wedding.

Before he knew it, the pastor was saying, "You may now kiss the bride," and the whole place was cheering.

Sophie and Bobby headed down the aisle, beaming proud and joyful smiles from ear to ear. Then Jason stepped to the center of the aisle, took Katie's arm and they followed behind the bride and groom.

Man. It was becoming clearer and clearer to him that, with Katie by his side, all was right with the world. Without her, nothing was. He felt his chest get tight when he thought about letting her go. Again.

Chapter Twenty-Four

Katie took a moment and looked around the reception, which was in a refinished barn at the edge of the lake a few blocks from the chapel. It retained enough of its rustic original architecture to lend itself well to 'country chic' events like Sophie and Bobby's wedding reception, but it had been completely outfitted with a commercial kitchen, a dance floor, sound system, and every amenity event-goers might need.

The best part was that both ends of the barn had huge, open double doors that led outside. One set led to a grove of trees, which was filled with twinkle lights tonight. The other set of doors looked right out onto the lake.

Katie sat at the head table with Chelle, giggling and gossiping yet again. It really was their default, and Katie liked that just fine.

Chelle leaned in close, and Katie could already see that she had a wicked look on her face.

"I know you did the dirty last night, girl. Don't even try to deny it," she said, waggling her eyebrows up and down for naughty emphasis.

"You don't *know* anything," Katie countered with a smirk.

"As good as," Chelle shot back. "Seriously, it was embarrassing how hard Jason was staring at you before, and today it's magnified tenfold. It's like he's the starving desert guy from cartoons and you've turned into a steak."

Katie shook her head. "I don't think I come out particularly well in that analogy. I'm basically just a piece of meat?"

Chelle laughed. "Don't go getting all feminist on me. At least in my analogy, Jason wants to eat you. That can't be bad, right?"

They both burst out laughing just as Jason returned to the table with their drinks. He chuckled as he set the glasses down. "Seems like I'm missing all the good stuff," he teased.

"The way I hear it, you're not missing much," Chelle said with a grin, and Katie elbowed her.

Just then, they heard the DJ announce that it was time for the toasts.

Oh, Lord, Katie thought. *Please don't let me bawl in front of all these people.*

Jason stood and tapped his fork against his glass, and the room quieted. He turned towards Sophie and Bobby, who were looking up at him with expectant faces.

A smile spread on his face as he picked up the microphone, and began. "I'm sure most of you know that Nick, Sophie's older brother, was my best friend. I spent more days and nights at the Hunter house than, well, than I spent at my own a lot of times. In truth, I've always thought of Sophie as my little sister in a lot of ways.

"Especially after we lost Nick. I stepped in and tried to fill that void. I tried to give her advice about school, about friends. Even about guys. I tried to tell her what I thought Nick would have wanted her to know—to hold out for someone who didn't just love her, but couldn't live without her. Someone who she didn't feel like she could live without either. Someone kind and honest and who treated her like the princess she is. I hadn't realized when I gave her those words of advice that I was describing my own baby brother. But man, I'm sure glad I was."

Jason, then, looked at Sophie and delivered the rest of the speech directly to her. "I can tell you from experience that Bobby is the best man I know. He has courage, he has integrity, and he has more loyalty in his little finger than most people have in their whole bodies. I know him, Sophie, and he will fight for you. He's loved you forever, and he'll love you forever to come. He's everything I think Nick would have wanted for you. He's everything I told you to hold out for. Like I said, Soph, I've always considered you my little sister, and now you actually are. Nothing could make me happier."

He turned back to the crowd and raised his glass. "To the happy couple."

"To the happy couple." The crowd echoed, raising their own glasses.

Jason handed Katie the microphone and sat down, she could feel his encouraging stare on her.

She turned to the crowd. "I'm not sure how I'm going to top that," she joked lightly, and the guests chuckled.

Katie opened her mouth to speak, but her throat closed from the tears that were threatening. She waited a few beats, getting herself under control.

She smiled and addressed the crowd again. "Wow, that's been happening a lot this weekend," she said lightly, and they chuckled again.

"I'm pretty sure I'm not the only one here who has been overcome by tears more than once as they've watched these two beautiful young people make a commitment to each other, one that signifies just how much they love each other. And you can see, just by looking at them, exactly how much that is.

"I've known Sophie since she was just a little thing. Sophie—or Sophiebell as she will always be to me—was only four years old when the Hunters moved next door. She was my shadow from the very first day, and that couldn't have made me happier. Sophie was the sister I never had. Since the first day I met her, she seemed to be bursting at the seams with love, joy, and happiness. But, I can honestly say that I have never seen her as happy as she is today. I love you, Sophiebell.

Turning to Bobby, Katie sniffed as she smiled, "Bobby, I can honestly say that until I came back two days ago, I probably had only heard you speak a total of ten words in all the years I'd known you."

The crowd chuckled and Katie paused before continuing, "But, from what I've seen the past few days, you are everything that Jason so eloquently said and more. It is obvious to anyone who spends time with the two of you that you are each other's perfect match. Your quiet strength balances Sophie's bubbly enthusiasm perfectly. You are truly the yin to her yang. I know that you two have the kind of love that will only grow stronger with each day, each month, each year that passes. I love you both."

Katie raised her glass. "To Bobby and Sophie."

The attendees echoed, their own glasses raised. "To Bobby and Sophie."

Katie sat down, and Jason put an arm around her shoulder. Chelle grasped her hand from the other side, and Katie felt (to quote *Anne of Green Gables*) pretty nearly perfectly happy.

They sat and chatted like that for a while with others coming up, intermittently, to tell either Jason or Katie how much they had enjoyed the toasts, and before Katie knew it, it was time for the first dance.

She got up from her seat and moved to the edge of the dance floor so she would have a better view. Sophie and Bobby looked into each other's eyes lovingly as they swayed to the music.

After the first dance, the father-daughter dance began. Mike joined Sophie on the dance floor, and the two of them laughed and talked as they moved around the floor. Most of all, they looked to be very happy.

Katie realized, maybe for the first time, that when she got married, there would be no father-daughter dance. She was missing a pretty critical portion of that equation.

She started to feel a little sad, and that quickly bled into feeling overwhelmed. That led to feeling claustrophobic in a room packed with people. The walls were closing in.

Oh, no, she thought. A panic attack is coming on.

She began to repeat the mantra to herself:

You can breathe. Just breathe. Breathe in and out slowly. You can breathe.

Where was a good old-fashioned brown paper lunch sack when you needed one?

The mantra wasn't working, she didn't have her bag or picture with her, but she knew she could not just duck out of the reception in the middle of the dance. She was the maid of freaking honor. People would probably notice.

That knowledge only made her feel more out of control and panicked, which fed into her ever-increasing symptoms, which made her feel out of control—vicious cycle, yadda yadda yadda. She needed to figure out how to stop it.

Her heartbeat was erratic, her palms were sweaty, her tongue and limbs were tingling, and her chest felt like an elephant was sitting on it.

She didn't know what to do.

Then, just when it was getting really bad, she felt a hand on the small of her back. Jason was standing beside her, and he leaned in to whisper in her ear. At first she was so far gone that she couldn't even understand what he was whispering to her, but then she deciphered his words.

"Are you okay? Or do I need to get you out of here?"

The tone in his voice, the heat of his breath on her neck, the weight of his hand on her lower back—all of it served to anchor her to the room.

She shook her head, signifying the fact that she didn't need to leave.

Screw the mantra, Katie thought. She obviously didn't need a picture when she had the real thing standing beside her, his mere presence seemed to be keeping the looming panic attack at bay.

After Jason had stood with her long enough to calm her down considerably, it was time for the wedding party to join the bride and groom. Jason led Katie to the floor and pulled her against him. He wrapped his arms around her tightly, and she melted into him. When she was in his arms, she felt so safe, so solid, so secure, so…perfect.

She closed her eyes and laid her head on his shoulder. They swayed back and forth in an almost hypnotic fashion, following the slow and lovely melody of the music. David Ryan Harris' *Pretty Girl* began playing.

Jason leaned down and whispered that he had chosen this song specifically for the wedding party dance because he knew that he would be dancing with her.

Katie focused in and made a point of listening to the lyrics, she'd always liked the song but had never really paid attention to the words. Now that she was listening, it was the sweetest song that she'd ever heard. It described basically the perfect girl and how much she was a part of the singer's soul.

She pulled back to look up at him, amazement filling her countenance. "Is that how you really feel about me?" she asked, her voice tinged with awe.

Jason leaned in and kissed her slowly and sweetly, just like the song had said. Forgetting completely that they were in a room full of people, she kissed him back, all her inhibitions dropping away for the duration of that one perfect kiss.

He looked into her eyes and answered her. "All that and more, Kit Kat."

As the song drew to a close, Katie felt utterly overwhelmed with emotion. She told Jason that she needed to have a minute for herself and headed for the restroom.

She sat down on the closed lid of the toilet in the stall, trying to slow her breathing and calm her frazzled nerves. So much had happened this weekend—some of it good, some of it bad, some of it great—but all of it had been *intense*. She just needed a moment to gather herself.

When she heard other people entering the bathroom, she pulled her feet up, not wanting to be engaged in conversation. She heard the distinctive voices of Lisa and Tiffany, two of the mean girls from high school, and they proceeded to prove that they had not yet reformed, even ten years later.

"God, could you believe it?"

"Ohmygod, I know exactly what you're talking about. You don't even need to say it."

"On three, we'll go together."

"One, two, three."

"Katie Lawson being a total slut." they said in unison.

"I know, right?"

"Totally, girl. You read my mind."

"Seriously. Can you believe she's such a whore? Just making out with Jason at Nick's sister's wedding, right in front of God and everyone."

"Including Nick's parents!"

"You're right. I didn't even think about Nick's parents being there."

"I guess she didn't either. She's such trash. I bet they hate Little Miss Perfect now."

"They should. Oh my God, I feel so totally sorry for Nick."

"I know, right? He was such a good guy, and his

girlfriend's such a slutbag."

Ironic, Katie thought to herself as the girls filed out, *coming from the mouths of two girls who had screwed Nick while he'd been her boyfriend.*

But she also couldn't deny that they had a point. She had behaved like that at Nick's sister's wedding. In front of his parents.

She just couldn't take any more of this. She shook her head. She was going to avoid Jason for the rest of the reception (even if it killed her) and then she was going to head back to the hotel (alone) and indulge in a (probably particularly raucous) shower concert. Maybe that would help her get her head on straight.

Chapter Twenty-Five

Katie stepped out of the shower, feeling slightly better. Her shower concert had been bittersweet, mainly focusing on titles such as "I Will Remember You" by Sarah McLachlan and "It Must Have Been Love" by Roxette. Still. Despite her melancholy repertoire, she felt that she had regained some of her composure and some of her perspective.

Which was, of course, immediately shattered upon opening the bathroom door and hearing a persistent pounding along with Jason's voice saying, "Katie. Open up. I know you're in there. I can hear you."

She shook her head, sighed, and quickly grabbed a towel and wrapped it around herself. She couldn't believe he had chased her up here.

No. That wasn't true. That actually seemed completely in character. She realized that what she couldn't believe was that he was going to see her looking like this.

She resigned herself to the fact that she was going to answer the door with her hair sopping wet, her face scrubbed of all makeup, and wearing nothing more fashionable (or flattering, thank you very much) than a fluffy terrycloth towel.

Great.

She pulled open the door, which he was still knocking on in a steady rhythm, and said indignantly, "Jason, I have neighbors, you know. They probably don't appreciate that."

"Well, then you should have..." he started to tease with a mischievous glint in his eye. But then she saw him stop short, taking in her appearance. He looked her up and down, slowly, his smile fading, the color draining from his face.

Damn, she thought ruefully. I must look worse than I thought.

He stepped inside, shutting the door behind him, never taking his eyes from her body.

"Did you need something, Jas?" she asked, growing more annoyed by the second.

"Yeah, I..." he trailed off and then started again. "God, you look so...you just look so..."

Holy crap, was he really going to insult her right now?

"Sexy," he finished almost reverently. "So unbelievably goddamn sexy."

Okay. That was a surprise. But she would take it. She smiled.

Enjoying the feeling of having the upper hand and tired of him being the one to always take the initiative, she decided to make a bold move. Completely out of character for her, but it felt good.

Wordlessly and immediately, she reached up, unfastened her towel from where she had hooked it under her arm, and dropped it to the floor, never breaking eye contact with him. She stood there, naked and unflinching under his hungry gaze, and felt herself becoming hotter and wetter. Jason brought out a bold eroticism in her that she had never experienced in her life, but she thought she could definitely get used to it.

Groaning, Jason reached out to grab the back of the desk chair he was standing next to in order to steady himself on his feet.

"Damn, Katie..." he breathed, looking her up and down. His gaze caused her to feel bolder, more empowered.

She took the two determined strides necessary to bring her to stand in front of him and immediately dropped to her knees. Still without speaking, she unzipped his fly and reached inside, pulling out his hard manhood.

He groaned even louder, tilting his head back and putting his other hand flat against the wall to effectively anchor himself in place.

She caressed up and down his shaft, delighting in how his member became even harder in her hands. She used both hands, alternately stroking up and down so that there was never a part of him she was not touching. She loved how his skin felt sliding against her hands—soft and velvety but hard as steel.

When she felt he had taken all he could of that particular delectable torture, she slipped him inside her mouth and began to move her head back and forth, applying slight pressure with her tongue all the way.

She varied the rhythm, pausing intermittently to pay special attention to areas where she got a particularly positive response to her mouth's hot and insistent caresses.

Jason breathed harder and harder until Katie was sure he was about to hyperventilate. She was momentarily concerned, but the strength of his grasp on the back of her head told her that he was in no danger of losing consciousness.

She smiled to herself. He was just having a good time.

As she continued to work his steel-hard shaft with her tongue and mouth, she let her fingers go searching through his pockets, both in his jacket and his pants. In the second pants pocket she explored, she came across what she was looking for and pulled out her prize triumphantly.

"Well!" she exclaimed, pulling back and rising gracefully to her feet, holding up the foil-wrapped condom she had found. "I see that you were very confident again, Jas."

He smiled, still clearly reeling from the touch of her velvet soft mouth. "I'd say it was warranted," he teased, his voice hoarse.

She laughed. "True. And since you thought ahead

and were responsible enough to bring this, I'd say it's only fair that we put it to good use."

As she said this, she took his hand and led him across the short expanse of floor to the bed. It was still unmade, the sheets rumpled from their adventures of the night before. She had been so wary of anyone finding out, of somehow sensing what had happened here, that she had left the 'Do Not Disturb' sign out all day.

She pushed him down on the bed so that he was sitting up, his back resting against the headboard. She felt his eyes on her as she tore open the condom packet and then unrolled the plastic tube onto his hard length. He shivered at even that small touch.

She smiled. She liked having that kind of power over him.

When she was finished, she put one hand on each of his shoulders, balancing as she swung her leg to the other side of him, and straddled his body effortlessly. She began to kiss him deeply as she lowered herself onto his shaft, shuddering with the pleasure that each new inch of him entering her caused to course through her body.

When she had settled down onto him entirely, she paused a moment, just enjoying the feeling of kissing him while he was buried deep inside her. She felt her muscles squeeze around him and he gave a small groan of pleasure.

Without ever breaking their kiss, she began to move

her hips up and down slowly but steadily. She began their lovemaking at a slow and languorous pace, one that she knew would build in speed and intensity before too long. She wanted to savor this slow and unhurried moving of their bodies together while she could.

She felt Jason's hands slide up her legs, over her hips, and come to rest firmly on her waist. He held on to her there as she moved her hips in their rhythm, anchoring the two of them together even more strongly.

She moaned with greater pleasure. She loved it when Jason put his strong hands on her like that. She could feel his large, powerful hands, hardened and roughened and muscled from years of construction work, and they nearly encircled her tiny, delicate waist. Every time she came face to face with Jason's pure, raw, physical power, it left her breathless. It made her feel calm, safe, and secure, but at the same time almost unbearably excited.

Her rhythm quickened, and at the same time, his hips began thrusting up to meet hers.

Katie threw her head back and arched her back, crying out in pure ecstasy.

Her hands moved up, tangling in Jason's brown hair that she loved to touch. So many times, even when she was younger, she had had the urge to reach out and brush it with her fingertips, to stroke it away from his face, to run her fingers through it, but she never could.

It was always off-limits.

Not anymore, though. She could bury her hands and her face in Jason's hair to her heart's content. There was no part of Jason's body that was off-limits to her now, and she found that idea unimaginably exciting.

"Oh, Jason. Oh yes..." she gasped as she felt herself getting closer.

As she continued to ride him, and as he continued to thrust up into her, she felt his mouth close over first one nipple and then the other. The hard point of his tongue was swirling around them, flicking them, sending electric jolts throughout her body, especially concentrated in the one area he was so deliciously burying himself in right at that moment.

"Oh, Jason, yes!" she cried, writhing in pure and intense pleasure. "Yes, that feels so good...I'm so...close!"

All of a sudden, the world fell out from under her and she felt as if she were doing somersaults, flipping through space.

It took her a moment to realize that this wasn't some incredibly realistic manifestation of a metaphor, a new way of experiencing an orgasm. No, she was actually now lying on her back. Jason had flipped her onto her back and climbed on top of her. He was now stroking her hair away from her face and looking into her eyes.

"I know, Katie...I know," he said, the wicked grin

back on his face.

"Know what?" she asked dreamily, lost in his eyes. As so often happened when she was lost in his eyes, she couldn't remember what she had just said, what he had just said, or much of anything else for that matter. She was completely enraptured by his gaze.

He smiled. She could tell he knew exactly what was going through her mind. He pretty much always did.

"I know that you were getting close," he whispered conspiratorially. "Which is exactly why I wasn't going to let it happen yet." he continued, his voice growing huskier. "This is going to last awhile. We're going to enjoy this."

With that, he began to plant sweet, gentle kisses all over her face and neck as he began to slowly but insistently pump into her again from this angle. Each time he thrust into her, he kissed her again in a new location.

Katie leaned back and decided to just enjoy this new sensation, this passivity. She liked the idea that her only responsibility was to feel the pleasure he was giving her. It was so different from how she normally felt, this whole sensation of being well taken care of, well cared for. She hadn't felt it since…well, since the last time she had seen Jason.

As he continued his steady rhythm, he trailed his tongue lightly over her chest until his mouth found her nipples again. As he sucked and licked each of them in turn, the need began to fire in her again, and she knew that she would no longer be able to maintain the passive and relaxed stance she had been enjoying.

Indescribable pleasure filled her body. She began to writhe, she began to moan, and her hands began to move ever more frantically on his body.

This time, it was she who began thrusting her hips up to meet his rhythm, and oh, it felt so good. She knew he wanted to prolong the encounter, but she also knew that she was nearing her breaking point.

When she could take it no longer, she gasped, a pleading note in her voice. "Please, Jason. I need to. I need to…"

A strangled cry tore from his throat at her desperate words, and he moaned, "Yes, Katie. Just let go. I want you to come so hard…"

His words were barely through being processed in her brain before she heeded them. Her core exploded in fireworks of pleasure, spasms tearing through her torso, her limbs clutching at Jason for all she was worth.

She heard herself crying out but barely recognized her own voice. Wave after wave of sensual gratification crashed over her.

As her body calmed and the stars flickering before her closed eyes began to fade, she became aware of Jason holding her gently and stroking her hair.

She opened her eyes, looking into his again. Uh-oh. This was dangerous territory. Better concentrate if she wanted to keep track of the conversation.

On his face was the most stunning expression of

affection and pride she had ever seen. It was an expression of love. She reached up and gently ran her fingers over his cheek, his chin. She just loved touching him.

"Did you…?" she asked tentatively.

He shook his head, a smile on his lips.

"I wanted to watch you," he said, grinning lopsidedly. "I didn't want to be distracted."

She grinned back widely. "Well, then why did you stop. Let's go."

He kissed her forehead. "I appreciate it, babe, but don't feel you have to do that for me. I'm just happy to have made you happy."

She laughed, running her fingers through his hair. "Number one, I think that, while there is probably a grain of truth in there, it's mostly bullshit. Number two," she added, naughtiness tingeing her voice, "who says I'm finished? I think I could definitely go for round two if you're interested."

He buried his head in her neck. "My God, you are the most amazing woman I have ever met," he breathed as he began to thrust inside of her again.

This time, there was no slow build-up. There was no romantic preamble. Their passion overtook them almost as soon as they began to move again, her already sensitized flesh causing her to quickly reach climax.

Their pleasure crested its peak simultaneously, and Katie did make a point to keep her eyes open and watch him as he lost control. Wow. He was definitely onto something with that. It was probably the most erotic thing she had ever seen, watching his face contort and his muscles bunch in ecstasy, knowing it was she who had made him feel that intense pleasure.

As soon as they came down from their massive mutual highs, exhaustion hit Katie like a ton of bricks. *No*, she thought as she felt herself being pulled down into sleep. *I want to stay up with Jason. I want to talk with him, to laugh, to snuggle, to spend every minute. There's not enough time...*

But it was no use. The emotional and physical exertion of the weekend had finally caught up with her, and sleep was dragging her into its steel embrace whether she liked it or not.

As if from far away, she heard Jason whisper, "I love you, Kit Kat. I love you like I never thought it was possible to love someone."

*Hmmmm...*she thought to herself as she drifted away. The last thought she had before she lost herself completely to slumber: *Maybe Kit Kat isn't such a bad nickname after all.*

Chapter Twenty-Six

The next morning, Katie awoke to the delicious, smoky aroma of sizzling bacon. She sat up and extended her arms above her head, feeling like a graceful cat as she stretched her muscles out as far as they would go.

"Jason?" she called, but she got no response.

She looked around the room and then spied a note sitting on the pillow he had used with a rose stretched across it.

She grabbed it and smiled as she unfolded it.

It read: "Kit Kat, I had to go downstairs early and take care of checking out the block of reserved rooms. I ordered room service for you—bacon and eggs just like you like them. Enjoy your breakfast. Take your time getting showered (sing as loud as you want—yes, I know that, too) and dressed. I'll see you downstairs. Love you."

She laughed and then immediately went to tuck the note into a safe pocket in her suitcase where it wouldn't get wrinkled. She was definitely keeping it. Forever.

Katie luxuriated in every single bite of her breakfast,

and her shower concert featured sappy titles such as "Reunited (And It Feels So Good)" and "Love Lifts Us Up Where We Belong."

After she got dressed, she headed downstairs, pulling her suitcase behind her and smiling a special little secret smile because only she knew what it contained—her note from Jason.

The first two people she saw when she disembarked from the elevator were her mom and Aunt Wendy. She hugged them both hard and did her best to put out of her mind the fact that she would be saying goodbye to them both today.

When she pulled away from the two women who were her entire family, she saw that the little group had been joined by Grandpa J, Grace, and Mike. Katie smiled. So maybe she should revise that—they might be her only blood relations, but they were far from her only family.

As the group chatted, largely about what an amazing job Wendy had done (which her aunt was lapping up, Katie thought with amusement), Grace pulled Katie aside to have a private conversation.

Oh, no, Katie thought. The hateful words, that had spewed from Lisa and Tiffany the night before, echoed in her mind. "*They probably totally hate her now.*"

"Katie, honey, I wanted to talk to you about Jason," Grace said carefully.

Katie's heart filled even further with dread.

"I know it must feel strange for you, what with Jason and Nick having been so close. Especially here with Nick's family all around."

Katie nodded. It was all she could do—her throat was too closed up to speak.

"Yeah. We could see that you were uncomfortable. Like you were looking over your shoulder. But, Katie, you have to know that Mike and I… We just want you to be happy, honey. If Jason makes you happy, that's a really good thing."

Katie's eyes filled, and she said hoarsely, "But…Nick…"

Grace shook her head determinedly, her eyes filling as well. "Nick would want that, too, Katie. He thought the sun rose and set on you, honey. He would never want to see you unhappy, and especially not because of him. He'd want you to move on."

The tears spilled down Katie's cheeks unchecked just as they did down Grace's.

"You have to know, Grace. You have to know, no matter what, a part of me will always love Nick. He'll always have a special place in my heart." Grace pulled Katie to her, holding her tightly.

"Thank you for that, Katie, sweetie," she said thick-ly.

The two women stood silently together, holding each other, their hearts communicating something too deep for mere words to express—until Katie heard a shrill cry coming from Aunt Wendy.

"Well, butter my butt and call me a biscuit," Aunt

Wendy exclaimed. "I think Jason's gonna strangle that man!"

Katie and the whole group ran outside as fast as their feet would carry them, running to the place Wendy had frantically been pointing at.

Jason had the guy she had been mentally referring to as Motorcycle Man, pinned up against the wall, his forearm at his throat. Motorcycle Man was grunting and trying to squirm away.

"Why are you stalking her?" Jason demanded harshly.

Katie could tell that the guy was trying to deny Jason's accusations, but Jason wasn't letting him get a word in edgewise. She could see Jason getting more and more agitated the more he yelled, and the kid just looked more and more terrified with each word that flew out of Jason's mouth.

"You've been following her around town, you let the air out of her tires, and now you're gonna deal with me!" Jason snarled as he reared back to punch the kid.

Grandpa J stepped up and put a hand on Jason's shoulder to stop him, saying sharply, "Stand down, son."

Grandpa J never talked in that sharp, militaristic tone to any of the kids, but they all respected him so much that it didn't take but once to be effective. Everyone standing around calmed down and stood at attention.

"Now, I don't know if this boy's been following

young Katie around town or not. But I know for a fact that he didn't let the air out of her tires."

Katie exclaimed, "How? Were you looking out the window? Did you see who did it?"

"I didn't need to be looking out the window to see one doggone thing. I let the air out of your tires, and I'm not ashamed to admit it."

Katie's jaw dropped, and the rest of the crowd looked at Grandpa J with wide, shocked eyes.

Grandpa J, for his part, just shrugged unconcernedly. "What? I thought you and the boy needed a little catch-up time."

"Are you kidding me?" Katie asked, disbelieving. Jason looked at her like he didn't believe it either.

Grandpa J waved them both off and turned his attention back to Motorcycle Man. "What's your name, son?"

His voice came out sounding strained because Jason still had him pinned up against the wall with a forearm across his throat, pressing against his windpipe. He made a valiant effort and croaked out, "CJ…CJ Lawson."

Jason dropped his arm from the kid's neck but still held him by his shirt, pressed up against the wall.

Alex stepped up, reached into CJs pocket, and pulled out his wallet. He flipped it open and then shook his head before holding it out and showing it around to everyone, reading the name out loud. "Craig Allen Lawson, Jr."

"Wait..." Katie said uncertainly, still feeling as if this whole encounter might be a dream and wishing she could make sense of what was going on. "That's my dad's name." Jason stepped away from CJ and put a protective arm around Katie's shoulders.

"It's *our* dad's name," CJ said nervously, clearing his throat a little.

"You're my... brother?" Katie asked, incredulous, as she took a step towards him.

Jason stepped between them, clearly not quite as eager to accept this explanation as a valid reason for the events of the past few days. He asked, a hostile tone tingeing his voice, "Why have you been following her?"

CJ continued to speak straight to Katie, and he sounded apologetic as he explained. "I only found out about you a few months ago. I didn't know exactly what to do when I first heard about you. I hired a private investigator, and they found you in San Francisco. I was planning on flying out there but the PI that was following you said that you'd boarded a plane headed to Chicago, which meant that you were probably headed home.

"I don't know what else to say. I took a chance, got on my bike, and headed to Harper's Crossing. Once I got there, though, I wasn't sure how to approach you. I didn't know if you knew anything about us."

"Us?" Katie asked, eyebrows raised. "Are there more of you?"

CJ smiled a crooked smile, and for the first time,

Katie started to notice a resemblance between herself and this stranger standing in front of her.

"There are four of us in total. I…um…*we* have two younger brothers, Caden and Corey, who are twins. And a little sister, Carrie." CJ shook his head a little. "My mom liked 'C' names."

Katie, still feeling a little shell-shocked, attempted to clarify. "So you're saying I have three brothers and a sister?"

CJ nodded his head.

Katie looked around the crowd frantically until she caught her mother's eye. Her mom looked pale but resolute, and she stepped forward when she saw that Katie was looking for her. "Did you know about this, Mom?" Katie asked.

Pam shook her head in the negative but added, "It doesn't entirely surprise me though."

CJ was looking increasingly uncomfortable to be the center of the laser-focused attention of the gathered crowd. Inclining his head to indicate the small café across the main street the hotel sat on, he asked Katie, "Do you think we can go get a coffee and talk about this some more?"

"Of course." Katie nodded, still reeling from the revelation. She needed to gather her thoughts, and she had about a zillion questions for her…brother. That was definitely going to take some getting used to.

As she began to move to the crosswalk, she felt Jason walking along beside her. She turned to him and laid her hand on his chest. "I'm fine, Jas, really."

"We need to get headed back soon," Jason said. He was speaking to Katie, but his eyes were on CJ, and they still held a healthy measure of suspicion.

Katie smiled indulgently. "Jas, you can go ahead and get going. Seriously. I'll catch a ride back with Mom or Aunt Wendy."

"Katie," Jason said. It was just one word, but the way Jason spoke it communicated volumes. He was asking her if she was okay. He was letting her know he wasn't happy about letting her go, even just across the street, with CJ, who was a virtual stranger. He was saying that he wanted to be there for her if she needed him. He was basically just being Jason.

She shook off the feelings that the simple act of him saying her name stirred up inside of her and decided that was better left for another time. Right now she needed to deal with CJ.

So she looked up into Jason's sexy brown eyes, eyes she could lose herself in, and smiled. "I'm fine, Jas. Really. Just go. I'll see you back in town."

Katie then squared her shoulders and turned to CJ, saying with a smile, "Coffee sounds great. Let's go."

Chapter Twenty-Seven

Jason watched as Katie stared silently out the passenger side window at the scenery flashing by. They had left Whisper Lake over an hour ago, and she had barely said two words to Jason in the intervening time. Actually, she had not *said* one single, solitary word to him.

Jason had watched her in the cafe from across the street in the hotel lobby. At first, Katie's body language was tense, and he could see that she was firing questions one right after another at CJ. For a moment, he almost felt sorry for the guy. He definitely knew what it felt like to be on the receiving end of Katie's rapid-fire questioning.

But after about ten minutes, she'd relaxed. Her posture changed, and she even laughed at a few of the things CJ said. He watched as CJ pulled out his phone and flipped through it, showing her pictures of their siblings, Jason assumed.

When she came back to the lobby after saying goodbye to her brother, she looked around, scanning the lobby for (he assumed) her mom or aunt.

Jason walked up to her and said, "It's just me, Kit Kat. Everyone else headed back." She just silently nodded her head and turned to walk towards his truck.

Since then, she had been staring out the window as if in a daze, still completely silent.

Jason recognized how selfish it was of him to co-opt the opportunity to have a long, unbroken conversation with her when he knew how badly she must want—and need—to talk with her mom and her aunt.

He also knew that this wasn't the right time to have the "Define the Relationship" talk. DTRs were stressful enough under normal circumstances, and immediately after having found out that your dad, who'd abandoned you, went on to have a family with four kids he did stick around for and take care of, was far from being normal circumstances.

He knew all of that. Logically, anyway. Unfortunately, no one had sent his heart the memo. He was somehow sure that if he didn't get another chance to talk to her before she got on that plane to head back to California, the walls she would put up once she was back in her comfort zone would mean a life sentence of heartbreak for him.

Well, he figured, *I better get the ball rolling. Every mile that passes is one less minute we have together.*

"I don't know what I like better, you pretending to be asleep like you did on the drive up here or you sitting there quietly in a fog," he teased lightly. He glanced over to her to gauge her reaction and saw that she just sat still.

"Look," he continued in a sincere tone, "I know you need to talk to your mom, and I am going to drop you off there. You'll have hours to talk to them before you need to catch your flight. But I just wanted—no, needed—to make sure you were okay. That *we* were okay. I knew that if I didn't drive you back, I would lose my chance."

She remained silent.

"Are you okay?"

"I'm fine," she replied flatly.

"So how did things go with CJ?"

"Fine," she repeated.

"Was he able to shed a little light on the bombshell he dropped?" Jason asked.

Katie shook her head, sighed, and pulled her knee up onto the seat so that she was facing towards Jason. "You're not gonna drop it, are you?"

He didn't answer. He just smiled.

She turned back to face forward. "He said that about a year ago his parents—my dad and his mom—moved to Florida, and they had a storage unit they kept in Iowa. They asked him to pack it up and send the contents to them in one of those portable storage containers. He did, and while he was loading the container, a box broke. Inside, he found several pictures of me and my mom with his dad. He also found divorce papers and several other things that made him suspicious.

"I guess he hasn't always had a great relationship with our dad so he asked his mom if she knew anything about it. She said she didn't and then immediately said that she needed to go. Her reaction made him even more suspicious, so he decided to hire a PI to find out whatever he could."

"Wow. That's a lot to take in. So you have three brothers and a sister, huh? Do they all live in Iowa?"

She smiled, softening as she talked about her siblings.

"The boys do, but get this: Carrie is in California. She goes to UCLA. How crazy is that?"

"Are you going to look her up? Are you planning on keeping in touch with CJ?" Jason asked. He knew that his voice sounded tense, but he couldn't seem to hide his concern. He didn't want to see her get hurt.

"Well, I'm definitely going to keep in touch with CJ. He hasn't told his brothers… er…*our* brothers and sister about me. I guess he wanted to meet me first, you know, to make sure he wasn't inviting crazy into his family. That's why he didn't come right out the first day he saw me at the bridal shop. He wanted to watch and see what I was like first. And also, I think he was nervous, you know?"

"I still don't like it, but I guess I can see where he was coming from." Jason paused for a moment, looking over at Katie with concern. "So how are you doing with all of this? Not just CJ, but the whole coming home, seeing everyone…us?"

Jason tried to make his voice sound casual, but he realized he was holding his breath waiting for her response.

Katie was silent for a moment, and Jason glanced over at her with trepidation. To his relief, he saw that she didn't look tense or sad or anything negative. She just looked thoughtful. This was exactly how she had always looked in school when she was trying to choose exactly the right words to express her point. He felt a sharp stab of love for her, his girl, the one who always wanted to say and do things *exactly* the right way.

"About CJ, I don't know. To be honest, this whole thing kind of has me feeling a little disconnected, you know? Like an out-of-body experience. I mean, growing up, all I wanted was to have brothers and sisters. You remember that."

Jason nodded.

"I would have done anything to have had them then. But how do you form bonds as adults? I mean, the best part of having siblings is your shared childhood, right?"

When she was silent for a few beats, Jason realized she might be waiting for a response, and that her question wasn't rhetorical. He said, "Yeah…I guess."

He loved his brothers, but Seth and Riley had gotten the hell out of Dodge the instant after graduation. As far as Alex and Bobby went, well, they were great, but they had also been a lot to deal with as teenagers. If he were honest, though, he would have to admit that he wouldn't know what to do without any of them.

Katie sighed and looked out the window. "And it was great seeing everyone again. It really was. I don't think that I ever stopped long enough to really feel *anything* since I left. Now that I've come back, it's like...it's made me realize how much I have actually missed everyone over the years. I know that sounds weird. I don't know how to explain it."

"No, I get it. The same thing happened to me when Alex came home after being gone for six years. I'd been so busy while he was gone, helping raise Bobby and keeping the business running, that I didn't even realize how much I'd missed having him around."

Jason was trying to keep things light and breezy. He knew she would get around to 'them,' but he had to let her do it in her own time. She didn't react well to being pushed—she never had. Also, he wasn't sure he would like what she said when she did, so now that the ball was rolling, he wasn't going to be overly eager in shoving it down the incline.

"As far as us, I mean, honestly, it kind of feels equally natural and totally weird that there even is an 'us,' Jas."

Okay, he told himself. *That's not a particularly auspicious beginning, but it could go either way.*

"I mean, I know that maybe it shouldn't be weird, and maybe I should just focus on the part that feels natural, like there always was an 'us,' but every time you touch me in front of Grace and Mike or *kiss* me in front of God and everyone like at the reception, I feel weird. Like we're doing something wrong."

"You feel like you're cheating on Nick," he said, unable to completely keep just a trace of the bitter irony he felt from his voice.

"Yeah, kind of," she admitted, shrugging. "And, we also have real lives, Jason. Separate lives. Ones I don't know if an 'us' fits into."

She took a deep breath, and when she continued, her voice was a little shaky. "I do love you, Jas. I always have. And this weekend with you, when it was just 'us,' was amazing. But I just don't know. I don't know how this will work—logistically."

He looked over and saw tears falling down her face. That was like a punch to the gut. He could barely stand to see Katie cry. The last thing Jason wanted was to be the cause of those tears. He knew that Katie was a 'processor.' She needed time to put things in their places, to organize her feelings. He didn't want to upset her by pushing the issue, but he also didn't want her to think that he was giving up on her, on them.

He reached over and rubbed her knee, trying to comfort her, but immediately he felt desire rise up in him. He knew that as long as he was drawing breath, he wouldn't be able to touch Katie and not be affected by it.

"Look, we don't have to decide anything today," he said soothingly. And that was true, even though he had already made his decision. He would do anything it took to be with this girl. "Today, all you have to worry about is talking to your mom and getting your cute little butt on that plane. The rest will take care of itself."

Or he would take care of it. But either way, she certainly didn't need to worry about it.

She nodded, and—to Jason's eye, at least—it looked as if she felt better, more secure, less tense.

As they turned onto Harper Lane, his chest ached. Even though she was still sitting right beside him, he was already feeling the loss of her leaving.

"No, Jas," she said with quiet resolve. "I don't want to bail on you again. I know we need to talk, to figure stuff out—"

He interrupted her as they pulled into the driveway of Katie's childhood home. "Katie, I have loved you and waited for you for almost twenty-five years. I'm not going anywhere."

An expression crossed her face that he couldn't quite place. It was gone before he was able to pinpoint it.

He opened the door and got her suitcases from behind the seat. As he came around the truck to head up to the front door, she flung her arms around his neck and buried her face in his shoulder.

He immediately dropped the luggage and wrapped his arms around her while lifting her off the ground. He held her with all of his might, hoping foolishly that somehow it would give her a reason to not get on that plane.

He knew he was being delusional.

After she gave him one last squeeze, she lifted her face and pressed her lips to his.

It was a sweet kiss. A kiss that felt like it held a promise. It didn't feel like a goodbye kiss. He set her down just as Aunt Wendy made her way out of the front door, followed by Pam.

"Your mama and I have been on pins and needles to find out what happened with Motorcycle Man."

"CJ," Katie corrected as they made their way into the house.

Aunt Wendy waved that aside. "He'll always be Motorcycle Man to me."

Jason set Katie's bags down. "All right, Kit Kat. Have a safe flight, and call me when you make it home."

Katie turned and looked at him with those big blues that had always done him in, and she smiled. With a twinkle in her eye, she said lightly, "I will. And thanks, Jas, for…everything. I love you." Then, she got on her tiptoes and kissed him right in front of her mom and Aunt Wendy. It might not mean she was staying or even that she had worked 'them' out in her head, but he did take it as a very good sign.

Chapter Twenty-Eight

Katie felt the wind whip past her face as the moisture from the damp grass seeped through her jeans at the knees.

She was freezing, but going back to the car to get a jacket just didn't seem like an option. She simply could not tear her eyes from the tombstone before her.

Katie wasn't even sure if her legs would even work at this point. Her body felt almost as if it were a foreign object she didn't know how to control.

She had no idea how long she had been there. It could have been an hour, but it just as easily could have been three. She had yelled, cried, laughed, cried, talked, cried…oh, and cried some more.

Emotionally, she felt better. Physically, she felt like a wet rag doll.

Through her mental fog, she heard a voice break through the rustling leaves behind her.

"Well now, what's my girl doing out here all by her lonesome?"

The voice penetrated her malaise, and she turned to see Grandpa J walking towards her. She smiled through the tears that were still falling down her face.

He knelt beside her. "Is this the first time you've been out to visit Nick?"

Katie nodded her head.

"Did you need some more privacy or do you think you could stand the company of an old man?" Grandpa J asked gently.

Katie didn't trust herself to form words so she just laid her head on Grandpa J's shoulder.

He wrapped his arm around her and the chill that had been seeping into her bones was replaced by a feeling of warmth and comfort.

"So you've had quite a couple of days. I'm here if you want to bend an ear."

Katie took a deep breath. "I don't even know where to start."

"Well, from what I hear, you found out my grandson here"—he motioned towards Nick's headstone—"was skirtin' around on you, both of y'all's best friend is in love with you, and on top of all that, you found out you had kinfolk you didn't know about."

Katie looked up at him in disbelief. First of all, she had not known that he had been aware of all of those facts, and secondly, she couldn't believe that he had been able to sum it up so succinctly.

"Yep, what you said," she smiled, and tears continued to flow down her face as she laid her head back against his wide comforting shoulder. She sniffed and was immediately handed a worn handkerchief by

Grandpa J. She blew her nose. The handkerchief felt so soft against her skin, and it smelled like home. She held it to her chest.

"Well, young lady, as far as my grandson goes, there is no excuse for his behavior. All I can say is that he was young, and while he did love you very much, he was just too stupid to act right. Now as far as Jason goes, now that boy has loved you somethin' fierce for as long as I can reckon. He's a good boy, Katie girl. He would take good care of you.

"Now your kin, well…I see how that one could throw you for quite a loop, but look at it this way—you got off that plane a few days ago not knowing that you had a good man that would do anything for you and that you had siblings to call your own. Now, as hard as it is to wrap your head around, ya gotta admit, it's not all bad."

"Well, yeah, when you put it like that." Katie sniffed again and hugged Grandpa J tight once more before sitting up straight and wiping her face.

"So what's holding you back, Katie girl?" Grandpa J asked gently.

Katie shook her head. "I don't know how to put it into words. I just…I want to be with Jason, I do. But every time I'm with him, especially if anyone sees us, I just feel so guilty. So ashamed, almost. I mean, especially Grace and Mike. I just don't…" She shook her head in confusion.

"You feel like you're cheating on Nick," Grandpa J

stated matter-of-factly.

Katie nodded solemnly. "Yes."

Grandpa J smiled. "Well, it makes sense you would feel that way. You're a good girl. You like to follow the rules."

Katie nodded her head vigorously.

"So being with Nick's best friend feels strange to a small part of you, but Katie, honey, there's no truth in it. Nick's gone, sweetheart. He's been gone a long time. And he would want you to be happy every bit as much as Grace and Mike and I do."

Katie started to cry again. "That's what Grace said, too."

Grandpa J chuckled sadly. "Honey, that's because it's true. Now, listen here. Do you know the first thing Grace said when Sophie told her that she was going to ask you to be her maid of honor?"

Katie shook her head.

"She said, 'Hmmm…maybe on the same weekend that you and Bobby vow your love, a new love will bloom between the maid of honor and the best man,' and Sophie replied, 'Mama, you read my mind.' Now does that sound like people who don't want you to be with Jason?"

Katie shook her head, amazed.

"Besides," Grandpa J said with a twinkle in his eyes. "Not that I'm trying to rush anything or put pressure on you, but I would just remind you that by virtue of the knot my beautiful granddaughter Sophie just tied with one of the Sloan boys, they are now my grandsons by marriage. If, say, a pretty blonde happened to marry one of them, she'd technically become my granddaughter if you look at it a certain way. Now you wouldn't deny an old man the hope that one of his favorite people might still become his granddaughter one day, would you?"

Katie laughed and threw her arms around him, hugging him hard. "I love you, Grandpa J," she whispered.

"Love you, too, Katie girl," he said affectionately. When she pulled back, he said, "Now, not that I'm complainin', mind you, but shouldn't you be up in the sky, headed back to California right about now?"

"I missed my flight," Katie said as she blew her nose again.

"Well now, I ran into your mama and she said that she and Wendy dropped you off at the airport in plenty of time."

Katie sighed. "I know, I just…I couldn't…leave."

A wide smile spread across Grandpa J's face as he stood and pulled Katie up into a bear hug that felt better than Christmas morning, her birthday, and anything chocolate combined. He said happily, "Welcome home, my Katie girl. Welcome home."

Katie smiled. It really did feel like home when Grandpa J said it. They stood for a moment in silence, looking at Nick's headstone and paying their respects until Grandpa J spoke again.

"Well, speaking of home, honey. You ready to get out of here and head there now?" he asked and Katie nodded. As they left the Harper's Crossing cemetery, Katie felt like a huge weight had been lifted off her shoulders.

She was really and truly *home*.

Chapter Twenty-Nine

Jason lay in bed looking at the blinking red light on his nightstand. It read 3:16, exactly four minutes later than the last time he had checked. He looked at his phone again to make sure that he hadn't somehow missed Katie's call. He had been tossing and turning for hours now, waiting to hear that Katie had made it home safely.

He climbed out of bed and headed to the kitchen to finish off the leftover pizza from dinner. As he opened the fridge, he heard a small knock on his front door.

In his experience, middle-of-the-night guests rarely brought good news.

Oh God, not her plane!

He ran to the front of the house, knocking over a lamp and a chair in his frantic race to the door, and threw it open, heart pounding, steeling himself to see a teary-eyed Pam or Wendy there. Or maybe they would send his brother. *Oh my God…*

It took him a few seconds to process who *was* actually standing on his porch, and then his heart simultaneously dropped and expanded.

Katie was here. On his doorstep. In Harper's Crossing—not in California. But this wasn't entirely happy news because he could see that she was upset. Her eyes were puffy and her nose was bright red.

He pulled her to him and she wrapped her arms tightly around him.

Closing the door behind them he asked, "What's wrong? Are you okay?" He tried to not sound as alarmed as he felt. She sniffed and nodded her head yes.

He pulled back slightly and cupped her face in his hands, wiping the tears that were falling down her cheeks with the pads of his thumbs.

"Baby, talk to me. Why are you crying?"

"I don't know why I'm still crying," she laughed, but there was more frustration than humor in it. "It's like I've opened a valve and I can't shut it off. I've been like this for hours. It started when I rented a car at the airport and it hasn't stopped since."

"You're upset because you missed your flight? That was hours ago. Where have you been?" Jason asked. This wasn't making any sense, and he needed to get some clarification on the subject.

"No, no," Katie smiled and rolled her eyes a little, and he felt his body relax. "I'm not crying because I missed my flight. I went to go visit Nick and then Grandpa J showed up. He wanted to tell Nick about the wedding."

Katie swayed against him, and he moved them to

the couch and sat down, pulling her onto his lap. She laid her head on his shoulder as he rubbed the palm of his hand up and down her back, waiting as patiently as he could for her to tell him what was going on. Her breathing got steadier and slower, and he was just about to check to see if she had fallen asleep when she broke the silence.

"I'm not going back to San Francisco, Jas."

He felt like his heart was going to jump out of his chest but he tried not to get too excited until he heard her out.

"I don't mean ever. Obviously I have to go back to tie up loose ends like, oh, I don't know…my *career*"—she laughed a little—"and my apartment, things like that. But then I'm coming back."

He still waited quietly to make sure there wasn't a catch. He needed to make sure that what he *thought* she was saying was what she was *really* saying.

When she didn't continue, he figured he would have to move this along if he was going to get the answers he so desperately needed.

"When did you decide this?" he asked carefully.

"I was sitting at the terminal, waiting for my flight, and I started hyperventilating. I got my paper bag out and started repeating a mantra my therapist had suggested, but neither of those things made it any better. In fact, it seemed like they were making the symptoms worse. At first I thought it was just all the leftover anxiety from the weekend."

"Why? What happened this weekend?" Jason asked innocently.

"Ha ha ha, real funny, Jas," She pursed her lips and tilted her head before swatting his arm and smiling.

It was a smile that reached all the way to her eyes, and he knew if he could just see that smile every day, he would be the luckiest man in the world.

"I kept telling myself that once I got home to San Francisco, I would be able to sort everything out and make sense of it all. But every time I thought about getting on the plane to head back home, the panic attack got worse. I closed my eyes and tried to just *will* the panic attack to stop. No dice.

"Then, I heard your voice telling me it was going to be okay. I felt your arms around me, and I started calming down. Once it had completely stopped, I decided I would just do some work until it was time to board the plane. Work has always kept my mind off of things before. But not this time. Nope. This time, instead of being my escape, it seemed to trigger even more intense symptoms.

"When I tried to calm down, the same thing happened. The only thing that stopped the attack was hearing your voice and imagining your arms around me. After I was breathing normally again, I thought about you, about this weekend, and about what my life would be like if I was here. You know, not just to visit, but if I lived here.

"And then, just like magic, my whole body relaxed,

and I knew, in that moment, that going back to California..." She barked out a short laugh again. "Well, it just wasn't an option. This is where I belong—with you in Harper's Crossing. You're my home, Jason."

"Hmmm," he said lightly, trying to mask the ecstatic tone he would have otherwise been using, "So, basically, you're moving home because I'm the 'Panic Attack Whisperer.' Is that right?"

Jason knew it was wrong to tease her, but honestly, he couldn't help himself. An irritated Katie Marie Lawson was still the cutest thing in the world to him.

She pursed her lips even tighter and tilted her head to the side while lifting her arm to swat at him. This time, however, he was ready for it, and he caught her arm mid-swing, using her own momentum to lift her up and lay her on the couch below him. He kissed her forehead, her cheeks, her lips. He needed her. He needed to touch her, to make sure that this wasn't a dream, that his Katie was really home and was really *his*.

"You're sure about this? You're really coming home?" He needed to hear it again. Just one more time.

She kissed him and smiled, a mischievous twinkle lighting up her eyes. She teased, "On one condition."

"Anything," he immediately shot back.

"Admit that *you* were the one who wrote on my name paper." Katie's blue eyes twinkled as she looked at him with a satisfied expression, clearly feeling she was about to win a quarter-century-long battle they had been engaged in.

Well, she might win this battle, but he had a plan to win the war.

"On one condition," he countered.

Her gaze turned suspicious. "What?"

"Marry me."

She stared at him, her expression frozen. Then he saw tears, once again, forming in her eyes.

He was just about to say, 'Never mind. Forget the whole *proposal* thing—obviously too soon,' when her lips turned upward into a grin and she spoke one simple word.

"Yes."

Adrenaline, relief, and joy all rushed through him. He felt like he had just won the lottery. Well, not that he knew what that felt like, but there was no way it could feel any better than this.

Katie looked at him, waiting for his response, and he couldn't have been happier to give it to her.

"Yes, Kit Kat," he admitted happily. "I was the one who wrote on your name paper."

Her eyes grew wide and she gasped as she pointed her finger up at him. "I *knew* it!"

He laughed and kissed her.

Katie was home. She was his. He was hers. And Jason knew, without a shadow of a doubt, that writing on her paper was the smartest thing he'd ever done.

Excerpt:

My Last – Riley & Chelle

THE CROSSROADS SERIES

Chelle awoke to the sound of a beating drum. Why would someone be playing a drum indoors? Especially this loudly?

She tried to open her eyes but found that her eyelids were encased in concrete. At least that was how it felt. They were heavy and felt abrasive and itchy on her delicate eyes. She tried even harder to open them, but resigned herself to the fact that it was a losing battle.

If she could just get the drummer to stop banging.

She decided that she needed to sit up. Maybe that simple act would help her open her eyes and become aware of her surroundings. When she tried to lift her head, however, she realized her mistake. *Huge* mistake. Her stomach rolled with nausea, and the banging sound became louder and was accompanied by sharp pains—pains that felt like ragged shards of glass being twisted viciously into her brain.

Note to self: vodka and pizza do not mix.

That was when she realized that there was no mystery drummer in the bedroom—although, if she didn't feel so crappy, she may not have objected to having a mystery drummer in her bedroom. No, the thump-thump-thumping she heard was the pounding of her own head.

She laid her head back down in defeat, but she did come up with a plan. She decided that she would lie perfectly still long enough for the nausea to pass, and then maybe she would just try and roll out of bed. *Gravity, FTW!*

She carefully placed her hands over her stomach and concentrated on breathing in through her nose and out through her mouth.

"You awake, Sleeping Beauty?"

At the sound of the deep voice, adrenaline overcame all of her symptoms and Chelle bolted upright in bed, her eyes flying open.

Adrenaline didn't help her vision, though, and it was pretty fuzzy. She was having a hard time focusing. She could just make out a shadowy figure sitting in the chair across from the bed. Just as she was getting ready to scream bloody murder, the figure spoke again.

"Chelle, it's Riley. Don't be scared."

The deep, sexy voice certainly sounded like Riley. From what she could make out of his features, the seated figure looked like a blurry version of Riley too. The frame was right—the blurry blob had Riley's wide, muscled shoulders and taut, sculpted waist. The rest of the features fit as well. She could barely make out dark blond hair and sun-kissed, tan skin.

But what in God's name would Riley Sloan be doing here?

"Riley?" Chelle spoke his name in disbelief. Trying to make some sort of sense of what was going on, she asked, "Is it... What are you... Why are you here?"

"Sightseeing."

"What?" she asked, bewildered.

"Sightseeing," he repeated.

"In my bedroom?" she murmured, puzzled. She rubbed her eyes, trying to clear her vision to see if he was really here, in the flesh. After all these years. Live and in person—and in a chair that sat only a few feet away from her.

Was it true? Or was he just a smoking hot hallucination?

Probably the latter, she concluded.

She was most likely experiencing the final stages of her complete and total mental meltdown.

Well, she thought sanguinely, *I can think of worse ways to lose my mind than imagining the sexiest man in the world in my bedroom with me. If I have to go crazy, at least I have company.*

Or at least I'm imagining I do…

The figment of her imagination smiled at her and said, "Jason called me. Katie was worried about you. She's been trying to get ahold of you for a few days. When she wasn't able to reach you, she wanted to fly home early to check on you. But since I was already in California, they asked if I could stop by and make sure you were doing all right."

Okay, so maybe not a figment of her addled imagination. She didn't imagine that some sexy hallucination she conjured up would sit there talking to her about phone calls and plane schedules.

"I haven't gotten any calls from her." She reached over to retrieve her phone from the nightstand but her arms were so heavy that she didn't quite make it.

"Your phone was dead. It's charging in the kitchen."

She tried to get out of bed, fueled by new urgency, saying, "I need to go call her."

However, it seemed that even new urgency was not

enough to overcome physical deficits, and this proved to be much trickier than she had assumed it would be. The blankets she lay in were wrapped around her tightly, and try as she might to free her arms and legs, it felt as though her limbs were filled with lead. She was having a tough time disentangling herself.

Riley stood and stepped towards her. She stopped writhing and just stared. Good *Lord* that was a mighty fine male specimen moving toward her. Riley was wearing a white v-neck t-shirt that he filled out like one of the models she used to drool over on the Calvin Klein billboards. Well, to be fair, she'd actually drooled over them because they'd reminded her of Riley…

He looked like a Greek god in jeans.

He stood beside her bed. "I already called them last night after I got here, and I let them know that you were okay."

He picked up a bottle of water that she hadn't noticed was sitting on the night stand.

"You got here last night?" she asked incredulously as he twisted the cap and handed the bottle to her. She took the proffered bottle, and as she did, her fingers brushed his.

Her body reacted as if she had received an electric shock. A zinging sensation raced from the pads of her fingertips where she had felt his hand beneath hers and zoomed all the way up her arm. She shivered.

Trying to cover up her completely out-of-proportion physical reaction to this innocent touch, she quickly brought the water bottle to her lips and started sipping from it. She had no idea if she had, in fact, been successful in concealing her reaction. Maybe he'd think she'd been…thirsty? It was worth a shot. When she looked up at him, he *did* seem to have a small smirk on his lips. But she could have been imagining it.

"Yes, I got here last night. The landlord let me in. I tried to wake you, but you were passed out cold."

"Where did you sleep?" she asked as she took another small sip of water. She definitely felt a little dehydrated—in addition to all of the other things she was definitely feeling.

"I didn't," he answered matter-of-factly.

Her brow furrowed. "You didn't sleep?"

He simply shook his head.

"At all?"

He shook his head again.

Chelle knew that she was still a little—well, maybe a lot—foggy-brained, but that simply didn't make any sense. She was certain she would be having the same reaction even if she were clear-headed. Why in the world would he not sleep?

Well, she thought dryly, *only one way to find out.*

"Why didn't you sleep?"

"I didn't want you to wake up and be scared that some guy was in the apartment. Plus, I didn't know how much you'd had to drink, so I wanted to make sure you were all right."

"So you just watched me sleep?" She smiled sheepishly before taking another drink of water. "Sorry. That must have been boring."

His voice dropped an octave and there was almost a growl to it as he said softly, "No, it wasn't."

She shivered again, this time solely from the baritone vibrations of his voice. Her eyes shot up to meet his. He looked down at her, his gaze intense and…hot. She felt a tightening in her stomach—and a fluttering a little farther south—from just the expression in his eyes alone.

Wow. He had such amazing eyes.

It was almost as if she could lose herself in them. They were deep and had always held so much emotion. She had forgotten what looking into them made her feel. It was like not eating a favorite food for several years. Obviously, you remembered how much you loved it, but the passing of time makes that memory almost academic.

Until, of course, you taste it again. Then, the flavors hitting your taste buds bring all the memories of every time you ever tasted that food flooding back to you at once, all the emotion connected to it, and you truly remember how much you loved it. And you're amazed that you could have ever forgotten.

When you put a forkful of that long-forgotten favorite food into your mouth again, it is like a mouth orgasm. This was like that. But with eyes. It was an eye orgasm. An *eyegasm*.

She felt her breath begin to quicken.

Riley took a step back from the side of the bed and cleared his throat. "Why don't you take a shower or a bath or whatever and I'll go make some breakfast."

He turned and started towards the bedroom door, walking with purpose.

"Umm, I'm not sure there's anything to make."

He stopped mid-exit. Without turning back to face her, he said lightly, "Then I'll go down to the market on the corner. Do you have any requests?"

Riley stood perfectly still, and Chelle took a moment to appreciate the view from the back. Man, he looked as good going as he did coming. His back muscles were taut beneath the thin white cotton of his t-shirt, and holy moly, he had a perfect rear-end. He had the kind of physique that people carved marble statues of. It really wasn't fair for one man to be that insanely hot.

"Chelle?" He turned back towards her, and she realized belatedly that she had let the silence go on an uncomfortably long time.

She immediately shot her gaze up to his face, her eyes becoming as big as saucers. Embarrassment caused heat to race up her face, coloring her cheeks a deep red, she was sure.

She was pretty certain that he had caught her staring at his backside, but he didn't make a comment about it. "Huh?" she asked innocently.

"What sounds good for breakfast?" The corners of his lips twitched as though he were trying to suppress a smile.

Well, even if she had been caught, at least Riley was too much of a gentleman to call her out on it.

"Oh, right. Umm, yeah. If you could just get me some orange juice and maybe bread for toast, that would be good," she stammered. She wasn't sure if her stomach could handle much more than that.

"Got it," he smiled and walked out of the room, shutting the door behind him—but not before he favored her with a small wink. She smiled weakly. So he *had* seen.

She flopped back on the bed, letting out a loud groan as she covered her face.

"Oh, and Chelle?" she heard him say as the door cracked back open.

She popped back up into a sitting position and said, "Yes?" in as non-nonchalant a tone as she could manage.

"Take a picture next time," he said, a light teasing tone playing at the edges of his voice. "It'll last longer."

Books by Melanie Shawn

THE CROSSROADS SERIES

My First – *Book 1*

My Last – *Book 2*

My Only – *Book 3*

My Everything – *Book 4*

Tempting Love – *Book 5*

Crazy Love – *Book 6*

Actually Love – *Book 7*

Fairytale Love – *Book 8*

My Love – *Book 8.5 (Novella)*

THE HOPE FALLS SERIES

Sweet Reunion – *#1*

Sweet Harmonies – *#2*

Sweet Victory – *#3*

Home Sweet Home – *#4*

One Sweet Day – Novella: Epilogue to Books 1-4

Snow Angel – *#5*

Snow Days – *#6*

Snowed In – *#7*

Let It Snow – *#8*

About the Author

Melanie Shawn is the writing team of sister duo Melanie and Shawna. Originally from Northern California, they both migrated south and now call So Cal their home.

Growing up, Melanie constantly had her head in a book and was always working on short stories, manuscripts, plays and poetry. After graduating magna cum laude from Pepperdine University, she went on to teach grades 2nd through 8th for five years. She now spends her days writing and taking care of her furry baby, a Lhasa Apso named Hercules. In her free time, her favorite activity is to curl up on the couch with that stubborn, funny mutt and binge-watch cable TV shows on DVD (preferably of at least eight seasons in length – a girl's gotta have her standards!).

Shawna always loved romance in any form – movie, song or literary. If it was a love story with a happy ending, Shawna was all about it! She proudly acknowledges that she is a romanceaholic. Her days are jam-packed with writing, being a wife, mom aka referee of two teens, and indulging in her second passion (dance!) as a Zumba instructor. In the little free time she has, she joins Melanie in marathon-watching DVDs of their favorite TV programs.

They have joined forces to create a world where True Love and Happily Ever After always has a Sexy Twist!

You can keep up with all the latest Melanie Shawn news, including new releases and contests, at:
melanieshawn.com
and
facebook.com/melanieshawnbooks

Printed in Great Britain
by Amazon.co.uk, Ltd.,
Marston Gate.